Powerless

By
Tarun Shah

AOS Publishing, 2025
Copyright © 2025 Tarun Shah

ISBN: 978-1-998662-56-2

Cover Design: Meredith Lindsay

Visit AOS Publishing's website:
www.aospublishing.com

For
Surendra and Mansukhlal,

Part 1

Chapter 1.1: 13:23:44
October 8th, 12:00

Visiting the I&MNG Power Plant was the final stop for the twelfth grade physics class at New Manotick Collegiate Institute. They had scheduled three tours during the day for their unit on energy production. The first stop was a solar farm in Islington on the east side of the Rideau River, about five minutes away from their school. Afterwards, they toured Chaudière Falls, almost half an hour north. They briefly learned about solar and hydroelectric energy, and wrapped up both tours before eleven in the morning.

Twenty students and their teacher arrived at the facility by bus around noon. The school bus drove itself around to the east wing and parked far away from the reactors. Once the bus turned itself off, within seconds, the warm outside air flooded inside, overwhelming the class. Within a couple of minutes of stopping, the tour guide mounted the bus to welcome the heat-stricken class. They did not need to return to school until three in the afternoon, so some students had deduced that this tour would be the longest part of their field trip.

The I&MNG Power Plant was one of the most noteworthy landmarks of the Manotick area. Although it only employed a few hundred people, it could generate power sufficient for the town of more than one hundred thousand residents, while exporting the remaining energy to hundreds of thousands more in neighbouring towns of the Greater Ottawa Area.

"Good afternoon," the guide announced. "Welcome to I&MNG Station. We are so delighted to have you here with us to learn about the wonderful world of nuclear energy. When you enter our facility, you will pass through our beautiful glass lobby. We will then take you to the control room, where from a safe distance, you can see all the machinery in action. After a brief lunch break, we will get a closer look at the machinery from above using our catwalk." The chatter of the students did not cease.

Mr. Glass noted the lack of alertness of his students. He hung one of the towels he used to dry himself on the bus seat behind him, and using his cane and the back of a seat to support himself, he stood up. "I expect all of you to pay attention to Dr. Montgomery. I don't want to see any childish behaviour like what happened at Chaudière. Do I make myself clear?"

The class immediately stopped talking and gave their undivided attention to the front of the bus.

Dr. Montgomery quietly bowed to their teacher, thanking him. "Excellent. We have been a proud staple in this town for almost twenty years. We see many groups full of eager, young students and we cannot wait for you to see how we contribute to your everyday lives. So, who is ready for a tour?" He pinned his pen between the clipboard and his lab coat. His smile faded as he noticed some of the students were fanning themselves with their caps or dabbing the sweat from their faces. "We also have air conditioning inside."

Upon hearing the news, almost every student immediately shot up from their seat and shoved their way off the bus. They followed Dr. Montgomery into the nuclear plant's lobby.

"Form a single file line, please," said their guide. "I trust you all have taken iodine pills before the trip. If you have not, I do have some on me. And I trust you have all signed your waivers, notifying us of any pregnancies, heart conditions, or miscellaneous health problems."

Mr. Glass did a count of every student as they left the bus and noticed three heads in the back seats. Sidney did not get up, and he had his arms wrapped around his head and nestled his body in between a corner of the window and the bus seat. One of his friends, Harriet, looked at him, sliding her thumb and index fingers along one corner of her lips to the other, then twisted an imaginary key next to her mouth, while Kyle, another one of

Sidney's friends as well as Harriet's boyfriend, stayed behind to console him.

"Are you okay, bro?" he asked, offering him his water bottle.

Sidney opened his eyes, took off his glasses, and cleaned the fog off the lenses with his shirt. "Thanks," Sidney answered, taking a swig from the bottle. "It's just a headache."

Harriet reached into her purse and grabbed an unmarked bottle, emptying a couple of white pills into her palm. "Tiens." She dumped them into his hand.

Sidney brought the pills up to his mouth and swallowed them, washing them down with Kyle's water. He tempered his breathing and allowed the pills to work their magic, but snapped out of his slumber when he felt his teacher approaching.

"What is going on here?" Mr. Glass asked. "Do you three require extra supervision?"

Sidney removed his head from the window and sat up straight. "It's my fault," he explained. "I just got a migraine, but I am good to go now." He slowly got up to his feet and walked into the aisle. Harriet and Kyle followed shortly afterwards.

The group travelled around the east wing of the plant, and two structures caught their eye. One was the brown translucent glass lobby where all the other students had entered, and the other was an old, dilapidated shack located on the west wing of the facility near the entrance. It was on the west wing of the plant, next to the chain link fence. None of them glanced at the old shack for more than a few seconds; it was not a pleasant sight.

As they walked into the lobby, they were greeted with a blast of cold air. They basked in comfort while joining the rest of the class.

Kyle eyed the tour guide, sensing his chipper attitude. "So, ready for the indoctrination?" he asked his friends. "Hari? Sid?"

Harriet rolled her eyes sarcastically. "Can't wait to hear about how this is the safest and cleanest energy in the world."

"I'm excited," Sidney answered sincerely. "My mother's been showing me what she has been doing here since I was young. I can't wait to impress her with what I learned when she's out and back to work again." He maneuvered himself through the crowd of students.

"They got to him," Harriet said, aside.

Kyle shook his head. "Shit. I forgot about his mother."

They both exchanged guilty looks. They were aware of the condition of Sidney's mother. She had been admitted to the hospital recently because of a couple of benign brain tumours. She was still recovering from a recent operation and needed to take some time away from her position as a safety inspector.

"Welcome, everyone, to our air-conditioned lobby, arguably the most popular part of our tour. Take some time to delouse, leave your bags here." Dr. Montgomery handed out the necessary hard hats, safety goggles, and lab coats to the group. "I cannot imagine what you guys have been through on your previous outdoor tours. For early October, it is unreasonably hot...but not as hot as the control rods in a nuclear reactor. Which can rise to...?" He paused, hoping that someone would finish his piece of trivia, but was disappointed when none of them responded to his witty commentary. "Nine hundred degrees Celsius." The guide drummed his pen upon his clipboard. "At that point, they would need to be replaced." He sighed. "Are you guys alright?"

The students scanned the room until one of them caught the eye of Mr. Glass. When they saw his disapproval, a few of them nodded hesitantly.

"Excellent." Their guide held the clipboard to his chest and tapped his fingers together enthusiastically. "Let's go." He waved to the class as he walked along a long narrow hallway to the control room.

The class entered a large area full of control panels and CCTV equipment. They got to see a day in the life of a technician while learning about the roles of fuel rods, what they were composed of, how they could slow down or speed up the rate of reaction, and how the resulting reaction created steam to power the turbines. They learned the differences between nuclear fusion and fission, and the plant's expansion plans. The lecture took approximately one hour. The students listened intently, as much of the information from the tour would be needed for the following Tuesday's test.

After a quick, fifteen-minute lunch break in the plant's cafeteria, they headed upstairs to the catwalk to get a closer look at a working reactor's heat exchanger.

Throughout the tour, Harriet had noticed many of the plant's workers looking at her intensely. Her father was a proud advocate for green energy and renewable technology, and was running for Parliament on a platform of prioritizing it above nuclear energy, which meant, in the long run, shutting down I&MNG. She was a notable figure in her father's campaign, but their eyes made her feel small. She hunched over, trying to avoid eye contact.

Kyle took her hand. "Your message is coming through, babe. They might hate you now, but they will love you and Vipesh when they transition to better jobs."

Harriet smiled and raised her head. The couple found Sidney at the front of the group. The class formed two crammed lines on the narrow catwalk. Despite the less-than-ideal conditions, everyone got a decent look at the reactor modules below, the heat exchangers in line with the catwalk, and the steam turbines above them.

"It was a pleasure to have you join us today." Dr. Montgomery pushed through the crowd. "Now, I want to talk to you about your future," he said, after getting enough elbow room.

Sidney listened with unwavering attention while a bored Kyle checked his watch. Harriet directed her gaze toward the heat exchanger, visible behind a pane of glass.

"This plant has been supplying the town and its surrounding areas for more than twenty years, and as I think about the next generation, about how hard my son has had it, I mainly think about how he will carry on my name and how he can service this town and neighbouring areas. While our output is much smaller than that of Chaudière Falls, we outperform Islington's solar farms. We have completed the environmental assessment for our plans to build two additional reactor units. With the expansion of Manotick and Riverside's suburban areas, we will need more warm, able bodies to produce enough energy to keep up with the growing community. A waterfall has a finite energy output, but we don't." He took a break to allow the information to sink into the minds of the students. "I don't know what you guys have planned for the future, but I hope I have piqued some of your interest."

Harriet gently nudged her boyfriend in the hip, keeping her eyes on the heat exchanger. Kyle raised his hand. Dr. Montgomery noticed an arm reaching far above the entire class. "Do you have a question?"

Kyle lowered his hand. "We don't have many fossil fuel plants remaining, so what were we replacing? And what do we do with the waste?" He smirked and confidently tipped his hard hat up. He looked over to his girlfriend, who waved him away, so he turned to his other friend.

Sidney stared at his ex-girlfriend, Yasmine, who was also in the front row, viewing the reactor. He smiled at her; she responded by glaring in disgust and turning away, hiding from him behind her other two friends, Emilia and Anthony. Feeling dejected, Sidney continued listening to the lecture.

The tour guide took some time to think before responding. "Good questions..." He looked down at his paper, scrolling through his list. "...Kyle. We have been replacing fossil fuels such as natural gas for many years. Alberta has been converting some of its oil and natural gas generating stations into nuclear plants. Other plants across Canada have been producing a surplus of energy, which we sell to other countries all across the world.

"And as for your second question, we have a nuclear bunker thousands of meters underground for disposing of waste. Not to mention, larger nuclear plants can repurpose their waste. In summation, disposing of waste has never been safer and easier, not to mention lucrative for our country." He tipped his hard hat upwards, mimicking Kyle. He then turned his head to scan for more raised hands, however during his scan, he noticed the heat exchanger's pressure gauge.

The pointer increased substantially. Despite not knowing the reason why, he did not draw attention to it. "Mr. Glass, you have such wonderful and engaging students, but we will have to continue our discussion on our way to the bus." He took his pager out of his pocket and tapped away, alerting everyone in the plant.

The students groaned at his request.

"It's still boiling outside," Harriet said, still focusing on the vessel, angling her hardhat upwards, holding onto the rim with both hands.

"Could we just wait in the lobby?" Kyle added.

"Dr. Montgomery, does it matter where you deliver your final words?" Mr. Glass asked. "Maybe it would be best if you speak in a place where the students could best understand you."

The guide took in a deep, calm breath. "I understand your concerns, and I shouldn't cause alarm; however, the pressure gauge on the heat exchanger's a little high, and I fear that—"

Tiny screws shot off the metal exoskeleton and hit the glass screen. Eight screws split the pane of glass. A seismic vibration shook the catwalk; the glass pane shattered a few seconds later. In a wild frenzy, students who were still upright ran away, but because of the narrowness of the catwalk, some didn't make it far. The students furthest from the rupture point made it to the stairs safely.

The pressure gauge flew off the reactor and broke some nearby pipes, releasing steam and heavy water into and around the area. A burst of high-pressure steam filled the core and separated the guide from the students, some of whom were unconscious. While the alarms blared and sirens coloured the room in a red light, Mr. Glass rounded up his students on an enclosed stairwell.

The guide shielded his face with his arms as he pierced the steam cloud to join the class.

Mr. Glass struggled to support himself with his cane while he counted his students. "Fourteen—we're missing six of them!"

Dr. Montgomery grabbed a CM-6M CBRN gas mask from a secure box located next to the entrance and ran back to the unconscious students on the catwalk. "Get your students back on the bus," he ordered before forcefully slamming the emergency button, sealing himself with the six other students. Another lab technician saw the group of frightened young students and escorted the class out. Mr. Glass moved to the back of the group.

"What happened to those kids?" a technician screamed. "How did this happen? Are they going to live?"

Every employee evacuated I&MNG, while the fourteen students and their teacher mounted the bus, still wearing lab coats and hard hats.

The class watched with horror as they saw the parking lot fill up with the plant workers and emergency vehicles. Four ambulances and two fire engines arrived on the scene and drove around to the west wing of the plant.

Mr. Glass dismounted the bus and tried to flag down several EMTs, most of whom did not pay attention. "They're in the viewing area, on the second floor, next to the control room on the west wing."

He sat on the steps until an older primary responder walked up to him. The responder wore a hairnet, face mask, and EMT scrubs, obscuring most of his face and body. "Sir, are you in charge here?"

He nodded his head. "My name is Spencer Glass, the senior physics teacher at New Manotick Collegiate Institute. We were on our yearly field trip, and the reactor just exploded."

The EMT looked above the Power Plant at the faint steam escaping the west wing for a few seconds. "The reactor did not explode; this is not a Chernobyl. It appears to be just a simple heat exchanger malfunction, but we are rushing everyone out." He took out his phone and hit record. "Can you tell me what happened, exactly?"

Mr. Glass started feeling a little delirious as he stood up from the bus's bottom step. "I'm not sure how it happened. I know that one of the pressure vessels broke the glass screen. A chain reaction caused part of the contraption to fall apart, and now six of my students are missing, and I don't know how they are doing—"

"Hang on." He walked around the bus, looking through the window at the remaining students. Once he performed his examination, he looked down in disappointment. "Do you know their names?"

Mr. Glass tilted his head, confused.

"The missing students. We will need to contact their parents or guardians."

"Yes," Mr. Glass took out his list and looked at all the names he had not checked off. "Yasmine Cartier-Williams, Kyle Cruz, Harriet Ganatra, Anthony Peters, Emilia Short, and Sid Tam-Adams."

"Thanks." He wrote the names down on his phone. "Did any of your students have messed-up hair or have hats that just seemingly fell off their heads for no reason?"

"I'm sorry?" He shifted his weight from his left leg. "I fail to see how that's relevant."

"Our team of paramedics is getting your students out of the building as we speak. If you could just answer my question, you and the rest of your class will be home much sooner."

"I don't know," Mr. Glass blurted out.

"Maybe I should talk to one of your students who might have seen a clearer picture—"

Mr. Glass stepped in front of the EMT, blocking him from entering the bus. "I don't think you should. They are too young, and it would be greatly appreciated if you could do your job."

He yielded his ground and stepped backwards. "I apologize. Tell the children that if they start to feel feverish to go to the ER, and that they should limit their exposure to other people. They should take iodine pills. I see some of them resting their arms or maybe feeling a bit feverish because of the heat. Everyone should keep hydrated."

Mr. Glass thanked the man and mounted the bus, shutting the door behind him. They left I&MNG two hours early.

Thirty minutes later, every victim had been collected in an ambulance and the four ambulances drove to Ottawa Hospital General. The old EMT entered his personal vehicle and trailed them.

On the west side of the Rideau River in Manotick, only about a five-minute walk west from the I&MNG Power Plant, was the campaign office of Vipesh Ganatra. The first-time candidate applied to run for the Canadian House of Commons in his old district. He was a former Civil Engineer whose proudest achievement was being one of the lead structural engineers behind the construction of the Morissette Bridge, which spanned across the Rideau River, connecting the towns of Manotick and Islington.

The red tied-arch bridge itself was not a marvel of engineering. It was a smaller, functioning replica of the Strandherd-Armstrong Bridge five kilometres north. But at the time of its construction, it was deemed too extravagant and expensive for the one-hundred-and-eighty-meter span.

The firm reasoned that it would be necessary. The beautiful design would attract more people, buses, and cars, and would help alleviate the load off of other older neighbouring bridges, prolonging their lifespan. However, the main idea floated by the

City of Ottawa was to join these two towns directly, as they had not always been well-acquainted.

Manotick was an old, semi-rural area with a small suburban population centre west of the Rideau River. Islington was a new, semi-urban neighbourhood on the east side, closer to the heart of Ottawa and consisting mainly of mid-rise superblocks and renewable energy initiatives. Its development came about during the resettlement of thousands of refugees and answered the question: 'Can we build a self-sustaining town, in every sense of the word, from scratch?' with a hesitant 'yes'.

The property values of other neighbouring towns increased, especially in Manotick. Some families did not like the urbanization of their small town, and both sides were initially against the idea of being physically connected; the significant demographic variances had put them at odds with each other. But when the bridge opened to the public, Manotick and Islington got to enjoy some commodities previously unknown to each other.

Children from Islington started crossing over to attend the less crowded schools in Manotick. Simultaneously, the residents of Manotick enjoyed newer cultural experiences not available to them locally. Traffic flow through the neighbourhoods increased and helped boost their respective local economies. The bridge significantly reduced the commute time between people who worked in one community and lived in another. Both towns recognized the firm's work and got to know the engineers and workers who made it possible.

Vipesh Ganatra had always been a dedicated public servant to Manotick and Islington, and to the Greater Ottawa Area. He had volunteered his free time to help those less fortunate in the downtown areas by working at the local kitchens or assembling teams to clean up the city. And now, he felt that he had accomplished enough from his work to move on to something a little more enticing: campaigning for the Canadian House of Commons.

After obtaining the minimum number of signatures from members in his district, and interviewing with the Green Party's figureheads, he became their nominee for the district of Ottawa Rural South. Despite living in Manotick, he had not won them over. They saw him as inexperienced and a long shot at winning against MP Guillaume Riviera, the nine-term incumbent whose proudest achievement was protecting I&MNG and their workers, the largest employer of the district of Ottawa Rural South.

Vipesh's new strategy was to win over young and unregistered voters by creating a youth base. He tasked his daughter, Harriet, with assembling students from her high school. Anyone who was looking to complete their required community service hours to graduate could join.

The volunteers would arrive at Vipesh's office every Friday, either to canvas the neighbourhood to install lawn signs on houses and any public spaces, or to stand in Manotick's Farmer's Market handing out informative pamphlets. This outreach squad also included Mr. Ganatra's niece and nephew, Vritikha and Varshil.

The two siblings arrived after school and noticed the dark, unoccupied office. Varshil turned on his phone's flashlight and tried flicking every switch, with no success. "Is there even supposed to be a meeting today?"

"There should be," Vritikha answered. "Our school had a power failure at one-twenty-three, but it didn't last this long."

"My school didn't have a power outage," Varshil said.

"I guess it only affected Manotick. I'm calling Kaka." She picked up her phone and dialled her uncle. Within seconds, it went to voicemail.

"Nothing." She put her phone back into her pocket. "Can you see if he tweeted anything?"

Her brother pulled out his phone and searched through his old messages. "I found something. Kaka posted this about two hours ago." Varshil read the message aloud. "'To all the good people of Manotick. I will keep everyone affected by the I&MNG

explosion in my heart and prayers today. They include my friends who work at the plant and some seniors of NMCI, including my daughter.'"

Vritikha backed up until she hit a wall; she lost balance and slid down until she fell on the floor.

"Next tweet says: 'I will be cancelling my interview with the CBC tomorrow and will be delaying all future campaign events until further notice. I know the election is only twenty days away, but I need to focus on my daughter during these times.' The final tweet says: 'I wish everyone affected a quick recovery. Hashtag Manotick Strong. Vipesh Ganatra P.Eng.'" Varshil closed the tweet. "Well, I guess that's why no one is here. Also, why couldn't he write this in a note and take a screenshot of it? Who still writes threads?" He spun around until he found his sister on the floor.

Varshil turned off his phone's flashlight when he noticed his sister was upset. She sat still, her arms crossed and her left leg straight with her right bent. She did not respond to anything he said and stared blankly into a dark corner of the office.

"Tikha, Hari's going to be okay." He looked through the recent news articles and found the one with the most optimistic and informative headline and scrolled through it. "See, see. There are no reported deaths, and only one person, an adult male, is in critical condition. According to this, the students are recovering at OHG."

"That's about forty-five minutes away from here," Vritikha said feeling a little relieved.

Both their phones buzzed simultaneously.

"Abba just texted. He's coming." Varshil walked to the exit, but halfway between the office and the front door, he noticed his sister was not by his side. He walked back into the dark office. "Need help getting back up?"

Vritikha nodded.

He crossed his arms and grabbed his sister's wrists while she grabbed his. He counted down from three and hoisted her up as she anchored her right foot against the wall's baseboard. Once she stood up properly, he let go of her. "There you go, back on your feet...or rather, foot."

"That joke was only funny the first ten thousand times you said it," Vritikha rolled her eyes at her younger brother. She pushed the door open and walked out of the office. "Come up with better material."

"I know," he snickered. "The jokes can be a little wooden."

"I'm ignoring you now."

"Good luck with that," Varshil snapped back. "Or should I say break a—"

"Bye!"

They waited patiently for a couple of minutes when the minivan pulled up. The two siblings sat in the backseat. Their youngest brother, Vijay, had joined their father in the passenger seat.

"How are you doing, *chhotes*?" their father asked.

"I'm fine; Varshil made many insensitive jokes about my leg," Vritikha answered.

"It was to distract her from Harriet," Varshil innocently defended himself.

She furrowed her eyebrows at him and stared angrily into his eyes, knowing this was typical behaviour from him. He passed out a few seconds later. She turned her head to her left, looking out the window. She slipped her headphones on, played *Fallout*, and allowed herself to get lost in the music.

Meanwhile, Vipan started lecturing his three children about the busy long weekend they would have, but stopped short when he noticed two of his children were inattentive. One was too busy listening to music on her headphones while the other was fast asleep. He asked his youngest son to get the attention of his older sister. Vijay reached back and snatched Vritikha's headphones off her head. Vritikha, irritated, swiped them back. Vijay then tried shaking his brother awake, but he would not budge.

Vritikha grabbed Varshil's face and stared into his shut eyelids long enough for him to wake up again.

"Where are we? How did I fall asleep that fast?" he shouted.

The minivan braked as they approached an orange-vested traffic coordinator. The family observed the police officers and firefighters but also a small crowd of activists on the other side of the tape. "As I was saying, Hari's checked out. She has bandages on her arm, but she is good to go to uOttawa tomorrow with Vritikha. But we need to gather back home at six p.m. tomorrow to listen to Vipesh Kaka's radio interview. And it's extra important that you are all on time because both Veera and Krishna will be here. We will be closing up early tomorrow, which means we will be extending our hours tonight and on Sunday and Monday. So, whoever has today will be working until ten at night. Understand?" He drove as soon as the traffic coordinator gestured to him to proceed into Islington.

Vipan was in a rush because he left his family restaurant unattended to pick up his children. On top of this, he was still trying to coordinate his younger brother's doomed campaign. His wife was in India while his oldest daughter was away studying in Toronto. His children understood the amount of pressure he and their family were under for the next twenty days.

Vritikha looked at her father through the rear-view mirror and nodded. "I can cover tonight." She pointed to the small group of protestors. "But how did that happen so quickly?"

Her father looked at the crowd. "A sit-in would need a permit. Like the climate strike happening at the Parliament tomorrow."

Varshil and Vijay turned to look through their sister's window.

"I don't see anyone trying to break it up," Vijay added.

Varshil looked on his phone for recent articles. "Should we even be driving this close? What if we all become fallout zombies?" He opened the sunroof and tried to find any smoke exiting from the cooling towers. Finding nothing, he sighed in relief.

"You are not in any danger in the car. They already set up a miniature exclusion zone and redirected traffic. The chances of a large-scale disaster happening now are virtually non-existent. They probably would have kept Hari longer if that were the case."

They drove across the Morissette Bridge, making their way back to Islington. Once the car parked in their complex, the family of four entered their restaurant. Varshil and Vijay took off, while Vritikha ascended the stairwell to her room to prepare for her shift.

She thought about what just happened and the whiplash she experienced learning about her cousin's health. Who else got injured in the explosion? Why, after many years of impeccable service, did it explode? Also, could it be the catalyst to finally shut down nuclear energy?

Vritikha put on her black button-up, black pants, and shawl while tying her hair into a bun. She descended the steps to their restaurant at five-thirty in the evening for her four-and-a-half-hour shift.

During every break, she perused through articles and second-by-second playbacks that recently came out. She found out it was a simple heat exchanger explosion. There was no indication that the power output exceeded its intended capacity, nor was there any indication of a terrorist attack, technician malpractice, or sudden natural disaster.

After her shift ended, she changed into her pyjamas, and while getting ready for bed, she continued to look for new headlines. By five in the morning, she gave up looking for answers and decided to get some much-needed sleep.

Part 1.2: Meeting #1
Sidney, October 8th, 21:00

"His vitals are higher than they should be. His heart rate clocks in at one hundred and eight beats per minute, and his blood pressure's one-twenty-six over ninety-one," a doctor says as he forces my left eye open. I can't say a word or get a good look at where I am. I try to raise my hand to block the flashlight, but I am too feeble.

"Sid, wake up," a male voice says. "Doctor Thompson, he's resurfaced." He waves to his left while the second doctor walks over to my right. Doctor Thompson starts talking to me about my condition. However, I can't understand much of it.

A loud, high-pitched ring overwhelms my ears, and if I had the strength, I would cover my face with a pillow. The other doctor, not Doctor Thompson, puts an otoscope in my left ear. The hot, stinging sensation makes its way through my eardrum.

I look at my left hand. A heart rate monitor is clipped onto my index finger. When I wiggle it, a sharp, stabbing jolt shoots down my arm, making my hand twitch a few seconds later. Suddenly, my back starts to contract as the bed folds me upwards. The doctors appear as two yellow smudges. The one on the left has something in hand.

"Can you tell us your full name?" asks Dr. Thompson.

"Sid Tam-Adams," I reply, staring vacantly at the doctor on my right.

"That's great. I'm going to ask you to do some exercises in your bed, so don't get up," the other doctor instructs me. As he gets closer, I can see he is holding a clipboard. "Hold your hands up and touch each finger to your thumb." I do so without saying another word. There is a bit of a delay and my hands tremble, but I complete the exercise as instructed.

"Alright, Sid, can you feel this?" Doctor Thompson takes a brush from a tray table and rubs the bristles against my left foot. I shake my head to indicate the lack of sensation. "How about this?" She puts a sharper object on my left foot, and I can feel it very faintly. I nod, and then she moves to my right foot, and I nod again.

"Great," she exclaims. "Can you now lift your foot and draw a six with your big toe?" She removes my blanket, revealing my bare legs in a hospital gown. I can only lift one leg slightly, and after eight seconds, I collapse. The ringing sound in my ears intensifies.

"Well, that's good for now," Doctor Thompson tells me. "Patient responds to questions without much hesitation, and nervous response time is also excellent. Although, pupillary response and fine motor skills are delayed and need time to improve." The other doctor puts his clipboard on the tray table to my left and moves closer. He is close enough for me to see the bright yellow hazmat suits both of them are wearing.

"Can you tell me the last thing you remember?" he asks.

"It was when Mr. Glass got soaked at Chaudière Falls," I answer. "He walked into the path of some rogue mist. Everyone laughed; he did not. I thought about how a rogue wave of mist could hit him and the timing worked out." I laugh, and the doctors laugh sympathetically. "Half an hour later, we arrived at I&MNG. It was thirty-something degrees outside, and I had a migraine. After that, my glasses fogged up and my friends gave me an aspirin. We toured the plant, I ran into my ex, and that's where they stopped. Do you have my glasses?" I ask. "I am starting to feel a little light-headed." The two doctors leave my vision, rummaging through the room.

"I'm sorry, Sid," the other doctor says. "They must have been damaged, so we had to dispose of them. Do you, by chance, have another pair at home?"

I nod.

"Great, we'll call your mom to see if she can bring them for you. They'll most likely be available first thing in the morning. Visiting hours are closing very soon."

"Thank you." I stare blankly at the curtain to my right.

The other doctor places a remote in my right hand. "If you need anything else, you can just push the big button, and one of us will come to see you." The remote has more buttons than I expected.

"Where am I?" I interject. "Is this Greber General?" I familiarized myself with some details since my other mother was admitted.

"No, you are at OHG," Doctor Thompson answers. "Greber is experiencing some power failures. They have been transferring several low-risk patients here."

"We have scanned you for hazardous radiation levels," the other doctor continues. "The readings from our Geiger counter show you have been exposed, but it's nothing too serious. We are taking extra precautions and will keep you isolated until your body passes the radiation. We'll test some more fine motor skills in the coming days and have scheduled an MRI scan for tomorrow morning. Your hearing seems to be returning, despite the acute tinnitus." The low ringing sound intensifies.

"When will I be released?" I ask. "How are my friends?"

"Sorry, Sid," the other doctor chimes in. "Your friends haven't even woken up yet."

I start to hyperventilate.

"They're stable and we are doing everything we can to speed up their recovery."

I cringe because I am partly annoyed with all the technical jargon, and partly nauseated from being blind. But I am getting hungry above everything else. However, I put all of that behind me. They are doing their jobs, and I am grateful for the care; it's likely a stressful time for them, and I do not want to be a huge inconvenience. "I'm good for now, just feeling a little peckish."

"You did very well today. Thank you for being so cooperative. Your dinner is to your left. Iodine pills are on the tray; take them as soon as you can." Doctor Thompson comes around the bed and places the tray of food and pills on my lap. It smells rancid, or maybe my sense of smell has been affected. But looking at cold mashed potatoes, stale, pre-packaged bread, and room-temperature meatloaf, it's probably both. On a normal day, I would be excited to eat something with meat, but I can't identify what kind of meat is on my tray. "We will be happy to assist you with anything else, just press the big button."

"Now, we do have to check on the other five students." The other doctor picks up his clipboard. They must be understaffed due to the influx of patients from the power outage.

"Four students," the first doctor argues while walking out of my room.

"There's Kyle Cruz, Emilia Short, Anthony Peters, Harriet Ganatra, and Yasmine Cartier-Williams."

"Ms. Ganatra was re..." I don't hear the rest of the sentence. Of the students mentioned, I am most familiar with Kyle, Harriet, and Yasmine. I really cannot fixate on my friends right now. There is nothing I can do for them at the moment.

I don't want to eat this food, so I set the tray back on the desk to my left. Since I can't see two feet in front of me, I have to feel for the countertop. I twist and flail my arm around until I hit something solid and flat, and slowly place the tray on the counter. It takes much longer than it should have and also drains me. Instead of eating, I lie on my back and stare at the ceiling.

But the realization hits me: I survived being in an explosion.

I just had a near-death experience and I need to reevaluate my existence and trajectory. I assume it's what most people do in my situation. Welcome to the first day of the rest of your life, Sid. Will you become a better person, or will you brush the experience off?

On a normal day, I would enjoy a good read. If I had my backpack with me, I could start *The Awakening* by Kate Chopin, a book Ms. Philips will assign us later in the semester. I had checked the book out of the school library right before our field trip and planned on having a quiet Thanksgiving long weekend at home. There is no TV remote, which, in hindsight, would exacerbate my tinnitus. With nothing else to do, I fall asleep.

"Sid?" someone says. The ringing returns to its regular volume. I turn my head to the right, and looking past the flickering light above them, a small figure moves behind the plastic curtain, slowly approaching me.

"Sid, *très bien*." It's a girl's voice. Her head blocks the blinking light, and her shadow flickers onto my body. Even though the curtain blurs her face, I can make out some details. She's a short girl with a dark brown pixie cut and one green streak on her left side, a diamond nose stud on her left nostril, one light brown eye and one blue eye, and a medium tan complexion, wearing a lot of form fitting yoga apparel. "I have been looking around this entire hospital. Everyone else is under but you." Harriet pulls up a chair and sits down beside me.

"I heard one of the doctors mention your name. How are you up already?" I ask.

"I was still conscious at the time," she replies. "I just had a bruise and some cuts on my left arm." She smiles, while showing me a large gauze bandage on her left shoulder.

"You really should not be here; I have been exposed to radiation. You could get hurt if you come too close." She tilts her head down and raises her eyebrows, not saying another word. We were in the same explosion; she had the same exposure as me. "Right. Can the doctors just let you in to see whomever you want?" I don't want to push her away, but how can she visit me when my mom and sisters aren't allowed?

"I told the nurses I am a relative, like a long-time family friend. We kind of look the same, *oui?*" She smiles half-heartedly.

Harriet is half-Indian and half-French-Canadian, so some nurses could think she is 'ethnically ambiguous.' It might work for a couple of students, but not everyone. "Sure, but we also are long-time friends." I smile at her.

"I thought you would look extremely sick or deformed, but I'm so relieved to see your mood hasn't changed, and that you don't look like shit."

While upright and leaning against the bed, I squint. "Well, I did feel like shit, then you showed up and blessed me with your energy."

"Do you know how to make a girl blush?" She quips, "Don't try to make Kyle jealous."

"How is he?" I ask.

Her smirk instantly disappears. "*Quoi?*"

"He was also admitted here. I overheard the doctors talk about him."

Her eyes start to water. "*Merde.*" She shuts her eyes and slaps her right temple. "I've got to go. Talk to you on Tuesday." She rushes out of my room, disappearing through the blinking light before turning a corner.

Most weekends, we would all hang out in Kyle's backyard. However, this weekend she will be going to uOttawa with her cousin, Tikha, and I will still be in this hospital for another week, at least.

"Focus on the positives," I tell myself. "I am alive. I will be getting my vision back tomorrow because Mom will visit me. I am not injured, or I am on some good painkillers." I am not sure if that is positive or not. However, the feeling is euphoric. And as much as I hate to compare myself to other people's misfortunes, it could be a lot worse. "I could be in a coma, or worse, awake and in an intense amount of pain."

This is my first time being a patient in a hospital. I visited Mother twice before both of her surgeries. She always made us feel at ease by telling us things could be worse, and now I feel like she was setting me up for unrealistic expectations. The best thing I can do is get a good night's rest. Using the remote, I flatten my bed. Once still, I close my eyes again.

The door creaks. My eyes shoot open again as I swivel my head to try to make out another figure protruding from the blinking light. "Harriet?"

"Hello, Sidney, I come in peace, and just want to talk."

It's a man's voice this time, low-pitched and a little raspy. His sentence feels a little ominous.

"It is not my intention to scare you," he clarifies. "You should not feel alarmed. I find something striking about your record."

The man keeps his distance, staying on the other side of the translucent curtain.

"So, you were just in a terrible accident?" he asks as if he already knows the answer. "I can read what your chart says, and you did make the news, but getting other people's perspectives is always a good idea. You were on the front lines. You saw how the accident happened, and most importantly, if it was..." He pauses. "...an accident?"

"Are you saying it was sabotage?" I ask. Who the hell is this guy? I don't think he's a doctor. "Did you blow up the plant?" I don't know why my mind jumped to such an extreme conclusion. I have never accused anyone of eco-terrorism upon first meeting them, but his entrance is enough for me to end my streak.

"You do not know me, Sidney. Sorry, Sid. I know that you prefer to be called Sid." He walks closer to me. "I am not a doctor; I am just a man. A man who sees some unusual activity coming from your most vital organ."

My neck starts to feel a little stiff, so I roll it around for a few seconds, my left side first. When I turn back to my right, I find him hovering over me, looking down at my thinly-covered body, centimetres from my bed. I push myself up with my elbows. He's not wearing any personal protective equipment. Instead, he has a standard but reasonably fitted tan, two-piece suit with brown loafers. He doesn't have a tie, nor is his top button done up. This man looks to be a fifty-something-year-old Caucasian male with a soft jawline and unblinking buggy eyes. His forehead has deep furrow lines, and he is slouched only a tiny amount. He has a full head of light brown hair, but it is beginning to turn grey, especially on the sides. For some reason, I think I have seen him before, but I can not remember where, exactly.

"I have to say, I'm flattered by your description, but your guess is about twenty years short." The man brings a smile to his face, baring his perfect teeth. I lie down and look the other way in disbelief. How did he know I was taking a mental picture of him?

My back involuntarily arches, and I sit up. The bed has not moved, I'm sitting up on my own.

"I'm getting sidetracked. So, Sid, do you believe things happen for a reason?" He places his hands on the bed frame and grips it tightly.

Last summer, I was vacationing with Kyle, Yasmine, and Harriet, who brought up the same point. I already know most of our defining, life-changing decisions are not in our control. I already know where my high school life is taking me and what courses are prerequisites to becoming a nuclear technician, like my mother.

But some things do happen for no reason, like Mother collapsing in the middle of our dining room a couple of days ago because of a tumour found in her brain. And then there is the explosion, which also seems unprovoked. Although it just so happened to affect our school trip.

I turn back, only to find him not by my side anymore. He's behind the translucent curtain.

"You took too long." The curtain flaps sporadically, and seconds later, an object strikes me across my right cheek. The force knocks me off my balance and I land on my bed. My ears ring even louder than before, and my cheek gets warmer—all my blood pools on the right side of my face.

"What the hell?" I yell in his general direction and sit up, using my strength. It is hard to make him out because of the flickering light. But if he's not by my side, who slapped me?

"Wow, you don't know anything, do you?" he chides. "And I feel like you are distracted by something." He turns around and looks to the hallway.

Suddenly, something shatters, the room goes dark, and pieces of glass rain onto the ground.

"What did you do?" I raise my voice at him.

"I just exhibited several of the abilities that you are capable of as well," the man answers, pushing the curtain aside and walking back to my bedside, grabbing my bedframe. "Whether it be reading minds, altering physical objects, molecules, energy, or even manipulating people. You can do it without lifting a finger." His buggy eyes get larger.

"So, you are reading my mind right now?" I cautiously ask him.

He chuckles. "I'm not the only one." He darts his eyes back and forth. "Now you try."

The ringing sound in my ears slowly dissipates. The PA system outside fills the room along with the sounds of ambulances outside my window. My vision also becomes clear; I can see past the man; the plastic curtain has a poorly sewn-on, opaque vinyl footing. The door behind him is old and beaten down with noticeable dents and stripped white paint. The floor is covered with shards of glass—he must have broken the flickering lightbulb. It's nice seeing and hearing again, although a gloomy hospital room is not the first thing I want to see.

"Oh, no, your vision is not restored. It is only temporary. I just adjusted the position of the optical sensor in your eye. You will be blind again tomorrow. But since you have no sensory limitations now, I want you to express yourself."

What do I know about myself? I have a migraine. I have never felt worse since waking up. My neck struggles to keep my head up and two cold plates are compressing both of my temples simultaneously.

"You know that is not what I meant when I said, 'express yourself', I mean visualize everything you are feeling."

"What does that mean?" I ask.

"It starts with a small, spontaneous particle and quickly transfers some energy to its neighbours. They become infected, and it spreads quickly and passionately until it is the only thought inside your brain. These thoughts will leave your body in waves, dancing among the physical matter, affecting the air around you and then the objects around the air." He gets more jovial as he recites his monologue. "It's a chain reaction that you can start with an idea, a spark."

The migraine keeps getting worse. I want to lie down, but my body feels stiff. I am stuck sitting up; I feel paralyzed.

"You cannot let your stiffness overwhelm you. You have to let it out somehow." The only part of my body not immobile is my head. He knows I have a migraine. He is doing this to me. I imagine myself going to where he is, underneath the broken light fixture, socking him in the face. I close my eyes.

The sound of a plastic sheet tearing shakes me. I immediately reopen my eyes and find the man on the floor. He moves his head aside, revealing a large hole between the vinyl footing and the translucent curtain.

I get out of bed, and in my bare feet, I walk to him. The heart rate monitor and IV drip bag drag alongside me. "Are you alright?"

He pushes me away before I can help him and uses part of the curtain to lift himself again. "You did alright, Sid; a little messy, but not a beginner's first mind pulse."

"First mind pulse?" I ask.

"You visualized punching me in the face and it translated. You let your mind shoot a large amplitude wave at me. I could feel what you were thinking. And that is only the beginning. If you don't want to be blind anymore, I will be in the shed next to the I&MNG tomorrow night. You know exactly where that is."

"I can't," I interject. "I have to stay here for at least another week. I have an MRI scan—"

"MRI?" he interrupts me. "I have to get you out before that." He stands up straight. "You'll be checked out by tomorrow. I will fill out the required paperwork and contact your mom." He touches my forehead; his hand lowers my internal temperature. He looks at me through narrow slits. "You are fine, Sid. Just get back to bed; your new life will begin tomorrow, at nine in the evening."

I walk to my bed and climb over the railing, making sure I do not trip on my hospital gown. I slide the rest of my body into bed, covering everything below my neck. I look to my left and see the tray of food.

Instead of the cold mashed potatoes, bread, and meatloaf, there is now a salad with Italian dressing on the side, a cooled quarter-litre carton of orange juice, and a brownie.

What happened to the old food? The only explanation I can think of is that I died in the explosion. He's the devil, and he's torturing me. Or this is a hallucination because of the painkillers.

If this is happening, I can no longer brush off the explosion as a mere sidenote in the story of my life.

Part 1.3: What Happened?
Sidney, October 9th, 9:00

I wake up and rub my eyes and my right cheek. My vision is back to being blurry. I touch my thumbs to each of my fingers, first the index, then the middle, ring, and pinky; the sensation in my hands is still there. But the heart rate sensor clip isn't clipped to my left index finger anymore, and a bandage has been installed in the crook of my arm.

The last thing I remember is a creepy man who came to my bed and slapped me without touching me. After he changed my food, I fell asleep. Years could have passed, and I might be much older; my family could still be waiting for me to wake up. Maybe they have given up hope. What if they are gone? What if I have been under for decades?

I rub my face again, but my worries quickly fade. This will be the first and only time I will be glad to have acne.

Footsteps approach and I roll myself into a fetal position on my bed, facing the door. The plastic curtain is gone.

"You're up, great." Dr. Thompson walks up to me, but she's now wearing regular, blue hospital scrubs instead of a yellow hazmat suit. "Your mom's outside signing you out."

She holds two bags out and hands them to me, one of which is a tote bag, the other a clear Ziploc labelled with my name containing my phone, wallet, house keys, and a pack of gum. "This bag has everything we found on you the day we admitted you. This one, your mom gave to us to give to you." I open the tote bag and find a change of clothes, my backup glasses, a toothbrush, toothpaste, and some deodorant.

I put my glasses on, and the intensity of my migraine decreases slightly. I can still feel some pressure on my temples, but I'm glad I can see. I'm in the same room, with a tray of old food to my left; it still has the salad, carton of orange juice, and brownie. To my right are the doors with a worn-down paint job.

Dr. Thompson takes the dinner tray and places my breakfast, a bowl of cereal, milk, and a cup of fruit, on the table. "Please eat." She takes one whiff of me and recoils. "And if you need to freshen up, the bathroom is to your right."

Every layer of bedding is damp, as if I had just come home from swim practice without showering afterwards. I swing my feet downwards and attempt to dismount my bed.

"Woah, Sid, take it easy." She holds her hand out and gently sits me back down. "Eat something first. I'm glad you're energetic, and your mood has changed significantly since you arrived. However, I need you to keep up your strength. I don't want you to create more holes through the curtains or step in the glass."

"I understand." I nod in agreement. "But what are you talking about?"

"A nurse found you in the middle of the night sleeping. The plastic curtain had a hole and she noticed pieces of broken glass on the ground. I wish we had noticed it sooner because it could have been bad for the hospital staff." She smiles. "Take it easy for the next few days; you'll be back to your old self before you know it." Doctor Thompson walks out, closing the door behind her.

I swing my legs back onto the bed, open the cereal container, and drink the cold milk as quickly as possible. Everything is pre-packaged and inorganic, and the fruit cup is preserved in liquid sugar syrup and seems to be entirely canned fruit. Mother never let me have this as a kid, and I understand why. One spoonful is enough to give me a sugar buzz. It tastes like processed sugar water with only the tiniest hint of pineapple. It's disgusting but addictive. I consume everything in less than two minutes and put my tray aside. My stomach churns.

I get up from my bed, slowly dismounting, looking down at my bare feet, ensuring every step lands. I heed her advice, as I am still barefoot, and walk to the bathroom.

The bathroom of the hospital suite is simple by design. It's a stand-up shower around one square meter in with a sink and a mirror next to a tankless toilet, sink. and mirror. And my bathroom comes with complimentary mini shampoo and conditioner bottles, although looking at the ingredients, they aren't high quality. My mother knows cosmetic chemistry and taught us how to look for cheap ingredients in our hygiene products, but these would do just for one day.

The first thing I do is look at my reflection. My black hair parts in every direction. Mother always compared my hair to that of a pineapple. I didn't understand why at the time, but I see it now. My hairstyle made me two centimetres taller on a good day; it now stands twice as high.

I remove my hospital gown and glasses and step into the shower. I'm still somehow sweating, so I decide to take a cold shower. My pores close as I wash all the sebum out of my hair and drool on my face.

I take an extra long time showering, because as I clean myself, I take some time to think. Doctor Thompson said she saw me yesterday, then the explosion must have happened yesterday. So I must have seen Harriet, and more importantly, the creepy man.

One of the worst migraines of my life came to me yesterday, which is a high bar to beat. Mother claims it's because I don't hydrate properly, and perhaps she's right. The only reason I hydrate is after long, strenuous, physical activities.

My stomach churns again, and then my breakfast shoots out of my mouth and onto the shower floor. I gargle with the shower water, removing any remaining traces from my mouth. As I finish washing the vomit down the drain, I turn off the water, grab a towel, and dry my body, armpits, and hair.

Even after a cold shower, my forehead feels a little warm. And looking in the mirror again, my complexion is a little redder than usual, as if I had an Asian glow, or in my case, half-Asian glow. I sweep my hair to the left and take a step forward. "I look fine," I tell myself.

"Sidney? Are you alright, baby?" Mom's quivering voice travels through the door.

"I'm fine. Give me five minutes."

"Alright, let me know if you need anything."

I vigorously brush my teeth to remove the smell of regurgitated processed sugar from my mouth. A small trickle of blood comes out, and then I gargle with the sink water. I apply the deodorant under my armpits and put my clothes and glasses on. I spin around, look at myself from all angles, smile, jump, and walk out of the bathroom. Mom needs me to be healthy; I can feel it.

I open the door to find Mom sitting on my bed, and upon seeing me, she immediately wipes a tear from her face. Her nose is red and scrunched up, and her mouth trembles slightly. She scoops me into her arms, squeezing tight enough to cut off the air from my lungs.

"Baby, you're okay." She kisses my cheek, my forehead, and every other inch of my face.

I can't see myself, but I'm sure I'm turning a dark shade of purple. "Mom, please." I barely get out a whisper. "You're squeezing too hard."

"Oh, sorry, sorry."

She loosens her grip on my diaphragm, and I collapse on the floor. I'm not exaggerating; her hugs are painful. It takes a few minutes for me to catch my breath.

"It's just..." she stammers. "I couldn't talk to you yesterday; doctors would just repeat the same lines to me. I didn't get any sleep, and only a couple of hours ago, they told me you could come home. I went through a rollercoaster of emotions, and..." she breathes a sigh of relief. "...I'm just glad you are here and in one piece." She hugs me gently this time, her arms softly caressing my shoulder blades. "Is anything broken?" She does a full pat-down of my body, starting at my face, moving to my shoulders and arms, looking individually at my fingers, and down my chest.

I stop her before she gets any lower. "I'm good, Mom," I tell her, taking her hands off my body. "Are Kat and Mindy here?"

"Yes, they are on this campus." Mom pulls me off the ground. "It's not a long trip, though. Your mother got transferred to the cancer centre after the power outage."

Shit, I completely forgot about Mother's second surgery.

"She doesn't know about your accident; could you pretend we got lost?" Mom asks me. "Extra stress can prolong her recovery."

I fake a smile. Mother hates when we lie to her, but I genuinely don't know what would cause her more stress. "Sure." As we exit the room, something rolls right in front of us.

A motionless body on a gurney covered by a thin, white bedsheet stops us from walking out of the room. It's haunting to see someone who so recently expired. The body's not pale. It also had cuts on its neck and burn marks along its face. I grab my chest and hyperventilate at the sight of it.

"*Excusez-moi, allez-vous bien, monsieur?*" A nurse approaches us.

"Yes, sir. I'm checking him out." My mom answers for me.

"Shall I fetch him a wheelchair?" The nurse suggests. "He may not be used to walking just yet."

"No." I breathe in and out through my nose. "I am fine. But that body?"

"Oh." He looks left and then back at us. "He risked his life to save those children at I&MNG. *Pauvre homme.* He's the only fatality..." He pauses. "...so far. Anyway, I hope you feel better." He leaves us behind and we continue towards the elevator silently. I walk a little slower, as I am still a little disoriented. Mom takes my hand and places it on her shoulder, giving me some extra support. She also takes my toiletry bag and matches my walking speed.

"I'll be honest, Sidney. It'll be hard for you to see Mother like this," Mom informs me. Mother has had two rounds of surgery to remove tumours from her frontal lobe. They diagnosed her with stage one meningioma in the summer. Mother warned us she had a family history after the first round of surgery, although we didn't imagine it would come back so soon.

The elevator dings, and we get in together. "Your sisters are already by her side; I haven't gotten a good look at her yet. From what Mindy texted, she's a lot thinner and paler than her first surgery. The tumours were larger, and we are lucky they won't affect her senses or fine motor skills." She presses the button, sealing the door. I feel my stomach drop a little as the elevator descends. "I got you." She grabs my arm, supporting me. "If there is a next time, we might consider radiation therapy or radiosurgery. I'm told she'll be a little slower, more emotional, have fits of rage and sadness, and occasional memory lapses." The elevator opens, and we get out at the same time. "But we will cross that bridge if we get there." I think she wanted to say 'when' but couldn't say it to me.

We exit the hospital building, and I try to walk a little faster to avoid one of the hottest days of the fall season. I don't feel hot, though; Mom's the one slowing us down this time. I direct the two of us to the Radiology Centre. I start to feel a little bit of a headache but it disappears the second we enter the air-conditioned lobby and stop to enjoy the breeze.

People here are much older than on my floor, although we see our fair share of children. The fluorescent lights are brighter, and the atmosphere and the workers are busier.

Mom lets go of my arm and talks to the receptionist. She gives us visitor passes and directs us to Mother's room. I have never seen her sick. When she had her first surgery, there was barely a scar, and the whole process of her noticing the tumour and getting it removed lasted less than a week.

Mom takes my hand and holds it gently as we stand in front of her door. She looks at me and exhales sharply. "Be strong. Can you do that for me?"

I nod and smile. "I'll do it for both of us." She opens the door to a much nicer room than where I was admitted. There are two beds; Mother is in one and my younger sister is in the other, playing games on Mother's phone, not paying attention. Mother is awake and looking back at us. I'm stunned to see just how emaciated she is. Her skin is paler, and her cheekbones and jawline are much more pronounced. Her forehead has a stitch pattern in the shape of a squished U with a distinct shaved pattern around the top of her head. When she looks at us, I try to maintain eye contact, but find it difficult. "Hi, Mother," I sheepishly say to her.

Mom runs to her and kneels by her bedside. They press their foreheads together and interlace their fingers. "Gen, I made it," Mother whispers, guiding her hand to Mom's chin. Mother wipes a tear from Mom's eye. "I'll be here for a few more days but I'll be coming home." They look at each other for a few seconds before engaging in some marital PDA. I give them some privacy and walk to the other bed, where Kat has made herself comfortable.

"Careful, there is a bump in the middle of the floor," Kat informs me, not taking her gaze from her phone.

"Thanks, Kat." The linoleum tile sticks out less than a centimetre above the rest. "Where's Mindy?"

"She told me, quote: 'I have a group project for my 'Print Journalism' course, and I'm meeting up with my team on campus, will come home tonight,' end quote." Mom groans. "Anyway, how are you doing?" Kat continues. "You—" She puts Mother's phone away, jumps off the bed, and walks towards me. She's a head shorter than I, so I crouch to her level. "What superpowers did you get from the—"

I put my index finger on her lips. "Keep your voice down. Mother doesn't know."

"What can you—you—" She trips over her words, and I get back up. Everything she says gives me a headache. I lean at the foot of Mother's bed. "What can you do? Can you fly, or do you have heat vision? What happens if you get angry? What if, what if, what if you can see things no one else can, or climb walls using your—"

"Oh, my god." I tower above her. "Shut up!"

Kat immediately steps back, her face puckers up, and she starts sniffling. I have never raised my voice at her before. I try to hold her, but she runs to Mother's bed. I should have known I would feel shitty after yelling at an eight-year-old for no good reason.

Mother gives me a dirty look. "Sidney, come here."

I walk over to her, hanging my head.

She puts her hand on my face. "You're so warm; come closer."

I crouch down; she puts her hand on my face. She wipes the corner of my mouth with her index finger. "What's this?" She shows me a drop of yellow liquid.

"We ate breakfast on the road," I lie.

She brings her finger to her nose and sniffs it. "Where did you even get this?" Mother had made us eat healthy organic foods at home. Sugary products or desserts rarely set foot on our property. I had tried to sneak some treats into my room, but Mom's a great detective and always found them.

"That's on me," Mom answers. "We stopped by the hospital's Tims."

"However, I was the one who felt famished," I continue the lie. "I asked for a mango smoothie—"

"Gen," Mother cuts me off. "I don't care about what he eats now, but I also don't want you guys to lie. And I especially don't want to see you bickering with your little sister." She grasps my face infirmly and looks back at me with her half-open eyes. "Sidney, I can't believe I'm saying this, since you're seventeen. You need to act like the man of the house."

Kat starts to well up again.

"Katherine, I will be back very soon. But for now, you listen to your big brother, okay?" She repositions my face again and turns it towards her, making sure she keeps eye contact. "You need to protect her and be patient, do you hear me?" Her grasp becomes weaker with every passing second. Soon she holds my face as if it were a delicate cloth.

I nod accordingly.

"Good, now Mommy's tired." Mother releases her grip from my face as her eyelids start closing. "I'm guessing Mindy's not coming."

"Mommy?" Kat raises her voice.

I run to her around the bed, forgetting about the uneven tile Kat warned about a few minutes ago. I momentarily lose my balance, but quickly regain it, and finally meet her by the other side.

"You see this?" Mom points to the heart rate monitor. "These squiggly lines here show her heart beating. She's just sleeping; she needs a lot of rest."

"Oh," Kat says glumly. As a superhero, I know what I need to do.

"I did get superpowers, Kat. One of them was super strength." I take her hand and walk her to the other bed. "Watch this." I grab her by her armpits and lift her as high as I can. Her pigtails strike me hard on my face, but she's giggling. Mom smiles at us.

"So what else can you do?" Kat erupts into laughter as I toss her up in the air.

"Isn't super strength enough?" I ask. "I could carry mountains, cars, and trains. I could move the sea, the oceans, the earth. But Mother told me my priority is to protect famil—"

I trip over the uneven tile in front of Mother's bed. Before I fall over, I toss Kat on the other bed and use an arm to cushion my fall. My knees and my chest absorb most of the impact of the fall. I lie face down for a few seconds.

The impact isn't as bad as I built it up. I barely feel much, and look at the uneven tile while still lying on the floor. Without touching it, I lift it. I focus on the tile and use my mind to shoot a wave at the piece; it hops a couple of centimetres in the air before cartwheeling to the wall, revealing uneven grout below. While getting up off the floor, I kick it into the far corner of the room away from anyone else. The floor looks worse, but people can see it's uneven, and I'll notify the hospital of a tripping hazard.

"Are you alright, Sidney?" Mom asks, staying by Mother's side. I pat down my face. There's no blood, tile dust, or dirt sticking to my face.

"I'm fine," I answer. "I have never been better." I stand back up and walk back towards Mom, holding my head high without missing a step.

Kat jumps down. "Where's the tile?"

And that was all the confirmation I needed: last night happened.

Part 1.4: What's Going to Happen?

I look at the time on my phone: five o'clock in the morning. I put my head on my pillow and close my eyes.

* * *

I will see gridlock; the street signs will say Slater and Bank. Harriet will be to my right as we walk on the sidewalk. The heat will be unbearable. We will follow the traffic due east, scanning up and down Slater Street. Harriet will inform me of the lack of collisions. We will walk until we reach Metcalfe and will head north to Wellington. We will notice a section of Wellington is barricaded as we approach Parliament. There will be a sea of people with signs saying, "Radioactively participating in my democracy," or "Cher-NO-byl." The picket signs change every time I look at them. There will be a protest on Parliament Hill. Harriet will be looking at her phone and will show me a text that says Sid is checking out of the hospital, then she will look up and smile. We will merge with the crowd for a couple of minutes then we will walk away. We will make it just in time to meet up with the rest of the faceless group at uOttawa. The first building we will visit is one of the dormitories. The tour guide will open the doors for us. Harriet and I will be the first to enter the building.

Harriet and I will enter our restaurant and sit in one of the booths. My brothers, Abba, Veera, and a young man with a boyish face and an adult body will join us at the table. The restaurant will be empty. Abba will quiet everyone down as we prepare to listen to Vipesh Uncle's interview. We will then eat some Palak Paneer, Chana Masala with some Naan and Bhatura. Meanwhile, Harriet will be eating some roti and vegetable biryani. After dinner, Harriet will leave with Vipesh, my brothers, and the boy-faced man. Meanwhile, Veera, Abba, and I will be cleaning up the restaurant. I will then open the door and walk upstairs to our apartment.

I will enter Ms. Stone's chemistry class. Our lab today will be creating aspirin from two ingredients: acetic anhydride and salicylic acid. Yasmine will be preparing the flask with salicylic acid while I obtain the hazardous acetic anhydride from the ventilation hood. While obtaining the pipette, I will look back and see Sid and will get scared. The bottle of acetic anhydride will fall with me and shatter. It will land far away from my face but on my lab coat. Ms. Stone will rush me into the chemical shower. The door will slam behind me and I will promptly slip. Lying down, I will close my eyes.

I will open my eyes again and find myself lying on some cold asphalt. I will look around and see a river and steel cables joining a red metal arch. Someone will be standing over me. It will be a man in a black hoodie and black pants. He will climb on top of me, place his hands on my throat, and squeeze until I cannot breathe. I will hit him, kick him, yell for help, but the roads will be empty. Then I will see another figure raise their hands, trying to fight back. They will be wearing white clothes and will have a couple of strands of red hair. My eyes will roll backwards.

* * *

I wake up hyperventilating and with misty eyes, unable to control myself. I grab my chest and feel the urge to scream, but I cover my mouth.

The adrenaline fades quickly, and I start to feel tired again. I breathe and think about how I got into this position. I was unable to sleep for the longest time. I check the time on my phone: it's now seven in the morning.

If I had slept for only two hours, I would have about two weeks for everything in those visions to happen. It starts with the protests and ends on the Morissette Bridge.

The door swings open. "Wake up, T. We have to depart in an hour." Harriet sprints to my side. She looks as good as ever. No hideous deformities from the explosion, no bandages or casts. She's just beautiful, bright Harriet, dressed in a white blouse, a short, grey dress skirt, and perfect makeup.

She's staring at the bed on the other side of my room. My older sister Veera is fast asleep. She arrived at midnight and hasn't said a word to me, even though I was awake then.

"Coming," I whisper as I climb out of my bed. But I lose my balance and fall on the floor, not realizing I don't have two legs to stand on. Thankfully, Ammi had the foresight to install an area rug in our room before we moved in. I fall gently onto my face. I'm in no pain; in fact, I feel comfortable enough to fall back asleep. Two hours isn't enough time to recharge. Harriet should understand, she shouldn't even be going on a tour; she was just in the hospital.

"*Allons-y.*" She grabs both my arms and crosses them, lifting my face off the ground and rolling me into my chair next to my desk. She lifts my left pyjama pants leg to expose my stump. "Do you need me to do this, or can you manage?" she asks sarcastically. She knows I've lived without a left leg for almost ten years now.

"I can manage." I grab my light, carbon-fibre prosthetic next to my desk and slide the fitted sleeve onto my stump. I slide the socket of the prosthetic and roll the pyjama leg up. Harriet leaves my room as I perform my daily checks. Using my phone, I calibrate my leg; I lean backwards, and it locks. I lean forward, and my knee bends. I sit down and lift my stump upwards; it kicks back up again. I wiggle my stump around and confirm friction is holding it in place. Everything is operational.

Now I need to pick something to wear to the tour at uOttawa. Harriet is wearing a miniskirt and a blouse, so I should probably dress similarly. The tour starts at ten in the morning, and it's already half-past seven. It would take an hour and a half to get there by the O-Train, so we would need to get to the station by half-past, which means we are in a rush to leave.

I grab the first two things I can find: black pants and a white button-down blouse, along with my hairbrush. I put them on and exit my room. Harriet is operating the stove. The smell of chai brewing on my stove perks me up and carries me to the kitchen table.

Harriet brings a chair out for me. "We knew chai would be just what you needed right now. It's what I need, too." She takes a sip from the pot.

"Thanks." I run the brush through my hair. "And also for helping me back up in my room."

"*Pas de problème.* Anything to help out a fallen comrade." She giggles as she continues to taste the pot. I give her a courtesy laugh. The joke's dumb, but it's better than most of the one-liners I get from Varshil.

There is only one thing I want to talk about right now because I have been losing sleep over it. How can she look so good after everything that happened? "So..." I struggle to find a way to bring up the explosion. "About the..." I stammer, hoping Harriet would eventually finish my sentence.

"Explosion?" Harriet winks.

I let out an audible sigh of relief. "I don't want to pry. I mean, I don't love sharing details about injuries."

"I can tell you. Of course, I'll tell you." Harriet pulls up a chair and sits down with a second cup of chai. "As you know, we went on a field trip to the nuclear power plant. Ten students were sent to the hospital, five of whom arrived unconscious, and the other five were treated with minor injuries. I just had minor injuries." She undoes a couple of buttons and pulls her collar over her shoulder, showing me a bruise about the size of a fist and a couple of stitches near her left triceps. "No one got too seriously hurt, thank goodness." She walks to our fridge. "But these will not heal." She rebuttons her blouse.

"Well, that's not exactly true," I say.

Harriet spins around, confused by what I said.

"No one died in the explosion, but the power outages did affect people, mainly freak accidents," I explain. Last night, I was trying to distract myself with some news to try and sleep fast. I tried to find some current events stories that were not particularly interesting in the first place. However, the biggest headlines were from the power plant explosion. Many stories compared the event to Chernobyl, but the more I read, the less catastrophic I&MNG seemed. It would be unfair to compare it to one of Canada's worst accidents, the Level 5 Chalk River Accident.

Based on the International Nuclear Event Scale, I would estimate the explosion as a Level 1 Anomaly. I'm not an expert in categorizing nuclear disasters, however, there were no expensive cleanup efforts, the plant only shut down for a couple of hours for minor repairs and is operating at a reduced output.

I did find out about all the hospitalized students; one of the students is my best friend, Yasmine. I tried texting her the night before. However, she still hasn't answered.

"*Oh, mon Dieu,*" Harriet exclaims. "It's horrible to think about the town of Manotick. They have houses, businesses, schools, and campaign offices that will all be affected by this tragedy." Harriet gets back up and turns off the stove. "Maybe we should be glad that more people didn't get hurt, eh? Anyway, you need to eat something before we go. Your dad will drop us off at Bowesville, which should save us some time in taking a bus to the train stop."

Typically, the bus connecting Riverside to Islington would only come every hour on a Saturday. The ride takes another ten minutes, so getting dropped off in a car is worth it. And Harriet would have no strong objections to taking Abba's electric minivan. She's pretty particular about the way she travels. She would only ride in a plug-in if she were desperate and never in a gas-powered car; she would rather walk.

"Thanks. Where is my dad?" I ask.

"He's in the restaurant, talking to my dad. As soon as he's done, he'll drive us."

I drink the chai, eat the apple and some handvo as fast as I can. I still feel exhausted, but I will try to sleep as much as possible on the bus. I have mastered the ability to fall asleep anywhere, as long as someone's protecting me, and Harriet seems well-rested enough.

"Hari?" Abba's powerful voice makes its way to our kitchen from downstairs. I continue to eat and drink my breakfast. "Your father just rescheduled his interview for six p.m. You two should be back before then." He enters the kitchen. "Anyway, are you girls ready for the first day of your university life?"

"It's just a tour, Vipan Uncle. I haven't even decided if I want to go there," Harriet answers.

"Ah, yes," Abba puts his phone back into his pocket. "But the tour is where you fall in love with the school. You can do all the research on your laptops about your program. But this is when you immerse yourself in the culture. Your real first college experience."

Harriet and I exchange looks. She raises an eyebrow and smirks; I mirror her expression.

"You know, within reason, don't do anything illegal or dangerous," Abba offers a quick correction. "Promise me you will keep each other safe. I don't want to have to deal with Vipesh Kaka again."

I would never do any such thing, I would never leave Harriet's side. I have been downtown, and it's a terrifying place for a teenage girl with limited mobility.

"What do you mean?" Harriet asks Abba.

"Your father is a sensitive man; when he heard you were in a terrible accident yesterday, he wanted to end his campaign to be by your side. And he was going to, until he heard you checked out."

Harriet sinks into her chair; her smirk turns sullen. "Yes, Uncle. We will be fine. I have everything I could ever need in my backpack."

"Excuse me for one second." I walk into my room, trying not to disturb Veera. I grab my purse and look inside: bus pass, phone, a serviette, money, mints, and earbuds. I'll never leave my house without my headphones. They help me drown out my surroundings and concentrate to see a calmer version of the future. My visions are boring most of the time. They are typically me walking by myself, eating food, or getting the answers to a future test.

They are supposed to be repetitive, but last night, something changed. These visions are completely different from the ones I had yesterday and the past nine weeks.

I erase the whiteboard above my bed and update the visions. I write down in Urdu:

بڑا احتجاج ، عشائیہ ، لیب حادثہ ، پل تصادم

(large protest, dinner, lab accident, bridge conflict)

Urdu is the only language no one in my family can read, aside from my Ammi. My Abba and siblings come into my room any time they want, but they wouldn't understand the writings on the wall. Given my two hours of sleep, the established dates for the final vision to occur must be between October twentieth to twenty-seventh. They always follow a sequential order.

What's going to happen to me on that bridge? I can't identify many features on the shadowy figure in black, so I might not have met him yet, like the faceless mob in our tour group. But as I meet more people, maybe he will reveal himself.

But the first thing I need to look out for is a protest on Parliament Hill. It will most likely happen today; I'm going downtown. I can never hear words coming out of their mouths, nor can I talk, but I infer what's happening based on later actions.

After writing everything down, I go to the bathroom, comb my hair, and apply some antiperspirant. I tie my hair into a bun behind my head and wash and moisturize my face.

My eyes are a little bloodshot, but hopefully the chai will kick in. I feel alright, not great, not terrible. I exit our apartment and enter Abba's car: it's now a quarter past eight.

Part 1.5: What's Happening?
Vritikha, October 9th, 9:30

I will see gridlock; the street signs will say Slater and Bank. Harriet will be to my right as we walk on the sidewalk. The heat will be unbearable. We will follow the traffic due east, scanning up and down Slater Street. Harriet will inform me of the lack of collisions. We will walk until we reach Metcalfe and will head north to Wellington. We will notice a section of Wellington is barricaded as we approach Parliament. There will be a sea of people with signs saying, "Radioactively participating in my democracy" or "Cher-NO-byl". The picket signs will change every time I look at them. There will be a protest on Parliament Hill. Harriet will be looking at her phone and will show me a text that says Sid is checking out of the hospital, then she will look up and smile. We will merge with the crowd for a couple of minutes, then will walk away. We will make it just in time to meet up with the rest of the faceless group at uOttawa. The first building we will visit is one of the dormitories. The tour guide will open the doors for us. Harriet and I will be the first to enter the building.

Harriet and I will enter our restaurant and sit in one of the booths. My brothers, Abba, Veera, and a young man with a boyish face and an adult body will join us at the table. The restaurant will be empty. Abba will quiet everyone down as we are preparing to listen to Vipesh Uncle's interview when—

I will be in my bed; Veera will be stroking my hair—

I will be carrying a backpack. Yasmine will be with me holding a bunch of lawn signs with Vipesh's face and name on them. We will canvas the neighbourhoods to put up some lawn signs for potential future voters in Manotick. We will get bothered by the heat, and Yasmine will be especially drained, sneezing every ten seconds—

I will be in the library now. Yasmine and I will be sitting at a table, trying to write up a lab report on why our aspirin was of poor quality. I will also have two stage plays to review, one of *Macbeth* and the other of *King Lear*—

The library computer and chair under me will suddenly change into an office computer. And the plastic chair will transform into an office chair with wheels. I will be in Vipesh's campaign office, calling people to encourage them to come out and vote—

I will still be in his office, except my attire will have changed. I will be standing and wearing a blazer and a skirt with leggings. We will be hearing the results of election night. He will lose—

I will be in my room, cutting my hair—

I will be outside on the Morissette Bridge again. The streetlights will be extremely dim. The figure in black will raise his hands. The ground underneath me will sink, a blue light will blind us, and four cables will snap spontaneously—

I will lie on the ground next to the riverbank, separated by a ridge connected to a road. Broken glass will line the asphalt. The two figures will fight; the one in white will be on the ground while the one in black will be kicking them. I will try to escape, but my left leg will be jammed.

* * *

I wake and place my hand on my chest, keeping my eyes closed. This has never happened to me before. Usually, I open a door or close my eyes to transport myself into a new part of a vision, but these abrupt scene changes in my visions leave me befuddled. I could never control my visions, but I always saw them change naturally. Now I can't even understand why the original rules I have come to learn and accept have changed so suddenly, making me feel more powerless than ever.

"T?" Harriet shakes me until my eyes open again. "Hey, we have to get off now." Most people around me have already gotten off the train.

"Where are we? And how long was I out?" I whisper. The air-conditioning is quite pleasant. I bring my hands up to rub my eyes.

"You don't want to do that." Harriet slaps my hands away before I touch my face. "You've been asleep for about an hour."

Is everything I just envisioned supposed to happen in a week? The election will occur on October twenty-eighth, which is in two weeks. According to my previous visions, the bridge fight vision is supposed to happen in about two weeks. It doesn't make sense; either the train or the people around me are giving me some terrible interference.

I take out my phone and write down my visions anyway, just in case: a protest, a dinner, canvassing, multitasking, telemarketing, Vipesh's loss, cutting my hair, four severed cables, and a collapsed bridge.

While writing the visions down, a news alert pops up, notifying everyone that the I&MNG accident has claimed its first real casualty. I put the phone back into my pocket. "The chai didn't do anything," I exclaim. We get up from the foul-smelling felt seats at the back of the carriage, sitting higher than everyone else. To my right is an all-glass building and the reflection of people outside, people in suits, people with bikes, small children, and shop owners and a bus. "This isn't a train," I reason. "And we're not at uOttawa."

"No shit," Harriet snarls. "We missed the O-Train. We had to take a hybrid bus, and we are stuck in the middle of downtown, ten minutes away from where we need to go, in thirty-five-degree weather." Her nostrils flare as she rants, and her accent changes from French-Canadian to North American.

I have seen Harriet angry or upset only a couple of times in her life. She can get a little obsessed or stressed because she's such a huge part of her father's campaign, but neither she nor her father are aggressive. The only time I have seen her truly emotional over anything non-campaign-related was when she had an abortion a week ago, and before that, it was when her mother died, which was ten years ago.

"Are you alright, Hari?" I ask her. I pause the song *Yellow Light* on my phone, keep my earbuds in place, and rub my eyes. A stinging sensation makes its way into my corneas and I try to blink the irritations out.

She looks down as she exits the bus; I join as soon as I regain my footing. The intense heat strikes the back of my neck and hands, the only areas of my body not covered. I make a mental note: never wear black pants in the middle of a heatwave. My real right leg is sweating a little while my carbon-fibre socket and sleeve create a makeshift oven for my stump. I could have worn my realistic silicon-skin leg. It would make me walk slower because it's a non-mechanical prosthetic, but I could wear something shorter without drawing attention to myself.

I follow her to the back of the bus. "*Pardon, monsieur?*" she asks the bus driver who is examining the engine. "*Qu'est-se-que se passe ici? Avec l'autobus?*"

"*Je ne sais pas. L'autobus est soudainement demeuré pour aucune raison,*" the driver answers. "*Mais il va fonctionner. Attendez, s'il vous plait, pour quelques minutes.*"

"Oh, for f...we can walk it," Harriet suggests. "Screw it, *merci.*" She thanks the bus driver, then grabs my wrist and hoists me eastward along Slater Street.

"Are you alright?" I repeat. "Did you take your pills?" It seems like an overreaction to the bus breaking down.

"I'm fine, it's not the bus. I spoke to my dad and everything's true. I can't believe he would give up the campaign so easily." We continue to walk along Slater Street. Even from Vipesh's point of view, I would be devastated if my only child got hurt. I would drop everything to be with her.

"But—"

"Even for me," she interrupts. "If something bad did happen to me, he should feel more of an incentive to campaign."

I have never seen someone so willing to fridge themselves before today, but that's Harriet; willing to sacrifice herself for the greater good.

"You should feel so lucky," I say, trying to blink out the irritations. "How many people can say they would give up everything for their only child?" Sometimes I wish I had the same kind of relationship with my Ammi or Abba, mainly when my brothers aggravate me. "I think you're overreacting. He's back in the race, and everything is good now." I twirl my hair around my fingers, neglecting to add the bit about a man dying. She doesn't need to know right now.

"He was overreacting, not me." She lets out one more remark and then turns her head to me. "What's wrong with you?"

I'm darting my eyes back and forth, blinking a lot, shutting my eyelids for a few seconds then opening them back up for a few more seconds. A miniature pulse starts throbbing inside them. I keep my hands in my pockets, even though they don't fit. "I accidentally rubbed my eyes on the bus."

"Keep them open," she tells me. We seek shade in an entranceway of a Bridgehead as she examines me. A gentle breeze washes over my eyes. "I don't see any irritation; your eyes aren't red. You should be fine. But if worse comes to worst, we can go to a bathroom, and you can flush them."

I cautiously nod along. She proceeds to take her backpack and opens two unmarked bottles; she turns them upside down and takes two pills, one white and another orange. "Do you want an aspirin or phenelzine?" she jokingly offers.

"No."

She swallows them simultaneously, without water. "Shall we?"

We walk for a good five minutes in silence. I start to slow down a little, feeling a little lightheaded. I take out a serviette from my purse and start dabbing my forehead. Unfortunately, I didn't pack a water bottle. A cooling breeze wipes across my face and jolts my head up. We are at the intersection of Metcalfe and Slater.

"How long will it take to get there?" I ask while waiting at the intersection.

"Around five to ten minutes," she answers.

"Okay, that's...manageable."

"Or on second thought, maybe we should blow off the tour, get something to eat, and then go home."

"We're halfway there, we can do this," I reason.

"I'm not feeling too hot," she says with a non-glistening, perfectly made-up face.

I want to scream at her, because she doesn't look like she's dying from the heat.

"I mean, I am boiling, but I just got out of the hospital. And I don't think you are feeling well, either. I said I didn't see any irritation in your eyes, but I know you're tired. How long did you sleep last night?"

She knows me so well, but I wish she knew the chai she made didn't wake me. "Two hours," I answer. "But it doesn't matter. I'll get a coffee at uOttawa."

"Two hours?" she raises her voice. "You know what, screw the tour. We've already done a lot of research. The environmental studies program is among my top three choices. I'm sure you've done a lot of research on the political science program. So, what else is there to see?"

She's right, I'd already made up my mind. uOttawa is my first choice, mainly for its location and program. Also, I can understand how tours could be traumatizing for her. The important thing is she's no longer thinking about her father and how he almost quit, so maybe the change of plans could be good for her. "Okay," I comply. "Where do you want to eat? Do you know any non-franchised, locally-sourced, vegan restaurants nearby?"

"I'm always prepared." She smiles at me and pulls out her phone.

A bus drives past us, the cool breeze of recirculated air cools me for a few seconds, and to make matters worse, it's the same one we were on a few minutes ago. "You've got to be kidding me. Harriet, we could have been there much faster if we stayed." But the real question is, how did I not see this coming?

"You sure about that?" She points to the massive queue of cars along Slater Street. The bus stops at Metcalfe behind the pileup and lets everyone off again. The number nine displayed on the bus turns into a couple of dashes, indicating it's out of service.

A hoard of annoyed bus riders file into a line and enter the Parliament O-Train station. Harriet opens maps on her phone. "Yeah, this whole area is shit. Both Slater and Albert are red. We have time to wait until the traffic thins out. After all, we need to get back by six o'clock. If we are blowing off the tour, we have about four and a half hours to wander the city." Harriet smiles for the first time since getting off the bus. "So that would give us around one and a half hours to eat and three hours to do anything else, and we would still have one hour to travel back home."

"Why, six o'clock?" I ask.

"Your dad mentioned something about having one of your old family friends over. Also, that's the time of my dad's interview with the CBC. We're all going to listen to it together. Where's your head at, girl?"

Abba briefed me in the car yesterday. The family friend is a boy named Krishna Sethi. Our families knew each other back in India before moving. He's now in his first-year studying Computer Sciences at Algonquin College. My visions show him with an uncanny, younger face because I haven't seen him in more than nine years and it's how I remember him.

"Hey." Harriet points to her left. "You see that crowd of people about two blocks up?"

I can't see where she's pointing, so I continue to walk toward the university, but she's very persistent. We turn left onto Metcalfe and continue to walk north in the blazing heat.

The sun from the south burns my neck as we walk towards the Parliament. "Where are we going? I thought we were going to eat."

"It's ten-thirty. But come on, T. We're downtown, and history is happening right now."

"Are you going to break out into song?" I quip.

"No," she frowns. "If this were the greatest city in the world, I might. But it cannot come close to the natural beauty of Montreal. It's not as eclectic as New York. Still, it is our home, and it beats that corporate shithole, Toronto. Where's your sense of adventure? *Allons-y!*"

She runs past me at full speed. I try to speedwalk, but I cannot keep up with her without manually adjusting the speed on my leg. She runs back towards me after a beat.

"You know I can't run," I politely inform her.

"Oh, because of that?" Harriet gestures towards my leg. "I know a guy like you, another Canadian AK amputee who ran halfway across the country."

"And then he died." I shut my eyes and groan. Sometimes, arguing with her is like talking with a stubborn reactionary.

"Maybe that was a little insensitive. I'll walk at your pace." She joins me by my side. "But I imagine you would be eager to check out the big city. Haven't you ever done this before? Have you ever just set yourself free? Forgotten about your deadlines and responsibilities momentarily and wander around aimlessly exploring, alone with nothing but your thoughts? We don't get many moments like these today, so you must savour them."

I shake my head. Being alone with my thoughts is terrifying most of the time. I always try to listen to music to keep my mind busy. The last time I set foot out of Islington was during summer school. We went inside the Greenbelt, to Chinatown. Yasmine, Harriet, Kyle, and I took twelfth-grade calculus, and Yasmine wanted to see her now ex-boyfriend. I make an exception for Bluesfest every July, but I'm just too busy being a waitress at my family's restaurant while saving enough money to pay for my university tuition.

As we continue to walk north, unintelligible dialogue becomes louder by the second.

"What's happening?" we ask simultaneously.

And then we see it: protestors complete with signs, bullhorns, and creative chants. They are a diverse group of people from an Indigenous people's group protesting how climate change will affect their homes and infrastructure to a group of students from varying schools across the Ottawa area demanding a secure future. There's even a group of retirees from a nursing home who don't want their graves to be flooded and want their grandchildren to have safe lives.

This is an organized climate awareness rally. And some of the signs are about the I&MNG explosion from yesterday. It gives them more ammunition to launch their grand gesture; many are masked because of the worsening air quality or bandaged because of stronger UV rays. Wellington Street is barricaded, and I start cheering at the lady leading some of the chants.

At this moment, I understand what Harriet's talking about. I forget about my schoolwork, running a restaurant, and getting choked by some shadowy figure. At this moment, I have a feeling of hope that things could get better. In this age of fast-spreading information, a large group of people could make a difference. The politicians will listen to us because we represent every age, race, and income demographic. I remove one earbud from my right ear. I allow my body to gravitate toward the crowds and give them a small smirk.

"Sid just got out of the hospital," Harriet elates, then looks up from her phone, and a twinkle develops in her eye. "What are you waiting for, comrade? *Vive la révolution!*"

Part 1.6: Drifting, Floating, Falling
Sidney, October 9th, 17:30

After encountering a dead body, visiting Mother, and sitting through an hour of driving, Mom, Kat, and I make our way to the farmer's market in Manotick. We spend up to two to three hours talking to our neighbours or scouring the aisles and looking for the best food to graze our tables.

Mom and Mr. Ganatra have a long conversation about the future of the plant workers. She voices her reasonable doubts but believes his intentions to transition plant workers to more renewable jobs. She's skeptical about the bill making its way through the legislature. She fears that given Mother's sick leave, she may be unable to work as long, and Mr. Ganatra doesn't do much to ease her doubts.

We arrive home around five-thirty in the evening. Kat and Mom carry everything into the house. I offer to help; however, she tells me to save my strength. We enter the common area and find our sister sitting at the dining room table, violently typing out her stories.

She's intensely fixated on her laptop and doesn't even notice us. A vein pops out of her forehead as she hunches over her computer. Neither Kat nor I would disturb her when she's in the zone. But Mom's not either of us.

"Mindy?" Mom gets her attention. "Come say hi to your brother."

Mindy lets out an annoyed sigh. "Hey, Sid, how are you feeling?" She doesn't even look up from her computer.

"He just got out of the hospital," she raises her voice sharply. "He's been through so much today." She clenches her teeth and furrows her eyebrows. "Get off your computer and give him a proper welcome back!"

Mindy shuts her laptop hastily then speed-walks to the door and hugs me. "Sorry, I couldn't come to see Mother today. I had a group project for Print Journalism. You know how two-term courses are, and my team couldn't coordinate another time, anyway. Welcome back, bro." The hug only lasts two seconds, and her greeting lasts only seven; however, I savour all nine seconds.

Since she started her final year of university, we've had only brief glimpses of her. She comes home some Saturdays for dinner; otherwise, she's MIA. "Thanks, Mindy. I do feel better." By the time I finish my sentence, she's already back at her computer. I wouldn't describe her as a workaholic, because she doesn't only spend time doing school work. She's rather obsessively organized and knows how to budget her time for school and her social life, planning her days to the minute.

Mindy's constantly advancing beyond her age, as she skipped the second and seventh grades. And she's still inclined to prove she deserves to be ahead. No one has ever said otherwise to her; however, this mentality helps her excel at anything and everything she wants. She tries to make time for her family; however, her schedule changed drastically after the news of Mother's surgeries. Mom was never too bothered by Mindy working too hard, but after the first surgery, Mom became annoyed at Mindy for spending more and more time away from us. Her fourth-year workload was much larger than anticipated, as she was prone to carrying everyone in her group, even redoing work she deemed inadequate.

Mom doesn't buy her excuses. "Help me with these bags, Mindy." She picks up half of the groceries and walks them into the kitchen.

"Can I finish this paragraph?" Mindy, still tapping away on her laptop, responds. "It will only take a minute."

"Sure, honey, I hope you get your article done soon. The world will need to know how a nineteen-year-old girl ended up at the bottom of the Rideau River. And I'll even write the headline." Mom puts the groceries on the kitchen floor and raises her hands above her head. "'Mom Cleans House All by Herself'." That's a long setup to arrive at not much of a punchline.

Mindy closes her computer softly and saunters to the front door, taking the grocery bags from Kat. "I'm doing this out of courtesy. I know you wouldn't do that to me, there are witnesses here." She brings them three meters from the front door, into the kitchen.

"No, it's because I'm your mom." She walks her back from the kitchen to the foyer. "This isn't going to be easy for anyone." She grabs her face firmly, so they are looking at each other eye to eye. "Your mother might not be the same when she comes back, which means everyone here needs to pick up some more work. And the best way to keep a healthy household is to be present, it's what she would want."

Mindy lets out a less-than-enthusiastic 'fine' before breaking from Mom's grasp. She picks up her laptop and gives it to Kat. "Can you put this in our room?"

Kat nods.

"Wait, kids." Mom signals for us to come over to her. Kat runs back to Mom. "One last thing before we break." She takes all three of us in her arms. Kat, Mindy, and I are all just bunched up together as we join the hug. "I love you guys."

I feel cozy in the family embrace even if it only lasts for half a minute, then we all go on our way. "Sidney, stay on the couch. Dinner will be ready soon. Katherine, keep an ear out for him."

"Okie." Kat runs to her room, probably to disappear in her games.

Mom and Mindy enter the kitchen, and I sit on the couch in the adjoining living area in front of a large window overlooking our backyard. I can hear everything from my position on the couch. Only a thin wall separates the kitchen from the dining area and living room. My parents love this house because of its small size and large yard. We have so much space in the warm months and are close at night and in winter.

In our large backyard is this year's disorganized blend of assorted produce. The berry bushes grow next to vegetables; carrots and celery crowd each other, and the vines of grapes and cucumbers wrap around the same trellises. The lush, green grass is populated with dandelions, ragweed, crabgrass; I feel bad for not spending more time gardening or maintaining our lawn.

We have cultivated our yards every summer since we moved into this house. I have lived here for basically my whole life. When Mindy and I were younger, we would have so much fun sowing seeds or planting flowers in our gardens and flowerbeds, getting a kick out of putting in some actual manual labour. We grew onions, leeks, potatoes, garlic, and peppers throughout the summer, and gourds in autumn. Mindy and I would run across the garden without any reason once the harvest season was over, tossing leftover scraps at each other. Mom and Mother would watch us together on the porch. In those days we had a surplus and sold our excess crops at the farmer's market.

We were also thinking about growing some tropical fruits. We knew the season was not long enough to produce anything edible; however, we did harvest a mango pit and got a seed to sprout, although no fruit came from that experiment.

As the years progressed and the heat advisory warnings increased, more time was spent indoors. And combined with our increasingly busy schedules, our crop yield significantly decreased. Mindy was not there to help create an organizational pattern, so we tried to recapture some of the enjoyment we had in our heyday. Kat began to plant seeds in an disorderly fashion. We then hoped that something would grow from the mess, and to our surprise, something did.

We didn't have a surplus of food this summer. The wildlife running through our minimally-fenced property consumed most of our yield. We're not farmers by any stretch of the word; we didn't depend monetarily on selling what we grew. We live in the largest cul-de-sac neighbourhood of our semi-rural town, but there are pastures within walking distance. Some are slowly being bought up and converted into soulless condominium complexes or new commercial spaces, prompting those farmers to move south.

I don't want to leave Manotick, especially not the Greater Ottawa Area. The furthest I would consider is Islington. I want to keep the coziness my family has cultivated in Manotick. I love how close we all are, but the drift has already started, and I will look no further than to Mindy and Mother.

While her conditions aren't ideal, they should improve. I could get a pass on not doing homework, given the circumstances. And since I have no other notifications, I throw my phone to my feet and lie on the couch.

But I have run into a problem; I'm bored. I already made myself comfortable, and I don't want to walk to my room to get my book; also, yelling at Kat to help me would take more energy than just making the ten necessary paces, as my room shares a wall with the living/dining room.

So I try to figure out other ways to preoccupy myself. On the adjacent coffee table is Mother's Kindle. It's not technically a screen because it doesn't shine blue light. Mother sits here reading whenever she has free time. When Mindy and I were little, Mother read fantasy books, like *The Chronicles of Narnia* or the *Earthsea Cycle.* When we got older, she would read murder mysteries by authors such as Agatha Christie and Arthur Conan Doyle.

I turn it on and see Mother is reading *The Doors of Stone.* The green backlit screen blinds me. Since I don't know how to operate the ancient technology, I compromise by holding it far away from my face. I extend my arms and lie down, scrolling through the collection of books. Some of my favourites show up:

Margaret Atwood, Ted Chiang, Philip K. Dick, etc. and as I scroll through the list of authors, I find *The Awakening* by Kate Chopin.

"Sidney?" Mom yells from the kitchen, startling me enough to lose grip of the Kindle. "Could you set the table for us, please?"

"'Kay." I shut my eyes, bracing for the impact on my face. After a few seconds, I open them and find the Kindle floating equidistant from my face and my hands. I concentrate as I had in the hospital room, and the Kindle flies farther away and almost hits the ceiling.

I look at my feet and keep the same thought. No one in my family is watching me, so it's the perfect time to experiment.

When I tilt my head upwards, the Kindle descends. I pick it up and place it a good arm's-length away from my head. I close my eyes and lower my hands, thinking about its placement in my head.

I fear the Kindle will dent my skull or crack one of my lenses; however, I keep still and find it hovering. I giggle, and to my surprise, it flies higher on its own. I laugh; I cannot believe what the man said in the hospital is true. It's applicable and controllable.

"Sid, whenever you're ready."

I panic and lose concentration; the Kindle falls downwards, and I squirm and brace for impact. But it comes within centimetres of my face. I manage to stop it right before it knocks me out.

No amount of money, good grades, or admiration from my friends compares to this moment. I made something hover with my mind. Now I know the abilities are connected to my emotions. Happiness is a slow, gradual ascent, being scared delivers a quick burst, and being inattentive makes them disappear.

Levitation is an exciting start, but thinking back to the list of abilities he mentioned—manipulating matter, controlling minds or changing chemical compounds—I hadn't scratched the surface of what I could do.

A pounding sensation in my forehead paralyzes me; my fingers twitch a little. I may be still dehydrated from the long day we had. I grab the table to keep myself from falling over.

"Katherine, dinner's ready," Mom yells. A one-person stampede approaches us as the stairs creak and groan. I grab my head as the headache intensifies. Mom catches me before I tumble and sits me down. "I'm sorry, baby; if it's too much, I'll get the bowls."

"I can do this." I get up, although I have nothing to prove. Once the stampede dies down, I walk to the kitchen and open the cabinet.

I count four bowls and plates. The smells in the kitchen are enough to make my stomach churn. Mom and Mindy have made minestrone and bread from scratch. Maybe organic food will balance the amount of sugar I had for breakfast.

The soup is relatively uncomplicated, just boiled vegetables, legumes, and noodles. As the growing season is ending, Mother has plans to use everything from the garden.

I grab a glass of water for myself and set the table for the four of us, bowl on the left side, plates in the center, and a spoon and butter knife on the right. I place a napkin underneath the two utensils. Mindy has a way of setting the table and even a seating arrangement. Mom and Mother sit on the edge across from each other, Mindy sits to the left of Mother, I sit next to the right of Mom, and Kat sits at the head.

When I open the pot, the fumes immediately fog up my glasses. It did help cleanse my pores as I fan the steam into my face. Mindy shuts the pot loudly, briefly reactivating my tinnitus. "We're not ready to eat yet." Mom comes in with the bread and starts slicing it.

"By the way, Sidney," Mom says. "You forgot to close the cabinet again." Before she sits down, I look at the kitchen through the open door and see the cabinets ajar, exposing the plates, bowls, and glasses. But instead of walking to the kitchen, I look at the cabinet and think about happier thoughts.

I was nine years old; our family had decided they wanted a third child. Since they had many complications from their previous pregnancies, they decided to adopt. I was excited to become an older sibling, and Mindy wanted me to experience the same pain I caused her. There weren't many choices back home; they had tried for almost a year before looking internationally. They also felt disheartened when they received eight rejections from local agencies. But I never forgot the feeling when they received their first approval. It was a long process, but it was worth it when our parents saw Katherine. She was an adorable, four-month-old baby girl from South Africa who was put up for adoption because her mom died in childbirth and her father could not be found.

We travelled to Cape Town to see her and got a feel for the culture to help her keep her roots. We also got briefed on her condition. She was born three months premature and had a recent surgery to fill a hole in her heart.

After a long, painful process, she was ready to come to Manotick with her new family. She had been worth the wait. We could not imagine any other child in place of Kat; she was so chubby and adorable, and as she grew, she only got more energetic and made our world much brighter.

I smile, look at the cabinet, and the two doors slam shut.

"Ow," Mom yells. I spin around quickly to find Mom fallen on her butt, cradling her elbow in her right hand, my smile fades.

"Mom?" Kat shouts.

Mindy rushes around the table to help her up. "Are you okay?" She brings Mom to her feet.

Mom brushes herself off and sits down. "I just lost balance for a second. It felt like a heavy breeze that came from nowhere and just knocked me onto my butt." She giggles to herself. "We should turn down the AC, but I'm fine."

We all look at her, concerned.

"I'm fine," she says. "I have suffered many worse falls on my patrols. We don't need any more reasons to go to the hospital today."

She laughs, but Mindy and Kat exchange confused looks.

I squint and inhale through my teeth silently; it's my fault. Mom fell backwards, and I was in front of her. I pushed so hard it rebounded and knocked her down as well.

The man warned me I had an unfocused but solid blow. If she was holding the knife, the situation could have been much worse. I need to focus on budgeting an appropriate amount of power. I've got a lot to learn.

Part 1.7: Blackout
Sidney, October 9ᵗʰ, 18:00

For the first time since the middle of the summer, all of us except Mother are eating together; but four out of five is a record for our family. Even if Mindy didn't stay late at university and Mother wasn't sick, Mom would usually work overtime, meaning Kat and I would be the only ones at home on the weekdays.

I finish drinking my second water, but the migraine persists, so I make chamomile tea. I walk to the kitchen and boil some water. Within about ten seconds, I have it ready. I dip the teabag in repeatedly and proceed back to the dining table.

"Sidney, could you turn the radio off?" Mom asks.

CBC is playing. "Welcome back to the program. Now let us introduce our next guest. He's the Green Party nominee running for Parliament in the Ottawa-Rural South's District; joining us over the phone is Mr. Vipesh Ganatra. Thank you for joining us today."

"Thank you for having me."

"Vipesh, did I say that right?"

"That's perfect. And thank you for having me back after I cancelled. My daughter was in a bad accident yesterday, but she's doing much better now."

"No problem—"

"Sidney?" Mom interrupts from the other room. I turn it off. I don't invest myself in politics but I want to support Mr. Ganatra. He has always been a father figure to me. From kindergarten until the second grade, I was good friends with Harriet and sought a male role model. Mr. Ganatra was the best candidate. When he and Harriet moved away in the third grade, I tried to find someone else to fill that hole, and when my search didn't pan out, I interrogated my parents about my real dad.

It didn't occur to me it was a selfish question, and by looking for a male role model, I was effectively saying my parents were not good enough for me. Neither one of them was comfortable answering me. After a long period of pestering them, Mother told me a story about how he was a superhero living in the sky. He could not be in my life because he was too busy saving other people. I told myself someday, if I was a good person, I could join him and make the world a better place.

At the time, I believed her. It was nice to hold on to the thought. Later in life, I understood why she told me a harmless lie, enough for me to never want to look for him again because I knew he had his own life. He's probably some random down-on-his-luck guy who needed money. There's no story to pursue, and I am now grateful for the two parents I have.

Mom smiles a little when I bring my tea to the table. Before I can even take a sip, she takes the mug and downs one big gulp, unbothered by the scalding hot temperature. I take a spoonful of soup in my bowl and tear off pieces of bread.

"Thank you, Sidney." She finishes her first bowl of soup. "I have some news for you guys."

The three of us turn our attention to her.

"Our precinct will be starting an investigation into the nuclear plant explosion."

Is this bad news? I start scooping vegetables into my mouth in anticipation. The carrots and potatoes have different textures, but everything tastes the same. Every minestrone I have ever had is bland, so I'm glad my taste buds are not tricking me. Both the vapours from the soup and the tea infuse into my skin, and it's more therapeutic to breathe in the fumes than to consume the food.

"Wasn't it bad equipment?" Kat plays with her food, making balls out of bread and creating a catapult with her spoon, trying to get them into her mouth, missing every time. "That's what the news guy said."

"That's just a theory," Mom corrects her. "We don't know yet." She takes another sip of my tea and lets out a delighted sigh. A part of me is annoyed because I made that tea for myself, but she didn't sleep at all last night, and even without my hospitalization, she rarely ever gets a good night's sleep.

As a police officer for the City of Ottawa, her job means she has to travel and always stay alert. She told Kat and me she was supposed to fill in paperwork to begin the investigation today. However, given the circumstances, she got the day off to be with her family. She loved her job, but the three of us hated that about her. She put her life on the line for everyone, especially people who disrespected her and her profession.

Frankly, I look back at myself and think about how stupid I was for even wanting to know my biological father. No matter what kind of crime fighter he was, he could never measure up to my real parents. No one is more like a superhero than the Inspectors. They work in hazardous places to make life safer; they are the real heroes.

"Isn't working the case a conflict of interest for you, given that your wife works there?" Mindy asks as she shoves pieces of bread in her mouth.

Mom finishes her second bowl of soup and serves herself a third. We know the signs of stress-eating; hopefully, she will ease up a little when Mother comes home. "I can see why you would think that. I don't want her to lose her job." She looks at me and smiles. "But the plant put my baby in the hospital, so in the end, my conflicts of interest cancel each other out."

"Mom," I groan at her, embarrassed. "I'm seventeen."

"You are also my baby." She reaches over to me and plants a wet kiss on my cheek. "Regardless, I will oversee junior detectives, and process paperwork and evidence. We are short-staffed, and my participation will be on a need basis." She takes another sip of my tea. "I will be starting tomorrow and will likely be swamped with other duties. We don't know how long the investigation will take. So, Mindy, Sidney, I need one of you to look after Kat and make dinner since Mommy won't return until Tuesday."

"I thought she was supposed to come back tomorrow," Mindy interjects.

"She was, but if you were with us at the hospital, you would've known that she is still going to need a lot of bed rest." Mom stares her down. "And that she will need a couple of days to recuperate."

"You keep telling us you don't want us to fight, but you keep attacking me for things I have no control over."

"I'm not attacking you." Mom sighs at her. Kat continues failing to launch bread balls into her mouth, oblivious to the fight in front of her.

"Yes, you are, and stop using that passive-aggressive voice, it doesn't work anymore."

"Don't ever take that tone with me," Mom barks.

Mindy looks across the table at me, darting her eyes from me to Mom, hoping I will support her. I respond by shovelling more food in my mouth since I don't want to add to the discussion. The inside of my mouth burns with every hot spoonful of soup, but it's much less painful than picking a side in their argument.

She redirects her ire to Mom. "I have a lot of work, and midterms are coming up. Should I just quit working as a teaching assistant? Maybe you would like it better if I dropped out, then I can be here forever." She scowls.

Mom forcefully gulps her soup down. "Don't ever say something that stupid. You would never forgive us if we made you do that. But as long as you live here, I expect you to be a part of the family, which means sacrificing a couple of days with your friends."

"So you don't want me to have a life anymore?" Mindy raises her voice again, then drops her spoon in the bowl, splashing soup across the table and hitting my hand. I wince as the splatter sears my skin. I try to use my napkin to soak up as much as possible. I'll run my hand under cold water the first chance I get.

"No!" Mom yells, she clenches her teeth and balls up her fist. She wants to bang the table, but resists the temptation and sighs. "Stop thinking about only yourself for a few minutes!"

My stomach churns violently. I understand why Mom made minestrone. We are all stressed today, so we all need to eat a lot of fiber. I haven't even finished my second bowl before Mom serves me a third. My stomach churns again.

"Okay." Mindy hangs her head. "The only class I don't have at night is on Tuesdays. I can come home instead of working on campus. I know it is not much, but I—"

"Thank you, that's everything I could ask for." Mom lowers her voice. "I know it's not easy to make sacrifices. But we can deal with them together, one night a week."

I sigh in relief as the quarrel at the dinner table is finally over. We eat in silence for a few minutes; Kat continues to play with her food. Mindy digs into her soup while I get served a fourth bowl. I down it pretty quickly. "So, Mom, what do you know about the explosion?"

"I cannot talk about it until the report becomes public," Mom answers. "But thanks for reminding me; my colleagues will need to talk to you and some of your classmates about what they saw."

My stomach churns again and I tap on my mug of tea. It feels cool enough to drink, so I take one moderate sip; my migraine decreases. "When exactly?" I fake a smile.

"It may be in a week or two, depending on what we can gather from the plant workers, security footage, and the specifications of all the equipment. We might not need your testimony but expect you to come in if we do. I can prep you on what to expect, but I can't conduct your interview."

My memory of the explosion is lacklustre at best. I remember I was with our class on the catwalk, and then Harriet and Kyle fell behind the rest of us. I remember pushing my way through to be closer to my friends and saw Yasmine, Emilia, and Anthony. My memories stop there. I'm not sure how great a witness I would be.

Mindy picks up the bowl and chugs it. "I'm done. If you need me, I'll be finishing my story in our room."

"Mindy, I do need you," Mom tells her.

She stops in her tracks. "But you guys are still eating. Can I just come later?"

"Keep an ear out for us," Mom reluctantly agrees. "Then come down when it's time to clean up."

Mindy nods and runs up the stairs to her room. I look at my right hand: the red burn marks look a little irritated, and the skin hasn't peeled off. The man in the hospital mentioned I could alter my chemical makeup, and my body is just a large cluster of cells; right now, there are many damaged top layers on my epidermis. But staring at my hand will not fix it. What I need to do is start small.

Kat places a ball of bread in the bowl of her spoon and smashes the stem, causing it to fly upwards. She has failed three times already, and the ball is about to hit her chin. I think of a simple happy memory: cheering her up in the hospital. With that, the ball budges slightly; it plops into her mouth.

She celebrates just as Mom turns around. "That's pretty impressive. Help me clean up the rest of the mess you made, please."

It's around half-past seven. Mom suggests I can go into my room and get an early night's sleep. The clicking sounds of ceramic bowls on metal cutlery are enough to give me another headache concentrated on my right temple. I walk towards my room next to the living room of our house. "Mom, can I go outside for a while? I need some fresh air."

"Sure," Mom answers. "But don't stay out too long."

The creepy old man said to meet up at nine in the evening. As soon as I go to the back door, the power goes out. I walk cautiously to find my phone. I remember that I threw it on the couch. Using my limited vision and my hand as a long cane, I guide myself around all the furniture. I eventually find it and turn on my flashlight.

I shine the light around the house. Mindy barges into the kitchen using her phone's flashlight and joins Mom and Kat. I'm just glad there's a part of her that always needs to be productive and helpful. Mom should be grateful she's finally helping without being asked.

I text Harriet; she is the only person I know who lives in Manotick.

<u>Do you have power in your house? And has Islington been affected?</u>

I sit and wait for a response.

<u>My house's not on grid</u>

<u>All of Manotick's gone</u>

<u>Islington's okay.</u>

I&MNG notifies everyone via an emergency alarm that Manotick, Riverside, and even parts of Barrhaven will be without electricity, so we should reduce our loads until further notice. It must be because of the nuclear plant explosion, and for some reason, I think the man has something to do with it.

Part 1.8: Meeting #2

It's not that cold outside. I would estimate the temperature to be around eighteen degrees with virtually no wind. A select few streetlights and stars nicely light up the sky. Mom's likely watching me from the couch in the living room. I don't blame her, but at the same time, I wish she wouldn't.

Being in the garden brings me back to a much simpler time. Mom was just a constable; even though she had long hours, we treasured the few hours a week we did have as a family. As she advanced through the ranks, she did get to reduce her hours, but we spent more time apart.

I remember being a sixteen-year-old boy with a girlfriend and an active social life, not wanting anything to do with my parents. What a stupid kid I was; now Yasmine's gone from my life, and I don't know how much time I have left with Mother. But I'm glad I've grown.

There is a shortcut to the plant if I hop over the fence. Then it's a straight shot south along Rideau Valley Drive North. Otherwise, it would take an extra six minutes to leave my cul-de-sac. It's only a nine-minute walk, or approximately one kilometre. What should I even expect?

I need to think this through. I'm going out, alone, at night, to a nuclear power plant, searching for a shack in the vicinity of a hazardous crime scene, to meet a mysterious older man who claims to have magical or superhuman powers. If Yasmine, Mindy, or Mother have not already called me an idiot for countless reasons, they will now.

But what I felt was real, the tile and Kindle lifting, nudging a bread ball towards Kat; those events happened. I have seen enough and done enough.

The walk is short and rather dull. Even the most developed cul-de-sac in the sleepy town of Manotick is way too safe. The only things I smell are the scent of nature, the dew on the grass, a hint of manure, wildflowers, and daisies and trilliums, all of which change when I arrive at the plant.

The smells change to something more metallic; my head throbs a little.

The chain-link fence is open and a lock is stored neatly by the gate. Two cameras mounted at the top of the gate's hinges point away from the entrance, away from me, and towards the building.

It turned dark about an hour ago; the only things illuminating the streets are the low-voltage LED streetlights, and they do a poor job of it.

It is precisely nine o'clock in the evening. The shack is close to the fenced area, left of the entrance, and far from the glass lobby. The shack looks like an eighteenth-century brown, monochromatic farmhouse, about the size of my living room, dining room, and kitchen combined, or about one hundred square meters. It's lined with vertical wood planks, and many are rotten or covered with mold. Some rusty nails on both sides of the entrance are sticking out at ankle level, calling out to any unsuspecting traveller who wants tetanus.

The shack door makes a loud, rusty, screeching sound as it moves. I look behind me, making sure not to hit the nails. It's empty, and the coast is clear; there's nothing stored inside. There are no lights that I can see; when I look up, the night sky is visible through a perforated hole around ten percent of the roof's area.

The door slams shut behind me. My feet leave the ground, and I hover for less than ten seconds, then fall onto my bare knees.

"Hello, Sid," a voice says. The sound reverberates around the shack for a few seconds. I can't match a face to a physical being. I probably should have taken another iodine pill; my head's still throbbing. "You're probably wondering a few things. What are you doing here? What happened yesterday? And why you, of all people?"

What on earth was I thinking?

I shuffle backwards on my knees out of the shed but struggle to find the door. I turn on my phone and use my flashlight to make out the door's outline. Suddenly, my phone dies, and I get knocked onto my chest and wince at the impact.

"You have no reason to feel agitated, Sid. You never did. Because of your age and your accelerated and powerful neural capacity, not only did you heal in record time, but you also never needed additional treatment."

I push myself off the ground and stand up. "But once you lose one of those..." He pauses. "...Well, I have bad news." I frantically search for the door again.

"The door is to your right." The whole shack illuminates. I drop to the ground again, burying my head in my stomach. My glasses dig into the bridge of my nose. After half a minute, I acclimatize to the light, unfurl myself, and see him. He stands far from me, still wearing a tan suit and uncomfortable shoes, but has aged a little. Noticeably, he has a slight turkey neck. His eyes are buggy but developing some large crow's feet.

"We are not here to judge my appearance." I'm pushed back until I hit the wall. I try not to think of anything, because I know he can read my mind; however, it's hard shutting everything off.

He walks over, and each step accelerates my heartbeats; he stops once he's within arm's reach of me.

He lifts me off the ground. I only feel a force pushing the soles of my shoes upwards; his arms remain by his sides. We are looking at each other eye-to-eye. My glasses levitate off my head and into his hands. Everything behind him is a blur.

"You still use these primitive things?" He tosses my glasses into a dark corner, disappearing from my limited field of vision.

They shatter. Simultaneously, everything goes dark again. This is a bad idea. This is such a bad idea. I try to wriggle out.

"So, what are you, negative four point zero on your left and two point two-five on your right?" he asks. "Your glasses prescription?"

"Oh, yes. What are you—"

"This will be over in less than a minute, and it will only be painful if you make it. Whatever you do, don't move, don't blink, and don't make a sound."

All the sounds and lights die in an instant. I can't even hear the babbling of the Rideau River. I don't want to make a sound, and I'm afraid to blink.

My eyes start to sting a little and a slight migraine comes back. He must be doing this to me. He gave me a migraine yesterday, and he is doing it to me now. I need to concentrate and knock him down.

"We are done." The man throws a coughing fit for a few seconds. "I would have finished faster, but your mind is always wandering. You don't trust me, do you?" He drops to his feet.

"Why...would I...trust you? What...did you do?" I check my shorts; my keys and phone are still with me. I check everything else; my belt is still intact; my shirt is untouched. "Seriously, what did you—" Something pushes me forward and I fall on my knees. My hands help cushion the fall, although my knees absorb my weight. And since I don't have a sufficient amount of body fat, it hurts to re-extend my legs and get back up.

"Ow!" the man suddenly yells. The shack lights turn on again. He stands twenty feet from me. His left hand clutches his right arm.

I run over to him. "Are you okay?" I extend my arm to him, but he swipes it away. This scene is playing out similarly to our first meeting. "I knocked you over again, didn't I?"

"Yes." He gets up on his feet. He smiles, showing the newly formed gap in his mouth. He is missing his top left lateral incisor. "Much better than last time, too. More focused, less messy."

"What are you talking about?" I scratch my forehead, right where the migraine is pressing.

"Fear, you felt it for the first time today."

It's not true. When we went to South Africa to get Kat, Mom and Mindy got malaria. I was scared something terrible would happen. I feared we might be leaving with fewer members of our family when we were supposed to come back with more. Mother tried to reassure me that would not be the case. She instilled a sense of hope that lives in me to this day. But they eventually recovered. It was just a bit of a scare and didn't last long.

Now, in this shack, I'm shitting myself. I have hyperventilated for the first time in my life. And most importantly, Mother isn't with me to put the pieces of my life back together. I'm on my own.

I contemplate what he says while staring blankly at the dusty corner on the far side of the shack. My broken glasses are entangled in a mass of cobwebs and floating dust particulates, and only one lens is cracked.

I'm not wearing my glasses. I can see distance. He fixed my eyesight and it's better than when I was wearing my glasses. The lights brighten a little.

"Why is my vision perfect? Did you give me Lasik?" I ask. "But where is the twenty-four-hour healing period?"

"I did more than just fix your eyes." He smiles. "I changed your food, read your mind, and controlled the energy influx in this shack. I would have done it in the hospital, but there were too many witnesses. Also, it was not dark enough." He sighs. "I guess I can trust you, and the explosion was just an accident after all." He exhales sharply. "I have many questions, none of which you can answer." He hangs his head in shame.

I look through the hole in the roof at the cloudless, star-lit sky. It's one of the beauties of our area; there are no large buildings and no light pollution. Even though the small hole does not offer much of a view, there are more stars in a small opening in the roof than in an open field in downtown Ottawa.

"Enjoying the view?" he asks.

"Yes. How did you fix my eyes?"

"Lasik carves out your corneas and reshapes your eyes. I did it without all the fancy technology. I numbed your eyes by temporarily cutting off your nerves so you would not feel anything, and..." He trails off. "...You do not care about the technical details, do you?"

"No, I do." Laser eye surgery is mainstream now, and I could have gone there at any time. However, my eyes were not that bad. "I am planning on applying to medical school. I wanted to do engineering physics, but it may not be an option anymore after the explosion." The sentence started out as a lie, but it might be true now.

"Anyway, I carved out your cornea and filled in the cracks. All of this could be done by replicating molecules and DNA strands on both a cellular and atomic level. I repaired your nerves."

"How is this possible?" I ask. "And why is this practice not everywhere?" I'm not interested in medical science or surgeries, but if he could fix my eyesight using only his superpowers, could I help my mother with her treatments? Replicating DNA strands is a revolutionary cure.

"We can generate waves with our mind. As a novice, you have been creating large amplitude waves that displace physical objects, which equate to a blunt pushing motion. Once you get better, you can generate smaller amplitude waves which rebound off air particles and wrap around objects, bringing them toward you instead of just pushing. And once you get good at seeing the particles, you can push molecules and atoms together, breaking them down or reassembling them. But you're not ready for that now."

"How do I get better? How do I create more finely-tuned waves that affect the molecular level?"

He smirks at me, revealing his now-imperfect smile. "By exercising your mind like any other muscle. They are tied to your emotions, and by training emotions or new feelings, you can access more abilities because you have explored more recesses of your mind. For example, you just felt fear. There are many more states to explore: happiness, anger, shock, disgust, despair, confusion, pain, and suffering, to name some. Your mind expands, and with the right view, you can do anything you want, within reason." He abruptly stops. "And to answer your other question, we don't use them because we have machines that do a better job than us, and it's taxing on my body."

The man leans on the wall, breathing heavily, clutching his head with both hands, and closing his eyes.

"Are you okay? Do I need to call someone? A family member, a hospice worker?"

"Are you still interested in learning?" he asks.

"Yes!" I answer proudly.

"Well, then, no." He tilts my head and looks at me directly with his wise eyes. "Go home. When you are ready and have explored every recess of your mind, I will come."

I nod accordingly and float through the doorway, narrowly avoiding the nails at the base of the door. Once outside, I fall onto my knees. Although, when will he come back? What do I have to do? Do I pay him for the Lasik? I don't think my procedure is covered by Ontario's Health Insurance Plan.

"Let's just say you are paying me in more than one way." His voice emanates from inside the shack.

I turn around and walk back to the shack, but the door slams in my face.

"Live your life, be in the moment."

The sounds of the Rideau River and the crickets in the fields return. There are no cars, no people, just the beautiful natural sounds of the outdoors.

I turn my phone back on and see it is nine minutes past nine p.m. To my surprise, it still has nine percent of its battery life. He must have killed my phone temporarily.

My eyes twitch involuntarily as I walk north back home, ending up at the Morisette Bridge. I stop for a second and look at my hands. As I blink, my field of vision shrinks, so I continue to blink for almost a minute. The dust particles on my hands enlarge in size. I focus on these particles as they flake off. In a few seconds, my palms start to sweat. I focus hard on them and squint, and with my mind, I imagine all the dead skin exfoliating from my body, falling like fresh snow, but much smaller.

The old cells exfoliate from my epidermis. I look at my hand and zoom in even closer, and see the spiderweb structure of connecting skin cells. My hands have never felt so smooth. I touch my cheeks, and it feels like someone else is caressing my face.

I try to zoom in even more, but I cannot make out the finer details of my body. I laugh. I don't even care how I appear to the outer world. These new eyes are perceptive and powerful.

I'm close already. Mother will be alright.

I break off into a sprint in excitement. The power plant is already about ten minutes away. I check my pulse, and I count around fifty beats in thirty seconds, so one hundred beats a minute. I keep running across the Morissette Bridge to Islington. I have time.

The air currents around me resemble a thick fog cycling around my hands, legs, and the bridge's cables. These currents interact with each other but the particles don't collide. They are constantly moving, vibrating, merging, and splitting up. I exhale and see the thick fog of particles exit my mouth. It looks like I am smoking without the tar and nicotine rolled up in filter paper.

Once I make it to Islington, I run back to Manotick, then north on Rideau Valley Drive North, and hop the fence to get to my backyard. It's still not even half-past nine. I lie down on my back, on some prickly weeds, far away from the gardens, and look up at the sky. The air currents coming off the giant fig tree and towards me enter my lungs. They spiral in a synchronized dance before getting sucked into my nose. After they leave my sight, I exhale around the air currents. These molecules split up based on their density. The large ones fall onto my body like tiny droplets of rain, roll off of me, and disappear in the grass below, while the tiny ones rise higher until they are gone.

My phone vibrates. I pull it out and find a text from Kyle. It takes a while for my eyes to recalibrate to the visible spectrum.

U up?

I smile and text him back.

Holy crap. When did you wake up?

I lie there, waiting for a response.

4 pm, it was insane. I have to tell u about it. Come over tmrw

I am sure I can hang out tomorrow; however, I should ask Mom. I'm also supposed to help out more around the house. But I still want to see him and I tell him everything. Although, I would probably have to protect my identity. I have this newfound power, and don't need Kyle to tell the whole class. I'm sure I will know what to do when the time comes; I have to live in the moment, after all.

I enter my house through the back door, trying not to disturb anyone. Mom and Kat are fast asleep on the couch. I place a blanket over them; Mom's earned this rest. They will be able to sleep well again. I must be the man of the house now.

I quietly laugh. I thought having more responsibilities would be exhausting, but this is living. I quietly walk into the kitchen to grab an Advil and a glass of water, and swallow the pill.

Everything happens for a reason.

Part 2

Part 2.1: Blackout II
Vritikha, October 9th, 17:55

"It's starting, everyone," Abba announces. "Varshil, Vijay, please come here."

Harriet and I enter the restaurant; the scent of Indian food and incense combined with the blast of air conditioning overpowers my senses. The hours of walking in extreme heat combined with my lack of sleep short-circuit my brain. I wander in as Abba charges at full speed in our direction.

"Vritikha, Hari. Why were you guys at the hospital today?" He places his hands on our backs and pulls us through the restaurant. While he drags us to our seats, my muscles relax. I immediately sit on the chair on the furthest left, as I need that specific seat for my leg. I lean back and stare at the ceiling while using the cold metal backrest to cool down my neck. Varshil and Vijay sit to my right on chairs while Veera and Abba sit in the booth.

"How did you know?" Harriet darts her eyes back and forth between Abba and me.

"I saw Vritikha's location on my phone, so why?" Abba answers.

I would explain to her that my parents needed to track me if I wanted to be trusted to have a phone in middle school. I thought it was unfair at first, and even though nothing terrible has happened to me since I got a phone, and even though we have lived in this country for almost a decade now, Ammi and Abba are always cautious. I would explain it was a two-way tracker, as I could also see my parents' location. And since I don't know how to drive, it's helpful when they need to pick me up from an obscure place. But I know she wouldn't understand or care for an explanation.

Harriet shakes her head. "We had time. I wanted to see if Kyle woke up." She keeps her eyes open and makes them tear up while her upper lip quivers slightly.

Since Harriet and I blew off the tour, we had some freedom. We ate at a Copper Branch in the Rideau Mall after an hour of protesting. We got some good pictures of the crowds, and at three-thirty, arrived at the hospital so Harriet could visit Kyle while I slept in the waiting room. I wanted to see Yasmine, but they wouldn't let me in. During my brief slumber, I had the same visions as I did in bed this morning. And at five-thirty pm, we bussed back to my apartment building.

"It's good that he's awake, but you shouldn't have cut it so close," Abba relents.

Harriet nods and smiles at Abba, then takes the chair to my right. I could have never gotten away with such a response. If I lied about blowing off the tour for any reason, I would have had my data plan cut off or been made to work in the kitchen, scrubbing dishes after hours for two weeks.

"Hey, Tikha, Hari, how was the tour?" my older sister asks. She walks up to me, pulls me out of the chair, and into her embrace. Her polyester hijab grazes my cheek as I rest my chin on her shoulder. "I'm sorry we did not get a proper hello this morning; I was exhausted."

It's the first time Veera has come back from Toronto Metropolitan. She usually comes home every month. However, since it's her final year of study and she recently connected with a boy over her third year, she sees fewer reasons to return. But it's Thanksgiving, so she has no choice.

"I...uh." I struggle to tell her that I'm an unfaithful student.

"Girls, sit." Abba gestures to the chairs. I hang my purse on the back, and Harriet deposits her backpack on a table behind her. I blink several times and pour chilled water into a glass to wake myself. The commercials end and our regularly-scheduled programming starts back up.

"Welcome back to the program. Now let us introduce our next guest. He's the Green Party nominee running for Parliament in the Ottawa-Rural South's District; joining us over the phone is Mr. Vipesh Ganatra. Thank you for joining us today."

"Thank you for having me here—"

"Focus!" Varshil makes the same joke whenever Vipesh is using his Canadian accent. He knows it's not a projector, but pretends the radio is broken. But it's a shame Vipesh has to use a fake voice to appeal to these voters.

"Varshil. Shut up," Abba orders. Their minor exchange makes it hard to hear a good portion of the interview.

"No problem, can you tell us a little about yourself? Namely, who you are, and why are you running?"

"Well, as you said, my name is Vipesh Ganatra. I am a father, a community organizer in Downtown Ottawa, and a professional engineer, in that order. Ten years ago, I was the lead structural engineer in charge of the design of the Morissette Bridge, connecting Manotick and Islington. In my spare time I love helping people in Downtown Ottawa and Centretown by handing out food and reporting, volunteering, and consulting for areas not sufficiently weatherproofed. I have always wrestled with running for office.

"As a structural engineer, I knew I wanted to improve the quality of life in my hometown. My work has improved infrastructure and reduced congestion, and as a result, helped improve our quality of health and mental awareness. When the bridge's design was completed and approved by the cities of Islington and Manotick, my wife tragically passed. Afterwards, my daughter and I moved closer to her maternal grandfather, and I took a job as an urban planner in Montreal. It was a good job in a beautiful city. However, after almost ten years, I had some time to think. It was a combination of feeling unfulfilled and seeing a lack of effort to combat climate change from the federal government that propelled me to run for office."

"So you mentioned your daughter was in an accident." The interviewer chimes in, "How is she doing?"

"She's a little banged up but she's a fighter. She's always been a passionate, vehement advocate for combating climate change, and one of the strongest people I know. When I entertained the idea of running for public office, I asked for her blessing; she told me I was a fool, because if I didn't run, she would."

"So, you have a lot to offer, but is climate change the only reason you are running?"

There is a little bit of a pause, which indicates that he is planning a good, strong answer.

"Climate change, or the climate crisis as we should call it, is the biggest reason I am running for the House of Commons. It's no longer an issue of when it will happen, but if we can mitigate the effects already happening. We have done alright by shutting down forty percent of fossil fuel plants across the country, but have only put a bandage on the problem by implementing nuclear energy worldwide. The large-scale implementation of a non-renewable energy source will cost us in the future. We have become complacent in thinking we have solved the problem when we have only slowed down temperature increases. Our country became the third-largest emitter of greenhouse gases by being the world's energy capital.

"The most accurate climate change scientists and models have constantly and consistently told us we have less than a decade before running out of nuclear material. We need to adopt renewable energy sources before that deadline. Otherwise, we will be right where we started, burning fossil fuels at an alarming rate, dooming this planet even further. Our country is huge and sparsely-populated. We can become a green lung by implementing the technology already at our disposal, while continuously researching and developing new technology and implementing alternative lifestyle changes."

He is direct and honest with his message. The comment on lifestyle changes probably won't bode well with the people in Manotick. Some have a very stubborn mindset and may not be open to change. I know this from canvassing the area and visiting those large properties with varying-sized houses; we have had our fair share of doors slammed in our faces. It's also unfortunate he did not mention the other reasons he's running, because his transportation plan would create more jobs, but I'm sure he will get there eventually.

"Thank you. So you mentioned climate change and the need to stop producing nuclear energy, but your district is home to a nuclear plant. Wouldn't the shift to renewable energy cause hundreds, maybe thousands of people to lose their jobs? And not just I&MNG, hundreds of thousands of people work in not just nuclear energy fields in Canada, but other non-renewable energy sectors."

He pauses. Abba is whispering to himself a Hindi mantra. I can not hear all of it over the radio. Harriet reaches behind her and takes an orange bottle of pills, dispensing one in her hand.

"We have already gotten rid of an energy source. Fossil fuels used to be how we obtained most of the energy we produced almost a hundred years ago, specifically natural gas and oil. When we started phasing them out, many Canadians saw an increase in their hydro bills because we shut them down without generating enough energy to meet demand. If elected, I will write and sponsor bills that will gradually phase out non-renewable energy sources, reducing our nuclear energy consumption and ending fossil fuel usage.

"We already have the technology to implement widespread change, but it doesn't mean we also can't keep improving; uncertainty is scary. As for jobs, I will oversee the implementation of transition programs. Our district and country want to move away from hazardous and non-sustainable ways of obtaining energy, but they don't have a choice because they need to make a living. I don't want to move away from the good people who break their backs or ruin their health so the rest of us can enjoy our lives. One of the towns in our district, Islington, is an experimental town built from scratch almost twenty years ago to be one hundred percent powered by renewables. Its construction was also carbon-neutral upon completion. It was a massive success. It helped resettle refugees from Syria, Iran, Algeria, Florida, and many other places rendered uninhabitable because of climate change. It boasts more than three hundred thousand people who live without fear of looming power outages."

"Do you think we can revitalize our entire electrical system in less than a decade? You mentioned Islington's carbon neutral, but still, it's a small population centre. Can this work nationally in a country of more than forty-five million people? Not to mention, we make most of our money from outsourcing energy around the world." There's doubt in the announcer's voice.

"I know, this is ambitious," says Vipesh. "We would have to overhaul and reconfigure our current system, but the sooner we do it, the better. Again, Islington is a good example of this. We had to cut down almost a hundred thousand trees in six months to accommodate many refugees coming into this country. We didn't do enough to combat climate change in the past, and parts of the Middle East and Africa became uninhabitable. We managed to replant twice as many trees in the greenbelt to offset our carbon footprint, but if we solved the problem earlier, we wouldn't need to resettle climate refugees.

"The only choice we have regarding the implementation of renewables is when we get to implement them. The solutions are expensive, but the cost of eight years of inaction will be trillions more. We have already resettled human lives, rebuilt infrastructure, and cured new diseases as a consequence of allowing the status quo to reign. The earth will get another chance at life, but humans may not if we don't do something. We have to give our children a fair chance to live long, prosperous lives. If we fail, they will have to clean up the mess we made, or worse, live in it."

Harriet and Abba get up and start clapping. Veera and Vijay join in later. Varshil gets up and walks away. Harriet tucks her pill away in her bag. Since radio interviews don't have applause breaks, we miss what immediately follows.

A young man walks to our table alongside Varshil.

"I want to apologize for my tardiness," he speaks. "What did I miss?"

Krishna arrives at the table. I expected him to sound more like an ESL telemarketer, not a sophisticated Indo-British anchorman who speaks the language better than I did in my first year living here. He also looks much different from when I last saw him. He's not the uncanny baby-faced man, but instead a taller, lightly tanned, dishevelled young adult. His long, messy hair drapes past his prominent cheekbones to his thin and patchy stubble, hiding a chiselled jawline.

And even though he's dressed like a homeless person, wearing oversized flannel shirts and jeans with rips near his knees, he looks well-fed. His general demeanour and wardrobe clash heavily with each other. He greets everyone at our table, shaking their hands, including mine and Harriet's. I smile without saying anything. I rub my eyes and get another look at him. He sits in front of me and next to Veera.

"You missed his stump speech," Vijay answers.

"Which was the biggest part of his interview," Varshil adds when Krishna gets to him.

"Thanks." Krishna smiles at my brothers.

"Krishna, I'm happy you could join us. Next time let's not wait this long." Abba gets up to pat him aggressively on the back.

"So..." Vijay says. "Are we still listening..."

"Oh, right. Everybody shut up," Abba scolds the room, even though he's the only one making noise. They have moved past energy and climate change because we don't even hear about his transportation policies or plans to implement free university for everyone.

"Well, we are close to being done," says the interviewer. "I will ask this: how do you feel about your chances of winning? The polls show you are in second place, but still far from your main competition, Guillaume Riviera."

He chuckles. "I feel pretty good about my chances. I have known this community for almost two decades and feel I helped shape it for the better. Even when I left for Montreal, I have kept my roots."

"And I only have one more question I want to ask before we go. Would you reach across the aisle in terms of supporting your PC or NDP MPs? How would you help bridge the gap we see today in our political discourse?"

"Well, as I previously said at the beginning of the interview, I'm very good at building bridges."

The radio announcer and Vipesh laugh over that remark, and so do we.

"I am uncompromising in my goals; I would not vote for any bill that does not have the interest of the planet and my district. Of course, even I must acknowledge that I would be a small coalition in a large and diverse House when I win. But I would help co-author bills and laws with my Progressive Conservatives, Liberals, Bloc Quebecois, and New Democratic Party MPs. I know the most important thing is to be civil, and I learned this while conversing with our incumbent MP, Guillaume Riviera. We disagree on some issues, however, he has been a respectable representative. I would be grateful to follow in his footsteps. I am glad to have brought forward so many issues to his time in office. By the end of this campaign, I hope our district will be a leading example of solidarity and respect for the planet."

"Thank you, Mr. Ganatra. That is all the time we have; I would like to thank you for tuning—"

Abba turns the radio off, looking neither proud nor defeated, just uncertain. Maybe it's the last sentence. He called MP Riviera a respectable representative when he's another status quo politician who bows to our corporate overlords. And while he's not always wrong about the issues, he's the biggest reason Vipesh is running, and everyone knows it.

"Wait," Varshil announces. "We didn't hear him tell everyone to go out and vote. There might be more."

"As soon as they sign off, it's done. I'm sure most of you are hungry. Let us go. Varshil, Vijay, come with me. Hari and Vritikha, set the table. Krishna, if you would like to wash up, Veera can show you where to go."

My brothers follow Abba into the kitchen, and Veera guides Krishna behind the kitchen to the restrooms. The only ones left at the table are Harriet and me.

I start setting the table for seven and catch a glimpse of Harriet smirking and raising her left eyebrow. "So..." Her grin grows larger, extending to the corners of her eyes.

"So...what?" I hesitantly ask, placing the bowls, plates, and cutlery down.

"I have never seen you look at someone like that before. I would ask what's up, but I see you, girl." She bobs her head from side to side. "I see you."

I'm not the kind of person who would fall for any guy, especially at first sight. His voice made me freeze; he's average-looking at best.

"I was caught off-guard," I defend myself. "I haven't seen him in a decade, he's changed."

"*D'accord.*" Harriet lets out a small sarcastic laugh, stands up, takes my right hand, and flips it around so that my palm faces upwards. She places her index and middle fingers on my wrist and feels for my pulse. After a few seconds, she raises her left eyebrow and smiles. "You are so in denial. He's no SSR, but I'm sure he cleans up well."

I try to turn my face away, but she pushes it back to her. "I felt like this when Kyle asked me out, and during the protest today. It's a rush, which gives me an idea." She lets go of my arm; I let it drop down to my waist. "Krishna also likes you, too. He was not paying attention to the interview. He had his focus..." She pauses. "...elsewhere. Anyway, he's a college student at Algonquin, and universities are places full of young, progressive, unregistered voters who—"

"No!" I yell and immediately step backwards, hitting my waist on the table behind me. "I am not—" I lower my voice. "I'm not going to dress up and flirt with a guy for this election."

She takes the plates and placemats and starts setting the table. "You want my dad to win, right?" She raises her eyebrows. "But you could just hang out with him and get with his friend group, and when the topic of politics comes up—"

"Forget it." I untuck my blouse and massage my waist. It does feel a little soft, but nothing is swollen or bruised. I made the stupid decision of not bringing an extra change of clothes. Harriet changed right after the climate protest in the bathroom of Rideau Mall and is now wearing a tank top and a hat, embellishing her father's campaign logo. She also proudly displays her battle scars from the explosion. If I didn't know any better, I would assume Harriet's original plan was to ditch the tour to advertise his campaign to a massive crowd.

"It's not happening," I inform her. "Not now, and not like that."

"It was just a stupid idea. *Je sais.*" Harriet finishes setting the table.

I thought she would have jumped on the fact I said 'not like that', instead of 'not now and not ever'. I didn't want to rule out the possibility entirely. But I don't want to build any kind of relationship on a lie.

"If you want to get some, it should be on your terms. You deserve to be happy." She darts her eyes down to her backpack.

"Hold on." She takes her phone out and turns it on. "Sid just texted me. Manotick has just lost power."

The rest of my family comes in with trays of food. My brothers bring over Palak paneer, Chana masala, vegetarian biryani, and stacks of roti and naan. Varshil sets the food trays on the table, immediately takes out his phone, and looks up news articles. Meanwhile, Veera and Krishna return together; he parks himself in front of me while she sits to his left.

"They say it's not in our neighbourhood," Varshil says. "Just confined to Manotick, Riverside, and parts of Barrhaven." He lets out a single content nose exhale.

"I guess that's good for Kaka," Vijay remarks.

"*Bhais!*" Veera snarls at our brothers. "What is wrong with you two? Those people might not get their power back for a long time."

"Your Didi is right. That was not very kind, *chhotes.*" Abba settles everything down and motions for everyone to sit at the table. Varshil starts to reach for some food. "Before we eat, we pray." Abba swats away Varshil's hand. "And don't worry, Hari. I have some dishes without paneer for you."

I grab Harriet's hand with my right and reach across the table to take Krishna's with my left. Veera leads us all; I rest my eyes only for a second as I start to feel my head get heavier. My elbows slide on the table and collapse under the weight of my head.

"T?" Harriet lifts my head by my hair bun. She repeatedly slaps my face until I slap her hands away.

"Sorry," I groan.

"You have to understand. It has been a long day for us; she slept on every bus and train we took; the heat would drain anyone," Harriet defends me.

"I'm fine," I raise my voice. I shake my head and neck. "I'll lead."

"No. We had waited long enough." Abba rips off pieces of his roti, scoops some spinach and chana masala, and shovels it into his mouth.

Everyone else follows his lead. I dab my roti with a serviette, absorbing excess ghee, and dig in. It tastes incredible, and I will lick my fingers clean every time; however, the excess ghee has caused some breakouts on my face, and it caused Abba to put on an extra five kilos, although Abba would claim the weight gain is from raising five children.

"So, Krishna." Abba breaks the silence. We usually don't speak during a meal, but it's understandable to break tradition for a close family friend. "How are you enjoying your first month here? How's the transition?"

"It wasn't difficult. I have been moving around, working various odd jobs for the past two years."

"Really? Where did you go?" Vijay asks.

"Buenos Aires, London, Johannesburg, Auckland, Shanghai, what's left of Miami. I took the time to explore, and learn new skills and languages while working as custodial staff everywhere I went. It was fast-moving and exciting, but now I'm just happy to put some skills to use." He brushes his hair to the side, tucking it behind his ears, and brushes some food out of his stubble.

"So, what's your plan after this? Are you going to Jammu or travelling some more?" Veera continues the conversation.

"I don't know," he responds. "I have not planned that far ahead. Right now, I am focused on my studies. I have just been learning maths and basic C++ coding. I'm enjoying it."

"Just wait until the final year rolls around," Vijay chimes in. "Veera's boyfriend is in Networking at the Toronto Metropolitan, and it's killing him."

"But Krishna should be a natural, unlike Neel," Varshil chirps.

"Neel's also Indian," Vijay corrects him.

"Sure, but Canadian-born coconut Indian, not real Indian."

While my brothers agree, Veera glares at the two of them without saying a word.

"Right, well, I will keep that in mind." Krishna laughs it off. "Mr. Ganatra." Krishna puts his food down.

"Please," Abba imposes. "It's Vipan Uncle."

Krishna's not our cousin, but we have a tradition for older family members to be called Uncle or Kaka or some variant.

"Well, Uncle. Thank you for having me here during Thanksgiving. All my friends are with their families, so it's nice to have home-cooked food with family instead of the cafeteria food I usually get at school. Although this is still very different from my mother's home cooking."

"It's a Gujarati and Punjabi-style fusion," I add. "Although we do have some khichdi if you are feeling homesick."

"No, this is more than enough. I have not eaten this much since my Mumma sent me off." He laughs. "Speaking of which, where is Mrs. Ganatra? I mean, where's Harsha Auntie?"

"Yes. Harsha's in India taking care of her mother, their Nani." Abba gestures to us. "Nani's been suffering from the late stages of dementia, and Auntie has been helping her for the past seven months."

"Oh, I'm sorry," Krishna apologizes.

"It's alright. She's in a place she loves. We were lucky to have her this long," Abba reassures him.

The rest of dinner is silent. We don't have that much after blowing through all the pleasantries. Mostly everyone wipes their plates clean. I take everyone's dishes into the back. I balance seven sets of plates, bowls, and cutlery. I stare at the knives balancing on the stack, so they don't fall and hurt me.

"Hari?" Abba asks. "Did you get enough food?"

She's not a gluttonous person. Even though we don't have many dairy-free options, she barely makes a dent in the meals we give her. I would assume her antidepressants would cause her to eat more, but she's very fit.

"Yes, Uncle, *merci.*"

I drop everything in the sink and take the remaining trays.

The door chimes ring. I infer it's Vipesh because of the loud footsteps running towards him. "Papa. You were incredible." Harriet appears to have forgotten she was mad at him for almost quitting, but she's happy now, so nothing else matters.

Vipesh hugs her and kisses her head. "*Merci, ma petite noix de coco.* But we have work to do."

I open the door and retrieve the empty pots, pans, and naan baskets. "Some people of Manotick are without power," Vipesh continues. "I have invited our neighbours to give them a place to recharge."

I have only been to Harriet's and Vipesh's new house once. It's large, even for a Manotick dwelling. Two of them live there, but they have about five bedrooms on a lot the size of a football field. I'm not sure how he can afford it on an engineer's salary.

"The invitation is open to everyone here," Vipesh adds. "We need a lot of help." Abba makes my brothers join them, to their dismay. They have a relatively low opinion of the town. I know they don't particularly love nature or the scent of outdoor fields and tranquillity, but I recognize it as a charm Islington doesn't have.

Krishna asks if he can help because he wants to get involved as much as he can despite not being able to vote. Vipesh graciously accepts. Varshil and Vijay immediately change their tunes and ask to ride with him. All they want to do is talk to him about his trips overseas and ask him about the nine languages he speaks.

The five of them leave shortly. Veera, Abba, and I stay behind to clean up. I resume my duties while Abba checks how much food is going to waste because of Harriet. Veera helps me in the kitchen, washing all sharp utensils for me. She leaves me after a few minutes.

Once the cleanup is done, I climb the stairs to our apartment and wash the sweat and smell of downtown out of all thirty-six inches of my hair, then change into my pyjamas. Veera rolls out her mat and begins her prayers. I hop into bed, remove my prosthetic, and massage some chafing cream into my stump, soothing a lot of the tension away.

I can't wait to fall asleep again. The new batch of visions is not making sense and I need answers as soon as possible. The time is ten-oh-one.

Part 2.2: Death?
Vritikha, October 11th, 00:30

Ms. Stone will be teaching us how to make aspirin. One of the ingredients, acetic anhydride, has hazardous vapours, so it will be kept in a ventilated area. I will try to obtain it, but Sid will approach me from behind, and I will get nervous and spill it on my lab coat. Ms. Stone will ensure the class there will be nothing to worry about as nothing will hit me or my clothes, and I will apologize. However, I will discard my lab coat and buy a new one. Sid and Harriet will finish first and have near-perfect purity. Yasmine and I will need to perform a make-up lab. Ms. Stone will inform us about the drug chemistry test on the Wednesday before the election. I will exit the classroom.

I will enter the gym for this district's Q and A; every candidate in our district will be there, even the fringe ones. Anyone will be able to ask whatever they want. I will sit still and watch Vipesh get hammered on every single question. In the end, MP Riviera will win over the crowd. His closing statement about community values and nuclear power plant employment will obtain way more applause than Vipesh's about climate change and future benefits. Vipesh will take us aside and tell us he's proud of our campaign. With that, we will leave the gym with our heads held high.

I will open my door, walk into my room, and collapse on the floor. I will be crying while listening to Anoushka Shankar through my headphones. Varshil and Vijay will check in on me, and I will tell him that my leg detached and I hit my head on the closet door. However, I will be twirling my hair around my hand. They will help me up, and I will exit my room, holding their arms.

Election night will come, and we will enter Vipesh's office space. Vipesh will receive a phone call informing him that he would lose the race to the incumbent, MP Guillaume Riviera. He will give a concession speech and call Riviera to congratulate him. However, he will not get an answer. He will tell the audience not to lose sight of what matters. I will enter Abba's car.

I will walk towards an old, rundown shack; the door will be wide open. There will be something lumpy in the corner. I will walk over to the lump and turn it over to find MP Riviera, dead, and a broken pair of glasses. I will run out of the shack and trip over some rusty nails, scratching my left shin; I will close my eyes.

I will open my eyes again, get up, and bolt. In the distance, the black hooded figure will quickly approach me. I will try to run away, but he will get close. I will shut my eyes.

I will get up. He will swing for my head but I will duck. He will try to sweep my legs, and I will jump. I will deliver a high kick using my good leg, but my knee socket will jam.

He will squeeze tighter and tighter, but I will muster the strength to pull back his hood and stare at his bushy eyebrows, dark eyes, thin face, large forehead, and jet-black hair swept to his left. It will be Sid.

The other figure in white will be running towards me. Sid will let go of my neck as I pass out.

* * *

I wake up slightly shaken. I should be freaking out. I remember these same visions from sleeping on the bus and in the hospital waiting room. However, there are some slight differences from before.

For example, there's no chemical shower this time, the last six visions will occur on the same day, and now I know the identity of the black hooded figure.

Why Sid? I have two classes with him this semester, Chemistry and English, but we don't talk at all. He's one of my cousin's closest friends and my best friend's ex-boyfriend. The only time I interacted with him was last summer, and he didn't seem like the psychopathic type.

Although, his and Yasmine's breakup was violent. Sid aggressively pushed her into the water when she took an embarrassing picture of him. Kyle and Harriet should have taken her side, but according to them, neither of them saw him do it. Of course, Sid denies the push, but I believe her. And now, I have future evidence to solidify her accusation.

I pat down my face and my chest. I'm dry, there's no blood, dirt, or rubble on my body. As I pat myself, a lamp turns on from the other side of our room.

"Tikha?" Veera wakes up and picks up her phone. "Are you okay? It's twelve-thirty in the morning." I've only slept for two and a half hours, longer than last night.

"Did you get strangled again?" she asks.

I don't slow down my breathing. "Yes." I stagger my breath. "But not just that."

She walks over to me and lies in my bed next to me. She puts her arm around me, and I nestle my head on her sternum.

"Just feel my chest rise and fall, and be in sync with me." Her breathing is slow and deep. I hear her heartbeat and feel her diaphragm rising and falling. It's calming how perfectly syncopated her heartbeats and breaths are. There are three heartbeats in between every breath. As I adjust to the light, I inhale and exhale synchronously with her.

"Do you want to tell me? Maybe we could pinpoint where everything went wrong."

Veera makes me feel like the world's weight won't kill me. But however good her intentions are, she's even less knowledgeable about my visions than I am. "You know we can't prevent it. Everything I dream comes true eventually."

"I know." Veera traces her fingers gently on my scalp. "But maybe running through these visions, we can think of where it can go wrong. You won't be able to prevent it, but maybe you can be in more control."

Veera may have a point. We always talk, but we never try to be proactive and run through them in depth, mainly because they haven't needed further analysis. I had night terrors of similar proportions ten years ago, but I decided to ignore them, and in doing so, I lost a leg. But I won't let it happen again.

So I tell her about today's visions, exactly how I remember them. I tell her about the chemistry class, the debate, the election, and finally, the bridge conflict. I omit the part where I attack Sid, about how I know it's Sid, and I skip over the person in white. She would have no use for that information.

"You said your leg will jam; you should be prepared. Try to get as far as you can from this guy," Veera suggests cheerfully. "Or maybe, find out who this dark hooded creature is and get to know him. He's disturbed, so if you save him, he might pay it forward."

It's a straightforward answer; I'm given the spot I am supposed to be at, the key players, and the rough timeframe. I don't get to control my motivation for being on location at the given time. Even though I should never go on the bridge, it wouldn't matter. These fragments are all I get. I don't get a connective tissue to piece everything together. "If I do that, Riviera still dies, and the black hooded figure gets away. Who knows what he'll do next?" I try hard to soften the bitterness. "But that's not my problem, is it?"

"It isn't your problem, but I know you, and you won't let it happen." She brings my head to her shoulder. "So, you said this happens sometime after election night. What were the results?"

"We will lose."

"Oh, no. I'm sorry, I know how hard you worked for Kaka." She looks at me and smiles. "Anyway, maybe he needs to win. If he wins, Riviera loses, and no one has a reason to kill him. You need to work every day and night to ensure he wins. It's easier said than done, but lives are at stake. You'll do what's right. And I'll be doing everything I can as well in Toronto."

She combs my hair with her fingers. We would do this to each other when we were younger. I would do the same, but her hair is flat from wearing a cap and hijab all the time.

"Are you feeling a little better?"

I nod to her. Even if nothing changes, I'm glad to have my sister with me.

"If you have any more information you would like to tell me, I would be happy to hear it and theorize more solutions, but I have to be on a train in nine hours, so I would like to sleep now."

The covers come off me. I'm wearing a yellow, cold-shoulder top. I move my left leg around until I hit my prosthetic. I feel a slight pinch on the tip of my stump and wince. "What day is it today?" I ask.

"Monday," she answers.

I check my phone; it's one in the morning on October eleventh. "So, Vipesh's interview?"

"That was two days ago, on the ninth. Do you not remember what happened today or a couple of hours ago?"

I shake my head.

"Since all your friends have just got checked out of the hospital, Harriet's boyfriend decided to throw a party to celebrate. You went to his house at about six or seven, and came back a couple of hours later." She pauses and moves towards me. "A boy named Sid dropped you off here. You were stoned or drunk or something, you could barely speak."

I don't remember anything. "I didn't drink or smoke or do anything." I try to convince myself. "And am I slurring my words now?" If I were tipsy, maybe it would explain all the inconsistencies in my visions.

"No, you're fine now. When you arrived home, you smelled bad. But I trusted you were safe."

Veera never touched drugs or alcohol because of her beliefs. I'm not as religious, because given that my existence as a clairvoyant is antithetical to those values, I couldn't call myself a follower. I tried beer once when I was in the eighth grade and hated everything about it: the bitter taste, the feeling of how it burned my tongue, and its ability to make me lose control over my own body. So I don't touch any recreational substances because I never want to have a night to forget.

"It's fine if you did," she reassures me. "Everyone attends parties in high school. Abba wanted you to go because he knew Harriet would be there."

There's a long and awkward pause. It's still nighttime, our apartment isn't spacious, and someone could be listening: our neighbours, brothers, or Abba. I change the subject.

"Wait, so Sid drove me home?" I say softly, with a hint of disgust.

"Yeah. Good kid. He also walked you in, made sure you were drinking enough water, held back your impossibly long hair while you...you know." She stops stroking my hair and steps away from me. "He stayed until he saw me, then I took over. I walked you up. He left a little after ten. And you passed out at around ten-thirty, and here we are. Is there anything else you want to know?"

Is Sid a good guy? He might be trying to better himself after pushing Yasmine. And she admitted she did provoke him by taking that picture, but it doesn't forgive him for almost drowning her. I could get on his good side or leave him be. The last thing I want to do is to give him ammunition for his future attack by having a sour opinion of him. I won't be intentionally cruel to him, which would inspire his dark origin. I have many questions, but I don't think Veera could answer them. "No," I finally answer.

"Alright, goodnight, and I hope we can talk again when I get back." Veera walks back to me and folds me into her arms. She walks back to her bed and sleeps facing me, smiling.

I change out of my clothes and put on my pyjamas. I remove my prosthetic and massage chafing cream into my stump like any other night. But before I forget, I write down the visions I just had on my whiteboard. I grab my purse and place it under my stump as I kneel on my bed. I list the following:

کیمسٹری حادثہ ، سوال و جواب کا نقصان ، رونا ، انتخابی نقصان ، لڑائی۔

(Chemistry accident, Q&A loss, crying, election loss, fight)

I write down something smaller underneath everything else, just one word:

موت؟

(Death?)

Writing my visions is a ritual. It serves no real purpose because I still remember every single vision I have ever had. They contain some of my most cherished memories and most haunting experiences. When I was just two years old, I predicted my brother. After an eight-hour rest, I said '*bhai*', the Urdu word for brother. A couple of days later, Ammi found out she was pregnant, and eight weeks later, she found out she was having a boy. The same night gave me a vision of walking with my older brother, Veera, my Nana, and Nani meeting three faceless people: two adults and one boy, not that much older than Veera. The next day, we met Mr. and Mrs. Sethi and their seven-year-old son, Krishna.

It's one-forty-three. I close my eyes.

I wake up again, and the same visions are laid out in the same order as the last set. It's three-forty-one. I try to fall asleep again.

I wake up, experiencing the same visions again. It's six-oh-two, and I close my eyes again.

I wake up for the final time and lie in bed. Veera has already left and it's time to face another day. At least I'm not only operating on two hours of sleep.

Part 2.3: Introduction to Waves
Sidney, October 12th, 14:30

Now that I'm approaching the end of the school day, I'm counting down the hours until I can see Mother back at home. The final class I have today is physics with Mr. Glass. Typically, it's when I'm the most attentive, but after he postponed the test to next week, my attention waned.

In the morning, I had chemistry with Ms. Stone. She walked us through the procedure for the aspirin lab this upcoming Friday. Some people in class pointed out I was not wearing my glasses today, even though they saw me without them at Kyle's party. They must all have amnesia from that night, but to be completely fair, I don't remember much, either.

One vivid memory I have is driving Tikha home. She ranted about her brothers, and I met one of them. He didn't say anything; I just waved to him, and he ran away. I thought Tikha and I would be friendly at the very least, but she barely acknowledged my existence.

The two of us had English with Ms. Philips. Today, we were given an important fifteen-percent-of-our-grade comparative essay assignment for *King Lear* and *Macbeth*, due in about a month. Although we sat at opposite ends of the class, I checked in with her, but she kept dodging me. Eventually, I got the hint, so I let her be.

After English, I had a two-hour spare, for which I tried to rearrange the chemical composition of my food like I saw that old man do in the hospital. I enhanced my field of vision on a salad I bought from the cafeteria and tried to change it into something meaty. I looked at the lettuce's composition and looked at a discarded bit of meatloaf. Their chemical structures varied immensely, and all I did was knock the food out of my hands.

I am nowhere near ready enough to alter their chemical makeup. It's fun trying to experiment with my powers and learn my limitations; however, it isn't getting me closer to helping Mother.

Finally, I sauntered to physics class to close out the end of the school day with Harriet and Kyle. Our classroom is on the first floor of our school and overlooks the parking lot where I parked Mom's Prius. I look outside the window and appreciate the scenery. The leaves on the deciduous trees are starting to change colours, either spotted green or orange. The only litter grazing the property is the cigarette butts from the seniors and juniors taking a smoke break outside the school's property line. It's the best weather we have had all week; a lovely, overcast twenty-three degrees. It's a shame the field trip didn't happen today.

"Mr. Tam-Adams?" Mr. Glass breaks my trance. I shake my body and give him my full attention. "We are still in class for another fifteen minutes."

Harriet nudges my arm as she stares at me with a stern expression. I pick up my pen and smile, looking at my lack of notes. We are learning about Kinematics.

At the front of the class, Mr. Glass and another student are holding a rope together. This particular student made it back to the bus but sported a sling due to foreign objects embedded in his arm. He was one of five other students who were unlucky and needed hospital attention. Luckily, today saw perfect attendance; everyone returned to class.

"Anyway, sound waves aren't always uniform, as you see here," Mr. Glass continues. Sometimes, they appear at a higher frequency; when this happens, there's a higher pitch. When there's a lower frequency, there's a lower pitch." He pauses to allow the class to awe and marvel at his presentation. "But let's say there is no medium. Chris, drop the rope." He complies. "Now, there is no medium for me to relay information. There is no collision between particles, and Chris cannot hear me."

On the other side of the classroom, I could hear Yasmine speak quietly to her table group. "I can't hear him, either. Maybe the lesson is over."

She's sitting with Emilia and Anthony on the furthest side of the class from our table. She's especially radiant today, sitting next to another window. The sunlight shines on her medium-brown complexion and long, straightened black hair, accentuating her dimpled cheeks and sparkling as it hits her perfect smile. Her smile is contagious; the room gets brighter when she grins. I haven't seen that side of her for months. We didn't end our relationship on good terms, but for a brief moment, I got to see that girl again.

My high-pitched laugh stops the lesson. She turns to me, and her beautiful, bubbly smile turns bitter. I glue my nose to my papers in response. I steal a glance back at her, but she's still angrily staring me down. I turn away again.

"If there is one thing you can take away from this lecture today, it's that sound waves need a medium to travel. Collisions need to happen for the transfer of energy from one particle to another, even if you are expelling unwanted energy, Ms. Williams. Or are you cackling to yourself, Mr. Tam-Adams." He stops his lecture; Chris goes back to his seat.

Mr. Glass takes a deep breath. "This classroom is tiny. I can hear everything you guys say." He walks towards us. His cane echoes every time it strikes the linoleum tiles. "We only get seventy-five minutes a day to learn about an essential subject, without which you could not enjoy the greatest necessities of life." He gestures to his left, towards the windows. "It's bad enough we are not allowed to go on our field trip again, and we must not learn the old-fashioned way by watching ancient videos on the internet. But you kids interrupting our class to crack jokes or count down the seconds until you go home are not the reason why I decided to teach. I expect your undivided attention, which means no texting on your phones, or holding hands during class."

He directs his scowl toward Harriet and Kyle. They let go of each other's hands and shuffle their chairs away from each other.

"Do I need to make a seating plan for this class?" Mr. Glass asks. "If you keep this up, I will."

The class freezes. Many of us are worried our teacher will erupt into a furious tantrum again. I already had PTSD from the last time.

When we were in grade ten science, I forgot to hand in an assignment by the due date. He was already on edge after Kyle accidentally dropped a piece of equipment for a lab, but my forgetting to hand in an assignment made him completely lose his shit. It wasn't my first time forgetting my homework for his class, but his rant shook the classroom. It covered many topics, including how easy our generation has it, how he put so much care into school back in his days, and how our behaviour is offensive to him. Veins popped out of his forehead and neck, and his eyes bulged out of his skull.

I wanted him to stop yelling, but I could not get a word out; I was petrified. After a few minutes, he grabbed his left arm and collapsed under his weight. It was an impactful and memorable performance; I even got a headache as he was rolled away on a stretcher. He broke a hip and took a year off to heal, but he returned this year to see us out as we graduated. I started studying extra hard for his tests, and when he assigned a CPT or a take-home quiz, I finished it way before the due date. Kyle and Yasmine weren't affected the same way I was, and while Harriet never had him, she was never frightened. But she's a good student, always scoring among the highest in the class. Science was never my best subject, although I know it will change after the explosion. And then I can help Mother and everything will be normal again.

The bell rings.

"Sid, come on, let's go." Kyle nudges me.

I immediately snap out of my daydream and notice everyone else is gone, even Harriet. "You okay, bro?"

I nod to him and walk with Kyle out of our class.

"It's okay, Sid. Mr. Glass can't hurt you anymore," he teases.

I humour his claim. "Mother's coming back today. I'm just happy, that's all."

"I know you were happy Sunday night. You were dominating beer pong," Kyle snaps back.

It was simple; much like when Kat threw bread balls in her mouth, I threw a ping pong ball a little short and pushed it in with my mind wave. I wanted Yasmine to be my partner so I could impress her with my new powers, but she didn't even come. Regardless, it was also easy playing against a couple of lightweights like Kyle and Harriet.

"Yeah, I remember. I didn't end up drinking at all that night." I sunk every shot. But I did end up with a migraine as intense as a morning-after hangover. And aside from driving Tikha home, I don't remember much.

"Yeah, buddy." Kyle puts me in a headlock and runs his knuckles into my hair vigorously, ruining my hairstyle. He's a head taller than I am and thirty kilos heavier, so I can't fight back.

Kyle changed a lot over the summer. He used to be tall, skinny, and skittish, like a giant praying mantis. But by August, he had bulked up, gotten a new hairstyle, and dyed his tips blond while keeping his brown roots. Suddenly, people did a double-take when they passed him in the hallway. I couldn't believe his transformation—not only his appearance, but also his attitude. He had not only become confident and decisive, but he was also striking. He made me feel ashamed of my twig-like arms and cylindrical torso. I run my fingers through my hair, sweeping it back to the left.

"Then what happened?" he asks. "You just disappeared after that."

"Tikha was pretty intoxicated, so I drove her home." Kyle and I exit the school through the back door and are greeted by another pleasant fall breeze.

In our haste, we forget to scan our surroundings, and I catch the eye of a swarm of news reporters. To put it more accurately, it's a group of three students who run an online blog. I don't know their names. They are an independent newspaper called the *Pulitzer Protégé of Canada*. Mindy initially founded the group as an extracurricular activity. Since she left high school, they have gained another kind of reputation. They are known for publishing personal stories without the subject's consent and researching to a point that could be considered doxing. Nothing they post is false, and it's free to read on their website, but they have a terrible habit of not staying out of people's lives.

I would love to acknowledge that I can see much further than I ever could with my glasses, but the sight of the reporters is unnerving. I pray they do not see us.

"Aww, such a nice guy. Too bad dementors are incapable of feeling anything," he mocks.

"Dementors?" I back away from him.

"It's the eyes; Tikha's eyes are so lifeless and dull until she looks at you. Then they burn an image in your mind and follow you wherever you go. You can't make eye contact with her for more than two seconds because your life force drains out of your body." He suddenly stops in his tracks. "I swear, when I woke up from that coma, her cold, expressionless face was the first thing I saw. Harriet tells me I was still drugged, but I know what I saw. That bitch is possessed and she possessed me."

I never really thought about Tikha much before Sunday. She didn't leave much of an impression the first time we met. Her distinctive limp on her left leg, and long, frizzy hair that grows past her waist set her apart; other than that, she looks like a generic bland Indian girl. And even though I don't know her well, I want to tell him Kyle he's being mean.

The three reporters notice us and walk in our direction. Each of them has their phones out. One has a tablet, while another carries a cheap home video camera, aimed at us.

"Excuse me; you two must be students from Mr. Glass's physics class?" the one with a microphone asks.

I don't look at them; I'm not in the mood to answer questions.

"We're writing about the I&MNG explosion. Can we talk for a second?"

"*Non, merci,*" Kyle responds in French. "*Nous sommes des étudiants de l'Asie et nous devons aller à la bibliothèque pour rechercher notre cours d'Histoire Mondiale.*"

I have no idea what he said, although I understand the words for 'Asia' and 'library'. It was a lie that no one would believe; why would Asian students be speaking French? I think he was hoping the French language sounded so foreign, they would leave us alone. Although I'm part Japanese, Kyle was ninety-percent European Caucasian, with a hint of Hispanic somewhere in his family's past. Plus, we're already outside, so we can't be heading to the library.

"I heard you two speaking perfect English two seconds ago," the reporter holding the tablet argues.

Kyle tries to walk back into the school, but the door locks behind him.

"Listen, please, we want to ask some questions for our story. It will only take five minutes," the student holding the tablet continues.

"We would rather not," I politely tell them. "I need to get home. My mother is coming back home today." We push through; Kyle and I continue walking toward my car.

The reporters still find a way to surround us. "Maeko Tamashiro, the safety inspector for I&MNG. How's she doing?" One of them stands to my right while the cameraman films us.

The fact he said her birth name, a name she does not use anymore, doesn't sit right with me.

"We do not want to contribute to your dumb extracurricular activity." I walk faster before I start to lose my temper. They move out of the way. I smile, and Kyle thanks them.

"Sid, what if—"

"Just go away!" I turn around, looking at their terrified faces. The air ripples around me as all three members fall over; the cameraman falls backwards as his camera hits the pavement before he does. The tablet screen shatters into a multi-coloured pixelated mess. The field correspondent gets tossed a couple of feet backwards, rolling on the hard parking lot asphalt. All of them rock around, groaning seconds after the fall. I bolt across the parking lot, and a panicked Kyle follows me. One of the worst migraines I have ever had throbs violently around a halo in my skull.

Kyle has also been a little roughed up; his hair on the top of his head is standing on its own. He removes some rocks that have lodged themselves into his hand.

Luckily, there are no students within our vicinity to witness my display of supernatural abilities. I keep looking around me, twisting my head, checking to see if anyone is following us.

We enter the car together. I'm in the driver's spot, he's in the passenger seat. We don't talk for about ten seconds as I think of how to diffuse the situation. I rest my head on the backrest and recline myself, looking at the ceiling, tending to my migraine.

"We did the right thing," I blurt out, tapping the steering wheel. "Those hagseeds had it coming. We have a right to privacy, and they can go right to hell."

"What the f—" He holds that consonant for a while. "What just happened there?" he finally asks.

"I must have startled them. By the way, when did you learn how to speak French?" I add, in an attempt to change the subject.

"Well, Harriet taught me a lot more than what I learned in ninth grade." He quickly sees through my misdirection and shakes his head. "But I'm not going to pretend that I did not see your hair stand up on its own and the air ripple around your..." He twirls his fingers above his head. He tries to remember where he saw them, because the words did not come from my mouth.

"Eyes, hair, head?" I lower my sun visor and lift the flap to expose the mirror, using my hands to comb my hair to the left again. I push the ignition button of my car, hoping to have a muffled conversation. Unfortunately, the Prius doesn't make a sound when starting up. "Let me just get this going." I put the car in drive and leave the parking lot. It starts revving as I push it past forty kilometres per hour. I don't look at Kyle. "This is going to sound crazy, but I can use my mind to control things around me. I haven't gotten far, though. I can only push and lower objects." I lie and neglect to tell him about my superior eyesight, because at this point, it's a novelty.

"Shit, dude." Kyle reclines himself, sinking into his seat. "Did you get it from the nuclear plant?" He somehow makes the realization sound sincere. "So, are you going to become a superhero now? We should test it out. Let's find a discrete location to see what you've got. Or are you a Carrie? Should I start being nice to you now?"

"I assure you, I won't kill everyone at prom, so long as no one dumps a bucket of pig's blood on my head," I joke. Kyle doesn't take my quip well, as he frantically tries to undo his seatbelt.

"Relax, bro." I put my hand on the dashboard in front of him. He freezes. "I don't even know where the school keeps its propane tanks or how to fray an entire electrical grid."

"I do feel better." He stops fidgeting and pushes my hand off the dashboard and back on the gearshift. "Mainly because Harriet told me our school is equipped with a geothermal heat pump, so the fact that you did not know is reassuring. However, that's not entirely your fault. They're so commonplace in Islington that I forget the school is one of a few places in Manotick that only recently converted. But I will need a contingency plan if you go ballistic."

As we approach a red light, I step on the brakes and stop at the Morissette Bridge. There is a lot of oncoming traffic. To my right, in the distance, an adequate number of protesters stand across the road from I&MNG, demanding that the plant be closed. Kyle looks out his window.

"I get it, but we could be preventing protests from getting out of hand, or stopping shootings in public areas, or preventing petty crimes." I list a bunch of options based on my current set of abilities. I cannot alter chemical makeup, but someday, I will.

"You can start there and work your way up," Kyle suggests. "You are the first of your kind, no one has seen anything like you yet. You could topple tyrannical governments or find the next supervillain of our times. I'm just throwing out ideas here." Kyle stops talking for a moment. "Wait, did you say 'we'?" He turns his head to me.

"You were in the explosion, too; you can probably do the same things I can. We can practice, I can teach you, and if you surpass me, you can teach me. Maybe this will be our new job. I can show you the old—"

Kyle squints hard and puckers up parts of his face. He looks as if he's going to shit himself.

"Kyle?" I shriek. "Not here; we need to find an open space. What I find is strong emotions like anger or fear are good triggers to get my powers up. Happy thoughts can help amplify, and no thoughts can help turn them off." I cross over the Morissette Bridge and open the windows to enjoy the warm autumn breeze. Kyle sticks his right hand out the window, allowing it to go up and down, depending on how he angles it.

"Can this qualify as a happiness trigger?" Kyle laughs. "We have it made."

"Maybe we are getting a little ahead of ourselves. We still need you to levitate something, or push or pull. It was what Mr. Glass taught us. We need to see the air particles collide and recoil, hitting other particles and transferring their energy around each other. That is how you do it. Your hand outside the car is constantly being hit with air molecules, forcing it up or down, and your hand's position directs it along. Do you need to see that?"

"Holy shit, I think I see it." He pulls his hand back into the car. I close the windows. He has learned well from physics class, but I haven't. I'm not ready to teach, but he's prepared to learn.

"Bro." Kyle smiles. We shake on it. "We will be the most powerful crime fighters in the world and dedicate our lives to the pursuit of justice."

Part 2.4: My Sweet Tea
Sidney, October 12th, 18:30

Since school ended, Kyle and I have been driving around downtown looking for any crimes in the area, like a robbery, a vandal, an assault, etc. As it turns out, it's not easy to happen upon a crime scene. I'm sure we can make a difference if Ottawa gives us a chance, but it's one of the most boring cities in the world. After a few hours, I get a migraine, so we head to *My Sweet Tea* in Centretown.

In grade eleven, it was my after-school job. My mom would drive me the twenty minutes I needed, and I would practice driving to get my G2.

Coming back to the poorly-lit tea shop brings back memories. Yasmine would visit me almost every weekend when I worked there, and daily during her summer school term. She would joke and say the only reason she went out with me was for all the free tea. I knew it was a joke because I only made her free tea once when I tried to get her back after she dumped me.

It was also about that time that I decided to quit. It was my final year, and Mother had just been admitted for the first time. I didn't need the money since I had saved enough for one year of post-secondary and could take out loans if necessary.

The owner's son is behind the register. He hides behind his phone most of the time. Only two people are working there, the cashier and the owner, Ms. Park. She's an old family friend of Mom's.

We avoid her sightline, order our teas, and sit in a booth. Kyle immediately orders a lychee milk tea, and I get a pineapple tapioca boba with thirty percent sugar and no ice. We sit in a booth in a far corner of the shop, unseen by everyone.

"Pineapple?" Kyle questions my drink choice. "Is that technically cannibalism?"

Why did I tell him about my mother's nickname for me? "I like pineapple." My face involuntarily twitches as I hide my embarrassment.

"I mean, you are what you eat and all." He laughs. "Although I know a pineapple has digestive enzymes, so maybe it's cannibalism the other way around." I'm relieved he didn't comment on the embodied carbon from importing the fruit across oceans. Harriet changed him, and her social justice reveals can get annoying after a while. Kyle wouldn't know what a geothermal heat pump was if it wasn't for her.

"If that is true—" I use my straw to suck up some boba pearls and aim the straw at his face. "This would be lethal." I shoot the pearls directly at him.

He releases a high-pitched scream and closes his eyes as they approach his face. They stop centimetres from his nose, suspended in mid-air. After a few seconds, he opens his eyes, realizing he's not in danger. He lets out an audible gasp and turns to the cashier, still tapping away on his phone. Kyle flicks the pearls back to me.

"I remember the first time I had control of my powers," I tell him. "I was in my dining room, and I saw an open cabinet. While thinking of my happiest memory, I just let it carry through, and just like that, the cabinet closed." I grip the padded seat below me as he processes.

Kyle takes a sip and sighs. "I know just what to think about." He closes his eyes and mumbles, "Harriet."

I cannot blame him for thinking about the cabin trip where he and Harriet hooked up for the first time. During the last week of August, we had gone to Orillia to stay at Kyle's father's cottage. The two of us and our significant others spent quality time in a mosquito-ridden but oxygen-rich township four and a half hours away from Ottawa.

Ever since the ninth grade, the two of us and Kyle's father spent the final week of August there. But last year, we were allowed to go without chaperones. I had just gotten my G2 and could drive by myself. I had to lie to Mother about the trip details; she would not let me drive for hours.

Harriet and I took turns driving Mr. Ganatra's Rivian truck. It took approximately six hours to make the four-and-a-half-hour-long trip. Harriet played her uncreatively named 'Capitalism Sucks' playlist consisting of songs such as *Price Tag, Imagine, Citizen of the Planet, Only the Young, Heaven is a Place on Earth,* and the entirety of the album *The Wall.*

The first day at the cottage was one of the greatest days of my life, at least when Harriet was not talking about her father's campaign. We swam in Lake Simcoe, played some board games Kyle had lying around, and had campfires outside. Harriet and Kyle got to know each other much better. But around the second night, I found out Mother had a massive migraine and needed to spend a couple of nights in the hospital; the doctors removed a small growth in her brain.

On the third day, I got lost in the woods during a game of hide-and-seek in the dark. We were a little stoned; we thought the smoke would repel mosquitoes. I got bitten a total of eight times on my legs and arms, and a couple of times on my face. We were unaware it was blackfly season. My ears puffed so that I looked like an elephant. Yasmine took a picture and set it as her lock screen background; I got a little upset with her. I was already in a bad mood after hearing about what happened to Mother, and I tried to grab her phone. She backed away, slipped, and fell into dark, cold, and shallow water. She flailed her arms uncontrollably, unable to bring herself up to the surface. I was in a lot of pain from the bites and was later physically restrained by Kyle while Harriet picked her up out of the water. When she stood back up, she screamed at me and immediately dumped me.

The blackfly problem got out of hand, and we stayed indoors. I brought all my favourite Studio Ghibli movies, although we only watched *Spirited Away, Princess Mononoke* and *Tales from Earthsea.* We then returned to Ottawa, and Yasmine has not spoken to me since.

"Sid." Kyle had opened his eyes already. "I'm not getting it; how did you do it?"

I'm not sure how to explain it except with the preamble that the old man told me.

"It starts with a small, spontaneous particle and transfers some energy to its neighbours. They become infected, and it spreads quickly until it's the only thought inside your brain." I don't remember every word, but I think I'm close.

He laughs. "Did you just make that up? Bro, that is either really deep or really dumb. The line between them is very blurry."

"What I mean is, concentrate, visualize what you want to happen, see it in your mind, and then see it right in front of you." I release my grip from my seat and cup my hands in front of me, preparing to catch Kyle's tea glass. Kyle puts his hands on his temples and puckers his face up. After holding his breath for eight seconds, he gives up and lets out one exacerbated and defeated exhale.

"Okay, I see what is happening. You're making me look like an idiot. Hilarious, Sidney."

I freeze. He only calls me 'Sidney' when he's trying to put me down.

"I don't know how you got Gerald, Topher, and Alex to volunteer to get roughed up or how you did that cool boba shot, but..." He smirks and raises his hands at me. "You got me."

"No." I take my tea and put my left hand close to me with my right hand further out. "Look at the cup. There's no joke." I look at the table to the left of the glass, rebounding a wave on the table so it hits the glass and pushes it to the right. The table absorbs most of the push, and the glass travels toward my right. I don't move my face or arms. Kyle's jaw drops. I palm the cup in my right hand and pick it up to take a sip. "Easy." I close my eyes and put the cup back down.

"What else can you do?" Kyle asks. "Moving objects is cool. But it's a party trick. I initially thought you could do something no one has ever seen before. Maybe I built it up in my head."

"No, you're not. I can shoot waves from my head, small and powerful waves. An old man told me what I could do. He mentioned I could deconstruct molecules, repair cells quickly, and manipulate energy."

"An old man?" Kyle questions.

"Yeah, he visited me after the explosion and told me everything. I saw him again on Saturday night."

Kyle drums his right four fingers along his glass. "How do I say this delicately? Did you go alone? Maybe you need to talk to someone about what happened in your state. Not me, like a trained professional, you might have some repressed memories you need to dig up."

"What are you implying?" I furrow my brows and grip my glass a little tighter.

"Well... you were on a lot of drugs and the experience could be very traumatizing." Kyle sinks into his seat. "I have read about this before. Some shady group 'adopts' a naïve boy or girl with a terrible home life and shows them that they are chosen to deliver some prophecy. They are then heavily experimented on and mindwiped of all their trauma. But for children naïve enough to believe any dumb thing an adult says, it's a real shitshow. Because a cult could very easily indoctrinate children into doing terrible things." He clicks his jaw as he stalls. "Or you have absorbed some energy you weren't supposed to and now have become a biological weapon. Have you spoken to the military at all? Look out for tails; they could be everywhere and take on any shape." He sits on his phone.

"None of that is true." I finish the rest of my tea, hoping it will calm me down. "I don't have a terrible home life, and the man didn't touch me. I remember being in the hospital and having a burst of energy come out my head and knocking the old man on the floor—"

"Hold it." He interrupts me. "You knocked an old man to the floor. Is he still alive? Maybe you're the one who's possessed." He rubs his hand on the tabletop softly. "...or drugged."

"Stop saying I'm drugged," I yell. "The man is still alive. I visited him the next day. He signed me out of the hospital and told me to go to an old shack near the power plant. He then fixed my eyes. I can now see cellular and atomic structures."

"That's impossible. Visible light is larger than atoms and compounds. They literally cannot be seen by the human eye, unless you're firing electrons out of your eyes."

He looks at me as if I'm full of shit. I can't believe he's using the 'that's impossible' line after seeing what I can do. He's okay with what he can see but draws the line at some other physical impossibilities. His stand-up routine is giving me a headache.

"I cannot believe I tried to spend the entire day with you, trying to unlock your abilities. Maybe you should go to that man, maybe everyone in the class should go. I'll take you there right now. I'll take the whole freaking class." I cannot believe the words that come out of my mouth. "Call Harriet."

"She's having a girls' night with Yasmine." Kyle texts on his phone. After finishing his text, he places his phone on the table and puts on a sympathetic face. "Listen, Sid. I want to believe you, I want to have these powers and fight crime together, and I believe you when you say you do as well. Maybe it's a family thing. Like you're so conditioned to radiation because your mother worked at I&MNG, and your grandfather worked at Fukushima, so I get why you have a higher tolerance. I said I felt something when you said those words, but now—"

My phone vibrates on the table and Kyle stops talking. Mom's video-calling me. I put my phone in front of my face.

"Hi, honey." She smiles. The quality of the video isn't very crisp. She keeps freezing and unfreezing, leaving behind a trail of pixels. "Where are you? It's seven o'clock, and guess who's back home with us?" She rotates her phone to show Mother. She's looking much better than when I last saw her. She still has noticeable bags under her eyes. However, her skin has more colour and her hair is still on her head, but she has a bandana tied around her head, covering the scars on her forehead. They are both sitting at the table, in their typical seating arrangement, alongside Mindy and Kat.

I strike my forehead with my palm in frustration. I have been looking forward to this moment for the entire weekend and got sidetracked.

"Sidney, where are you?" Mother barks at me. "We are all waiting for you." She pauses for a while and squints her eyes at me. "And what's wrong with your hair?" She brings the phone closer to her until the screen takes up her entire face. "Have you been keeping hydrated?"

"Miriam, you don't have to worry about him." Mom defends me but expresses her concern. "Let me do the talking, alright? Don't stress yourself out. But Sidney, will you be home for dinner?"

"Yes, Mom," I reassure them. "Kyle and I were drinking tea before you called. We were just about to leave."

Mom takes the phone back and smiles at me. "That's great, baby. Get home soon. Love you."

"Love you, too." I immediately turn off my phone's video feed and then comb my hair back to the left until it's perfect.

"Let's go." I take my keys and put my phone in my back pocket. "We can make a brief stop at the plant, and then I'll take you back home."

"I texted my mom; she's coming to pick me up. Can we put a pin in this, maybe tomorrow or Thursday or something? It's getting late. Besides, I heard what your mom said."

He's right. The whole day, I was looking forward to seeing Mother. Perhaps some other time I could talk to Harriet and everyone else. Also, Kyle lived on the other side of the river in Islington. The plant was in Manotick, it would be a bit of a detour.

"Excuse me, guys." Ms. Park's son approaches us with an Interac machine in hand. "If you guys are leaving, you will have to pay." I worked beside him for almost a week, yet I never got a good look at him since he was always on his phone. I don't think he remembers me. And only now do I see his nametag: Liam.

I immediately slip him a ten-dollar bill while Kyle takes out his wallet and tries to decide how he should pay. He has about five different cards. On the one hand, I know how wealthy Kyle is. His family can afford a house in Islington and a summer home. But seeing the old Kyle, the one who takes minutes on the most trivial decisions, is comforting. Even though Harriet fixed Kyle's rigidity, I miss the quirks of my old friend.

"Why didn't you ask us to pay before we got these?" I ask Liam.

He sighs through his nose. "I don't know." He slurs his words and maintains that fundamental, expressionless tone. He immediately turns away and continues to text on his phone. I'm glad I didn't tip him.

"What a dick," Kyle comments. I exit the booth, while he remains seated.

"Hang on." I focus on Liam's elbow and shoot a wave at his funny bone. Doing so would cause him to lose his grip for a minute. He hisses as he grabs his right elbow and drops his phone. Then I push the door open and send his phone out the door in one motion. He runs straight into the door face-first and screams. Rubbing his nose, he exits the tea shop.

Kyle and I have a good laugh about this. "Who's possessed or drugged now?" I smirk. I walk away from Kyle, giggling to myself.

My laughter ends when I see some blood on the glass pane.

I descend the steps to Somerset Drive to find it's dark out. It's only seven o'clock at night, but for some reason, I'm not used to it. Liam's frantically tapping on his watch.

His phone lights up the sidewalk. I can't believe how far I made it travel from his hands. The screen lights up Liam's face and reveals some blood dripping down his nose to his lip. He smears it on his sweater's sleeve. I offer to call someone or wait for an ambulance, but he ignores me and ascends the steps back to the shop. I instruct him to pinch the bridge of his nose and look downwards.

I take out my keys and try to summon my car. The atmosphere is quite different in Centretown than it is in Manotick. The area is much more alive. It does not shut down at eight like Manotick does. Some buildings are much older and date back more than one hundred and fifty years to the beginning of the creation of Canada. They represent an older time in Ottawa's history. The houses all look the same: single-garaged, red-brick, three-storey, semi-detached dwellings. If the lights are on, they're occupied, otherwise, the properties are either condemned or abandoned.

I get within ten meters of my car when a gust of wind pushes me off balance. Someone walks around and then stops when they are above me.

He doesn't say a word, nor can I make out any discernible features on him. I try to move, but I cannot. My feet stick to the ground. My first guess is Kyle finally caught up. However, I know he's nowhere near as tall, and I cannot make out his face because his head blocks the only streetlight in the area.

Suddenly, the streetlight explodes, raining down pieces of glass onto the sidewalk, and darkening the alley.

My following assumption is that it's a homeless person. I try to get my wallet to give him money, but my hands and fingers lock. My muscles stiffen, first my feet and hands, then my legs and arms. I temper my breath and try to look upwards but my head can no longer tilt. My final guess is Liam, who somehow figured out I made his phone leap out of his hands, but it could not be him, as blood is not dripping down onto the sidewalks.

The sound of my heartbeat overpowers my ears; I try to muster up a few words to make an apology. My mouth could open a little bit, but only to let the air out of my lungs. My legs turn to rubber and I collapse to my knees. The sharp aggregate embeds itself into my body. After every second another body part loses mobility. My eyelids get heavier, my facial muscles sag, and my arms droop down while my fingers release their grip; and my keys ring as they strike the ground. Then my chest hits the sidewalk, and finally the right side of my head. As my eyelids shut, I look at the only thing I can see: his shoes.

While it is very dark, I can see the textures and patterns in the linings. They are brown Oxford pump loafers. I know exactly who it is.

Part 2.5: Meeting #3
Sidney, October 13ᵗʰ, 00:34

"Now, what in the world were you thinking?" the man yells at me.

He said he would visit me when I was ready to take the next steps. I smile in anticipation. My eyes don't take long to adjust to my surroundings. I'm in the old shack again, standing up with my arms above my head. I take a step forward, but my arms pull me back. My butt slides on the dirty shack floor until my back hits a cold, metal tube. My hands are locked in handcuffs, attached to a vertical pipe mounted to the wall. His voice agitates the shack. I shiver. For the first time this month, I feel cold.

I cough and wheeze. "What's going on?" I try to stand up, but my legs can barely support my weight, and my arms feel like they are dislocating from my shoulders. "Where's Kyle?" I yell.

"I've contacted your mom and told her you are spending the night at your friend's place. And I contacted your friend to let him know you are safely home."

He's not going to teach me how to progress. I must fight my way out; otherwise, I would succumb to the terrible acts he wants to bestow upon me. He knows about Kyle's and my experiment, but it was uneventful. If he laid a finger on him, I would do him much worse than I did to those reporters.

"Reporters?"

I forgot he could read my mind. Every chain link is rusted over, and I need to break one. The chain vibrates gently, and the top of my head starts to throb. "I know things got a little insane back there—"

"A little?!" he interrupts me. "What part of you thought: 'Oh, I have these new powers, I can, nay, I *must* abuse them however I want? There are no consequences for me. I don't have to abide by anything except what I feel.'"

"That was not my intention. I just—" I cough. "I just—" I blank out. I don't know what I'm doing.

The old man is in the shack somewhere, but out of sight. There's no light anywhere, so I look through an infrared lens. I can adjust the wavelength of my eyes to see different spectra, and in doing so, see a warm, glowing body in front of me. He must be behind the other side of the wall, outside the shack.

"I'm having a hard time understanding my place in this world." I pace my breathing and resist the urge to cough. My lungs clear up; I'm winded instead of asthmatic. "I know I can do much more with what I have." I take a deep breath through my nose. "You told me to live my life and be in the moment to expand my powers, that's exactly what I am doing."

"Let me get something through to you," the old man pleads. "If you keep acting irresponsibly..." He pauses. "...well, you should be so lucky that I found you before the police did."

I know what he means. The police would not see things my way; they would see me as the aggressor. By hurting other people in the process, I lower myself. It's a lesson taught to an eight-year-old, but I guess at this moment I am dumber than a child.

Something metallic hits the concrete floor. The sound rings in my ears. A screw rolls right next to my shoes. It's covered in rust, around a half-inch in length, Philips's head with a stripped drive. The c-channel above me holding the chain is missing one screw. A simple tug could make the channel wobble a little, but there are more screws attached.

"Do the police know about us and our powers? What else do they know?" I ask. If that is the case, does Mom know?

"They don't know about your powers or anyone else's. At least, the force as a collective does not know." The man's ominous laugh echoes and shakes the chains and shack. I wince and try to use my biceps to cover my ears. "For a minute, let us consider a hypothetical situation. Let us say there is a powerful person. Let us call him Will. Will discovers he can use his powers to do anything. All he needs to do is visualize what he wants and make it happen. Will starts small, for example, counterfeiting money. He reasons that it's fine, as he's doing it for a noble cause. These unmarked bills are going to help less fortunate people. However, it works too well. It becomes so lucrative that he gives up having a job and travels the world undetected and untraceable. However, the migraines are killing him, and he starts to slip up because he wants to minimize the pain. Now would be the perfect time for the police to show up. The authorities catch Will with large stacks of unsolicited bills. Will could willingly surrender himself and go to jail. That is, if he is lucky. Will would not go down without a fight. After all, he is fighting 'the man'. He thinks he has an elevated status, especially since he is protesting what he deems an oppressive regime. He becomes dangerous, evades laws, and eventually, he is caught. Will would no longer be Will."

"So, you want me to be apathetic?" I whisper.

"Yes! People see us as scary and mysterious. Exercise in restraint and don't get caught."

"Don't get caught? By you or by the authorities?"

"Do you want to try to catch a bullet, or run for the rest of your life? Because I can prepare you for that right now. It will make my job a lot easier." A gun cocks in the distance. "Run, boy."

It's the word 'boy' that snaps me back to reality. I panic and run to the left, but the shackles restrict me and pull me back to the wall. I hit my waist on the cold pipe again. "I don't know how to use these powers." I'm going to die. I repeat: "I'm going to die." I close my eyes.

Another screw hits the floor again. The noise is much quieter and dissipates much faster. This one is newer, silver, unstripped, and two inches long. I try yanking my chains forward, and the chain has more give. However, I'm still attached. Every time I have a correct epiphany, a screw falls.

"So, is there some mad conspiracy? A secret society I need to be aware of that is retconning our civilization with propaganda made to make everyone powerless and submissive?"

"I'm too busy to fall into rabbit holes."

"Are you God?" I don't know why I said that. It just seems like a possibility, given all the crazy shit I've already witnessed.

"No. But I will level with you on something. I don't know our origin story or why we are so few in numbers." He softens his voice. "But I would be lying if I said I did not have a theory. Maybe they started stoning people because of suspected witchcraft. For fear of dying, the witches hid away. I'd like to think we're moving past burning at the stake, but many people still have that mentality." My head starts to palpitate again, I cringe and sink under my weight.

"So..." I ask. "The Salem Witch Trials were real and not just hysteria?"

"No, they were hysteria." He raises his voice. "Even if one person may or may not have done one supernatural thing, hundreds of innocent people were killed for no reason."

Everything suddenly goes quiet again. Another gust of wind picks up some dirt and debris in the shed.

"That's just speculation. Besides, we all have theories. But the more time you start thinking about what happened, the less time you spend in the real world. What starts as a small itch consumes every idle second of your mind. It becomes all you can think about, and you lose yourself in a conspiracy of your own making."

Dust particles fly off the ground and spin into a mini tornado, then collapse. "I'm only you because I don't want our lineage to die out after me. I won't live forever. You're not God, either. Would people believe their God is some tiny, biracial, teenage boy, born in an irrelevant part of the world, who probably hasn't lifted anything heavier than a bag of milk?"

I furrow my brows. I don't care about the insults; I want to get out of here.

"I should have known this would happen. Teenagers and young adults have raging hormones that cause them to rebel against authority." He lets out an exasperated sigh. "You know in a decade or maybe a few years, it will be your job to keep younger people like yourself in check. I don't want this to come back to me, and you won't, either."

"Fine, I get it!" I clench my teeth. But strangely enough, I do understand what he's saying.

"Let me ask you this, Sidney," he continues. "If you were to meet someone who told you they could see your future, predict insignificant trivia like what you will eat in the future or large benchmarks such as when you die with one hundred percent certainty, what would your first reaction be?"

He's asking me if I believe in psychics. My parents have always told me gypsy magic is a con. They told me they were scam artists at worst, or performers who use vague gestures and phrases to fool their subjects.

"The fact that you are taking this long to answer shows that you are not ready for the unabridged truth."

"Wait, if I exist in this state, and you exist," I hypothesize. "Real psychics can as well?" I raise my voice, unsure of where I'm going with this claim. He doesn't respond, so I formulate a definite epiphany. "I'm not saying my mom was lying to me, but she was going off the information she had. I guess I should, too."

Another screw falls to the ground; one is like the second one, almost brand new. It's not a great epiphany. After all, I'm probably not immune to propaganda. Stories from psychics are compelling, but they are still fibs.

"If psychics exist, if we exist..." I take a deep breath in and exhale. "...why can we not just change this? Why do we hide in shacks? Why does the Illuminati, or whatever they are called, do this?"

He laughs, in a much more friendly demeanour; no dust picks up off the ground. "You would think there is some secret society resisting, coordinating attacks. It's understandable to think that since there are underground societies for mascots or nerds who love certain media franchises to the extreme. Some people dedicate their lives to certain causes or identities, so why not this one?" He coughs again; the wood panels in front of me vibrate back and forth and wood chips flake off. "Look ahead." He raises his voice.

I guess I need some foresight to comprehend his plan.

"No. I mean literally, look forward."

Those wood chip particles start to grow in size. They spin and accumulate into large strands, and the strands replicate to form a pink blob. The mass snakes around itself and coagulates into a soft and wet brain floating in mid-air, joined by a couple of eyes floating in front of it. The eyes blink autonomously. I back up quickly until I hit the cold, metal pipe. Within a couple of minutes, the rest of the man's head forms: eyelids, ears, skull, hair, jawbone, etc. until he is just a talking head, staring at me. I should look away, but I can't. His heart, lungs, stomach, and intestines connect and a rib cage confines his internal organs. After the skeleton is formed, the muscles and skin wrap around the body. A dress shirt and a tan blazer clothe his midsection.

I look away when his bottom half reconfigures but get the all-clear when the sound of shoes clicks on the ground. He takes a step towards me, no longer floating in mid-air. The final body parts needed are his arms and hands. They start at the shoulders; the bones reconnect to their sockets and the muscular, blood and skin branch out until his hands come together. As soon as his body is fully reconstituted, he wiggles his fingers, touching his thumbs to his index fingers, middle fingers, ring, and pinkies.

He brushes some residual dust off his clothes and looks me in the eyes. "You know I did ask those same questions. Then I realized I was just a guy who worked at a nuclear plant. I thought if

I could show the world what people like us could do, more would step up. Unfortunately, people are extremely disappointed to see how vast our powers are in our imaginations, our abilities are so limited in practice. We don't fly around or run faster than the speed of light. The physical limits of our world won't allow it. And even if they could, we cannot be there all the time to stop crime because we need jobs and money to survive, and superhero work doesn't pay the bills.

"There are some publicized cases of superhuman abilities, but they're useless. They don't fight crime, and they sure as hell don't keep us safe from bad guys. And with us, there's nothing we cannot do that a machine has not already done." He steps back to give me some more space. He has some new wrinkles around his eyes and greyer hair strands near his ears. He hunches even more, and while he is still taller than me, he has shrunk to the point where I can look at his face without straining my neck. He seemingly gained ten years in a week, but still not in his late seventies.

I finally recognize him. He worked at the nuclear power plant; I'm 'paying him' with taxes. I'm not interested in local, provincial, or federal politics, but we had a picture with his face on our lawn for the two election cycles prior.

"You're Guillaume Riviera." A shiver jolts down my back. I don't have the heart to tell him my friend's dad is trying to unseat him.

"I guess you've been to a Q and A session before. I'm impressed. Most teenagers could not point out their MP in a lineup." He pats my face and turns around. I wipe my cheek using my shoulder to remove some of the dead skin cells he left behind. "You see, the problem with people like us is that the majority are the wrong type of people. They are often born without knowledge of the powers they hold. If they are, they are either underprivileged or just bad people. You've used the word 'telekinetic' to describe us, when in fact, another t-word is used by many people today: 'terrorist'." He cracks his back by pushing on his spine from behind and raising his head. It's the loudest sound I've ever heard coming from a human body.

"Most do it unintentionally, but mob mentality is powerful. They don't show off. Most of them either get one moment of glory before dying or propagate brain waves to hypnotize their subjects into doing their bidding. It takes less energy and is less taxing on the body. Some of history's greatest monsters were people like us. No mere mortal would even go toe-to-toe with them. The witches act like witches because the world treats them like terrorists."

The shed starts to feel a lot smaller with him inside of it. I don't feel winded anymore, but my lungs are still heavy breathing in old man dust.

"You are lucky, Sidney. You and your still-developing mind live in a well-off part of town, and the worst thing you will feel is a mild headache."

I groan at him in frustration; these are not mild headaches.

"But if you do not exercise restraint, you can receive a brain palpitation or a nosebleed. If you are unlucky, your hair will change colour and fall out, your eyes will turn red, or worst case, your skull could crack, but that would only happen once you have unlocked your full potential. Once you reach the age where your brain is one hundred percent developed, every use of your powers could take days, weeks, months, or years off your life expectancy. Phasing through a wall is—" He suddenly stops talking and falls to his knees while gasping for air.

I'm still attached to the wall so I need to come up with another epiphany to help him and then escape. "One thing I can understand is, you have been in this game longer than I have. I will keep a low profile and help in small ways to stay alive. Hopefully, one day, we can emerge from the shadows and live harmoniously. But that day is not now."

Mr. Riviera looks up at the c-channel. Something hits me on the head. I shake it off, and it hits the floor. It's a bolt about a quarter inch in diameter and about four inches in length, and with the gentlest of nudges, I walk forward and bring my arms to myself.

"Step to your right and watch your head." Mr. Riviera closes his eyes.

The slightest yank causes the whole pipe to detach. It falls in a straight line and avoids hitting both of us. The sound of collision rings in my ears, briefly reactivating my tinnitus. I close my eyes until the noise is gone.

My arms feel nine times lighter. I rotate them around in their sockets; they are extremely sore after hanging up for so long. I stretch as I walk to Mr. Riviera, and help him to a more comfortable stance, dragging the pipe alongside me. I sit him down with his back against the wall. He looks at me, slowly breathing in and out, without saying a word.

"So..." I wonder. "Are you going to get me out of these, or is there something else I need to learn?"

"Right." He pulls a key out of his pocket. "There is just some arthritis in my joints and lesions in my head. As you get old, you..." He stands me up, takes my right hand, twists the key in the keyhole on my wrist and releases me. He does the same to my left. "You know, for your sake of mind, I won't tell you. Anyway, there is one more thing you should know before you go."

He pulls out an EpiPen from his pocket.

I shake my head. "What's that?"

"This is just a warning; I can easily take these powers away. Just don't do anything stupid, no more crime-fighting, if that's what you call what you did, and don't tell anyone about this."

"Wouldn't epinephrine make me stronger?" I ask. "My senses would be sent into overdrive, would they not?"

"For ten minutes, but an overdose will overwhelm your system." His sinister laugh grows louder. "You will feel like you are on top of the world, bursting with energy until it reaches your brain. You start to experience some light-headedness and nausea, your hands shake, and your muscles disconnect from your mind. The shot will coarse through your entire body as your brain starts to shut down. Your heart will beat two hundred times a minute, and you will wish you were dead because you will become immobile. Your body will release tension, and you will be on the floor, shitting and pissing yourself while saliva bubbles out of your mouth and your eyelids flutter faster than a hummingbird's wing beat. The worst part of all is..." He lifts my chin and stares into my eyes. "You thought you felt powerless before, but you have no idea what it truly feels like." He arches his back and towers over me.

"So you're not going to shoot me?"

"I don't have a gun, that sound was just me manipulating airwaves."

"Can you wipe my mind?" I ask, reaching into my pocket and trying to turn on the record button on my phone. "I'm assuming that's what you did to Kyle."

"Put your phone away," he yells. "You're lucky I didn't smash that thing."

I bring my hands above my head and remain seated.

He shakes his head at me. "I will not wipe your mind. You need to remember this moment, what it is like to submit, to be less than someone else. You need to have the right thoughts and ensure you are inhabiting this reality and not one of your design. Do not use your powers for any selfish purpose, and make amends with anyone you have wronged. And do not try to seek out anyone else to teach them about their powers. If I find someone else in this small, low-density town, you'll know."

I don't want the evil government to know about my abilities so they can tell other people about what I can do or experiment on me. Although, one member of the government does know.

How can I trust him? He didn't even seem to be upset with me for hurting four innocent civilians.

Who came up with these rules in the first place, and why are they so strongly enforced? We idolize people with superhuman abilities. Finding out they exist would break the news, until they move on to the next big story.

I take out my phone. It is one-oh-eight in the morning, and I have a two-hour-old text message from my mother.

I'd better see your grades in physics get better.

My car fob is also in my pocket; however, my car is nowhere near me.

Shit, I am going to have to deal with the impound lot and pay a fine to get the car back.

I messed up. I will have to get used to walking from now on. Mother is still mad at me for that road trip to Orillia, so no doubt I will lose car privileges. On the long, lonely road, I observe over my shoulder. There are no tails, no military officials, and no scary, black jeeps trailing me. I breathe in the fresh Manotick countryside air, no more dust or dead skin cells.

But I have so many more questions. How did Mr. Riviera disintegrate? If waves come from my brain, how is my skull not already fractured? Am I not allowed to help my mother? Can I trust him?

I open the shed again, only to find it empty with dancing specs of dust caught in a synchronous upward spiral, exiting through the hole in the roof.

Part 2.6: A Colourful Canvas
Vritikha, October 15th, 16:00

One week has passed since the I&MNG explosion, and everything has more or less returned to normal. Yasmine and I are canvassing neighbourhoods again, but instead of leaving the comforts of Islington superblocks, we walk around Manotick. It's an area that typically votes Liberal or PC, but we are desperate for new voters.

Most lawn signs in Manotick are for the Tories but are shifting more towards Liberal after the explosion. I don't want to generalize about the people in this neighbourhood. However, Yasmine and I have gotten too many lectures about the explosion staged to get Vipesh up in the polls. It's an insane conspiracy, because the opposite happened. MP Riviera promised to keep jobs in the nuclear sector and to implement more safety measures, and combined with his dishevelled look, his popularity rose.

In Manotick, there are only two large neighbourhoods. The first one where Vipesh resides is close to the campaign office, and the other is north of I&MNG and west of the Morrisette Bridge. Yasmine and I have been walking around the first neighbourhood for thirty minutes. When people weren't ignoring us, they called us names such as 'The Burning Green Party', 'Communism Lite', 'Spoilers', and 'the Blackberry Party', because 'no one understands why [we] are still a thing'. That one kind of hurt.

Yasmine didn't want to come there originally because she didn't want to run into Sid, but Harriet somehow convinced her. Sid and Harriet's houses are at the end of their court, close to Rideau Valley Drive North. The sound of the Rideau River is the only thing we can hear aside from a single car passing by. As we walk by the two houses, I stop and admire the landscape. The contrast between their homes is remarkable. Sid's house is a small but charming wooden two-story, fully detached house with three separate flowerbeds in the front yard, next to a twenty-meter-long driveway with overhead powerlines on a massive property.

Vipesh's house is a much larger mansion entirely off the grid. When he bought it ten years ago, it looked like Sid's, but he did a lot of renovating and expanding for his daughter and wife. Auntie Isabelle had a hand in designing the expansion to accommodate the net-zero design, and it's a shame she never got to see its completion, her husband's campaign, the many milestones in her daughter's life, and many more to come.

A woman exits Sid's house. She's a mid-to-late-forties Caucasian woman with light, auburn hair tied up in a ponytail, translucent green eyes, and a sun-kissed complexion. She runs across the long driveway to greet us. I met Sid's mom once when she had driven me back from Centretown after summer school. At the time, she and Sid were strangers to me, but she seems to think we are well acquainted.

She stands in front of us in her full police uniform. I casually walk behind Yasmine.

"Hi Yasmine, Tikha, it's been a while. How have you girls been?" she asks us with the friendly demeanour of a small-town woman.

"We're good." Yasmine sighs as she plays with the cross on her necklace. "V and I are going around, handing out lawn signs."

From what Yasmine told me during summer school, she loves spending time with his family. Their calm and loving household is preferable to hers. "How is Ms. Tamashiro?" Her smile fades. "Harriet told me. I'm really sorry." She's trying her hardest not to bring 'him' up.

Sid's mom smiles. "She's doing well and misses you." Yasmine starts to glow a little. "She's back home and taking it easy. She's not going to the plant as much. We're hopeful this is the last time." She sounds cautiously optimistic, carefully choosing her words and not trying to upset us.

"That's good to hear, Inspector." Yasmine looks up at the sun and wipes off sweat from her face.

"Sweetie, Ms. Adams is fine."

"Alright, Ms. Adams, do you want a lawn sign on your house?" I gesture to Yasmine, holding the signs. I want to move along and get out of the heat; it was nowhere near as hot as the day of the protest, but to Yasmine, anything above twenty-five degrees is too much. She's wearing a bandana around her hair, but it's still accumulating moisture and revealing her natural curls.

"Of course." She smiles. "We support Mr. Ganatra." She looks at her phone and gasps to herself. "Anyway, while I have you here, I should mention we won't require anyone from your class for an interview anymore. We are about to wrap up the investigation. So, you can tell your physics class we won't be probing anyone." She gets into her Prius and drives off.

"She seems nice," I remark to myself. There's a little resemblance between her and Sid. I have been giving him space but still receive the same visions every night.

"Is that why you hid behind me?" Yasmine sarcastically asks. "I guess no one would see you if you hid behind the Black girl."

My heart speeds up. "I..." I could not get any words out. "Umm..."

"Relax, V." She grabs me by my shoulders. "I'm just messing with you. Ms. Adams is cool. I'll record their address. Could you find a good place to put the sign?"

I breathe a loud sigh of relief and remind myself this is her weird, messed-up sense of humour. "What's that about an interview?" I ask.

"Harriet told me that the 'pigs', as she calls them, are doing an investigation into the explosion, and we could be brought in for questioning. Anyway, let's plant the sign and get out of here." She picks up the signs and walks closer to the house. I follow her.

I walk around and look for a place on the lawn to install the sign and ruffle through my bag of tools, trying to find the mallet.

Sometimes, I wish I had obtained my driver's license. Even though there's only one car for our entire family, lugging around all this equipment in the heat isn't ideal. We have to rely on Manotick's terrible public transportation. One or two lines would take us into Islington, and none would take us around Manotick. Traffic is too bearable, even during rush hour, so no one bothers providing routes for us car-less serfs.

Even though I love the area, with its openness, nature, and gravel riverbank near the Rideau, there are drawbacks to a small town. Islington spoiled me; its compact design makes life easy. Any life essentials were within walking distance. Cars can only drive in one lane on major streets, while buses, bikes, and pedestrians take up the most area on the road. Frankly, there's no reason to have a car. Abba only uses it to drive to places outside of Islington, either my school or downtown.

"Are you good, V?" She taps on my shoulder. "Vritikha?" She taps on my shoulder again.

"Yeah." I sigh. "We had asked everyone in this neighbourhood if they wanted signs, so our final stop of the day would be I&MNG."

Buses come every thirty minutes, so we decide to walk there. Due to the neighbourhood's bizarre geography, it would take us fifteen minutes to get there, but if we bypass property lines, we could hop over a fence walk on Rideau Valley Drive North and make it there in less than nine.

We walk through Ms. Adam's yard, carefully trying not to step on any lush vegetation or in the gardens. At the fence, Yasmine tucks in both her legs and hops over. Even while wearing a sundress, she effortlessly clears the hurdle. The fence is only about a meter tall; however, I have never done something like this before.

I use my phone to lock my left leg. I can't let my left leg buckle; otherwise, I will eat shit. I have faith that friction will keep my sleeve inside the socket. I straddle my body using my arms and plant my right leg on the ground on the other side of the fence. Once I get a proper footing, I hobble backwards on my right leg until my left foot falls off the fence, then anchor myself on the soil.

I could have just taken off my leg and hopped the fence in half the time, but I haven't told Yasmine about my condition, and despite our relationship, I still don't feel we are in that place yet. We only met each other in summer school last August. We talk a lot, mainly when she needs a distraction from her parents' constant fighting, which means she calls every other night. I unlock my leg and walk with her southbound on Rideau Valley Drive North.

"Why did you insist we go outside today?" Yasmine complains. We have only spent an hour outdoors walking in the neighbourhoods for the campaign. So far, we have only put up eight, which is more than I expected.

"It's not that bad."

She glares at me as beads of sweat roll down her forehead, past her face, and drip onto the campaign shirt she's wearing over her sundress. "I hate you right now. How are you able to walk around in jeans?"

"They're leggings," I clarify. "And I was born in India. This is as cold as it would get." I try to lighten the mood. "I was made for this weather." I fidget around with my hair. I lived in a mountainous range; it would snow fairly regularly.

"Sure, I guess that makes sense. I've never been to Barbados." Yasmine stops to take a breath and places the yard signs on the sidewalks. "Can we just stop, please? It's too much."

"What do you want to do?" I ask.

Yasmine scans the area until she sees something across the street. "Let's go under that tree and get out of the sun."

I nod, and we cross the road without hesitation. We are close to the nuclear plant, within the sight of college-aged protesters. I avert my gaze.

After the protest on Parliament Hill, I have become disillusioned by these kinds of demonstrations. It's great seeing so much support, but it's all for show.

Many elected officials, including MP Riviera, showed up at Parliament Hill. Attending it was fun, but the afterimage was depressing and hypocritical. Some of the protestors left their signs at the gates of Parliament. The street became littered with fliers for upcoming events or fliers that Harriet had handed out. I tried to pick up as much as I could, but Harriet wanted to see Kyle, so I left while the Parliament was still a mess.

Under the tree, I lean on the trunk, taking the weight off my feet.

"This is much better." Yasmine sits down on the sidewalk. She starts playing with the pinecones around her. "By the way, why didn't you change after the lab accident?"

"I didn't get any dangerous chemicals on me, just the lab coat." I bend my right leg.

"I saw you handle the bottle. Ms. Stone said not to touch it and use the pipette."

I twirl the hair next to my waist around my hands. "If anything splashed on me, I would have felt something. Besides, it's Sid's fault; he scared the crap out of me. His face looks like a police sketch of a serial killer." I stop twirling my hair. We had the longest conversation without mentioning 'him', and it's my fault this time. Vijay saw him when he dropped me off after the party at Kyle's and described him in detail. He could not keep his mouth shut and spoke about Sid's cheekbone structure, thick eyebrows, large eyes, and very lean and pasty face. But I made the connection to a serial killer.

"Wow, I didn't even think about that. He is skinny, and his eyes are very close together. He does look like a serial killer." We both laugh.

"Were there other times he hurt you before your trip?"

She looks at me uncomfortably. I thought 'serial' meant more than once. Maybe there could be a pattern, and I could lock him up before the election.

"You don't have to answer that, sorry, I don't want to open old scars."

"No, it was just that one time. But one time is too many."

"I agree." I move closer to her. "Good for you for seeing the signs and not taking any more shit."

"Damn, girl." Yasmine lights up. "I didn't think you had it in you to drag his ass like that."

"Yeah, Kyle and him also recently got called into the principal's office for attacking Gerald, Topher, and Alex. He should be in jail," I say, continuing to please her, and apparently, I don't go too far.

She shrugs. "Somehow, neither of them got detention."

"Maybe his mom got him off," I float. "Pig."

She cringes. "I was with you up until that last part. Leave his mom out of this. But this is great. You know I have never thanked you for being there for me after the breakup."

"Of course," I tell her. "By the way, has he been different since he was in that explosion?" I open up my notes on my phone.

Yasmine chucks another pinecone across the road and sneezes. "Not really, he just stopped wearing his glasses. Also, he's losing focus during class. But I guess that is something you could explain."

"What do you mean?"

"Sometimes I see your expression wander, or you just close your eyes for a few minutes for no reason."

I close my eyes. "Maybe this is about his mother."

"His expression wanders just like that. But you're right," she shouts. My eyes suddenly shoot open. "He got the call that she was sick the day before he pushed me. He must have felt terrible."

I'm not sure I can completely relate to what he's going through. I didn't know his mother was sick until today. I'm not in the same boat as he is with my Nani, and it might sound a little sociopathic, but I'm not concerned for her. I have great memories of her when I lived with her twelve years ago. We would play *duboo*, a tabletop game similar to *carrom* but a lot more chaotic. She would beat me every time. I wouldn't take the game seriously because I enjoyed running around the table with my two legs and sliding the disks, bouncing them off every wall on the board like a six-year-old would. And because she would anticipate all of my moves, she was very competitive. We would also chase each other around our village, down the hills, and in the marketplace. I choose to remember the strategic and energetic Nani, and I lost her over a decade ago. She's a very different person than the Nani who meekly waves at her grandchildren through a video call.

My head starts to itch a little. My hair is covered in little burs, clumps of dirt, and pine needles. I brush off my shirt. Unfortunately, the white cotton is stained.

"I think we had enough of a break. We should go back." I look around the base of the tree. I have the bag of tools and the flyers for the Q and A session, but something's missing. "Yaz, where are the signs?"

Yasmine gets up, hitting her head on one of the branches. It knocks loose a pinecone and hits my head. "There." She points across the road, right next to the group of protesters.

I shake my head and use the branches of the tree to pick myself off the ground, but I get even more pine needles and burs in my hair. I pick out debris while crossing the street. Yasmine picks up the signs. Someone taps me on my shoulder. I turn around to see one of the protesters.

"Excuse me, miss, do you think it is okay to throw pinecones at us?" one of the college students asks. He has a fresh bandage on his nose and some swelling around his bridge. He has another cut on his shin that is still dripping, although I don't know how long his wound has been open. "We have a right to be here, kid! We have the required paperwork to picket, and you won't silence us!"

He continues to yell at me; I freeze and close my eyes. There are plenty of things I can try to get out of this. The first would be to run, which I haven't done since my physiotherapy appointments. Or I can try to speak Urdu and confuse him, but I'm sure that would allow him to talk condescendingly to me. Or I could fight. I clench my right fist.

"Sir." Yasmine pushes me aside, mid-brainstorm. "It was my fault. I threw the pinecones. We were taking a break from canvassing. We are on your side." She picks up the lawn signs and shows them to him. "Our guy, her uncle, is Vipesh Ganatra, who will shut down this old explosion-filled, child-injuring, polluting nightmare if elected. Would you like a sign for your lawn?" she offers. "And I could patch up your wound." She reaches into my bag to grab some gauze and rolls it around his leg, securing it with a metal pin. "You're going to be alright. My ex certified me a year ago." She cuts the roll and steps back, placing the remainder in my bag.

The protestor looks at her, intrigued. "I don't live here. I'm from Centretown. But I do know someone in my group who would like it. Thank you so much. Sorry I yelled."

"V?" I reopen my eyes and unfurl my fist.

"You will need to provide us with an address so we can collect it after the election." I pull out the address book and give it to him to sign. "There will be a Q and A for every candidate, including Mr. Ganatra and MP Riviera. It's happening tonight at six if anyone in your group—"

He hands me the address book and leaves without saying anything else.

Yasmine drags me off. She pulls out some pine needles from behind my head and tosses them. "You look great, let's go." She looks at her phone. "How is it already five-thirty? We need to get to the Q and A."

I open up maps and search for routes. "We can walk for ten minutes and get there right before six. Or we could take a cab and get there in five."

Yasmine takes out her phone and orders a cab to my younger brother's high school in Islington. "Be on the lookout for a white Prius." She groans. "A white Prius? Why does everything I encounter today go back to Sid?" she laments. "We ran into his mom, you got spooked by him in class, we came across some protestors in a town from which he used to work, and now we're getting picked up by a Prius, the same model he drives."

Yasmine believes in divine intervention, but sometimes it's like grasping at straws. "I feel like you are reading too much into this." I straddle the backpack on my right shoulder and shift my weight off my prosthetic.

"It's not just that. When I was studying World History with Harriet on Tuesday night, she kept defending him and telling me what a great friend he was when they were kids, and that it was also partly my fault for taking the picture." She scrunches up her face and sneezes again. "Shit, it's already allergy season, isn't it?"

"It's not your fault. He escalated it when he got physical, but if he is on your mind so much, maybe there are some unresolved issues. If you think about Sid when the most common type of car is brought up, he must constantly be on your mind. But don't give him the benefit of the doubt, he's still the guy who hurt you, and there's no excuse." Although Harriet has a point. Yasmine admitted to taking a picture of him without his consent, and he kept saying no.

She doesn't say anything afterwards, but based on her puzzled expression, she might be taking what I said to heart. The sun begins to set, and the temperature drops. We are far away from the protesters as well as the second neighbourhood. We only installed nine signs and didn't canvas the second neighbourhood.

The Rideau River babbles quietly as we enter the taxi. It has a lovely, peaceful rhythm and is louder than the Prius' engine. I focus on the sounds of the engine as everything else gets drowned out. The time is five-thirty-five.

Part 2.7: A Colourful Canvas
Vritikha, October 15th, 17:40

I will enter the gym for this district's Q and A and every candidate in our district will be there, even the fringe ones. Anyone will be able to ask whatever they want. I will sit still and watch Vipesh get hammered on every single question. In the end, MP Riviera will win over the crowd. His closing statement about community values and nuclear power plant employment will obtain way more applause than Vipesh's about climate change and future benefits. Vipesh will take us aside and tell us he's proud of our campaign. With that, we will leave the gym with our heads held high.

* * *

Yasmine taps my shoulder. The vision clears from my head. We walk in through the side entrance of the middle school. Harriet summons me into Vipesh's dressing room, which is the music room. Yasmine continues into the gymnasium with the remaining signs in hand.

My brothers and my father are with Vipesh in his dressing room. I deposit the bag of tools at the door and join my family around Vipesh's chair.

Harriet scrolls through the headlines, looking at the newest polls. "You are about ten points on average behind Riviera," she tells her father. "When you first signed up, you were last, and now you have pulled forward." She bites her lower lip. "But not far enough." She circles his chair. "The PC and NDP party candidates are polling behind you at around nineteen and nine, respectively. The Libs have around thirty-eight percent of the share, while you are at twenty-eight."

It's a loss. There is no way to shift ten points in a week.

Even if we get the second-choice votes of the NDP, we will still lose. And it gets even worse; the polls will likely swing to the

Liberals even more after the Q and A. I lean on the wall behind me, defeated.

"Well, as I said, we have made so much ground here, MP Riviera cannot ignore the issues we brought up. Our popularity exploded." Vipesh tries to console himself.

It's the same hollow line he used during the interview. He walks towards the exit, expressionless.

"What about the explosion?" I blurt out, pushing myself from the wall. Vipesh stops and turns his head to me, raising an eyebrow. "Riviera's main talking point is mentioning how he keeps the district employed. But after it sent ten kids to the hospital, people are protesting. You can talk about how it's dangerous to the planet and how harmful it is to your health. If there's any time to make a case, it's now." If I were a different person, I would tap my fingers together and grin sinisterly.

Vipesh never mentioned the explosion in an attack ad. He never ran attack ads. It's a terrible strategy, but he didn't want to add to toxic political discourse; instead, he favoured uniting people to deliver a positive campaign. But it wasn't working.

"That's politicizing the suffering of the injured students and plant workers and using them as pawns in a divisive game," Vipesh talks back.

I shamefully lean back on the wall and hang my head. He's one of the most positive people in the world, and I upset him. What was I thinking?

"I know you are trying to help, Vritikha." He holds my chin. "You have given some great ideas. However, this is the last chance we get some good points in. I need to talk about the core issues of our campaign, not resort to baseless divisiveness."

"What if you had our permission?" Harriet says as she finishes texting. She puts down her phone on his makeup desk. She half-smirks, taking her father's hand. Vipesh hastily turns around and is guided back in his makeup chair. "The students who were casualties in the explosion overwhelmingly support your agenda. And I am not just saying that as your daughter. I was one of them, so you have my permission, Papa." Her head blocks the light, casting a shadow on her father. "The public will love your no-nonsense breath of fresh air, both figuratively and literally. Everyone else is proposing more of the same delaying tactics, but you will get shit done." She grins at me, winking.

I give her a half-smirk and politely nod as she fixes his suit and tie.

"*Voulez-vous gagner?*"

Vipesh gives his daughter an uncomfortable smile. He turns his attention to me. "I don't like what's happening here." He points to Harriet and me, wagging his hand between us. She has successfully trapped him. "Vritikha, you're supposed to be a good influence on her." He lets out a brief exhale before directing his focus back to Harriet. "*Ma petite noix de coco,*" he soothes his daughter. "You resemble your mother more and more each day in both your appearance and actions. I don't know whether I should be proud because you are continuing her fight, or terrified because you could lead a revolution better than hers." He puts his hand under her chin, tilting her head so his eyes meet hers. He turns her head to the side and kisses her left cheek. Harriet blushes as he takes his hand away from her face.

He grabs his cue cards, adjusts his blazer, and runs his hands down his slicked-back hair. He uses part of his cowlick to cover the large, brownish-red scar that starts at the tip of his right eyebrow and stops short of his ear. Once he has perfected his look, he struts out of the room. Harriet gives herself a few seconds before following him out.

Vijay waits to ensure Vipesh has left. "We're screwed, right?" He's sitting next to the drum kit with a couple of sticks in his hand.

"Yeah," Varshil adds. "Tikha, there's a guitar right there, play us out." He takes the conductor's baton and taps one of the music stands.

"Boys!" Abba yells. His voice shakes the room and makes its way into the halls. The people pouring into the gymnasium stop in their tracks. He turns around, embarrassed and outraged. "This is no way to behave." He drags Vijay off the drumkit by his shirt collar and grabs Varshil by the wrist. "Now we will proceed into the gym and sit down without making any noise." Abba lets go and brushes the creases out of Vijay's shirt. "चलो" (Let's go). "You, too, Vritikha."

I follow the boys into the gymnasium, but someone grabs my shoulders from behind. "Hey, babe." His hot breath runs down my back as his hand runs down my body then grabs my butt. I freeze in place and shudder. "I can't wait to celebrate a victory later tonight."

He spins me around, throwing me back into his arms. It's Kyle, and I lose balance and grab his shirt. While still holding onto him, I reposition my stance.

His dumb smirk instantly fades as I make eye contact with him. "Oh shit, Tikha."

I drag his face down to my level. "Don't ever touch me like that!"

His eyelids flutter, his eyes roll back into his skull, and his body goes limp. He falls on top of me. I catch him and use every ounce of strength I have to keep him upright.

I accidentally put him to sleep. I don't like to make eye contact with people, because if I focus on someone in a state of anger or annoyance, they pass out, similarly to how I can make myself pass out so quickly. Sometimes, I put Varshil to sleep when he irritates me or makes a dumb leg joke, but that's it. Kyle came out of nowhere and punctured my bubble. Harriet and I were both wearing the same campaign shirts, and he recognized me from the back, maybe I could forgive the mistake, but not the butt grab.

I lock my left leg and am now able to support his weight. I built up my upper body strength in physiotherapy because I couldn't rely on my legs, so I sometimes needed arm and core strength to help me off the ground.

He must weigh over ninety kilograms; it produces a terrible strain on my back. His back and arm muscles relax a little through his clothes. Maybe I understand what Harriet sees in him, but it's a long process to turn him into a proper gentleman. I can't support him forever; I need to wake him up. I only need to come into direct contact with him again to wake him up in the same state he fell asleep.

Harriet signals my attention. Luckily, I'm in the doorway, so Kyle's out of her sight. I panic and throw him into the music room. He lands on the ground in a limp, dead man's pose. The carpet on the music room floor is padded, so he shouldn't get any brain damage. But would anyone notice if he did?

After Kyle is out of sight, I unlock my leg and walk out of the music room.

* * *

The gymnasium in Vijay's middle school comfortably fits around five hundred people, but the crowd only occupies about a quarter of the seats. I find my family in the front row and find a cheap plastic chair to the left of Harriet. As I sit down, my stump starts to cramp. I periodically get phantom pains in my stump; the muscles stiffen up as my brain still thinks my left leg is still attached to my body. It comes and goes as it pleases. I try to distract myself by looking up at the stage.

The nominees line up from left to right: Vipesh, the NDP and PC nominees, and finally, MP Riviera. Riviera has pronounced wrinkles around his forehead, cheeks, and neck, bags around his eyes and his hairline looks thinner. His clothes are more loose-fitting and I would assume a rich guy like him should have a proper tailor. Maybe he's just so assured in his victory that he could show up looking like shit and still emerge as the winner. One of his appeals is that he can pass for much younger than he is. He would never admit it, but he has gotten hair plugs and

Botox, and while there's nothing wrong with that, I wish he would own it.

The Q and A begins, and the first question is about nuclear power and I&MNG. The purpose is for the audience members to ask questions of the nominees. It's not meant as a platform to attack other nominees, but it doesn't stop them from doing so. Since the NDP and Conservative nominees need to gain some ground, they attack Vipesh and Riviera.

We knew Vipesh had an uphill battle to win against a nine-term incumbent who protected this district's most essential and staffed industry. We hoped the implementation of Ranked Choice Voting could have helped us swing in the polls; all it did was strengthen the Liberal base, but it's still better than the status quo plurality voting.

Vipesh doesn't exactly have a perfect track record. Along with his lack of experience and nationality, he also took many hours off work. Harriet would frequently get in trouble at school; it's in part because she lost her mom, but she has always been a little troubled. The Morisette Bridge was delayed by months because it failed to meet certification deadlines. Large infrastructure projects are rarely completed on time, but some have spun this as him not being committed.

Another story about him came out a while ago about a twenty-year-old Vipesh while attending McGill. He joined a group of people protesting a pipeline cutting through an Indigenous reserve and the theft of non-Canadian land to appease the Albertan sands. Isabelle Court, Harriet's mother, led these efforts. One protest got out of hand when the RCMP thought Vipesh punctured a line, causing hundreds of thousands of litres of gas to leak. He was even arrested for that protest. I thought it would make him look badass, but unfortunately, many did not see it as I did.

Anyway, these quote-unquote scandals are nothing compared to Riviera, who's a lobbyist for nuclear energy. He used to be a board member of a nuclear plant in Quebec before entering politics and greenlit I&MNG. He tried so many angles to keep nuclear energy cheap via deregulation.

He was initially against the development of Islington and bringing in climate refugees from uninhabitable countries. Downtown Ottawa was becoming overcrowded, and we had to give them a safe home; they had nowhere else to go and our country had oil-stained hands.

Not to mention, he routinely undermined safety inspections for his plant. Any of these would be enough to derail a re-election campaign, or so I thought.

A couple of dumb scandals are enough to delegitimize many of the real ones. One rumour circulating the internet is his role as a deep-state cult who drugs children, kidnaps them, and locks them up in shacks for some nefarious purpose. It originated about thirty years ago and has mostly died down; however, I have seen the topic brought up again online as recently as yesterday. I feel stupid for even giving it a second thought. There are many legitimate reasons to criticize Riviera, but these conspiracies are the only 'scandals' mentioned onstage.

Still, Riviera is suave and charismatic. Back in his time when he was first starting in politics, his constituents called him the next Pierre Elliot Trudeau, except even more of a hard-lined 'centrist'. He was known as GUR, pronounced as *'Guerre'*, French for 'war'. He was seventy-four during the last election and lived up to his reputation, but not today. Now he's just an old man letting everyone trample him.

Harriet is currently on her phone. She sends out the following eight messages to both Kyle and Sid:

<u>Where r u?</u>

<u>R u coming?</u>

<u>Don't come</u>

<u>It's really bad.</u>

<u>These nominees are f-ing hypocrites</u>

<u>My dad is dying out there.</u>
<u>Nvm I need u</u>
<u>WTF!!!!!!!!</u>

It's not a good look for one of the nominees' children to be distracted with her phone, but she looks upset. I get up from my chair and limp out of the gymnasium, each step inflaming my phantom pain.

* * *

I find Kyle still lying on the floor. I touch his hand and look into his mind's eye. Within a few seconds, his back flexes, and he immediately pushes me away.

"Dementor!" Kyle shrieks. "Why are you here? What are we doing?"

"Nothing happened. You just passed out. We are going to the Q and A?" I twirl my hair around my fingers again, trying to look innocent.

"Right." He laughs nervously. "Let's go." We only have thirty minutes left. He gets up off the ground and walks into the hallway. It's half-past eight; he misses most of the discussion. I follow him into the hallway.

He walks faster than me, opens the door for himself, and I sneak in through it while it's closing.

Riviera talks about family values and creating a stable home, or something tried that had helped win previous elections. He says his signature messages he has been saying for decades: "This is a nuclear family, one where every atom is in its place." And: "This plant creates a home, a life, and a future." They garner some applause, not great, not terrible.

"I told you six o'clock," Harriet angrily whispers. I scratch the back of my neck.

"Hi, babe." Kyle tries to kiss her, but she turns away before he makes contact. "He's killing it, right?"

"Did you not get my texts?" Harriet scolds him, causing some annoyance in the crowd. "Where were you?" Her French accent slips a little.

I retake my seat next to Harriet while Kyle sits on her right. He reaches into her back pocket, but she slaps his hand away. The crowd cheers at Riviera's final remarks. I rub my stump. The pain is starting to lessen, but only by a little; two hours is so far the longest phantom pain I have experienced.

It's time for Vipesh's closing remarks. I scratch behind my neck again. I know how it's going to end.

Vipesh stares at something in the distance and looks as if he has seen a ghost. I look behind me and see a figure in the background run away, obscuring himself behind a door. Vipesh puts down his cue cards. He pushes his hair back and reveals the large scar on his right temple to the crowd. It's a simple gesture, yet the crowd does not make another sound as we anticipate what will come.

"I have been talking about climate change the wrong way." He stops using his fake Canadian accent and instead talks with his thin Gujarati one. "It is not just a political issue. It encompasses many other larger threats related to the district, this country, and this planet: income inequality, poverty, and wars. They are all being exacerbated because we just got too comfortable accepting that there is no solution surrounding changing the current status. It took an explosion to get us to talk about energy production. But it took that same world-ending threat to open our eyes to the imbalances of our world, and it serves as a constant reminder that we are all living on this planet. We cannot wait any longer for more once-in-a-lifetime disasters to start a conversation.

"We have been documenting Nuclear Disasters for hundreds of years, and we know the catastrophes that arise from them. We have all had to hear endless coverage of the I&MNG explosion. It has dominated the news cycle, however, for the wrong reasons. I can talk endlessly about the ten students harmed in the explosion, one of whom was my daughter. But we are all fed up with these stories because they do not tell us anything about how we handle our children's futures. This explosion is no one's fault.

"But I know I'm not alone when I say I never want this to happen again, and I know we already have technology to fix this. We already have reliable alternative energy sources, and we should be investing our time and capital into them while continuing to innovate; that's what nuclear energy was supposed to do, and now we're going to run out of it. We cannot get comfortable anymore. We have already passed the dangerous tipping point concerning the global average temperature increase, but as long as we are here, we can still reverse course. The safety of our next generation is at stake. If the planet were a dying family member, we would do anything and everything to help it. I know I did and would again."

He places his microphone down gently, bashfully. Harriet takes Kyle's hand and looks up at her father with large, misty eyes. She sheds a tear, putting her pill bottle back into her purse.

I'm blown away. Vipesh brought up the explosion in a non-divisive way. And he probably gained a lot of sympathy points just by playing the dead wife card. Abba jumps up and applauds. It's much bigger than Riviera's applause. I don't care if I sound biased, but Vipesh Ganatra won the night; it happily goes against every vision I had.

The other two candidates say their piece, and the event disbands. Vipesh descends the stage while Riviera exits the side entrance. Harriet jumps on her father, hugging him and wrapping her legs around him. We all get our chance to fawn over Vipesh. Someone taps my shoulder, but I know it's not Kyle.

Krishna wears a solid, mustard yellow polo shirt and blue jeans that fit him well. His hair is combed and his beard is trimmed. Harriet is right; he does clean up nicely.

"Good evening." I unconsciously mimic his accent. "Fancy seeing you here." I cringe at my words. "I don't know why I spoke like that. What are you doing here?" I correct my voice and speak in my Canadian accent.

"Oh, hi there," he responds, using a half-assed Minnesotan accent. "That was quite a show, eh? Sorry a-boot not making it for everything."

"You didn't miss all that much. If you saw the closing statements, that was all you needed to hear."

"Oh, yeah, for sure. That's enough of that," he corrects his accent. "I believe there are details I missed. I would like an informed mind to tell me about every important 'campaign issue'," he smirks. "Perhaps over dinner next Saturday?"

I don't understand why; he can't vote, so why would he want to know about campaign issues? And he doesn't need me; Vipesh is here if he has questions.

"T?" Harriet whisper-yells, and slugs my arm. Her eyes dart back and forth, then she drags me aside. She turns to Krishna. "We, too, need to discuss campaign issues. *Vous comprenez. Oui?*" She pulls me by my sleeve to a corner away from everyone.

I rub my shoulder where she punched me. "You're not supposed to hit an amputee."

"Did they amputate your brain? You see what he's doing?"

It takes a few seconds for me to realize what 'dinner' means. I don't understand what changed from our Thanksgiving dinner. Why would he take an interest in me? But I retain the feeling of optimism from Vipesh's speech.

Harriet and I walk back to Krishna. "Sure, I would love to talk to you about the campaign," I giggle. "Pass me your phone." He hands me his Blackberry and I drop my contact information onto his with just two button clicks. "Let me know about any specific issue you would like to discuss."

Harriet gives me her nod of approval.

He laughs. "Brilliant. I can't wait to discuss 'politics'." He turns away to talk to my brothers.

How can a voice render me speechless?

Harriet and I walk back to Vipesh. "The livestream of this has many positive comments on your performance." Varshil scrolls through his phone. "They're calling it the highlight of the evening. I have to ask, what made you change your mind, Kaka?"

"I saw Sid at the entrance and got the idea," Vipesh answers. "His family has been through a lot, and I need to show them it gets better. Where is he?"

"He is talking to MP Riviera," Vijay answers.

Harriet had asked Sid to volunteer for Vipesh's campaign, but he declined. Maybe he's working for Riviera's campaign; his mother works for I&MNG, and he would want her to keep her job. But if that were the case, why would Ms. Adams publicly support Vipesh? And if Sid is working for Riviera, why would he want to kill him?

I scratch the back of my neck and cringe at the stinging sensation, but at least my phantom pain is gone.

Part 3

Part 3.1: Meeting #4
Sidney, October 22nd, 21:30

"Nine days ago, you were abusing your powers," says Mr. Riviera. "Your mind is nowhere near developed enough."

"That was ten...never mind." I went to the Q and A last Friday because I had some questions. Harriet texted me the debate address, which was at Pierre Poilièvre Public School in Islington. I found Riviera and waved to him across the stage. I wanted to talk, but he told me he could not be seen with me, and to see him next Friday in the same place. He also told me I should come every Friday, and if I didn't, he would find me. I told him about my interactions with the three students and how I injured them with just a powerful wave, as well as the subsequent principal meeting with Gerald, Topher, Alex, and Kyle. We didn't get in trouble because no one saw a punch being thrown.

In the week leading up to lesson number four, I tried being patient. I thought everything would come into focus by now. Mr. Riviera had been stonewalling me, and even though I'm in no rush now, I need to be ready.

"Could abusing my powers also be a way of expanding my mind?"

"Yes, it would be like pulling a muscle."

For the past week, I tried looking for people like us on the internet, looking at threads online, and discovering someone with similar abilities. It was a lost cause; I couldn't find anyone.

"Are you dumb?" He places his hand on the wall of the wood sidings. "We find each other. When I found you at the plant, I detected a small brainwave pulse. You could tune into the frequency once your mind has fully expanded."

"How?"

"I already told you, by tuning into your emotions. You can unlock one hundred percent of your mind's capabilities before you reach the age of twenty-five, but I've never seen it happen."

"Unlock one hundred percent?" I scoff. "This better not be one of those 'most people only use ten percent of their brain' situations, but we can use one hundred percent. You told me to have an open mind, but I'm calling bullshit."

"Not at all." The wood sidings creak as he pushes himself off the wall. "Not everyone can do what we do. A more apt comparison is working out." He walks towards me. "When you decide to go to the gym for the first time, you have to discover your limits before applying a progressive overload. The last thing you want is to strain yourself, physically or emotionally." He stops directly in front of me. "So you need to train your emotional muscles like any other kind in your body."

"How am I supposed to train emotions?"

"I don't know what to tell you. Were you expecting to be in a field with projectiles barreling toward you, and then you could use your brainwaves to deflect them? Maybe when you're ready, we could go one-on-one and see who knocks the other down first," he mocks.

"Can we do that? It sounds much more exciting and practical."

"If you have a problem with this, take it up with biology. We train by channeling emotions; I don't make the rules, but I also don't want to see you end up like Will."

He's in the middle of a campaign and setting aside his time to help me, so I should listen. The key to getting my old life back is with this aged government official.

"You need to understand something, Sidney." He walks closer to me. "You can go back to normal just by leaving. But deep down, you know nothing will be normal again." He clicks his tongue. "You probably don't even know what normal is."

"I know what normal is; I used to have it until this year. My parents are not normal by societal standards, but they have given me a great upbringing. My friends are eccentric, but they like me for me, and I do them as well. And who the hell are you to judge me and tell me what is normal? This..." I shake my arms in a circular motion. "...is not normal."

He starts to chuckle; the echo is making me uncomfortable. "Did I ever say that was a bad thing?" The lights gradually dim; I still have no idea where they are or how they work. The ground starts to shake, and I lose my balance temporarily. I fall to my knees, using my hand to stabilize myself on the floor. Mr. Riviera stays perfectly still during all of this.

"Feel that?" he asks. I get back up on my feet. "You think you have all the answers, but this idea of normalcy is not universal. I want you to remember the last time you felt normal, at least by your definition. To help you, imagine a time when your mind did not wander; you were just completely in the moment, and knew your place."

"So you want me to find my happy place?" I ask, confused.

"Happiness can act as a trigger; I want you to find a plain place. Your state of mind should be...present. Just a moment when you were okay, and you wanted nothing more because you were not fantasizing about anything else."

The most recent memory comes to mind: last summer, the first Monday of August, working at *My Sweet Tea* while the rest of my friends were taking summer school classes.

* * *

I was manning the register on the hottest day of the year. My job was to process orders and give change while Ms. Park did the tea-making. I enjoyed a nice breeze from the Air Conditioning, especially while the weather outside could reach at least forty degrees.

On that day, it was dry with no cloud cover and no chance it would rain in the next few days. The weather network told the public to stay indoors unless they were wearing a high degree of SPF. It was the perfect day to get a cold bubble tea. It would cool off hot people, soothe the dehydrated, and/or energize the hypoglycemic.

In the middle of the day, we had lines stretching out the door; despite the weather warnings, they were desperate for refreshments and had parasols to prove it. We had to process an average of fifty customers an hour. We didn't have time to breathe, just process orders quickly and efficiently.

At half-past one, Kyle would always visit me and take about ten minutes to order. On that day, he brought a girl. She was slightly smaller than I, with light brown skin, a nose stud, and short, sky-blue dyed hair. I didn't know who it was, so I decided to play dumb with Kyle and treat them like everyone else. "Welcome to My Sweet Tea. Can I take your order?"

"Sid?" the girl said. I froze. "*C'est votre voisine,* Harriet."

"Hari? Why are you here, and where the f—" I stopped myself before completing the sentence. It was still the middle of the day, and I spotted small children in line. "What can I get you two, and how did you meet?"

In my years of knowing her, she was standoffish and hid behind whatever was available. She would get in trouble with teachers and other students because she had some selective mutism. And now, she was more confident, happier, and outspoken. Living in a big city for ten years must have changed her. Her voice threw me off, because she didn't have a French accent ten years ago.

"Well, what does the chef recommend?" Kyle asked, further stalling the wait time.

"We have two specials, Salted Strawberry Crème and Goji Berry, both Milk Teas, and you can read everything else on the menu." I pointed above me. We had about thirty options from which to choose, but he hadn't decided on a signature drink.

Kyle looked at the menu, increasingly confused, while the rest of the line grew impatient. "Do you not have samples?"

I rolled my eyes. "No."

"Can I just choose a bunch of fruits I like and customize?" he asked.

"*Non*, and choose quickly," Harriet said. "You're not the only person in line. It's all tea, and it's all good." She smiled at me.

I mouthed a 'thank you' to her.

"Fine, I'll just take a Goji Berry Milk Tea. I don't like strawberry."

Harriet scowled. She would have preferred locally-sourced fruits.

"Hari. You want anything? Chai?" Kyle asked her.

Back when we were best friends, her mother made some soothing chai. Every week when I went to her house during our playdates, she would bring it out, along with an assortment of snacks. It was one of my few remaining memories of Mrs. Court.

I smiled. "Sorry, we don't have chai. Also, it's forty degrees outside. My Sweet Tea has many kinds of tea from East Asian countries. I guess chai just slipped Ms. Parks' mind. It would not have been as good as yours, anyway."

"*D'accord; rien pour moi, merci monsieur serveur. Au revoir.*"

I had no idea what she said, but I assumed she didn't want anything. She gave me a reusable mug and metal straw for Kyle's order, and I served the next customers in line.

As they were leaving the café, Harriet turned to me. "We'll catch up again at the end, hopefully before Orillia."

The rest of the day was uneventful, and no customer was as eccentric as Kyle and Harriet.

It was three in the afternoon, and the temperature dropped to thirty degrees. We ran out of tea and decided to close up early. As I cleaned up my work area and the tables in the shop, I was greeted by two more customers. Yasmine came into the shop and walked to the counter. She also had a friend tag along with her. This other girl was just a little slower, walking with a bit of a limp and with her chin down most times. She resembled Harriet. Her height, overall body type, and some facial features were very similar, although her skin tone was darker.

Yasmine leaned over for a quick kiss over the counter, while I was cleaning it. She reeked of body odour and sweat. "Are you just about done, Pineapples?"

Why did I tell her my mother's nickname for me?

"Do you guys have green tea?" the other girl asked.

"Sorry we ran out," I apologized. "But would you happen to know a Harriet Ganatra?" I asked, praying that the question was not racist.

"Yeah, she's her cousin," Yasmine answered. "Also, V goes to NMCI."

"How do you know Harriet? Why am I now just hearing she's back and when did she insert herself into our friend group?"

"Relax, Pineapples. We got to know each other over summer school. She's been here since July, living with V's family until they find a place of their own. Her father relocated so he could run for Parliament. Apparently, the PM will call an election sometime this week. Anyway, you'll get to know her on our trip." It was strange Kyle invited a girl he barely knew on our trip. But I let it pass because it was Harriet.

"Hey, umm..." I signalled the other girl.

"Vritikha," she answered.

"Vree-ti-kah..." I butchered her name badly. "Can I offer you some water?"

She shook her head. "No, thanks. Also, call me TEE-kha if that's easier."

I don't think she knew my name, which made me feel better about not knowing hers. I did a final sweep behind the counter and exited with Yasmine and Tikha.

My phone vibrated from across the room. Ms. Park would not allow distractions on the job, so I retrieved it after punching myself out. Mom texted me she was outside the shop, waiting in her Prius. She greeted me, kissed my forehead, and handed me the keys. I was practicing driving because my G2 test was coming up. Mom insisted on driving Tikha home. Tikha initially refused, but accepted after realizing a bus from Chinatown to Islington would take an hour.

As I was driving back home, Yasmine and Tikha sat in the back seats while Mom was in the passenger seat. Mom blasted the AC, and Tikha fell asleep almost instantaneously. "Seriously, how are you not dying right now? The seats are literally sticking to my skin," Yasmine complained.

"I did spend about six hours in an air-conditioned shop," I answered. "Also, mind over matter, and genetics. I don't sweat that much, especially when it is only twenty-ish outside. Like, what's up with that?"

"Sidney," Mom admonished me in her gentle voice. "What do you have to say for yourself?"

I sighed. "Sorry, my Queen." I look at her in the rear-view mirror as she cringes. She hated the pet name, but since mine was Pineapples, it became our thing.

We arrived at Tikha's apartment complex, and I backed into a spot in front of a restaurant called 'Ganatra and Ganju: Indian Cuisine and Sweets'. I turned around while Yasmine nudged her awake.

Tikha's eyes shot open. I would estimate she was out for only ten minutes. She looked in the mirror. My eyes met hers; she looked a little faded. She thanked me, and left sluggishly, limping into the restaurant. We took off immediately afterwards.

"So, your friend?" I inquired. "She's interesting. How did the two of you meet?"

"Well..." Yasmine looked aside. "'Friend' is a stretch. We met during calc. She didn't really have anyone to talk to, even her cousin wouldn't sit with her. She seemed nice and I got to know her better when I saw her skills. She knew how to solve complex derivatives intuitively."

"So, you befriended the socially awkward nerd just to get ahead?" I deduced. "Nice."

Yasmine hesitantly shook her head. "I can't see myself being her friend."

"Maybe you should try. Don't they say 'blessed be the meek, for they shall inherit the earth'?" I gloated proudly, using her own spells against her.

"Clearly, they never met V. She's..." Yasmine fanned herself. I had the air conditioning on full blast, but it wasn't enough for her. "...a recluse. I'm no stranger to awkward nerds." She gestured over to me. "But you're nothing like her. She doesn't put any effort into how she presents herself. You've seen those dark circles around her eyes, how she slouches. She's the kind of person that harbours a dark secret, except I don't want to know what it is."

"Yeah, the kind of people you would find on a watchlist."

"Sidney, Yasmine." Mom interrupted our conversation. We had both forgotten she was in the car with us. "It's not kind to talk about anyone in that manner." The car went silent for a long time until we drove across the Morissette Bridge into Manotick.

"Wait, I thought we were going downtown," Yasmine said.

"I need to get some Advil. Then we can go."

"Sidney, you're not taking the car downtown," Mom informed me.

Yasmine smiled, but then she looked at me, confused. "Don't you work at a tea shop? Why do you get so many headaches?"

I smirked at her and raised an eyebrow. "Isn't it ironic?" I took a right off the Morrisette bridge and drove along Rideau Valley Drive North.

We arrived at our house and noticed our neighbour to the left's house was for sale.

The three of us entered our house. While Yasmine greeted Kat, I raided our pantry for pills. "Why don't you keep some on you?" Mother's voice came from across the living room. "I keep reminding you to take them when you leave. You need to learn how to take care of yourself, Sidney."

"Miriam?" Mom nagged her while she tried to pull Kat off of Yasmine.

Mother was lying on the couch in the adjoining living room, reading her Kindle. "Sorry, let me try that again. Hi, baby, how was work today? And how's your driving? Will you be ready for the test?" She walked over to hug Yasmine. "And Yasmine, sweetie, how are you doing?"

"I'm great. Thank you for helping me with points of inflection and concavity, Ms. Tamashiro."

"I'm also doing well," I said to my mother. "My driving was perfect, and I just came to get some medication for my headache, then we will be gone." I pocketed a couple of pills and grabbed Yasmine's hand, dragging her to the door.

"Oh, baby." Mom walked over to me and grabbed my face, examining it. "Maybe you should stay home if your head is hurting."

Mother then joined the two of us and held me. "By the way, you cannot go out anyway. Mr. Ganatra invited the whole family over to his place for dinner."

"His place?" Yasmine asked. "He's found a place already?"

"Right next to us, actually." Mindy descended the steps and joined the conversation. "Our old neighbours are about to become our new neighbours. It was like they never left."

"Mindy, Katherine, come in here." Mom opened her arms. My two sisters came into the family group hug.

I remembered everything about that night. Mother drove Yasmine home, and then the five of us had a lovely regular dinner with Harriet and Mr. Ganatra at their house. As I recall, it was the last time the five of us were in a room together. Mindy and her friends went to Florida to prepare for their International News course. I passed my driving test, went to Orillia, got a call alerting me of Mother's first surgery, got dumped, and started my senior year.

Nothing was the same afterward.

* * *

I wake up, still in the shed. My vertigo is still shaken up.

"That was so sweet," MP Riviera says. "But a little schmaltzy at times."

I get up from the shed using the imperfections of the wood panels to hoist myself. "How did it feel so real?"

"You know, whenever you remember something, you are not thinking about the actual event, just the last time you remember it," he added. "Maybe there were some details you omitted because they were minute. But this memory was recalled over and over again. Why do you hold onto it?"

Why did I remember Kyle's two-minute soliloquy on bubble tea? Why did I remember the last family hug I had? It's a boring memory.

"It was a boring memory, but it was the calm before the storm." He sits down. "You strive to go back there because right now, your state of mind is... shit."

I can admit he can be straight-shooting, something I wouldn't expect from a politician, but what is typical politician behaviour is his lack of real answers.

"It was a simpler time. However, nothing about your life from now on will be like that anymore." He coughs. "That was a moment where your thoughts ran clear, and you could concentrate on the now. The right concentration techniques can allow your mind to run uncluttered."

I look at him, confused. "You keep telling me to 'live in the moment', and now you tell me to anchor myself to these memories to better concentrate on the now? That doesn't seem to compute."

"You live in the moment whenever you want to power yourself up, but you use your calm memories to help you suppress violent fits, something you desperately need to do so you don't cause a scene." He groans. "I thought I made that obvious."

I rub my neck and feel a bald spot behind my right ear. "What the hell did you do?" I ask, getting back up.

"I needed direct access to your memories, so I removed some of your hair. Most of us go bald because brainwaves pass through cerebral fluid, the skull bone, muscle tissue, skin, and finally, hair. It should grow back in a couple of days, Harry."

"Sid," I correct him.

"When you're older, your memory slips up," he explains. "But ask yourself this: do you want your old life back? You can have it. I'll change your eyesight back to the way it was. Your glasses are still in the corner of the shed. Just say the word."

On one hand, I want that life back. It was a time before Mother got those terrible seizures and Yasmine and I were on good terms; my migraines were nowhere near as intense. But most importantly, no creepy old men were kidnapping me, offering confusing life lessons; but with my current problems, I can't go back.

Mr. Riviera is gone and a gust of large dust particles exiting through the hole in the roof takes his place. I walk out of the shed. The time is ten o'clock. I take in the crisp, semi-rural air around me. There should be a way for me to have the best of both worlds; I can find some balance.

Part 3.2: Little Conversations All Around

A couple of weeks ago, I had this recurring vision. I will be on the floor, crying. It started the night I met Krishna, one night after the power plant explosion. A week earlier, Krishna asked me if I wanted to 'discuss campaign policies' over dinner; I accepted. The future changed significantly on the day of the debate; maybe it would change again.

Since Veera was home for reading week, she helped me curl my hair and pin it down the back. She helped me apply makeup. I usually only made myself up a couple of times a year for various religious holidays, but not as much as I'm doing now. I wear a skirt cut below my knees, a green floral blouse, a thin coat, and leggings. The leggings allow me to wear my slightly heavier, silicon skin, realistic-looking prosthetic, which means my limp would be more evident and I will walk slower, as this leg is not mechanical. I don't recognize the person in the mirror, but I like the way she looks.

The date could end badly; it could be a date where we find out we have nothing in common because he's so well-travelled and experienced in culture and I'm not. But there is some connection between my crying vision and my final vision. I will do whatever it takes to bridge the gap.

Regardless, I like Krishna. Despite being many years older than me and legally an adult, he seems like a cool, down-to-earth guy. He shows up in a gas-guzzling Corolla, wearing a white polo shirt and dark jeans. His hair is tied back in a bun and a trimmed beard. He greets me at the restaurant, walks me to his car, and opens the door for me. He says I 'look nice', and I return the compliment, glad Veera's hard work is yielding good results.

As he drives, he gives me an eighteen-minute speech about how similar London and Ottawa are because of their architecture, gardens, and canals. We even speak Urdu in the car. However, I do struggle to continue the conversation. Other than with Ammi, the only Urdu I speak is for my job, which means I can only converse on a few topics—the washroom is in the back, swing a right, but don't go up the stairs. Do you need more serviettes? The food is vegetarian and eggless, but not Jain. We take cash or debit above fifteen dollars, etc.

Krishna has a BBC radio voice I could listen to for hours. When we get to the restaurant, he finally asks me something about myself, namely what I want to do after high school.

I tell him about my political aspirations and there's a slight hiccup when I ask him about his political identity. I know it's terrible etiquette, but I see highly conflicting worldviews as a dealbreaker. His political beliefs could be best defined as milquetoast liberalism. There are some disagreements, particularly in his identifying as 'politically neutral' and 'loves finding compromises'.

Krishna further elaborates on how he left high school to travel the world. Although his family disowned him for not finishing his secondary education, he didn't regret it. When he had enough fun, he saved up to move to Ottawa to get an education, mainly because it was so cheap. He then shows me all the low-resolution pictures of every city on his Blackberry.

We finish eating in Byward Market. I have never eaten Lo Mein until today. While I struggle to use chopsticks and shamefully ask for a fork, he speaks Mandarin to the waiter, further displaying his world experience. I grab the check before he can, and we leave.

Afterwards, we walk in Confederation Park. The perfectly aligned light posts beautifully illuminate the Ottawa River, the East Block, the Bell Tower of Parliament, the wilting plants, and multi-coloured trees.

Krishna takes out a round pouch from his back pocket, unzips it, and pulls out a pocket-sized blanket, laying it on the ground. He takes my left hand as I put my entire weight on my right leg. My left leg extends outward as my right leg is in a tree pose. It's a little tricky trying to maneuver into a cross-legged sitting position.

"I know I have been talking a lot about myself. So tell me about yourself, and not about your political stances."

"What do you mean?" I ask. "I told you a lot about myself." I try to reach for some strands of my hair but am unable to as they are pinned back and not easy to twirl.

"Yes, you told me about your future, how you want to go to Ottawa University and study Political Science. That has not happened yet. Tell me about yourself now. You have talked a lot about politics, and I'm delighted you have found your passion, but I know there must be more to the story of Vritikha Ganatra." He emphasizes my name by moving his hands in an arc motion while raising his pitch as high as he allows before dropping it back down. "I know this is a controversial opinion, but I think there's more to a woman than her political philosophy."

I lean away from him, bringing my chin closer to my neck, raising my left eyebrow at him.

"All I'm trying to say is, I don't like you for your future. I like you for who you are now, and I would like to get to know that person a little better."

He has his hand on my fake knee. My heart beats louder, and I develop short, rapid breaths. I move slowly away from him, enough so his hand gently falls off my prosthetic. Politics is a big part of me and certainly has taken up a lot of my online media presence. I don't post about myself, and only use social media to tell my circle about my uncle's events or share stories which benefit his cause. But the truth is I don't think my life is worth sharing online, it would just get repetitive after a while. "What would you like to know?"

"Well, you have told me about your restaurant and campaign job." He puts his hand on my knee again. "I have told you about what my friends from Algonquin College do after school, as we don't spend much time in Nepean. But what do you do with your friends in Islington? What do you do for fun?"

My face changes and warps through many emotions. It starts as confusion, then morphs into sadness, until I finally settle on existential dread.

He and his friends spend a lot of time going to the pubs in Gatineau or attending house parties. These are two things Abba would never let me do by myself, even when I turn eighteen. If I turn eighteen, to be more accurate.

I spend most of my time working at our restaurant, volunteering for the campaign, or just listening to music in my room. My very uneventful, slow life is by design because a crazy night ten years ago led to my amputation.

And I succeeded. I have a comfortable routine and I don't stray away from it. I go to school, do homework, cheat on tests by getting the answers in my visions, work in my family's restaurant when asked, and then sleep. It's not going to change until I go to university. Although I might not make it; I could die on the Morissette Bridge soon. Why does my boring life lead to an unceremonious death?

My stomach growls, and a pit grows in my abdomen. I curl into a fetal position to minimize the pain, pulling my left leg to me, and burying my face into the grass. "I don't feel good." The blades of grass graze my cheek and make their way through my hair, much like Veera's gentle fingers. It tempers me enough so I can collect my thoughts. "I'm sorry for ruining this night. I understand if you don't want to call me or see me again." I try to get back up but haven't worn this leg in a long time, so I struggle to push myself off the ground. "However, I should tell you my family enjoys your company. I hope we can—" I lose balance and fall on my back, looking at the night sky, or at least the parts of the sky that are not cloudy or bathed in a hideously orange glow. "Stupid downtown air and light pollution," I mutter aside.

"Vritikha." Krishna takes me by my right hand and pulls me off the ground. "I think I should take you home. It might be my fault. I did not think the restaurant would give you food poisoning." He easily maneuvers me around until I regain my balance. When he finally lifts me, I position my feet and stabilize myself. He pats me on the shoulder and looks me in the eyes. "You still look great, though."

He smiles at me, as we walk away from Confederation Park and pass by Chateau Laurier. It's approaching Halloween, so decorations, cobwebs, and pumpkins line the path's entrance.

"I can tell you more things about me," I blurt out. "You don't know everything about my family. You have met my two younger brothers and my older sister. But I do also have an older brother."

"I remember Vishatan, but I haven't seen him since I was twelve. Where is he?"

In total, I have four older brothers, four older sisters, and two younger brothers. My parents only have five surviving children. First is my oldest brother, whom I have not seen in ten years. No one in my family knows where he is or what he is doing with himself, but I will never forget the last thing he did, and it hurts to hear his name again.

In the six years since he was born, Ammi had four more children, all of whom had been either miscarried or stillborn. Veera and her twin brother, Viral, survived, but Viral only lived for two weeks. After two years, she gave birth to my brother, Varun, who passed away after a year. Two years later, I was born. Two years after that, Varshil was born, and two years after him, Vijay.

"He lives somewhere in Japan. He's twenty-seven. I don't know why I mentioned him, though. We barely see him." I scratch the back of my neck and then push my hair aside. Using a hair tie around my wrist, I tie it back up in a simple bun. I don't know what else I can say about myself. I am an avid reader of political philosophy, but I doubt he wants to talk about the works of Naomi Klein or Andreas Malm.

"I play the piano and the guitar," I say, and it's not technically a lie. "I was pretty good for a while." We stop at a traffic light. "I stopped playing in high school because I had to prioritize my homework and waitressing first." I scratch the back of my neck again. The truth is, I just lost interest. I used to play instruments because they helped me relax so I could have more peaceful and controlled visions. But my parents saw potential in me to go professional with my talent. My visions, as a result, got a little darker. I was playing because they wanted me to get better, not because I wanted to play music, so I quit. However, I am getting back into it on my terms. I'm in the Jazz Band this year, but since I have been busy with the campaign, I was allowed to join in November.

"Do you listen to a lot of music, then?" He directs my attention to the earbuds peeking out of my purse. I brought earbuds in case I got bored, but I haven't used them all night. I'm proud of myself; I didn't need to distract my mind, although I was close. I shove them back into my purse.

"Yes," I chuckle. "Every July, I go to Bluesfest at LeBreton Flats. The first year we came to this country, my family went there to experience the culture of Canada." He holds his focus and nods along as if he's invested in my story. "My siblings weren't happy about leaving our home country, and I was pretty broken up about it, too, but I..." I pause because I'm about to mention my leg. "...I found something that made me fall in love with this land. I saw the union of cultures in one small area. People came from all over the world to listen to their favourite bands. I believe it's the way to unite all of us." There is an awkward beat between us. "Sorry, I didn't mean to get political."

"I don't mind this kind of politics, although I assumed it was a relaxation method. I thought music was a way to shut out your surroundings. Like how most people walk around with their headphones on and ignore the world around them."

"Excuse me?" I look at his forehead instead of his eyes.

"I didn't mean any offence. I like…" He stammers for a few seconds, looking up and breaking eye contact. "…Noori or Junoon. I have some music to put on in the background whilst doing homework or cleaning." He must be an old soul because I have not heard of either of those bands. Krishna looks back at me. "I guess I'm not as refined as you."

I shrug my shoulders. "I have brought many friends to Bluesfest in the years since." In elementary school, I brought a couple of friends whom I no longer see. They found out about my leg, and things just got weird. Since then I only bring Harriet or Yasmine. "But you are right. I do shut out the world occasionally, but not for Bluesfest. I go there to connect to the people around me and truly experience the culture. Some of my favourite bands have performed there—*Of Monsters and Men, Dear Rouge, Marianas Trench.*"

He spins around and walks backwards in front of me. "Hmm, I have not heard those names in a long time. And I didn't peg you for an alt-rock kind of girl. I just pictured you as someone who would enjoy more mellow and calm music because it's cool and mysterious, like you."

I raise an eyebrow at him. "Cool and mysterious?"

"I mean it as a compliment. I already knew you were a fan of Anoushka Shankar and played for the Jazz Band at school. So in my mind, you seemed so laid-back, not the kind of girl who would belt and scream in her room. But enlighten me, and I will accept my errors."

"I would not say she's my favourite artist." However, I do listen to her an unhealthy amount. "Her music embodies my very existence, particularly songs from the album *Traveller*. If I ever feel too Canadian, I play a song from *Traveller* and am transported back. One arrangement in particular, *Buleria con*

Ricardo, showcases a conversation between an older culture and a newer one. It's two halves to a song, like there are two halves to me, and they don't have to stay separate all the time. Near the end of the track, they combine into one distinct melody, and it's one of the most beautiful arrangements I have ever heard."

Another reason I listen to music is I like to mimic walking at a metronomic pace. I find a song with a pronounced beat and rhythm which matches my steps. When I walk without music, all I can focus on is my limp.

Krishna opens his mouth, but I still have more to say. "And I am not a fan of jazz. I play in the Jazz Band because it's the only one our school offers." I try to keep my thoughts short and respectable in length and tone. "Music should follow a logical sequence. There are a limited number of chords and progressions. Four-chord songs work so well because they are pleasant, and you can derive unique songs from the same progressions. Notes sound good together because they follow the conventional rules of math. Jazz throws all rules out the window and says any group of notes can come and go. When you veer so dramatically off course, it's just chaos."

"Wow." Krishna gets caught off-guard. "When it comes to music, you are kind of...conservative."

I raise my hand and pause to try to formulate a proper rebuttal. But the mention of order and chaos proves he's right. "Shit."

"That's not a bad thing; ideology, like most things in life, exists across spectra, and people are diverse and complex." He raises an eyebrow at me, and I reluctantly nod. "And I'm not a fan of freeform jazz, but I see some appeal. A true musician would not be bogged down by 'the rules of math', and breaking those rules can be beautiful. Even now, the cars honking represent a new culture, and the wind rustling on the nearby nature represents an old culture. They are having little conversations all around us."

Krishna starts singing nonsensical notes, riffing in the middle of the street.

Despite the awkwardness, I can appreciate how confident he is. While he walks along Mackenzie Avenue, I get a little closer to him. I close my eyes to wipe away a tear because I'm laughing pretty hard at his dumb riff.

* * *

A red smart car going seventy on Wellington Avenue will take a right onto Mackenzie.

* * *

My vision cuts itself short. I look to my left and see a red smart car taking a right turn without slowing down. Krishna, who's still riffing in the middle of the intersection, doesn't seem to notice. I quickly grab his hand and pull him back onto the sidewalk. He steps closer to me, but I momentarily lose balance. He places his right hand on my waist; our eyes lock on each other.

* * *

I will be on a stage, standing underneath a canopy. Abba, Ammi, and the rest of my entire extended family will be sitting in the audience. But to my right, Krishna will be wearing a turban, a red and golden jubbah, and a red and white flower garland. I will wear an orange sari and will have Mehndi tattoos over my arms. There will be magnolias decorating the canopy and a metal pan of tropical fruit. Ammi and Abba won't look that much different. Krishna won't look much older, but neither Veera nor my older brother will be present.

* * *

"Hey," Krishna yells. "Are you alright?"

I nod to him. How long was I out?

He scans up and down my body and removes his hands from my waist. "I should not have done that. Let me take you home."

I have no more words to say, and he doesn't say anything else as we walk to his Corolla. The lack of a conversation is a little worrying. One thing I like about Krishna is his ability to speak about anything. I know he's not a music buff, but the fact that he tried to talk to me about my interests shows the kind of person he is. I don't know if he feels embarrassed that I saved his life, or if he just wanted to give me space after accidentally grabbing my waist.

"Can you input your address for me?" he asks when we get in his car.

I nod and take out my phone. Abba has been texting me:
When are you coming home? It's getting late.
I have some notes on your comparative essay.
I put my phone down without texting him back. There's something more concerning at the moment than a comparative essay. For the first time in my life, I wasn't asleep when I got a vision. I needed direct contact with someone and to lock eyes with them with a worried mindset. I rarely make eye contact because it usually puts people to sleep. But Krishna didn't collapse, and I got a one-second vision about a future which wouldn't happen soon, but would happen in the not-too-distant future, because it's our wedding.

"How's your stomach?"

"I'm fine. It was nothing." I scratch the back of my neck again.

He pulls into our parking lot in front of the restaurant. "Anyway, here we are." He parks and puts his hand on my shoulder. "Thanks for saving my life back there."

"Thanks for helping me up after I fell. Also, I apologize for my stomach. It wasn't the food; you just asked me about what I did for fun, and I couldn't give a straight answer." I give him a courtesy smile after telling my half-truth.

"Vritikha." His face softens as he looks into my eyes. "You apologize a lot, but what you just did took a lot of courage to admit. Maybe I was a little too forward, but the last thing I want to do is to make you uncomfortable." Him saying my full name in his voice is enough for me to make a move.

I lean in and pucker my lips. When we lock, I try to conjure another vision, but all I can feel is his sharp stubble scratching my lips and chin. I separate after a few seconds and rest my forehead on his, our noses barely touching.

* * *

Krishna will look at me before disappearing around a corner of the banquet wall. He will be smiling as he leaves my sight. The staff around me will be busy putting away chairs. My younger brothers and parents will be by my side.

* * *

I can't lie and say I felt nothing from our kiss; the vision I got for a few seconds had to mean something, but I don't feel any sparks. When I try to get closer to Krishna, somehow, my visions show us further away. The scene changes instantly, and I have no idea why.

"By the way, this Thursday, my uncle is hosting a party at his office. My brothers and I would love to see you if you're interested." I gesture to his wrinkled polo and jeans. "You would have to dress up a little better."

He narrows his eyes into slits.

"I'm sorry for talking about the election again and I'm sorry for apologizing yet again. And I'm sorry for killing the mood. I just thought this was a way to see you again, and I realize this is not the time—"

"It's just that it's a Thursday." He leans away. "It might not work out with my schedule, but I'll see." His smile calms me down. "I will let you know."

He opens the door for me. I exit and watch him leave the parking lot in his fuel-inefficient monstrosity.

Abba is manning the phone in the vestibule of our restaurant while my brothers wait tables. All of them ask me about our date. I tell them it went well while scratching my neck. I lug myself and my heavy realistic leg upstairs.

Tonight has probably been one of the most awkward and out-of-body experiences I have ever had. But I don't feel like crying on my bedroom floor. I found a new way to produce visions instantly. I don't know how, but Krishna made it happen, and the future changed again.

Two visions haven't happened yet: crying on the floor in my room and the bridge conflict.

I fall backwards onto my bed and remove my leggings, leg, and silicon pad so my stump can breathe. Abba left the outline for my comparative essay on my desk, complete with comments and suggestions.

If my visions are adaptable, I need to find out how and why Sid and the plant explosion are connected. I would need to look into Sid's eyes to find out our future, and with my subpar essay outline, I think I have the perfect cover.

Part 3.3: The Socially Awkward Nerd(s)
Sidney, October 25ᵗʰ, 15:00

A strange thing happened today. Tikha asked me for help with her comparative essay. I have heard many rumours of the Great Tikha Ganatra, who single handedly got one hundred percent in calculus and advanced functions, and who would ace every test in Chemistry and Biology, but somehow underperformed in labs. As far as I knew, I had never seen her ask anyone for help. And for her to ask me, someone who has never actually helped anyone with their work, it's strange. I accept the new opportunity, because maybe it could be another way of expanding my mind.

We had shared many classes, including tenth-grade science with Mr. Glass, but we had never interacted until summer. The only time I would hear her talk was during English when we did table reads. Our class was not that big, so everyone got a turn to read lines aloud, and Ms. Philips would tell her to read the lines of Cordelia for *King Lear* or the Witches for *Macbeth*.

She told me to meet her in the library after school to work together.

I also heard she isn't particularly good at English. Even though she has a near-perfect North American accent, she would sometimes slur her j's and pronounce them as x's, her ch's as sh's, or roll her r's longer than necessary.

Regardless, I'm not in any position to judge. I was raised in the same small cul-de-sac for my entire life and would probably never relocate, even for university. I only know one language, unless you count the small amount of Japanese I picked up from hearing Mother speak on the rarest occasion, or when I watch anime or read manga. I have forgotten almost all the French I learned in school.

I find the least sticky table with a computer and place my bag over anything unhygienic. Our school's library is the second largest room in the building, right after the cafeteria. The study rooms are unavailable to book on such short notice, but the tables are available. The library isn't an ideal work environment; it's too loud to do any actual reading and too quiet for people not to hear our barely audible conversations.

Tikha arrives at my table wearing her headphones and listening to Indian music at a deafening volume. She puts her headphones around her neck and deposits her stuff on the seat between us. She then places her hand right on top of mine and looks straight into my eyes, widening them enough for me to see some white above and below her irises.

Kyle's right when he says it's impossible to look directly at her. It feels like she's staring directly into my soul or past it to my new bald spot near my right ear.

Her iris is a dark shade of dark brown, almost indistinguishable from the black of her pupil. It looks like a dark void or a cat's eye. She's not displaying her typical expressionless face. I describe it as a 'partially constipated and intense stare'. The whites of her eyes are bloodshot, and the dark circles around her eyes are even bigger.

"Are you alright? You look tired," I ask her.

She releases her grip after nine seconds. She has a surprising amount of strength for such a small and frail-looking girl, enough for me to be unable to move.

"Yeah." She immediately breaks eye contact with me, and I see her face change back to her default expressionless expression. "I got nothing. Anyway, I have my outline here. My father looked at it yesterday and left some very detailed comments." She gives me a small but seemingly genuine chuckle.

"What topic did you choose?" I ask. Three topics were available to us. We could 'compare and contrast: the role of women in both works, the protagonists' tragic flaw, or the role of the monarchy and providence', which meant comparing God's roles and class structure; no one took the last question (except

Mindy and me). The women's topic is the more popular option because the tragic flaw topic is more challenging. The main difference between these two questions is that there are many aspects to tackle with the female question, but only one to tackle with the tragic flaw.

"I took the tragic flaw question," she responds, looking down at her paper. "I know everyone else is taking the women's question, but I like a challenge." She fidgets her hair around her fingers.

I read her outline and find she doesn't have much of a thesis. "What exactly are you trying to argue? You're just summarizing the plays."

"I am trying to argue their tragic flaws come from different places. King Lear's first scene is just him getting his ego fed by his daughters, while Macbeth is a loyal servant to Duncan until a prophecy tells him he can become king. His ambition made him impatient."

"That's not the basis of a comparative essay." I take mine out of my bag and show her. "I talk about how it's the break from the traditional bloodline that made the respective kingdoms crumble and how they were brought back with legitimate heirs."

Tikha brings her chair closer. "Is that really what happened?" She looks behind her. "They said he was ahead of his time, but he still believes in Social Darwinism and that only the elites can man a kingdom properly."

She's not speaking to me directly. It's exhausting trying to engage with someone who injects politics into everything. She's a lot like her cousin, except nowhere near as boisterous. And it's not fair to look at the stories through our modern lens.

Tikha moves her chair backwards and looks up. I track her head and find Yasmine towering over us.

She takes one look at me and hisses. "V, we're supposed to be working on chemistry today, did you forget?" She puts her hands on her hips. Harriet and I had finished working on our lab on Sunday, but they needed to redo their experiment since their chemistry accident. She points to me. "What's he doing here?"

"Hi, Yasmine." I smile at her. "I am just helping her out with English."

"Yasmine, sit down. I can work on both Chem and Lit."

"You won't even know I'm here." I extend my hand to the seat right next to Tikha. She logs onto the computer, positioning herself to avoid my eye line.

I look through the rest of her outline. Many of her points were repetitive or not arguments at all. "Tikha? You have a good grasp of how to write your essay. You need to work organizing arguments and finding good quotes to support them."

"So basically, you're asking her to rewrite her entire outline?" Yasmine raises her voice at me.

"I didn't say that." I take a deep breath and whisper. "I said she knew how to structure her essay into points, however—"

"She has to come up with new points?" She wipes her forehead.

I reluctantly nod; if she has to rewrite a thesis, she might have to develop new topics for her body paragraphs, and she might need new arguments.

"What the hell, Yasmine? She can speak for herself." I try my hardest not to think of anything hurtful, bad thoughts lead to powerful emotions. "She asked for my help, and I'm just giving her my honest criticism." I exhale, trying to remember the good times we had. I think back to another time I was in the moment, where I was perfectly content.

It was in grade ten and we were at our school's semi-formal. I saw her across the room looking beautiful in a short yellow dress, wearing opened-toed wedges. Kyle and I were going as friends, but I wanted nothing more than to ask her to dance during a slow song. He said I didn't know her well enough but told me it was a good idea because no one else would ask her. He kept going back and forth.

At that point, Yasmine and I had only spoken a few times, but I knew she liked me a little. I approached her, the song *Perfect* played over the speakers, and everyone on the floor was slow dancing. My palms were clammy, my face flushed, and a slight headache developed.

When I finally got to her, Yasmine dabbed her forehead and cheeks with the cloth napkin on her table. I asked her if she wanted to dance. Immediately afterwards, my heart sank and my belt constricted; I thought I would faint if she said no.

To my surprise, she said yes. At the time, I didn't know if she just felt bad for me after she saw Mr. Glass scream at me for four minutes straight or if she genuinely liked me for the adorkable guy I was. She later told me it was both. Hand in hand, we walked to the dance floor. I wore ill-fitting dress shoes that gave me three centimetres of height. She didn't know how to walk properly in her wedges. I knew this because I looked at our feet for ninety percent of our dance to ensure I wasn't stepping on them. She put her hands on my shoulders, and I did on her waist. She was still taller than me, which added to my self-consciousness.

We danced around for the two remaining minutes. And suddenly, when the song was over, she leaned over and kissed me on the lips. I was too scared to make a move and was glad she did. But she became embarrassed afterwards and ran away from me. She would later claim she felt something push her face backwards and she overcorrected her neck position. A few days later, I formally asked her out, but she said yes, and we dated for over a year.

I based my relationship with Yasmine on my own parents' relationship. My parents had this perfect meet-cute story during their time at university. Mother was in her first year of university playing in a scavenger hunt. She played the role of a lost international student in a foreign city and Mom prevented her from veering too far from her map. Mom later exchanged numbers with Mother 'if she ever got lost again'. It was perfect, and I wanted it.

Yasmine got her braces off around the beginning of the eleventh grade, while I had a late growth spurt. And as we got more confident, we started to role-play. It began as a fantasy we both had. I may have liked this version of myself; I was stronger and would take charge and try to act tough to impress Yasmine. She started to outwit me, either by putting me down or by stroking my ego and manipulating me with her wits or her body.

We had fun and even told each other those three magic words, and we kept that charade going until she dumped me. Since August, I have wanted to get back together with her, but remembering where we came from and how far we veered away from who we originally were, I'm okay with us not being together anymore.

"It's due on Wednesday." Tikha slips in some words. "I will be fine. Sid gave some good advice."

I manage to cool myself off. Mr. Riviera's advice works.

"No, this is so passive, Sid." She slides her chair over to me and looks directly at me. Her almond-coloured irises are much easier to look at, despite the hostility they carry. "If you have a problem with her essay, say it. Don't make her try to guess it, it will end with her essay being irreparable after years of bottling up problems."

"This isn't about the essay. Is this about your parents?" Tikha asks while stroking her shoulder. Yasmine's parents' story was much different than mine. Mr. Cartier is an eighth-generation Canadian, while Ms. Williams is an immigrant from Barbados. They each wanted Yasmine to be more like them and saw the act of raising her as a competition to shape her like themselves. I only visited them once in the eleventh grade and it was the most painful three hours of my life. Yasmine wanted to spend more time with my family.

"They are finally splitting up." Yasmine smiles, moving her chair back to the computer and towards Tikha. "I knew this would happen eventually. What didn't occur to me is that my mom will be moving back to Bridgetown. So by the end of the year, I need to decide whether I want to stay here in Islington with my dad or move to another country altogether." Her smile fades.

"I'm sorry," I say, although I know Yasmine would not move to Barbados; she wouldn't last a day in a country with only two seasons.

"I hope you stay here." Tikha hugs her, running her fingers through her hair. "Even though we can still talk online. Harriet and I would miss you." They smile together. "You have a long time to make that decision. Don't hold your breath."

"Terrible choice of words," I interject before slamming my hands over my mouth.

"Asshole!" Yasmine yells, and the entire library stops what they were doing to look back at us. "Why the hell would you bring that up again?"

"I'm sorry." I hang my head in shame.

"You know, that's the first time you apologized. Do you have any idea what it was like in that cold and dark body of water?"

A librarian approaches us, which prompts her to whisper.

She turns her head back to me. "Every time I looked at you, all I could see was you screaming at me, then feeling your hands shoving me to the ground, and being unable to breathe."

The librarian returns to her desk as Yasmine takes out her phone. "I deleted that picture because I don't want the reminder of that moment, or you." She rests her fist on the table. "At this point, I should just count myself lucky that I did not get knocked up and become forced to raise a child out of wedlock. I'd relive that scene for the rest of my life." She fans herself.

Now I finally understand her anger towards me, and she's right to hold the grudge. I didn't push her, but I didn't help her, either. I have never felt as humiliated as I am right now.

Suddenly, a draft blows her papers off the table. While keeping my head down, I fall off the chair and recollect them. A migraine wraps around my head like a halo. No one speaks for the next few minutes, so I peruse Tikha's outline. In fairness, the quotes she chooses are pretty solid, and when she's not summarizing the plot, she does a decent job at stringing together the themes of both plays.

"Anyway." I keep my head down. "This is solid. I especially like comparing and contrasting how a tragic flaw could get these characters redeemed."

Tikha smiles as she shuffles her chair towards me.

"So you're not going to respond?" Yasmine looks back at me. I shrivel up again.

Can't...believe...doing this...

A monotonous voice speaks. Neither Yasmine nor Tikha's mouths are open. Tikha's chair squeaks as she stands up. Yasmine slides her chair backwards.

"Yasmine..." A stern expression develops on Tikha's face. "I know I'm supposed to be on your side, and I want to be." She raises her voice sharply. "But I have heard you rant about Sid for the past week, and it's too much; you're the one who keeps bringing it up." She walks over to her and proceeds to whisper. "I am sorry about your parents, but it doesn't give you the right to act like this. Frankly, I don't think you are even over him. And why him? It's beneath you to let a dumb guy occupy your thoughts like this."

Yasmine stands in shock. It's true what they say: the whole room shakes when the quiet kid snaps. "I think I should go," she whispers, and picks up her phone. "Harriet's been texting me for the past ten minutes about World History." She logs off the computer, grabs her notes, and leaves our table to enter one of the private study rooms. Harriet and Kyle are in there as well. The librarian comes to our table and demands we leave.

I put my books in my bag, as does Tikha. She grabs her backpack and purse, and we leave the library. I zoom in and enhance on Harriet, because my new eyes have that capability. Harriet's neck has four small but distinct red marks. I get a good look at her until it becomes creepy, which is only about nine seconds, the same length as one Tikha stare.

We sit outside the room in the hallways against the lockers. Tikha hangs her head down in shame.

Why...I...do...that? ... didn't ...solve anything...

The voice appears again; it sounds like Tikha, but her mouth doesn't move.

"That was incredible," I tell her.

She turns back to me. "You're not off the hook, either."

"I know," I sigh. "At least I know now." She looks into my eyes again, pinning my arms against the lockers. She squints and, after another nine seconds, breaks her stare.

Why...can't...create...vision...

Her mouth doesn't move when those words are spoken, yet there's no one else in the hallway. "Did you say something?" I ask. "Why can't create...vision?"

"No, I didn't say anything. But why did you push Yasmine?"

"I didn't push her." I raise my fist and lightly tap the locker instead of slamming my fist.

"Then what did you apologize for?" She leans forward and pins my hands between hers and the lockers again, widening her large cat eyes. "Tell me everything," she yells, and furrows her eyebrows at me, staring deeply into my soul.

My eyelids droop in seconds, and my neck turns to rubber. I don't have enough time to adjust my hands as they slide across the lockers backwards away from Tikha towards the floor.

She grabs my two hands with one hand while grabbing a clump of my hair with her other, then looks into my eyes. She helps me reclaim my balance and leans me against the lockers.

I have no idea what came over me. I think my soul left my body.

Tikha massages her left calf and picks up her stuff, embarrassed at what transpired. "You know what," she says as she walks away. "You have given me more than enough help today." She stammers, "I'm sorry—"

"She took a picture of me in the aftermath of getting eaten by blackflies." I stand up.

She turns around.

"I was in a lot of pain and was more irritable. Also, I had just gotten news about my mother's condition," I explain. "I walked towards her in a fury and she walked backwards. Eventually, she slipped off a ridge and fell into a shallow part of a lake. I should have helped her up, that's why I apologized. I did yell at her, and maybe I got a little too close, but I didn't touch her."

She cranes her neck, trying to match my height. "You swear?" She doesn't squint, nor does she bug out her eyes. She wraps her pinky around mine.

"On my mother's treatments," I say, with a clear mindset.

She stares at me silently, and after nine seconds, she releases her pinky and collects her belongings. "This is going to sound crazy, but I believe you. But I also believe her, in that I believe that's how she recalls the event."

I understand what she is saying, but I don't know why she's trying to play both sides.

"Maybe you two need a moderator to talk things over. Not me, though; I'm still going to take her side publicly." I nod to her, indicating that I respect her choice because at least she knows my truth. She taps her fingers on the lockers. "Do you have any more notes for me?" she awkwardly transitions.

I nod. "Your final sentence where you say 'both tragic heroes had their flaws which were a product of their environment. Although King Lear managed to obtain an iota of redemption, Macbeth had a chance at redemption and did not take it'. That's a good note of comparing and contrasting. Your ending is excellent. You should be good to submit this for Wednesday." I smile at her and take a step backwards.

"Thank you." She smiles and leaves.

"Can I ask what was with the staring?" I wipe my hands and pull my backpack off the floor.

"I was wondering if you got contacts or laser eye surgery. I have never seen you without your glasses," Tikha answers. She wraps some strands of hair around her fingers. "Anyway, thank you so much for your help today." She sighs. "By the way, when I said 'dumb guy', I meant the fascination was dumb, not that you were."

"Sure, I believe you." I wink at her.

"By the way, can your family make it to our election night party? It's semi-formal. So, don't wear a hoodie."

Is that a joke? "I was not planning on wearing one, but your uncle had already invited us; we'll be there."

"Great, thanks. I'll see you later." She slips the headphones around her ears and plays her loud Indian music as she limps away.

Kyle's right; Tikha's strange, and I don't know what's wrong with her. For all of her quirks, she's a good listener and wants to do right every way she sees it. She can be reserved but is also great at calling her friends out. We could be friendly if she doesn't do that uncomfortable staring thing again or talk too much about politics.

Maybe she's like Mr. Riviera; he was able to make me lose consciousness with just a stare. And why does she now suddenly want to talk to me after all these years? I need to speak to Mr. Riviera about her. She wasn't at the nuclear plant during the explosion, but she has some metaphysical abilities, just not like mine.

Part 3.4: Election Night
Vritikha, October 28th, 19:00

All of our hard work will culminate in today's results. Our campaign staff of more than thirty people are setting up the office in preparation for the announcement. We are moving desks and chairs out of the main floor space, bringing food from our restaurant, and contacting anyone who wants to come.

Aside from the student volunteers, the paid central positions are people Vipesh met while volunteering at shelters and soup kitchens or people he knew from his alma mater or previous workplaces. This group of people are doctors, restaurant owners, family, etc. The only similarity they have is that none have run an official political campaign.

The latest batch of polls shows Vipesh only a few points behind MP Riviera. I know compelling speeches at a Q and A existed, but I didn't think they had that much sway over people's opinions. And the boost is indirectly attributed to Sid. If he hadn't shown up at the last second, Vipesh wouldn't have given that speech, and wouldn't have been within striking range of the incumbent.

We are proud of what we did, but we didn't want to spend too much on an expensive party just to be disappointed. This location is also close to I&MNG and the shed where MP Riviera could meet his death. As soon as we have a projected winner, I will walk to the plant, prevent his death, and intercept the perpetrator, who may or may not be Sid.

The reason I'm saying 'may or may not' is because my visions from the past three days were inconsistent, but on my whiteboard, I mapped out the three possible paths that could happen.

On Monday, I got Sid to help me with my essay while also joining Yasmine to help with chemistry. I looked into his eyes three times to pinpoint where we would end up in the future, like what happened between me and Krishna. I could not get a vision the first two times, but I did the third time. I was with him; we were sitting at a table, he was wearing an orange shirt and had his hair cut shorter, and he was laughing uncontrollably. Maybe we will be friendly in the future. In this vision, Vipesh will win, and nothing is in the shed.

On Tuesday, Sid, Harriet, Yasmine, and I studied for the upcoming drug chemistry test. After a while, we moved our discussion to Harriet's house. Sid and Yasmine had resolved their issues. According to Harriet, they watched a couple of movies until about seven in the evening. In this vision, there was a tie, and there would be a recount. When I went out to the shed, there was nothing as well. Yet, I still had an encounter with the white hooded figure with red hair. They looked at me, then fled.

On Wednesday, I avoided Sid as much as I could to see how the future would change. I was doing some last-minute volunteering for the campaign, cold-calling residents to come to the polls. After about six pm, I went home, waited tables, and fell asleep a few hours later. In my vision, Vipesh lost. I went to the shed and found a deceased Mr. Riviera, and it ended with Sid throwing me in the river while the white hooded figure tried to stop him.

Earlier today, Harriet and I tried to get kids to convince their parents to come out and vote. I was unsuccessful, but Harriet managed to get a few to promise to talk to their older relatives before being stopped by our principal for promoting a political campaign on school grounds. For the comparative essay outline, I received a seventy-eight. Ms. Phillips called it a significant improvement over my other work.

I want to find Sid and thank him for his help; maybe with a good foundation he won't throw me off a bridge or strangle me. He has not appeared yet, and the polls have already closed. We are all anxious to hear the results. The last vision told me Vipesh would lose, but it could be different now.

I don't even know what to think anymore.

No one has announced anything yet; Riviera and Vipesh are the two candidates remaining and it's too close to call. The volunteers and guests spend most of their time mingling around the office and eating the food Abba brought from our restaurant. I wander around, waiting for Yasmine, Sid, or Krishna.

In the meantime, I fade into the background listening to Krishna's music recommendation. I love the musical fusion that is Sufi rock. One song in particular, *Sayonee*, seems oddly prophetic. It's about a boy trying to find his soulmate, and it couldn't be a coincidence that I got a vision of mine and Krishna's wedding.

"Tikha?" Vijay tugs on my blazer sleeve. I slip my earbuds into my blazer pockets. "Ammi wants to talk to all of us." He drags me across the room to Abba. She's video calling on Abba's phone. Nani's lying in her bed, not looking at the camera. At this time, they are probably just waking up.

"Good morning, Ammi," I say.

"In Urdu, Talibah," Ammi orders.

"Good morning, Nani, how are you?" I repeat myself in her language.

Ammi moves the camera so we can get a better look at Nani.

"She just woke up, but she was talking yesterday." Ammi responds.

In these last stages of dementia, Nani would barely string together random nonsensical words and thoughts.

"What did she say?" Abba asks her in Hindi, he understands some words but isn't conversant.

"She said Vipesh would win tonight and that she's praying for it."

The four of us on the Canadian end of the call exchange looks. We weren't aware Nani even knew Vipesh was running in an election; after all, he's her son-in-law's brother, but we would be thrilled if she did speak.

"So she knows he's running?" Varshil asks.

"Yes, Rajya. I tell her stories about her grandchildren. She wants to know if Abba is taking good care of you." She stops talking and looks around at the four of us, noticing a missing family member. *"She also wants to know, where is Natasha?"*

"She got dumped," Vijay replies in English.

Abba glares at Vijay for a few seconds, then looks back to his phone. *"You can tell Nani that I'm taking care of everything and that Natasha is enjoying her reading week. As of now, we are all just waiting for the big news."*

Ammi takes her phone and brings it with her to the kitchen.

"Thank you, Vipan. Anyway, it's almost breakfast. Nani is hungry. I will check in on our daughter later today." She waves to us and then says in English, "I love you, *betas*, tell me good news."

"Love you, Ammi," the three of us say in unison. We disband while Abba continues his conversation with Ammi.

There are now approximately forty to fifty people in the office. I stop scanning the room when I see Kyle and Harriet talking in a corner. She catches my eye and waves him away.

"Allo," Harriet joins me. She's wearing a green sleeveless dress. Her scars from the explosion are on full display and her hair is dyed all green. I'm wearing what I previously wore on my date with Krishna, with the addition of a dark black blazer instead of a light coat, complete with my realistic-looking prosthetic and tights.

"When did you have time to colour your hair?" I ask.

"I did it myself after school. Anyway, how are you feeling? Excited? Nervous?" She smiles, scratching the scar on her left arm.

I run through my list of bad things in my head: my grandmother has dementia, we are in the middle of a campaign that could end catastrophically for everyone, including MP

Riviera, I'm unconsciously checking my phone to see if a boy I barely know will attend this event, and I might die in a few hours.

"Not bad," I answer. "It's a lot, but nothing I haven't handled before." I scratch the back of my neck. "How about you?"

"I'm great. By the way, how did your date go?" Harriet seemingly springs it out of nowhere.

I blush. The campaign has been eating up a lot of her time, so, understandably, she forgot. "He's an interesting person. And he's mature for a twenty-two-year-old man. His face and beard are prickly." I feel my face to see if scratch marks are still on my cheeks and sigh when I cannot feel them.

"No...*Oh, mon Dieu.*" She squints her eyes and smiles with her entire face, shaking her head side to side again. She walks in front of me, grabbing my sleeve. "How was it? Tell me everything." She giggles like a young child.

"It was not some crazy heart-stopping experience. It was just a kiss with no hidden subtext." I scratch behind my neck. "And besides, I invited him here, but he hasn't responded to my texts. And there are some problems. We don't have that much in common. He left his family to pursue his dreams, he's free-spirited but 'wants to stay politically neutral'."

Her happy smirk fades. We both knew people who tried to seek some non-existent 'enlightened centrist position'. They see the government giving people basic human rights as 'handouts' instead of recognizing the absence of basic human rights as policy failures of the government.

"*C'est domage.*" Harriet shakes her head from side to side while clicking her tongue pitifully. "I spent all that time talking you up for nothing?"

"You what?" I raise my voice at her.

"I was helping a comrade." She places a hand on my shoulder. "I didn't make him do anything he didn't already want to do. I just told him how you were one of the living reincarnations of Shakuntala Devi and that you had a beautiful mind. I didn't say anything that wasn't at least partially true, and he believed it because I meant every word. When he asked about 'campaign issues', that was all him."

"Oh." My face begins to flush as a smile slowly creeps onto my face. We exit the office and she takes her hand off my shoulder. It's a pleasant eighteen degrees outdoors, and while it's dark, there are some dim streetlights around. The change from the stuffy office to a temperate outdoors is pleasing.

"I know what your problem is, T." Harriet nudges me, and we walk about the parking lot. "You're so concerned that things will just turn out badly, they end up that way. Do you know what I mean?"

I shake my head.

"There is just so much going on in that head of yours. You always think the worst possible thing could happen, so you unconsciously prepare yourself for disaster because it's easier than just being disappointed all the time. It's a self-fulfilling prophecy, also known as doomerism." She tilts her head at me.

"It's called being realistic," I defend myself. I know it's a bad mindset, but if the worst possible event happened to me at such a young age, it could happen again. And it could happen today.

"I get it, I know it's hard to be optimistic when so much is at stake. And the ruling elites certainly aren't giving us many reasons to be positive."

I raise an eyebrow at her. "Are you talking about the election or Krishna?

"Yes," she flatly responds. "But you can change him. Before I met Kyle, he was so clueless about the state of our planet. But I loved the challenge, and look at him now. You can do that to him. You're more powerful than you think."

"I don't think Krishna's coming. So what should I do, by myself?"

She exhales through her teeth. "The only thing you can do now. Take in this fresh air around you. Breathe, let your hair down. Then, you can walk to that tree right over there, and then take more deep breaths." She takes out a compostable bag with a joint and an electric USB arc lighter, and I know it's not a metaphor.

I back away slowly and in shock.

"*Quoi?* It's just pine needles and oregano." She leans in. "*Et un peu de hasch*," she whispers.

"What?" I yell.

"I know you support the legalization of all recreational drugs."

"Just because I support legalization doesn't mean I plan on using them," I object.

"Why? Because of what it would do to your body? Or your mind?" Harriet puts on a fake frown. "If the government is so concerned about the killing of brain cells, they would push the minimum age restriction to twenty-five, when our brains stop developing." She weakens her grip on the bag. "Anyway, think about it. You must be dealing with a lot."

She drops the bag, but I catch it before it hits the ground. "By the way, the results are coming soon, so if you do light that, let me know. I'm going to need a few hits later if we lose." Harriet takes off and enters through the front entrance doors.

In the days leading up to the election, she has been putting out fires where she sees them and has been taking antidepressants far more frequently. If I were her, I would break down every day.

I follow her terrible advice or rather half of it. I walk over to the tree to the right of the building and breathe. In through my nose, out through my mouth, my lungs have never felt so light. Maybe, I don't have to go to the shed. There is no immediate threat. I could just put in an anonymous tip and wait for the police to deal with a problem I have no business pursuing.

"Yo, Hari," a boy's voice calls out. I look out in the distance and see two figures approaching me. I realize I'm still holding a plastic bag filled with contraband. I don't have pockets big enough on my blazer. With no other option, and in a moment of panic, I remove my prosthetic and shove the bag into my socket, then stomp it down until it's hidden. However, there's not enough room for both my stump and the bag of drugs, so I'll have a much bigger limp; friction won't be my friend for now.

The two people approach me, one tall, one short, holding each other's hands. It's Sid walking hand-in-hand with a small Black girl. He's dressed in a standard two-piece suit, black jacket and pants, a grey dress shirt with the top button undone, and no tie. She's wearing a cute grey dress with a bow at the back, and her hair is done up in two pigtails behind her head. He covers the little girl's ears. "Shit. Sorry, Tikha, I thought you were Harriet. But you look wonderful tonight." He smiles, removing his hands from her head. I guess he had the foresight to cover her ears, but not to stop himself from swearing. "Not that you did not before. I like the bun on top."

I give him a courtesy smile. "Thanks. You two look wonderful as well. Did you do something different with your hair?"

"Right." Sid runs his hands through his head. "I just combed it the other way. I've had it this way for a week. By the way, this is my little sister, Kat." He brings the little girl forward.

"I'm adopted," she proudly exclaims.

I subconsciously nod along with him and smile down at her. "Hi, I'm Tikha, Vipesh Ganatra's niece, Harriet's cousin." I reach out and shake her tiny hand. "Aren't you an elegant young lady?"

"I think you need your glasses again, Sidney." Kat teases her older brother. "They don't look anything alike." She looks back at me. "But I already know I like you better."

"I know they don't," Sid tries to explain. "It's just that from a distance and under poor lighting they—"

"It's fine, I get that a lot." I cut him off, relieving him of some awkwardness. Harriet and I are about the same approximate height and weight; from a distance I could understand our silhouettes looking similar. But we do have noticeable differences. She has piercings on her ears and nose, her skin tone is lighter, and she has much shorter hair—and two legs. "It was a fifty-fifty chance; you'll get it next time."

While we walk into the building, the plastic bag sinks in my prosthetic. It squishes about my stump with every other step I take; it's almost as uncomfortable as phantom pain. "Are your parents coming?" I ask. It would be good to have a cop on the scene, and she could probably de-escalate her son.

"They're trying to find parking, so they dropped us off in front," he says as he continues to walk hand-in-hand with his sister. They are cute together, and he seems like a good older brother. How does he become the rage-filled black-hooded figure in my vision?

Sid opens the door to celebratory cheers. Harriet runs over to us. She squeezes me and lifts me a couple of centimetres off the floor. My stump momentarily detaches itself from my prosthetic. She immediately notices it and puts me down. I readjust myself.

"We won?" I ask.

She nods as she jumps around and hugs Sid and Kat as well. "Based on the current results, we are projected to get party status; unfortunately, we are not part of the coalition, but we are on the floor."

Crisis averted. I need to make sure we are following the best timeline. While Harriet, Sid, and Kat join the crowd, I exit the party as discretely as possible. I shift against the wall, not trying to draw attention to myself. It's only a five-minute walk to I&MNG and the shed, where there might or might not be a dead body.

Part 3.5: A Happy Ending
Sidney, October 28th, 20:30

As the office celebrates Mr. Ganatra's victory, Harriet, Kat, and I walk deeper into the crowd. I don't recognize many people here.

The campaign office is a relic from the twenties. The area rug is likely full of asbestos; above us are flimsy ceiling tiles covering the vents. The lights are long fluorescent tubes either white or yellow, which light the room unevenly. For a Green Party candidate, it's a little hypocritical not to use LEDs.

I quickly find Mom in the crowd and leave Kat with her while I stand next to Kyle, all decked out in a new eighteen-hundred-dollar pin-striped suit. I'm wearing the same suit I wore to semi-formal two years ago; I did grow into it. I compliment him and tell him Harriet's a lucky girl. He pats me on the back and teases me for not joining a winning campaign.

How was I supposed to know he would win? Mr. Ganatra had a hard battle against the most powerful man in the world.

Mr. Ganatra stands on a chair while Harriet gives him a microphone. He taps it with the ring on his pinky finger, and the crowd's chatter quiets when hearing the microphone's feedback.

"First of all, thank you to everyone for coming out here tonight," he starts.

Everyone applauds for a moment.

"To be completely honest, something no politician has ever said."

The crowd laughs.

"This was not the result I was planning for..." He pauses, stepping off the chair. "To have this district flipped to the Green Party, to see a record number of people come out to vote for our message, to have zero problems tabulating votes, for something like that to occur, it would have to take an act of Gods. However, I know they can't take all the credit. That must go to my amazing staff and my family, canvassing neighbourhoods and marketplaces, putting up signs, and reciting the issues that matter. They spent countless hours laying the groundwork."

"We counted the hours. Can you sign off on them?" one of Tikha's brothers shouts; not the one I saw earlier this month, he looks a little older. Everyone laughs.

"Yes, Varshil, and to all the students who helped, come see me later today. Anyway, I would like to give a special thanks to some people. First, there's my older brother, Vipan, who's had the most difficult job in the world for forty-five years, my nieces and nephews."

Mr. Ganatra takes his daughter by the hand and drags her to him, holding her in his left arm. "And the biggest thanks I want to give is to the girl who was with me when I started. She encouraged me to run and stood by my side every day of her life."

I'm unsure why he's setting up a reveal. It's Harriet, and it would be weird if he didn't single her out. He places a hand under her chin, and they smile at each other. "She called me after the explosion to tell me to keep going because she knew what was important. And a week ago, I had told her I did not know how I felt about her coming up with ideas on her own." He takes her hand and gives her a boost up onto a chair. "I didn't know if I was proud or terrified of her ambition." He lets out a short exhale of disbelief. "I was a fool for second-guessing her; I couldn't be prouder, and I would say that regardless of the result of this election. Harriet Isabelle Ganatra, you remind me why I volunteered for these communities and fought vigorously for our district." He gets a little choked up. "If your mother could be with us right now, she would break down to find that her little girl blossomed into the intelligent, beautiful, and accomplished young woman standing here."

Harriet tears up at her father's words.

"None of this would have happened without your spark."

She wipes a tear off her cheek and jumps from her chair. She wraps her arms around her father while holding onto him.

The crowd applauds again for a minute. I look at my mother. She uses the tip of her bandana to wipe tears away. Ever since her surgery, she has become a little more emotional. I take her hand, look her in her eyes, and smile. She wraps her arms around my waist and pulls me to her.

She lets me go and points to my other side. I look down to find a pair of open-toed wedges and bright yellow nail polish. I scan up and find the feet are connected to a girl wearing a yellow satin dress cut a couple of centimetres above her knees. When I finally make my way up to Yasmine's face, her head is adorned with curly and voluminous hair. I had only ever seen her with straight hair. My jaw drops.

The day after our rough exchange in the library, Harriet trapped us together until we smoothed out our issues. On Tuesday night, we even hung out after school at Harriet's house. I would go so far as to call us friends now.

"Hey." Her face flushes but not with anger, and she smiles with a perfect braceless mouth.

It takes me a couple of seconds to reconvene. I forcibly push my jaw back into position. "Yasmine, congratulations. I was wrong for not joining."

She takes my hand. "I need to tell you something." She pulls me through the crowd and towards the lobby of the building. I take it all in, the vaulted ceilings two stories above me, the floors made of red marble, the ambience, the cooler temperatures—it's quite a juxtaposition. And it reminds me of the banquet hall where we had our semi-formal.

"I want to apologize formally." Yasmine releases my hand. She looks me in my eyes, I stare at her forehead and focus. "We both made mistakes, and I cannot believe it took my friend calling me a bitch for me to realize this but, here it goes." She clears her throat. "I'm sorry." I take a step backwards. I cannot hear her inner monologue talk over her words.

I can hear Tikha's thoughts, but why not hers?

"I had no right to treat you like that on our trip," she continues. "You eventually apologized, and it's hypocritical for me not to accept it." She taps the cross in between her collarbones.

"You don't have to apologize," I reassure her. "You have a lot going on at home."

"No," she cuts me off. "Everyone has a lot going on at home and I have been dealing with it for seventeen years. I can't keep using my parents' shitty relationship as a crutch." She holds my hand. "I was mad at myself for thinking I was responsible for my parents falling out, but they chose to stay in an unhappy relationship because they thought it would benefit me and made me think their unhappiness was my fault." She takes my other hand. "I had to act two different ways for them. Every day in this town I'm reminded of how everybody looks and acts so differently than me. But seeing Mr. Ganatra during the debate, and now his victory speech, hiding nothing. He seemed so happy." She lets go and brings her hand up to her hair, combing through some strands and pulling on a lock until it extends past her breast. Once she lets go, it springs back to her shoulder. "This is my natural hair. I have been straightening it every day because, quote, 'I was not supposed to look like that'. My mom told me there were many things she had to do to fit in, so I changed myself. I pretended to be the perfect daughter in a 'happy family'. And then I remembered during that dance in the middle of grade ten, you showed up. I thought, 'Here comes this boy who doesn't look like anyone else here. He might know what I'm going through'."

I nod to her. I didn't realize someone like her could have insecurities. I lean back and hit a wall.

"When we were studying for the chemistry test a couple of nights ago, it was the most fun I have had with you."

As much as that comment hurt, because it meant our relationship was unmemorable and bland, it was fun. The actual studying portion only took ten minutes, Tikha just told us what would be on the test, and she must have stolen the questions from Ms. Stone. After we 'studied', all four of us watched some movies at Harriet's. Around seven at night, I got a phone call from my parents telling me to come home for dinner. Mother fell asleep and Mindy left, so I missed dinner, but didn't regret it.

"I guess it was fun," I admit. "I had never seen *Fight Club* or *V for Vendetta*. It was strange how they changed from their source material."

"That's not the point. It wasn't the movies. There was no pressure to try to be anyone else." She smiles. "I'd like to try this again, and based on your jaw drop, I think you feel the same way."

If this were two months ago, I would have jumped at the opportunity, but I know now we're not good together. I loved a fabricated version of Yasmine. "This is a lot," I say with reverence. The last thing I want to do is to hurt her, and with these new powers, I could do worse than what happened in Orillia. "But what would be different this time?"

"We already know our bugs, so we know what not to do." She lifts her right leg, undoes the buckle on her shoe, removes it from her foot, and throws it towards the office door. And then, with her left hand, she does the same thing with her left shoe, throwing them beside each other. "But I first want to see if the magic is still here." She stands at the same height as me. She runs her hand on my chest, undoing another button. Then she pulls the collar of my blazer towards her, pressing her lips against mine.

I close my eyes and can feel the difference. It's not just her curly hair colliding with my temples or her lips being more forceful. As I breathe with my nose, I notice she isn't sweating, and she smells amazing. We pull away from each other at the same time. She blinks three times in succession and her bright almond-coloured eyes sparkle. A smile grows across her cheekbones, highlighting her dimples, and revealing her perfect teeth. She flips her hair from side to side. "This time, I made the first move, and will freely admit it."

"Woah," I pause, breathing in through my nose and out through my mouth. "It's absolutely incredible to see you become the best version of yourself. But there has to be more than just that one night. Am I crazy for thinking that?"

"It was something Mr. Ganatra said tonight." She walks me closer to the door outside. "I didn't think we would win. It made me think we would be okay, as a country and a—"

The door suddenly swings open, swinging towards us. A cold breeze wafts toward us both. And through the shadows, Tikha emerges from the front door, with her long hair back in its natural unkempt and frizzy state. A final round of thundering applause comes from Mr. Ganatra's office.

"Sid? Yaz?" Tikha walks closer to us. "What are you doing out here?"

"We were catching up," I answer.

Tikha smiles at me and puts a hand on her chest, sighing in relief.

Thank God he's not at the plant, but why is she touching him like that?

"Yeah, just catching up," Yasmine answers. She lets go of me and brushes my chest.

Oh, no.

"So you two are...why?" Tikha points to the two of us. "And how? After what he did?" Her voice gets louder and higher with every question.

"I thought you said you believed me?" I ask her.

She walks towards me and looks at me with her bulging cat eyes. I turn my head away from her.

"Relax, V. Water under the bridge," Yasmine defends. "You convinced me that I was wrong."

She looks away from us.

Who could have seen this coming?

"Who could have seen what coming?" I ask Tikha.

The two girls look at me funny for a few seconds. They turn their heads back to each other as Tikha pretends she didn't think what I just heard.

"I promise, nothing will change between us." She links her arm around me. "You know what? I just remembered Harriet mentioned you were seeing that boy from Algonquin. Maybe the four of us could all do something together. What do you say?"

"Sure, I'll ask him; I am happy for the two of you." She twirls some strands of hair around her fingers. "But Sid, I'm watching you. If you hurt Yaz again, I will put you to sleep." She puts her hand down.

I wait for a wink, but it doesn't come. And then I immediately flashback to her intense stare and how my soul almost left my body last Monday. Her caution is justified, but she also said she believed me. I don't understand how she operates. "What were you doing outside?" I hastily change the subject.

"I just went to get some air." She strokes her hair. "Everything's good." She looks up at us, gives a polite half-smile, and stops touching her hair. "What's happening in the office?"

"I think your uncle is delivering a victory speech." Yasmine picks up her shoes. "I'm not sure if he's still doing it. Now that he's a politician, his speeches could last up to an hour, and they go around in circles. But let's try to make it back for the ending."

The three of us walk back. There is still something off about her, and I don't know what it could be. Maybe she knows about my powers. I haven't abused them for a couple of weeks. I don't have to, because Mother's getting better.

Tikha is limping again, and her stockings are torn on her left shin, although she doesn't have any visible cuts or blood.

"That looks pretty bad." I point to her left ankle.

"No, it's nothing to worry about. It didn't break any skin." She disappears into the crowd.

Yasmine brings me back to her. "As I was saying, the country listened to our problems because they got a better system in place. We can get a better system in place as well."

"Alright." I'm put at ease by this, although maybe it has something to do with her parents. She can act like she always knew they were growing apart, however I know divorces can still be upsetting. She could need another excuse to stay in Islington.

"Hey." Harriet spins me around so we face each other. She grabs onto my blazer and jumps up and down. Her green hair bounces all over the place. "I just heard the news. *Félicitations, Sid.*"

"Felicitations to you too, first daughter of Ottawa Rural South."

She giggles. "I like the sound of that. I should get a title; I have more influence than the Senators at this point."

While I don't think she has more influence than the worst hockey team in the league, I let her have her moment. It's her night as much as Mr. Ganatra's.

"I'm kidding." She combs some hair out of her face. "I see Ms. Tamashiro is doing well." I look over to Yasmine, who seems genuinely happy to be with her parents.

Even though they are splitting up, they seem to be enjoying the night, until they notice me and give me the same dirty look Yasmine gave me for the past couple of months. Even though Yasmine has forgiven me, her parents might not have. But I can fix it. After all, I managed to get Yasmine back without even using my powers. However, it's premature to call Yasmine 'Ms. Tamashiro'.

"No, *tata*. I meant your mother." Harriet forcefully swings my head back to her. "Anyway, this nightmare is finally over, and I promise I will be more available to you."

"To what are you referring?"

"I know what your mother is going through, and want to guide you through it. One friend helping out another." She rubs my left arm. "But first, I've got to clean up this place. *À bientôt,* Sid." Harriet skips across the room gleefully.

My parents summon me from across the room. Mr. Ganatra appears to have finished his speech and the crowd resumes mingling. I rejoin our family.

Mr. Ganatra welcomes us in all his glory, standing tall and triumphant. I shake his hand. "Congratulations, Mr. Ganatra." I correct myself. "Sorry, MP Ganatra."

"Mr. Ganatra is fine, Sidney. You don't need to be so formal. How long have we known each other?" He turns his attention to the rest of the family. "Thanks for coming, Genevieve, Miriam, and Katherine. I guess Mindy couldn't make it. Take some food home with you."

"Thanks, Vipesh," Mother says. "But I can't eat anything spicy. It does not agree with me now."

"Will do; I'm eating for the two of us," Mom speaks with a mouth full of food. "Give my regards to your brother; we'll have to check out his restaurant sometime. We cannot wait to see what change you bring."

Mr. Ganatra laughs. "The night is still young; we have yet to achieve party status. But I'm hopeful." He leaves while Kat runs to the self-serve station.

"Sidney." Mom pulls me aside. "We will be leaving soon. Mother is feeling a little tired." Kat returns with two large plates of food, and Mother takes some rice while Mom eats everything else.

Mom is already eating more than her second plate of food for the night; she's a little stressed about the future.

Before the explosion, they had only voted for Mr. Riviera because he kept I&MNG running. Mother's condition may have played a role in their decision to change their votes.

Kat thought Mom's work at the plant made her sick. It's unlikely, especially since Mother has a family history of cancer and no one else from the plant suffers from similar maladies.

But now that Mr. Ganatra has won, they will likely shut the plant down. Everyone could get new jobs in a similar industry. Mother could still work, so everyone wins, all except Mr. Riviera. However, he's in his seventies. I can imagine he will enjoy a long and well-earned retirement. I should check in on him tomorrow; he's not looking good lately, but tomorrow is the last time. I don't need to learn anymore.

When it comes to my family, I'm not worried. Everything is looking up.

Part 3.6: Everything's Back to Normal...
Vritikha, October 29th, 00:00

As we clean up, I look forward to sleeping for a total of nine hours again. Abba's allowing us to skip school today because we had worked so hard over the past two weeks. We were never allowed to miss school for any reason, not even for Diwali or Eid, but it depends on what happens tonight.

Ever since the first vision I got on October eighth, I have not slept for more than two hours at a time without waking up regularly. And for the past few days, I have only been getting ten minutes of uninterrupted sleep and waking up fifty times a night.

After hearing the results, I walked to the nuclear plant. Surprisingly, the gates were open, and to the far left, there was the old shed from my visions. It was empty except for an old pipe, some handcuffs, and an old pair of broken glasses. I only spent a few minutes there and snagged my leggings on some nails when I left. I felt my left leg bump into something, but I didn't notice the rip until Sid saw my left ankle.

When I got back, I asked Vipesh Kaka whether he heard from MP Riviera, and he said he had. MP Riviera congratulated him on his victory and gave him some advice for his first day in the House of Commons. Vipesh told us the Green Party had achieved Party status by reaching the minimum requirement of twelve seats across the country. Unfortunately, it came at the expense of the Conservative Party forming a minority government. We achieved a more diverse house, unseated a flawed incumbent, and every major party will have a voice in the Parliament, but it still feels like a loss.

The campaign may be over, but with a conservative minority government, we have a lot of protesting ahead of us.

I try my hardest not to sleep in the car. Varshil and Vijay pass out immediately in the backseats. As we drive across the Morissette Bridge, the Rideau River barely makes a sound.

Where does the phrase 'water under the bridge' come from? I thought the bridge symbolizing Sid and Yasmine's relationship was not only burnt, but that its remains would have flooded nearby areas.

My visions portrayed the river as raging rapids and the sky as overcast to the point where it just became too foggy to make out any constellations. But it isn't; the sky is clear and full of stars. Maybe it's the end of my clairvoyance; there are too many inconsistencies. I'll wait tables, get good grades by actually studying, and be less dour because I won't be held back by my visions. I could even start praying again since I'm no longer a walking contradiction.

We arrive in our parking lot at around twelve-fifteen. Abba carries Vijay over his shoulder, while I shake Varshil until he wakes up. As long as they're not dead, I can wake anyone up. He mumbles until I look at his head; his eyelids shoot open.

"Did I miss Krishna?" he grumbles.

I nod. He didn't show up but wanted to make it up to my brothers and me by taking us to a movie.

Varshil and I walk through the restaurant and make it upstairs slowly and quietly. I enter my room; Veera is already asleep. My brothers go to their respective rooms without freshening themselves up, while Abba calls Ammi to tell her the good news. We don't turn on any lights or even shake a doorknob.

I throw my nice clothes into a corner of the room. I toss my stockings in the garbage, take off my realistic-looking leg, put on my pyjamas, and apply some cream on my stump. I have experienced many muscle cramps due to my extraneous physical activities, so the chafing cream soothes my pain and helps me fall asleep even faster.

I lie down.

* * *

I will be in MP Riviera's office. I will be wearing a blouse and black dress pants. He will have nothing on his desk except a glass of water and many packed boxes behind him. He will be wearing a loose-fitting T-shirt and jeans. I will talk to him about his visions and why he ended up dead in some of them. He will be paying attention. He will determine that I'm clairvoyant and explain the frequent memory gaps, as someone who spends too much time in this state will fail to tell the difference between real life and a vision. He will walk over to me with a cane, hunched over even more than when I saw him at the debate. He will get close to me, and before he can touch my face, I will panic and speed-walk away. I will only take three steps until I walk face-first into the door. But he will bring a chair for me to fall into and take the glass of water on his desk. It will turn into ice. He will place the glass on my forehead. He will look into my eyes willingly but won't faint. He will tell me I can turn off my visions if I want. I will thank him for his time and open the door to leave.

I will walk into my room wearing a yellow, cold-shoulder top and faded blue jeans. My hair will be in nine rubber bands along the entire length. I will shut my eyes and use scissors to cut it. About twenty-seven inches of hair will fall into a transparent bag. I will pick out about ten or so strands and roll them for a string of the same diameter as a piece of yarn. I will be looking at a board I cannot understand. I will see a list of names such as Mr. Riviera, Mr. Glass, Vipesh, Sid, Ms. Tamashiro, Harriet, and Yasmine. They will all be connected in some spiderweb. I will step back and try to examine it until someone interrupts me. I will turn over the web to reveal a whiteboard. I will take a scarf, wrap it around my head, throw one end of the scarf over my shoulder, and form a very poor hijab. I will open the door to let Harriet in. She will bring a box of assorted stuff into my room. We will exit together.

I will exit a movie theatre room alongside Krishna. I am in a red flannel shirt and dark jeans. Varshil and Vijay will come up to us alongside some of their faceless friends. He will drive the three of us back to our building. We will have a moment, and he will lean across the gear shift in his car, but will accidentally slip and touch my inner thigh. I will panic and jump out of the car, collapsing on the pavement. I will close my eyes for a brief second.

I will open my eyes and find myself on a hardwood floor. We will be in Vipesh's new office in the Parliament; he will be giving us a tour. He will have eight different pictures of Harriet on his desk. The walls will be lined with blueprints for some of his engineering projects: the I&MNG glass lobby, the Morissette Bridge, and his house in Manotick. I close my eyes again and freeze.

I open them and find myself talking to Yasmine and asking her many questions about the power plant explosions. I will then move to Kyle, Emilia, Anthony, Chris, Peter, Lionel, Sage, etc. I will cycle through everyone in the physics class. Everyone but Sid will pay me any attention. Sid and I will walk out the door, but I will trip over a step.

I will collapse on the cold asphalt again and turn over to look at those red arches, but the cables will be severed. The sky will be dark and overcast, and the rapids below me will be raging. My stomach will drop, and the two hooded figures, black and white, will fall into the water with me. I will drown.

*　*　*

I wake up, gasping for air and reach for my phone. It's a quarter past three in the morning on October twenty-eight. It must have been three hours. "Why?" I ask myself.

"Why, what?" Veera turns the lights on and gets out of her bed. She crouches by my bedside without climbing into my bed or even touching me. "What did you see?" She's used to the routine. I don't deserve her.

"Why does this keep happening?" I ask. "I just want one day where I don't have nightmare-inducing visions." Mr. Riviera's life may not be on the line anymore, but based on my last vision, it's more than just mine. I don't think I can turn them off. Sid might become a killer, but given the choice of Sid dying or not dying, I choose not dying. He hasn't strangled me...yet.

She runs her hands through my hair, picking up a couple of strands. "It must have been pretty bad, you're shedding." She gets up in a state of shock. "*Halla,* today was supposed to be the day. I completely forgot." She climbs into my bed and puts her arms around me. "I'm so glad you're okay. Did you fight the figure in black? What happened?"

"Vipesh uncle won. MP Riviera is still alive. Sid is happy and somehow is back with Yasmine. Everything's fine." I trail off. "But it doesn't make sense. There's something off about Vipesh's win. It was just too easy."

"I guess you're right, Vritikha. A seasoned, well-respected incumbent lost his re-election to an Indian outsider with no real political experience in a quasi-rural district armed only with a powerful message and a bold plan for the future." She giggles. "It sounds like a fantasy wish-fulfillment story, but we should be glad it happened here and now." If this is considered fantasy wish-fulfillment, it's kind of depressing; we barely eked out a victory and many factors out of our control needed to happen so we could win.

"How do you know so much?"

Veera stands up again. "I'm aware of a lot of the news surrounding the election. In Toronto, we received hours of news coverage of the nuclear plant explosion. Panels discussed why it happened for weeks. It was not even an explosion, but it was the perfect October surprise for this election cycle."

She's right, it was a perfect October surprise. "What were the theories?" I ask. Maybe one of them had to be correct.

"Off the top of my head: faulty equipment, cutting costs on repairs, shabby inspections, corrupted unions, corrupted MPs, an act of God, liberal tampering, secret societies—"

"Wait," I interrupt her. "Maybe it wasn't an accident at all. Maybe the Liberals tampered with the machinery."

Veera silently climbs back into her bed. "When I said Liberal tampering, it was an idea proposed by a far-right conspiracy blog. The investigation concluded that it was just faulty machinery, and they have ruled out foul play."

"Which is what they want us to think." I take off my covers and put a foot on the floor. My heart rate rises. "Maybe the Liberals tampered with the machinery so they could show a false sense of unity. Maybe they put in some faulty machinery to get more funding for the plant and to bring in more jobs."

While I am delighted about this breakthrough, Veera holds a pillow over her ears while facing away from me. "What if someone tampered with the security footage to hide some horrible act? It was even possible that MP Riviera wanted an easy out for the election. He does know about clairvoyants. Maybe he manufactured his demise because he didn't want to die."

"Veera, why aren't you saying anything?" I whisper to her.

"Vritikha!" She throws the pillow to her feet and whisper-yells: "I helped you when your life was in danger, but you are really pushing it with this conspiratorial bullshit. Even if any of this was true, you still have no evidence. So shut up about your fever dreams and go to sleep." She reaches across to her feet and picks up her pillow, still facing away from me.

The last time she spoke so angrily to me was when we just moved here. She didn't want to leave Jammu behind and blamed me and my then-upcoming amputation. She resented me every day until she left for Toronto Metropolitan. She would hide my leg or refuse to help me if I fell. It was a long time ago, and we only grew closer since moving away. She changed because she became more religious and became isolated in the big city.

"I'm sorry, I'm just tired and a little bit upset. Maybe we can talk about this tomorrow." Veera lowers her voice and puts on a more sympathetic tone. "I want to help you, just not now." She takes the pillow off her head and lies down.

I concede. I feel like I had just had a memory gaff, because there must be another explanation for why she got mad. In one moment, I became the person I despised so much. But my visions are the first place to begin.

My phone buzzes, and I open my notifications to find that Mr. Riviera has emailed me. He has pictures of me on the grounds of I&MNG 'illegally' and says he will send out a warrant if I don't meet up with him next Friday at nine p.m. I don't have a choice now but to let the vision play out. But I do have one thing over him.

He and Sid have some kind of relationship; they were together the night of the Q and A, the night when he dropped in the polls. He knows something, but I can't just accuse Sid or Mr. Riviera without proof. Besides, acting nice to Sid is what gave us the victory.

Ms. Adams is an Inspector for the Greater Ottawa Area, so I could ask her for help. However, I will need to look at a different angle if I want her to reopen the investigation. But before anything, I need to enjoy the time I have left with Krishna, although maybe that's a bad idea. I don't want to put him in harm's way.

Nothing can be normal again until I resolve these visions. I thought I prevented my death, but I may have only delayed it.

Part 4

Part 4.1: A Fly Caught in a Web
Vritikha, November 11th, 16:00, Two Weeks Later

"Anytime I try to talk to someone about the nuclear plant explosion, they write me off. It can be the result of two things. The first is that they must all be trying to hide something. Or they do not know anything and are just annoyed with me. I am not ruling that out, but they were at the centre of this whole incident. How are none of them trying to figure this thing out as well?"

Veera and I are video chatting, but her screen freezes on her confused expression.

"I'll reset the video feed." I sit on my bed.

"The connection's fine," she tells me. "I am just confused about why you called me. I told you to call when you have something conclusive." She sighs exhaustively and mutters to herself in Farsi. I get a basic understanding of what she means, since some words are similar to Urdu. It's something along the lines of: *"She will never stop"*.

"I have conducted a lot of interviews since you left." I take my whiteboard off the wall, turn it around, and place it on my bed.

"Hold on." She picks up her mug of chai and takes a loud sip. "I'm ready."

I angle the phone to show her the web I have created. It's a work in progress. The back of my whiteboard has pictures of every person of interest. I didn't print actual images, instead opting to write their names paired with a crude sketch attached to the board with tape. They include the physics class and Mr. Glass, the former MP, the current MP, the sole casualty, and the police force in charge of the investigation. Other pictures on the board are the election, the plant, and the perpetrator.

"At the centre of this is the nuclear plant explosion. That's when these visions started. Before this, I had common visions: getting the answers to tests, applying to universities, working in our restaurant, a party." I move the phone over to the centre of the board labelled 'the explosion'. "Then everything changed on October eighth. The explosion at I&MNG Power Plant injured ten children; five were put on life support, either due to blunt force trauma or respiratory problems due to the release of high-power steam. There are also some casualties: a plant worker, and a traffic collision outside of Riverside that might have been due to a traffic light failing or just a coincidence. The jury is still out on that one." I move the phone over to show the names of the victims. "Now the police investigation has concluded that the machinery was nearing the end of its service life. The safety inspector, Miriam Tamashiro, should have reported this, except she was conveniently out of the picture. Her alibi is that she had surgery and was recovering, which checks out, so that was a dead end. Anyway, keep in mind the plant isn't that old; only about twenty years old. Who has been representing our district for much longer than that?" I pivot my phone to show her who. "Mr. Guillaume Riviera. He has been a big supporter of nuclear energy. He was part of the board of directors of I&MNG before entering politics. He supposedly divested himself before entering politics but has done everything to protect the plant and the workers. He was in first place in his re-election bid but Vipesh Kaka slowly gained ground.

"Suddenly, the explosion happens and Riviera rises about ten points. His response was one of protection and unity, saying he would defend the plant's future. The Q and A comes; according to my visions, he's supposed to win. But Vipesh Kaka emerges triumphant. Then the news becomes clear: nuclear energy is terrible, and I&MNG should be decommissioned. Kaka rises in the polls and ends up being within the margin of error. And throughout the days leading up to election night, my visions kept changing. But against all odds, Kaka wins." I pivot my phone to show Vipesh connected to the campaign and the explosion. "Riviera does not have an alibi as to where he was at the time of the explosion. As soon as I had that vision about him, he emailed me to organize a meeting. Everything happened in the vision that happened two Fridays ago. He knew what I was thinking and anticipated my every move; he even got me to forget to ask about Sid. Somehow, he knew about my visions, about my leg, and told me he knew he would not be getting another full term even if he won the election. He almost convinced me to stop looking, but why would he care about what I do with myself? He would not tell me where he was at the time of the explosion. This is where it gets interesting." I shut my eyes in order not to get excited. "A plant worker claims they saw him about ten minutes after the explosion, talking to Mr. Spencer Glass, the physics teacher of NMCI." I lower my tone. "I don't know why I'm introducing him like that. He doesn't have anything to do with anything." I move my phone to his position to show his connections to the students and the plant. "He claimed he was talking to a nosy reporter posing as a first responder. Mr. Glass gave Mr. Riviera the names of the students who went missing. So that was a dead end. And Mr. Glass only seemed to be hurt by the explosion. Field trip funding got cut because of this. But I showed him a picture of Mr. Riviera. He said he looked similar, but PPE obscured every part of his face, so he could not be sure. He said there were some noticeable differences, but he recognized the buggy eyes and dark brown hair, though saw a sizeable age gap between them."

I show Veera the connections Mr. Riviera has on the web. He has strands connecting him to the election, Sid, the plant, the explosion, Vipesh, and me. "Everything connects to him somehow, and this whole thing has to start or end with him." I sit on my bed, turn the phone to me, and look at my right foot. "I know everything, and yet something is missing. I hope someone or something could help tie up this last loose end." I hold the loose end that connects the explosion to the perpetrator.

My phone screen displays the call list, the last person being Veera Ganatra. The video call ended at four-oh-four pm, lasting eight minutes.

I drop the loose end and call her back. She picks up within five seconds. "What the hell?" I tell her. "I was in the middle of—"

She raises her fist above her head. "I checked out when you started talking about Mr. Riviera," she groans. "Would he create a heat exchanger malfunction that would hurt future recruits? It killed I&MNG's plans to expand. So either it was a colossal miscalculation, or he didn't do it."

I lean back against the board, defeated.

"But I'll humour you for a second. Did you watch the security tapes of the plant? Did you track down the receipts of the guilty parties? Who benefited the most from this?" She raises an eyebrow at me.

"I did watch the security tapes of the plant, I spoke to Inspector Adams, and since she closed the investigation, I had access to the tapes. The clips showed no suspicious activity, not even any overlapping action on the loading docks to the faulty reactor," I explain. "The heat exchanger only started acting up just as the physics class showed up. The feed's framerate was eleven-point-ninety-seven frames per second, so the footage was not doctored." I wanted to distract Inspector Adams and make off with the surveillance footage to further analyze it, but I didn't need a vision to tell me my half-baked plan would end badly for me. I don't think Inspector Adams was hiding anything, I just wanted to make sure, and I would do whatever it takes to close this investigation.

Veera's accusation clicks in. "Are you talking about Kaka?" I raise my voice. "Sure, he had something to gain from all of this, but the only reason he's on this web is that he won the election. He has an alibi; he was at a farmer's market at the time of the explosion, and Inspector Adams interviewed him. He was about to drop out because the explosion hurt Hari. If you want to talk about a colossal miscalculation, that's a big one. The only loose end is Mr. Riviera."

"I'm not saying it was Kaka, but it took me three minutes to come up with that theory and it makes just as much sense as yours," she says. "You understand how ridiculous you sound, concocting these conspiracies. You're starting to act like a reactionary." She sighs and finishes her remaining chai.

I grip my phone tighter and almost break the case.

"I'm sorry, but I had to use that word, otherwise I wouldn't get through to you. I do want to help, Vritikha. I want you to be happy, healthy, and alive—most importantly, alive. And I am glad we are doing this." I loosen the grip on my phone. "I miss our little talks, but I want to hear how you are doing. How is Jazz Band? Do you need help with your uni admissions? Or Krishna, how did your movie date go?"

Veera's been the first person in our family I go to if I have big news about myself. The last time we spoke over a video call was before the night before the field trip to I&MNG. "Okay, I'll stop."

Veera's mood does not appear to change.

"I could stay here, in Islington. I won't take the Morissette Bridge to go to school. I will avoid school, avoid Mr. Riviera or anyone associated with him. Just speak to the people in my building."

"No." She tenses up her face. "You need to find a way to live with yourself. You have tried everything to change them, and it didn't work. I know you won't let the problem be, but this is self-destructive. I can't always be there for you, so call Krishna, and tell him about your visions. Because if he cannot handle this part of you, he doesn't deserve you. But if you annoy him like you're doing to me, you don't deserve him."

I don't know how to respond, but she's right.

She sighs again. "Just know you might not be able to change everything again. Keep yourself out of danger and accept whatever victories you can get. I love you, please stay safe."

"Love you, too." The call ends and I put my phone on my desk.

What am I doing with my life? I have been trying everything to change my visions again: talking to random people, trying to come out of my social circle, attending Halloween parties, participating in today's assembly commemorating the military-industrial complex, messing up orders, deliberately getting wrong answers on tests, but nothing changes.

As for Krishna, we went to see a movie together while my brothers went with their friends. We went to Manotick, as the prices of admission there were cheap. The film was a murder mystery about a group of kids discovering a dead body during their lake trips. It was so forgettable that I forgot most of the plot and the title. I then invited him to come to our Diwali party on Saturday, and he said he'd come.

I collapse on my bed, put my earbuds in, and listen to my music. The song *Desperate Measures* plays, and the timing could not be more perfect. There's a reason I let these visions control large portions of my life. The worst timeline can still happen and I won't settle for the small victories. I accepted a small victory when I was seven because the alternative was death.

Even though Mr. Riviera is no longer part of the equation, he's still a variable. Sid is still a variable. I'm not just trying to save myself; I can still stop him from becoming the bad man in my vision.

"Vritikha?" I wake back up and remove one earbud. Abba doesn't open the door. I get up and put the whiteboard on the wall. "Hari's here. Have you finished clearing Veera's side of the room?"

"Yes, everything is gone." I tell him the truth. Since Vipesh Kaka won the election, he needed to move closer to downtown.

Abba arranged to have Harriet live with us in our tiny four-bedroom, two-bath, one-hundred-square-meter apartment. Harriet agreed to share a room with me; Varshil and Vijay would also share, and Veera would have her own during the winter break.

I descend the stairs through the restaurant and to the parking lot, and find Sid talking to Vipesh. Since he's the only friend of Harriet's with a car, he helped her move. I stand in the vestibule of our restaurant out of sight of them. Much like a fly on a wall, I'm present but not observed. I have an epiphany; I need to hear this conversation.

"Harriet has just been relentless in trying to get me to talk about my mother. I respect her intentions, but nothing has happened since her surgery six weeks ago. She's fine. I'm fine. It's fine," he overcompensates.

"Well, she's just looking out for you," Vipesh explains. "You know, she's been in your shoes before..." He pauses. "...with her mom." There's a beat between them as the internal cogs of Sid's mind turn.

"Oh, shit." Sid paces in his spot. "I'm so sorry, Mr. Ganatra. I completely forgot."

"It's alright, Sidney," Mr. Ganatra reassures him. Vipesh places his hands on Sid's shoulders. "I think about Isabelle every day and I remember everything about her. The day we met was one of the best days of my life, and the day I lost her was one of the saddest. She was one of the most considerate and intelligent people I have ever met. She was tough and outspoken, and no matter what I do in the future, I will always keep her with me."

"So, this campaign. You ran because of Mrs. Court?"

"No, I ran for the betterment of this district and our country," Vipesh explains. "But she was with me every step of the way. She lives on through Harriet." I emerge from the vestibule and try to help. "Harriet is wrong about one thing; you don't necessarily have to talk it out. People have their ways of coping." Vipesh takes his hands off him. "My way of healing was running. I felt guilty because I wasn't able to be with her before she died. I was just too busy working on that damn bridge." He pauses and gulps. "Sorry, I don't mean to unload this all on you."

"I understand, Mr. Ganatra." Sid bows to him. "Again, I'm fine."

"All I'm trying to say is if something bad does happen, remember what she loves. If you keep that in mind, it will be like she's always with you. So how can you make her happy? What does she love above all else?"

I walk towards this conversation to Sid's car. Sid looks at me and sighs with relief. "Hey Tikha, can you take this, please?" He hands me a box containing a yoga mat, incense sticks, and a foam roller. "It's the last one." He then enters his Prius and sits motionless.

Vipesh passes him a business card through the window. "If you ever want to talk about it, with someone much more..." He pauses for comedic effect. "...old, then let me know."

Harriet walks out of the restaurant as soon as Vipesh stops talking, and he walks away from Sid's car to his daughter. He embraces her for half a minute, blocking the doorway, and then puts her at arm's length, lifting her head to meet his eyes. "I want you to help out around the house. You are part of their family, so I expect you to pull your weight."

"I know, Papa." Harriet's face flushes. "I'll be cleaning up in the kitchen after hours, and then I can work my way up to waiting tables." She shakes her head. "Pending an interview with the boss."

He smiles back. "I'll put in a good word for you. Remember to take your pills every day."

"I promise she'll be good, Vipesh." Kyle walks up to her from behind, rests his chin on her head, and wraps his hands around her stomach.

Harriet giggles. "Babe, stop. Not in front of my dad." She pushes her boyfriend backwards. He releases his grip and stands up to tower over Vipesh.

"Well," he says, sucking air through his teeth. "You two will be living much closer to each other." Vipesh is not the biggest fan of Kyle. And for Vipesh to not like someone is saying something. But Kyle's everything Harriet wants, so for her sake, he tolerates him. "And as for you, Kyle." He raises his voice sharply. "If you hurt her, I will make sure you never see the light of day again." Vipesh grins, prompting Kyle to take another step back. "I'm kidding." Except he isn't. Vipesh hugs and kisses his daughter goodbye while maintaining eye contact with Kyle. Kyle's smug grin fades to a cold, dumb stare.

"*Je t'aime. Appelle-moi chaque soir, et s'il vous plaît, prenez vos médicaments.*" Vipesh walks to his Rivian and drives out of the parking lot.

"He's just messing with you, babe." Harriet brings him in. "He's playing the role of a protective father. *C'est bon.*"

"*Oui, c'est bon.*" He nervously laughs. "Anyway, he won't have time to go after me because he'll be too busy singlehandedly changing the world."

"Well, not singlehandedly. There's still a lot more we should be doing."

"Like what? We won and he's in the house. I did my part."

She rolls her eyes and looks over at me. "Oh, great. T has my last box. Can you take that upstairs? If it's too much I'll do it."

"It's no problem." I let them pass me and walk upstairs with the box; I can balance it with my right hand while holding the rail with my left. It's not too heavy, but it's large and unbalanced. A thirty-second climb takes one-and-a-half minutes with the shift in the centre of gravity.

"Thank you, T." She holds the door to the upstairs door open. I put the box of yoga and meditation stuff on her bed. It's the closest to the window on the opposite side of the door. When the coast is clear, I take my whiteboard off the wall to look at my conspiracy web.

I know what it is, and I'm not ashamed to call it a conspiracy web, or a web I somehow entangled myself in. I still believe Mr. Riviera has something to do with it. He has the most connections: to the plant, the campaign, and the workers, in total, he has ten. Vipesh has one less, and next is Harriet and Sid, who have two each. Everyone else only has one.

Harriet barges into our room with Kyle. I quickly turn the whiteboard around and hang it on my wall. "So here it is. It's cozy, and my roommate seems pretty cool." Harriet nods at me.

Kyle rolls his eyes. I furrow my brows and stare at his forehead. He shuffles backwards in a fright.

"Be nice, she's not a serial killer. You should look at it when I'm fully moved in, and preferably with less people." She hands me a mug of chai, mouthing the words 'thank you'. I start to sip. Something tastes off about it. I know she uses oat milk, as it's the best of the plant-based milks to pair with chai, but it doesn't hit the same.

"Fewer people," he says. "Preferably with fewer people."

"But it's nice. *N'est-ce pas?* The view is decent. You can see…" Harriet jumps on her bed and looks out the window. "…an entire parking lot from here." She squints for a few seconds. "Sid's just sitting in his car. What's he doing?"

"Sid's just being Sid." Kyle scoffs and pulls Harriet to him, collapsing on the bed next to him. She caresses his face.

"Now, that's my cue to leave." I take the mug and exit so they can have the room to themselves.

I sit out in the hall and continue to drink the chai. I wonder how our roommate situation will work. Harriet is much more social than Veera. Will I need to kick myself out of our room when she wants to be alone with Kyle? Once I finish drinking, Kyle leaves our room. I place the mug in the dishwasher, then open the door to our room.

"*Ferme la porte!*" Harriet yells. I continue to walk in. "Don't you knock, T?" She's sitting on the floor, staring at the back of my whiteboard. "How long have you been working on this?" I push her away, take the board, and hang it back up. My leg isn't locked, so I almost take a nosedive to the ground. Harriet catches me before I fall. I get off my bed as she puts my whiteboard back up.

"Only a few days. Why?"

"Because it looks like the vision board of a serial killer."

"Why did you take it down?"

"I just noticed something was sticking out, like a black piece of yarn, but much thicker and... fibrous." She pauses and glances at me. She jumps off my bed and lands right in front of me, then touches all around my neck and head. She feels around my head for what is underneath. "*Oh, mon Dieu.* Is that why you're suddenly wearing a hijab? Is that your hair?" Her French accent slips as she yells.

For the past two weeks, I have been losing sleep and clumps of my hair keep falling out. I have just been wearing a scarf and trying not to draw attention to the bald patches on my head. I keep telling them I'm fine; I know I'm lying, and I know I'm fidgeting with my hair more and more.

After four and a half years, I decided to cut my hair so I wouldn't have something to play with. It happened the same way it did in my vision; I put in elastics and cut it, so only nine inches remained on my head. As it turns out, the scissors in my hand were not that bad. Sharp objects in other people's possession are scary. Then I got the idea to make the board a couple of days later, and I figured since I had long strands to connect the important events, I might as well make good use of it. It's not like I would show it to anyone else, except Veera, and now Harriet. I had only used about ten percent of my hair, and the rest was still in a bag in a closet ready to go if I see more connections. I fashioned it into a thread just by rolling it around. It had the strength to maintain its shape.

It started as one strand connecting the nuclear plant explosion to Mr. Riviera. And I thought maybe it also related to the election, to a rise in polls, and before I knew it, I had a whole web.

"I know this can look a little off-putting, but it's all in service to an investigation I'm trying to solve." I pause, waiting for Harriet to interrupt me again.

"So this is why you have been annoying everyone in my physics class. Take a good look at yourself."

"No one told you to look at this or to take my whiteboard off the walls, and no one told you to snoop around my room," I scream at her.

Harriet hangs her head. "You're right." She takes her pill bottle out of her box. "I overstepped. I should have just told you about that loose end." She falls to the ground, sitting on her feet and back resting on the bedframe. "We are supposed to be roommates. But our first day together is off to a terrible start. I'm sorry, comrade." She sighs heavily. Her head dangles weakly on her neck as she looks at the floor.

Very few people get to know the real Harriet Ganatra. She's not always the charming, extroverted girl she presents herself to be. I join her on the floor.

"It's just that I did not expect for my dad's leaving to hit me this hard. It's been the two of us for ten years, and now he's gone."

"I get it." I envy her ability to sit comfortably anywhere, especially on her feet. "I haven't seen my mother in around ten months." I try to sympathize, but I shut my eyes shamefully. Our pains are not the same. I haven't seen my mother in less than ten months. She hasn't seen hers in almost ten years; she has no parents now. "I'm sorry—"

"Don't apologize. It's fine." She does not change her expression or her posture.

I move my head under her face to look at her. "I don't know what it is like to lose one parent. But I want to give you something you've never had."

She looks up a little.

"Because we are more than just comrades. We're sisters."

She's still sad, but she's looking at me and not at the ground. "I think I failed already."

"You're doing a great job so far. Veera and I had problems when we were sleeping in the same room. But now we're the best of friends." I scratch behind my neck, I think Veera might resent me now. "We fight, but we always call each other out on our shit, and we never go to bed angry." I lean up against the bed again. "Varshil and Vijay don't always get along, but they band together when they want to irritate the crap out of me. We, too, will present a united front."

She looks into my eyes, tilting her head and fluttering her eyelids while a smile slowly creeps onto her face. I mirror her expression and her smile grows as a result. "Can I tell you something?"

I nod. She brings her bottle of antidepressants to me. "I know this will sound silly, but I thought when my dad got elected, something would have changed."

She's not the only one. My impending death visions haven't changed. "I have been taking these things more often. I feel bloated from excessive use." Harriet shakes the bottle. Only about three or four pills rattle in the container. "Sometimes, I don't think they work. But I know this always does." She sets her pill bottle aside and touches my shin tube, just above my pylon.

"Surround yourself with people who make you happy. People who make you laugh, who help you when you're in need. People who genuinely care. They are the ones worth keeping in your life. Everyone else is just passing through," I effortlessly quote. Harriet may not have her father anymore, but she has four people in this apartment who care for her. And soon, it will be six.

"Marx?" She giggles. "Nice. I do want positive change, and even with my dad in the house, we have a lot of work to do."

"Yes, we do," I tell her. She quickly lunges towards me and places her arms around my body. The hug pushes my spine backwards, gently cracking it on my metal bed frame. She nuzzles her left cheek on my scarf as I hear her giggle slightly. I place my arms around her and join her embrace.

I don't know why I thought Yasmine was my best friend. Ever since she and Sid got back together, we haven't been as close. Harriet, however, has always been here for me, even when she lived in Montreal, and I want to do the same for her. Even though she has Kyle, she still makes time for me, and if something greater happens between Krishna and me, I won't let it change us.

She releases her grip and jumps up, removing her sweatshirt to reveal her form-fitting tank top. I believe her when she says she feels bloated but she looks great. "Thank you." She brings her suitcase and box of yoga stuff into our shared step-in closet, then unrolls her yoga mat on the carpet. She lies on her stomach and pushes herself into an upward dog.

"Your police procedural board is kind of impressive. At first, I freaked out when I saw hair and tape and pictures of our faces. But I guess I would be a hypocrite if I didn't believe in repurposing materials." She laughs and transitions into a runner's pose. "I guess it's harmless. You can have obsessions, as long as you're not hurting yourself or anyone else." She completes a warrior pose. "Care to join me?"

"After you cracked my spine, I'm going to do Shavasana on my bed." I get up off the floor and then collapse on my bed. I check the time on my phone: five p.m. I close my eyes.

Part 4.2: Ice Cold Lips
Sidney, November 12th, 13:00

In physics class, I think we are learning about kinematics, but I can't focus. I'm sitting right next to Harriet, and I'm formulating an escape plan if she wants to get me to open up about my feelings.

After the office party for Mr. Ganatra, she said she wanted to be there for me, and she has been for the past two weeks. And when I spoke to Mr. Ganatra about what she was doing, he did the same thing. Mother has returned to work with no serious health complications for over a month now.

But when Mr. Ganatra said: "What does your mother love above all else?" he threw me off. I couldn't answer his question. She's my mother, so I knew I could say she loved her children more than everything else; but it's a reductive way of thinking about who she is as a woman. I've known her my entire life, but I don't know much about her life before me.

I sat in my car for ten minutes pondering the question, then drove home. Mom gave me a time limit to help Harriet move to Islington. Afterwards, I gave Mother the keys as she read on her Kindle. She asked me how I did on my physics test. I told her it went well.

Waves come to me far more intuitively than energy, kinematics, or power because I can see their behaviour as they propagate out of my head. I even learned about chemical compositions and what different molecules looked like at an atomic scale. I just have to count the number of protons in the atom and make the reaction by pushing small amplitude waves at these particles. I have been getting much stronger migraines, but it's worth it to further my learning.

Every day I scan Mother's head, trying to see if another tumour will develop, and so far none have.

"Sid?" Mr. Glass hands me back my test. "Congratulations."

"Thank you." I look at my scantron and see I got a ninety on the bottom. This has never happened to me, and not even to Mindy. I could have gotten more if I studied harder, but I'm still proud of my result.

"What did you guys get?" Yasmine asks us. "Seventy-eight."

"Seventy," Kyle answers first.

"Eighty-eight." Harriet smiles and turns her test to the group.

"Not too good," I lie. "Sixty-nine."

"Really?" Yasmine responds.

"Nice," Kyle and Harriet say simultaneously.

"Maybe that is why Mr. Glass congratulated you," Kyle responds.

I'm not typically one to make those kinds of jokes, because they don't originate organically. I just chose the lowest mark out of the four of us and subtracted one point. Harriet would get the highest, followed by Yasmine, then Kyle, and finally me.

"If you think about it, though," Kyle puts an arm on my shoulder. "It's more impressive that Sid got that. He knew which answers to get right and wrong to get the perfect number."

I bring my index finger right beside my nose and swiftly flick in his direction.

The bell dismisses us to our two-hour spare. "Anyway, I'll see you guys later." I get up and walk out the door to my locker, which I have only started using right after losing the car.

"Sid," Harriet calls me before I exit the room. "Come to Gatineau with us."

"Sorry." I politely decline their invitation. I don't want to go with them, partly because I do not want another Harriet lecture, this time with Yasmine around. "I have a lot of homework."

"Oh, right, it's Friday," Harriet says. "Can you skip whatever it is you do?"

I haven't seen Mr. Riviera in weeks, nor do I plan on it today. I didn't show up for the last two meetings, yet I could hear him in my dreams every Friday night. I don't typically remember dreams; they usually disappear the second I wake up, but the ones with Mr. Riviera stick with me. Regardless, I do have a lot of homework. We have to write a pre-lab for the upcoming titration experiment and the essay is due on Monday. I budgeted my work to do everything on Friday to have enough free time to spend with Yasmine.

"Come on, Pineapples." Yasmine tugs at my arm. "It'll be fun."

"We're still on for Saturday, right?" I ask her, and she nods. I kiss her goodbye and walk away.

On Saturday, I'm planning to go downtown with her, maybe go to a tearoom, but I would want her in a calm setting so I could have a serious conversation about the trajectory of our new relationship. The first week back as boyfriend and girlfriend has been great, but we have fallen back into our old personalities. We both recognize the problems between us, but nothing has fundamentally changed. I'm still acting like someone I hate, albeit to a lesser extent. I don't want to break up, but I don't know how to progress.

However, the biggest reason I need to sit down with her is because I cannot get on her parents' good side. Even though she forgave me, her parents still see me as the guy who tried to drown their daughter. They disagree on almost everything but are united on this one issue, and Yasmine is fully aware. She claims she doesn't care, but I couldn't, in good conscience, let her ruin her relationship with her parents.

"*Pourquoi?*" Harriet exclaims as I turn away. "We need to enjoy the fall colours while we still can. Skip this one Friday."

I walk away from the conversation and into the library, but find it is too loud to work. Usually, if I want quiet, I sit in my car, but I can't anymore.

I give up and decide to go home. I will have the house all to myself. Kat still has school. Mom, Mother, and Mindy are still at their respective jobs. As I walk towards my locker, Kyle stations himself in my path near my locker.

"I take it Harriet did not drag you on her nature walk?" he teases me. "Why?"

I stare at his forehead. I have been practicing reading minds with Tikha when she asked me about the Nuclear Plant explosion, and that's frankly all she thinks about when I get close to her. It sucks because I can only read her mind, when I would rather read literally anyone else's.

"I'm not in the mood right now." I stick my head into my locker.

"You know." He takes a step closer to me. I quietly grab my *Macbeth* and *King Lear* copies and chemistry textbook and drop them in my backpack. "Ever since you discovered that you could shoot waves out of your head, you have changed."

"Yeah, no shit. People change after a chemical explosion, even if nothing else does." My home life certainly is not any different. Even after Mom and Mindy's feud a month ago, Mindy resumed her rigorous school and work schedule. Even though Mother is close to being unemployed, she still needs to go back periodically to help decommission the plant. Mom's dream of having everyone home once a week became unrealistic, as everyone's too busy for family time.

"I know chemically you have changed, but also emotionally. You're not the same plucky boy you used to be. What happened to our plans to fight crime together?" Kyle asks.

"Firstly, you can't do anything," I snap back. "But I will stand up to any evil supervillain I come across in the future. However, right now, at this moment, I have my own shit to deal with, which means you and your girlfriend need to stop bothering me." I shut my locker, but he obstructs my path. I try to push him away but can't make him budge.

"Oh. This is about what Harriet's dad said." He smirks. "You don't need to worry about that, there's nothing you can do."

"It's not about that," I argue, and without telling him he's wrong, I stand my ground. "But while we're on the topic, can you tell Harriet to stop with the existential morality speeches?"

He lowers his arm. "You can ask her, she's a free woman. But now I know it is about what Vipesh said. Why else are you being so distant? It's not like you at all."

"Maybe you would know what it's like if you had parents present in your life." I grab my hoodie, slip it on, and hoist my knapsack over my shoulder.

He puts his arm back to block me from leaving. "I manage fine, and even if you lose your mother, you still have a backup."

I slam my locker shut.

"Come on." He nervously chuckles. "It's just a joke...because you have two moms. I didn't mean anything by it. We joke about it all the time; you poke fun at my parents' divorce and how they leave me in the house all the time. Don't be more offended than they would be."

Without blinking, I focus on his jaw. I start breathing in and out through my nose, teeth grinding, and fists clenched. I zoom in on each cell through his skin and see the influx of airborne particles flowing through his mouth.

"For as long as I have known you, Kyle, you've had such a bad habit of running your mouth." I take a step closer to him and crane my neck. "First, it was because of your indecisiveness, but since last summer you have been acting more like a douche, tossing me around like your very own ragdoll and saying whatever the hell you want. Frankly, I've had it."

I zoom in so that I can look at his atomic structure. Resting atop his moist lips are a cluster of vibrating water droplets inside a droplet. I shoot a wave at each particle to dampen their movement. These water droplets freeze on both his upper and lower lips.

I look into his eyes. "You really need to learn when to shut up."

"Mnph" He tries to inhale. His teeth move inside his mouth, but he can't make out words. He drops his right hand, and his backpack and water bottle clang on the hard-tiled floor. He places his hands over his mouth, then collapses on the floor, squirming around.

The remaining people near us stop whatever they are doing and form a circle around Kyle as he rolls around on the floor. I leave through the crowd's frenzy.

I don't know why he couldn't speak. If he loses one way of communicating, he has a backup: writing on a notepad. And even with this alternative talking method, nothing can hide the pain and the damage to one's original mouth. Talking will never be the same again. Maybe he'll finally know what it's like to have a debilitating problem thrown into his life without any warning, one he's neither qualified nor mature enough to handle.

I can't help Kyle in this case. I didn't get recertified in First Aid, and there's no procedure for treating ice-cold lips.

No one could determine the real reason he stopped talking; no one saw me touch him. He wasn't coughing up blood, nor did he have a history of asthma. But he does have a history of choking up, especially when it comes to simple dichotomies.

Yasmine and I discussed Harriet and Kyle's relationship a week ago. Yasmine said Kyle changed when he started dating Harriet. I tried to argue that Harriet was not always like she is right now; people bring out certain personality traits, even bringing out the best in each other to be more compatible. I guess Yasmine and I can relate to Kyle and Harriet. How could I not see this change? He improved for Harriet, but he's not the friend I made at the beginning of the ninth grade.

Ambulances stop in front of the school's entrance as I make my way outside. I gulp. Why would he need one? He didn't get frostbite, did he? The paramedics run past me with a stretcher. Mr. Glass greets them at the front entrance.

I exit the building when a cool breeze sweeps across my face and makes me shiver. I zip up my coat and put the hood over my head. It's only ten degrees, which is warmer than usual for Manotick in November.

Harriet keeps telling me it should start to snow about now, or at least drop below zero. In my lifetime, I have never seen it snow until at least early January, and only for a couple of weeks a year. But she's a *Québécoise* girl, so she's probably used to snow in the middle of August and temperatures reaching forty-below.

For the past month, I have been walking everywhere. It's long and monotonous, but peaceful. It only takes about six minutes to get from my house to the school. The scenery's not remarkably beautiful like the trails of Gatineau, nor are they lonely like the nine-minute walk from our house to I&MNG at night, but it's nice. I should give up my parking pass at school.

My eyes start to throb when I get home. I reach into my backpack, grab a bottle of homemade aspirin, and pop a pill into my mouth. I learned the recipe from school, and my knowledge of chemistry helped me make perfect pills. My phone vibrates, notifying me of a couple of missed calls from Harriet.

Part 4.3: Lost in Japan
Sidney, November 12th, 14:30

My forehead drips in anticipation. I unzip my hoodie and sit on my front step. It would be terrible if I ignored her. I never told her about my powers, nor Yasmine. The only person who knows is Kyle, but it's possible he told her. Or maybe she wants to talk. I never told her our conversations about my mother were making me uncomfortable. Maybe I could start there.

I video-call her and she answers within seconds. Her eyeliner is dripping down her face, her cheeks and nose are red, and her lips are trembling.

"Sorry, I could not pick you up earlier. I was in the library. What's wrong?" I inquire.

She blows her nose and wipes her face, smudging a bit of her eyeshadow. "Sorry, I'm a mess right now. I just heard that Kyle was just taken to a hospital." She softly exhales.

"Holy shit," I exclaim. "Why?"

"He couldn't breathe. He hit his head after collapsing, and they had to force open his airway, and, and..." she stammers. "First my dad leaves, now this happens."

I try to act cool. "Is he okay now?" I have gone too far. I just wanted him to be quiet for long enough for me to move away. "Where are you? I'll come to get you, and we can see him." I unlock the door to my house, grab the keys to the Prius, and exit.

"He regained consciousness. He's at Greber right now. His mom told me they're going to keep him at least until tomorrow."

If his mom showed up for this, it must have been severe. "That's good, isn't it?"

"*Oui,*" Harriet answers. "But that's not the reason I called earlier. Kyle will not be able to make it to the movie tomorrow. So, do you want to come?"

Kyle and Harriet were supposed to see this murder mystery-type movie. I'm a fan of Agatha Christie and films with a large central cast of multi-dimensional characters, but I'm not a fan of the theatre experience. I prefer a nice, closed space with friends. "I have plans with Yasmine tomorrow."

Her lower lip trembles a little. "I don't think that's going to happen." She turns her phone to Yasmine, who's about two meters from the screen. I can see her in her entirety. Her backdrop is picturesque—maple, oak, and birch trees lined along a monochromatic gravel path. The leaves are a majestic orange, red, and yellow, one colour entirely designated to a single tree. The ground is completely free from debris or leaves. Yasmine, in all her glory, stands dazed in the middle of the path. Her face is redder and more puffed up. She's having trouble keeping her balance, spinning around with her head in the crook of her arm, sneezing and coughing into it all the while.

"Hey, Pineapples. We just started our walk." Yasmine spins around, sneezing into her shoulder again. "And I'm allergic to everything out here." She coughs violently into her arm, snot dripping down her face.

Harriet turns the camera back to her. "She's on a lot of medication."

Yasmine brings the phone to her face. There's no more background, just her puffy yet still beautiful face. "I won't even have time to finish my paper about the collapse of the Soviet Union."

"I'm on my way." I walk towards the Prius.

"We're fine," Harriet interrupts me. "We don't need a 'straight' 'white' 'man' to come to our rescue." She giggles while using air quotes around all the adjectives. "Worst case scenario, we'll take a cab." She turns the phone back to her. "Although I do wish you'd come."

"You mean I should have driven you guys there?" I joke.

"No, I know you lost your car privileges, and I don't want a ride in your green-washed toy, either. You would really like these trails, there are no bugs anywhere."

"I'll see about the movie. I have some homework to complete. Thanks for the offer."

"Bye, Sid." Yasmine also waves goodbye and blows me a kiss. I turn off my phone. Maybe it's possible to finish my homework and then go with Harriet.

I re-enter my house and put the keys back in the bowl near the front door. Our dining room table appears to have a bright yellow candle. It's inside one of our glasses, and there doesn't appear to be a label. It smells exactly like our garden. I don't know where we could have gotten it.

I grab my backpack and head to my room, then take out my books and laptop and spread them across my desk. Since I aced physics, chemistry is my worst subject by far. My job for the titration pre-lab is to write up a procedure to titrate acids and buffers into a strong base. I have to just copy the textbook and formulate a hypothesis based on what I learned in class. I should be doing this with Harriet; she knows chemistry better than I do.

Tikha also does well, but as far as I know, she only understands what to do on the day of the experiment. And while I have no proof of this claim, she never seems to have her work done until the night before, or sometimes the morning of class. I could never ask for her help, because she always changes the subject.

Since a couple of weeks ago, she has been hounding everyone in my physics class about the nuclear plant explosion, even though it happened more than a month ago. I indulged her at first because I can humour a good mystery, but it has been getting a little intrusive. She's even talking to Mom at her precinct. And her 'investigation' is taking a toll on her mental health. According to Harriet, her service at her family's restaurant has caused many people to leave unsatisfied reviews. She'll tire herself out eventually, although I thought the same thing about Harriet and her consoling lectures; those Ganatra girls are extremely persistent.

I finish the chemistry lab, and while taking a break, I begin reading *The Awakening* for the second time.

Although I don't need to grind tonight. Since Yasmine won't be available tomorrow, I can take my time this weekend. I alternate between doing my homework and looking at the pictures she and Harriet had posted online. They look fantastic in the autumn foliage. Yasmine poses, holding on to a tree, popping her leg up, while Harriet is squatting right next to her. Another picture has Harriet in a deep, meditative stand, sitting underneath a maple tree, closing her eyes and putting her hands on her lap. There are many pictures of Harriet showing off her flexibility.

Suddenly, the lights in my room go out and the Wi-Fi disconnects. I groan and close my laptop, and at the same time hear the clatter of metallic cookware on the kitchen floor.

Ever since the plant shut down, we have been experiencing many intermittent power outages. Mother told us Islington wasn't designed to accommodate the extra load capacity necessary to service the gap left by I&MNG. She also mentioned all the equipment and material was sold to other nuclear facilities across Canada. It's a rare case where no one's happy: not environmentalists, the economy, or the citizens of either town. The only people who benefit are the people picking at the carcasses of I&MNG.

I run out of my room and to the kitchen to find Mother on the floor holding her head.

"Mother?" Her head has a little bit of a bump. I zoom in even further and don't see any cancerous cells. She's healthy; I sigh in relief and help her back onto her feet.

"Can you get me an ice pack? And a couple of ice cubes." She picks up the pot on the floor. "But don't keep the freezer open for too long." I oblige and retrieve the objects for her. She puts the ice pack on her head and the ice cubes in a bowl of water.

The power comes on shortly; the oven timer reboots, and the kettle beeps. The lights turn back on and illuminate the kitchen counter. There's a bowl of soaked and uncooked rice, ice-cold water, rice vinegar, long, thin strips of cucumbers and imitation crab, avocados marinated in a spice mixture, dried sheets of seaweed, a tube of wasabi, and a jar of ginger slices. She has already completed three rolls of sushi.

"Are you making sushi?" I don't remember the last time she cooked for us. Mother would usually come home from her shift at seven at night, and either Mom or Mindy would be the ones to make dinner. "Do you know what you are doing?"

"It does not take that much electricity to make. And there are some things you never forget. It's my first day of being unemployed, and I have so much free time. I can travel to Islington to pick up all these specialty ingredients." She takes a large chef's knife in her right hand and takes one of the rolls, slicing it into seven pieces. She cuts an imitation crab roll cleanly, as they are all approximately the same height, and even the end piece looks appetizing. "You know I gave this to your mom the first time we met."

"I don't remember sushi in the scavenger hunt," I inquire.

"The university scavenger hunt was only the ending. It's a really long story."

I stand up straight. "There's more?"

"It's a little heavy, so be warned."

I nod; maybe I could learn a little more about the woman I'm trying to save and answer Mr. Ganatra's question.

"I guess you are old enough." She turns on the kettle and starts to boil some water. She removes the bandana from her head and reveals her surgical scar. The hair on her forehead is regrowing, although I could still see the original incision starting and ending on both of her temples. "I was younger than

Katherine, only five years old. It was a scary time. I was living in Japan with my father, and I had one of the worst migraines of my life. I was bedridden on a Friday morning, and I could not attend school. I felt my body shake, but as it turns out, it was the aftershock of an earthquake.

"I was scooped out of my bed by a neighbour. We left our apartment and got to higher ground, because as it turned out, a tsunami breached our seawall. He took me far from our apartment because it was in the twenty-kilometre exclusion zone. While my father tended to a power emergency, we hid away as we watched the flood wash over our town.

"Many lives were lost in the aftermath. The Japanese government was unable to locate my father, and with nowhere else to go, they sent me to Tokyo and put me in a home for other lost kids. I experienced the longest four years of my life; everyone and everything I knew was gone. I rarely left my room and only communicated through a tablet. One day I was alone in my room, while all the other children were playing outside, and I heard somebody screaming, but not in Japanese.

"I recognized some words, like 'Momma', 'Daddy', and 'Help', then saw a red-headed, Caucasian girl getting pushed around by pedestrians. It was a busy street, but she stuck out to no one except me. I tapped on the window until she saw me.

"I directed her to come to the courtyard using hand signals, then I brought my tablet to translate everything. Then I notified my caretaker about her situation, and he tried to contact anyone he could to get hold of her parents. In the meantime, she told me she was hungry, so I shared my lunch with her, this exact meal. She told me her name, 'Gen with a G', because I would keep calling her Sen. Even though we could not speak each other's languages, we connected. We spent nine hours together, and she never left my side. Afterward, her parents picked her up. They were upset that I fed her seafood but grateful I found her. The family of Canadian tourists never returned to Japan.

"But I never forgot her, and every boy I dated after meeting her did not make me feel the same way she did. I had to see her again; I learned English by taking courses in school and by listening to *girl in red* I proceeded to 'stalk' her online to find out where she was in the world. When I found her, I pretended to get lost during the scavenger hunt. She won't admit it, but I did sucker her into going out with me. She told me, 'Here's my number; let me know if you get lost again'."

Mother picks up the rice and tastes it; she takes it off the element and brings it to the cutting board lined with seaweed. She puts the pot down, walks over to the dining room entrance, and looks out to our backyard. "If your mom were to tell this same story, she would tell you that I saved her that day forty years ago, but she got me to come out of my room and made me feel less alone; I wouldn't be where I am without her."

I momentarily lose balance and catch myself on the kitchen counter. I have no words.

A few seconds later, a muffled "holy shit" comes from the ceiling.

Mother looks up. "Sometimes I forget how thin the walls in this house are." She looks back at me. "Sidney? Are you okay?" She helps me up off the counter.

I spring towards her and hug her. "Why didn't you tell us about this?"

"I wanted to wait until you were mature enough. I told myself by not telling you I was protecting you—but protecting you from what?" She sighs softly and we separate from our embrace. "The real reason is that I wasn't ready to tell you until now, but I cannot hide this part of myself anymore. I didn't tell your mom my story until years after we were married." She evens out the bed of rice and spreads it over the dried seaweed. "I never wanted you, Mindy, or Katherine to go through what I did, but I should have told you so you could better prepare yourselves for such an eventuality, like my episodes. And I feel like I failed as a parent."

I grab my chest and stammer, trying to think of something just as beautiful to say. "You worked with radioactive materials," I lament. "Every time I hear reported crime on the news, I worry about Mom. Both of you always made us worry about your state of being; by those metrics alone, you did great."

The wrinkles on her forehead disappear as a smile grows around her eyes and below her cheeks. I don't remember the last time she made that face. The room starts to feel much brighter.

"I guess I have finally become an old woman, regaling you with tales from half a century ago about how hard life used to be. It's only a matter of time until you have to help me go to the bathroom."

"No," I interject. "And please don't joke about that."

"Sorry." She spins around. "But do you have any questions?"

"No, I just..." I exhale sharply. "I just wanted what you two had for so long." I shrug my shoulders. "But I guess I am having doubts about Yasmine."

She rushes over to my side and grabs my shoulders. "What's wrong? Did Yasmine break my baby's heart again?"

I shake my head. "It's just that we got back together under the pretense that things were changing for the better. But I don't think anything has changed between us. And we are still making the same mistakes."

Mother runs her hand through my hair. "Oh, Sidney, I saw this coming from a mile away. There is someone else, isn't there?"

"Who?" I ask, genuinely curious as to why she would think that. "Kyle, Tikha, Emilia?" I gulp. "Harriet?" I raise my voice sharply.

She tilts her head at me, raising an eyebrow. "You did say you wanted a relationship like your mom and mine. You two met as young children, became friends, lost touch for a decade, and reconnected as young adults. And on top of everything, a nuclear disaster forced its way into your stories. Do I need to go on?"

"No!" I yell. "I have been avoiding her for the past two weeks."

She giggles.

"Not like that," I correct her. "She has been overly sentimental, trying to get me to open up my feelings about you...in a worst-case scenario." I regret saying it, but I'm telling the truth, and she would appreciate it.

"I'm not going to be around forever, but I'm also not going away anytime soon. She cares about you, more than any other friend you have ever had." She grabs my face with a firm grip again. "I remember when you were younger. You were quite the reserved, prickly child. It's one of the few things you've inherited from me. Opening up is hard, but Harriet cracked you. And because of her hard work, the rest of us found the very soft, sweet interior you got from your mom."

I move her hand down. "I thought you liked Yasmine."

"I do like Yasmine. She's funny, intelligent, beautiful, and loves you for you. But if she's not making you happy, that's what I care about the most. You two were very cute at first, but cuteness doesn't last forever. As you get older, you might want something different, someone that might challenge you, and I can think of no better person than Harriet." She starts pinching my cheek. "I think you know she loves pineapples." She licks her lips in a cartoonish way and starts moving my arm to her mouth, biting air, acting as if she wants to devour me.

"Mother." I remove my arm from her grasp. "Stop that. I'm not a baby anymore. It's just weird."

She gives me an insincere frown, dragging a fake tear down her cheek. "You could be fifty years old, married with three kids, and running the biggest company in the world, and you will still be my little Pineapple." Mother turns around with a lighter step.

It's ridiculous to suggest I'm falling for Harriet. There's too much history between us. Also, she's with Kyle.

The front door swings open, and a heavily-uniformed Mom emerges from the foyer. "Miriam, something smells good." Mom embraces Mother from behind and kisses her while taking the scarf around her neck and throwing it over her shoulder. She walks over to me, kissing me on the top of my head. "And that candle on the table? Did you make that?"

"Yes, I used all the remaining vegetables from our garden." Mother completes another roll. "I spoke to Mindy; she'll be coming home tonight. We will finally all be under the same roof."

Mom quietly cheers. She walks up to me and smiles, kissing me on the forehead. "How was your day, Sidney?"

"It was pretty good; I got a ninety on my physics test."

"That's great, baby." She lifts me, spins me around, and places me back down. "I'm so proud of you."

"And here I was worried you were taking too much after your mom." Mother takes strips of cucumbers and imitation crab, placing them on the bed of rice. "But you probably don't want to follow in my footsteps anymore. You'll have plenty of time to decide what you want to do with your life. Maybe something today jogged your creative muscles."

"I don't know about that. The only other thing that happened today is Kyle being sent to the hospital. That didn't do much to inspire me." I cringe at how dismissively I reveal his hospitalization.

"Sidney. Why did you not lead with that?" Mom grabs me again. "Is he okay? How are you feeling? Should I call Maria?" She looks over to an unconcerned Mother.

"He's fine; Harriet told me he had trouble breathing." I try to break free, but Mom knows how to restrain me effectively.

"What did you do to him?" Mother keeps her back to me.

"Nothing," I answer. "He's a foot taller and has thirty pounds on me."

"What did you do to him?" she asks again.

"Miriam, we are talking about our son. Do you think he could hurt anyone?" Mom releases me from her grip and manhandles my face, hands, and chest, feeling around for bruises or some other kind of evidence I got maimed. "He's clean. I don't even see any concealer. I'm going to get changed." Mom leaves the kitchen and ascends the creaky stairs to the master bedroom.

Mother cuts the last roll up and arranges the sushi on the tray. "Sidney." She turns to me and looks me up and down. "I'm going to ask you one last time, what did you do to him?"

"What could I even do?" I couldn't tell her what happened because she wouldn't be satisfied with my explanation. I turn away from her and walk out of the kitchen.

"Was it because of Harriet?" Mother continues.

"Nothing is about Harriet." I storm out of the kitchen.

"Then what was it, and if you deny it, you..." She pauses "You..."

A loud thud hits the kitchen floor behind me. "Mother?" I turn around to see her convulsing on the floor. "Mother?" I gasp. Her eyes roll back into her head as she foams from her mouth. I scan her head again, and a small but volatile clump of cells spreads around her frontal lobe, pushing on her skull. I know what I need to do, but have no idea how I can help. When she needs me most, I'm unable to save her. "Mommy?" I tremble, keeping my distance.

The stairs creak loudly as the steps get louder and louder. Mom enters the kitchen. "Sidney, stop standing there like an idiot. Get me a couple of towels."

I zoom out to my normal vision and shake my head. Without much hesitation, I pass her two on the kitchen counter. She places one into Mother's mouth and another underneath her waist. She rolls her into a semi-prone position and then pushes me out of the kitchen. The stairs creak again. "Take care of..." Kat walks into the room and produces an ear-piercing scream at the sight of Mother. I pick her up and drag her into my room, slamming the door behind me. I hug her tight while she sobs uncontrollably. I rub her head and pick her up, trying to make her feel better, but nothing is working. I kneel beside her. "I think it's just going to be the two of us for dinner."

"But what about Mommy?" Kat asks.

"She'll be okay. She told me she's not going away any time soon." I focus on her forehead. "She gets stronger after every episode." I look at her mind on an atomic level, through the hair, skin, bone, and brain. The neurons and cells firing are so complex in their structure. I want to increase the production of dopamine, but have no idea how, or where the happiness centre of her brain is, even if there is one. I'm sure any other person with my abilities would do the same because I have no idea how to console her.

"Not like this." Kat wipes her face on my sweater. "My birth mom left me, and then my dad didn't want me either. And now Mommy's leaving. Am I bad luck?"

I sometimes forget she had a family before us. I don't know how she remembers her biological mother; we had told her she died, but we didn't tell her how. She's eight years old, she can't be feeling guilty.

"Kat?" I look at her and raise her chin with two fingers. She looks up at me with misty eyes and soft, red-brown cheeks. I move her bangs away from her face as I wipe off some of her tears. "This is not your fault. She was yelling at me about what happened to one of my friends." I rest her head between my shoulder and neck.

But what if it is my fault? She had a seizure after confronting me about Kyle, and I unintentionally hurt him.

Paramedics barge into our house, which causes Kat to well up even more. Indistinct chatter comes from the other side of the door. I have no idea how minds work, and looking at her complex cerebral structure makes me feel dumb. I hold her tighter and reassure her everything will be alright.

She pushes me away.

My phone buzzes with a text from Mom.

<u>Coast is clear. Feed Katherine and clean up. Going to the ER.</u>

We exit together. I try to hold her hand, but she swats it away. I grab everything we need for dinner from the kitchen while Kat pouts in her seat. While eating, I ask her what happened with the rest of her day at school, but she doesn't want to talk. I toss some pieces into my mouth to try and goad her into doing the same; she doesn't look at me. She's eating like a grownup, quietly and slowly, and after eating a few pieces of imitation crab, she dismisses herself.

"Kat?" I say with reverence. "Katherine, can you help me clean up?"

"No, Sidney," she barks. "You clean up the mess you made." She runs away without saying another word.

Kat might be partially correct. Mother hates it when we lie to each other; the last time I lied to her was on her hospital bed, and before that, it was right before her second episode. It's my mess; it all leads back to me hurting Kyle. So after cleaning up everything and putting the leftover rolls in containers, I check the time: eight-forty-five p.m. I need to fix this.

Part 4.4: Meeting #8
Sidney, November 12ᵗʰ, 21:00

Why would I break into a nuclear plant just to talk to Mr. Riviera, even though I said I wouldn't go back? Because I'm desperate to fix everything in my life. My powers are the only way I can help Mother. He has never shown me something simple, like healing an open wound or anything physical or applicable, but I'll be more direct with him; no more kowtowing.

When I took swimming lessons, I got into the pool and submerged myself. I was then able to apply those steps to real-life situations. I could hold my breath or save someone who was drowning. If my school taught me the basics of chemistry and physics without lab experiments, I'd complain. I love watching chemicals change. Science would not be as fun without it. And after getting my vision fixed and looking at things on an atomic or cellular level, science has been so much more fascinating. I know there are otherworldly applications to these powers, and I will discover them if it's the last thing I do.

I have taken everything Mr. Riviera said to heart, and I know I'm close to finishing. I had a dream two weeks ago, which would have been the sixth meeting, where I was in the shed at I&MNG with no one else but the disembodied voice of Mr. Riviera. He tells me that I am putting negative energy out. It sounds like hokey pseudo-science, but he explains it takes a consistent effort to keep a clear mindset, and an agitated mind is a dangerous one. I told him about Harriet trying to console me for the past five days and that I could walk away if it bothered me. Otherwise, I need to find a way for it not to bother me. So I did. I walked away from this dream and Harriet anytime she wanted to talk about my mother.

And last week, which would have been the seventh meeting, I had a similar dream where I was in the shed. He just told me to remember the worst day of my life. And I told him aloud that it was the day Mother was admitted, and he said to me that he was scanning my activity. He deduced I had not even felt despair. While it was a bad day, it wasn't bad enough. He said a complete state of hopelessness should help me better understand my livelihood. Because if I were to live ethically, even when nothing goes my way, I could finally progress to the next stage.

Those two dreams felt real because I would pass out on Friday at nine o'clock and wake up less than ten minutes later. Since then, I have been trying to chase the feeling of hopelessness and despair. I thought, 'Perhaps I could study my ass off for a physics test only to get an unsatisfactory grade, and it would make me realize it would be futile to get into university'. However, I aced the test, and my parents approved my choice to not follow in Mother's footsteps.

I arrive at I&MNG, but the gates are locked. The metallic smell is still strong, but the ambient air is much colder. I know Mr. Riviera has some connections, which must be why I was allowed to stroll in every Friday. I climb the fence, snagging my right pant leg on the unelectrified barbed wire. I fall on my stomach. After dusting myself off, I walk through the shed's wide open door.

I take a few steps inside; the door doesn't slam shut like every other lesson.

"Look who's back." I spin around to find something, a shadow, a light, but nothing catches my eye.

I take in the surroundings; the shed's wooden panels have deteriorated even more. The hole in the roof has gotten bigger. The night sky is overcast, and I can hear everything: the occasional car passing by, crickets, and the babbling of the Rideau. "I know, I just want to—"

"Let me stop you right there. I have scanned your mind and your wave production centres. You're not fully developed."

"Tell me how to get better at using these powers," I order. "It's an emergency. And don't give me this 'I'm not ready' bullshit," I scream. "Lives are at stake. I'm trying to be better; I'm trying to help people. You fixed my eyes; I want to learn what you did."

"How far have you gotten in your medical school degree?" he mocks.

"What? This is about our powers. Just show me how—"

"Do you think I magicked my way into fixing your eyes?" he asked. *"I guess my experience in ophthalmology and quantum mechanics means nothing to you."*

"Going through medical school would take eight years. She can't wait that long."

"Why do you want to be super powerful?"

"Who wouldn't? I don't need a reason."

"And yet you still have one and need to say it, to me and to yourself. Your mind cannot develop if you keep it sheltered. You can't force development."

He doesn't seem to remember he forced development during our second meeting in early October. He manufactured the perfect scenario for me to feel fear. I legitimately thought he would assault me in an empty shack.

"That was not the fear you felt that night," he chuckles. *"Fear is deeply rooted in your psyche. You did feel it for the first time that day, but it came much earlier."*

I was scared that I could have died during the explosion.

"Not that; dig deeper."

I was also afraid of losing Mother. If I lived in another country, she could be dead due to a low-grade tumour. I can't be the man of the house; I'm still a kid. I don't know shit about anything, and it's not her time; I only just started to get to know this amazing woman and there's so much more to her life. And I couldn't even console my younger sister; she deserves every opportunity in the world as I did. These facts make me feel powerless.

"Fine, I plan on using my powers for selfish reasons, but it does not negate the fact that I am trying to help someone," I scream. "Just help me!"

"I guess you have completed your transformation from a naïve small-town boy into a whiny little bitch."

I clench my teeth as hard as I can. "Do you think this is funny?"

"I think it's funny that you think you are owed something. If I tell you you're not ready, then that's final. But if you'd like a second opinion, you can go seek one." His laughter echoes in my head. *"Right, you can't detect other people's brainwaves, because you're not developed enough."*

"Where are you?" I yell. "You've seen what I did to Kyle. That was nothing." I know I can handle myself against him. The last time I saw him was during our fifth meeting, the Friday after the election. His stoop shrunk him to my height, and he wore large-rimmed glasses as any old man would. He was stuttering his words, shaking and shuffling with every step. He had used his powers for too long and started to look much older than his mid-to-late-seventies.

He asked me about my life and who I was before I met him. I told him I was just a normal kid who aspired to work at the nuclear plant and follow in Mother's footsteps or work alongside her. He could sense I was lying and knew I never wanted it for myself. He instructed me that if I didn't tell her soon, I would resent her for the rest of my life. He suggested that I should tell my parents the truth.

I asked him if this was the current path he wanted. He didn't say another word.

"Come out and face me, asshole," I scream. "Or are you scared?"

I change my field of vision to the Infrared Spectrum, but there's no warm body anywhere.

"I'm not here, Sidney."

A sharp pit builds up in my stomach and buckles my knees. I left Kat home alone for no reason.

"And I know what you did to your tall friend. You instigated that fight; you took things too far and now you are suffering something we old people call 'consequences'. But I can help. Do you want to fast-track your expansion?"

"Yes." I get up and smile a little bit. "I'll do anything."

"Leave!" he yells, and that awful ear-splitting ring returns. I hug my head as the wood creaks louder and louder. *"It's your fault she's sick."*

"It's not my fault." I defend myself, "Sure I sometimes stress her out, but what kid doesn't? It's not my fault lies cause her extra stress."

"So you know you cause your mother extra stress and yet you keep doing it? What's wrong with you? But even if that wasn't the case, you have an unhealthy codependent relationship with her. So build yourself anew, but don't get caught."

This disembodied voice is now suggesting something completely counterintuitive. After everything I did today, I couldn't even think about leaving.

"I had given up my family to become powerful. It's a necessary sacrifice. Any loved ones will become obstacles to hold you back."

Based on what Harriet has told me about Mr. Riviera, very little is known about his personal life. He kept his family out of the media's spotlight. There are videos of him dating back twenty or thirty years in his early campaign days, but there's no mention of a wife, sibling, or descendants.

"It's not easy," he explains. *"These progressions shouldn't come easy. I had just discovered that I did some terrible things to the people I cared for when other people threatened them."*

A gust of wind blows into my right ear, across my face, and cools down my already cold body.

"You felt that?"

I nod.

"I just felt your head nod up and down. Your mind is expanding, but it's not enough. I have just been trying to get you to act out, but you are resilient, which is not good in this case."

He doesn't care about me. "This is an emergency," I murmur.

"It's always an emergency. Your generation wants everything done fast and doesn't care about the chaos it might bring. That's just not how it works."

"Just because that's how you did it doesn't mean that's how I want to do it. I'm daring you to have a free and open mind."

"Go home, Sidney." The shack shakes again as dust rains down from the ceiling. *"I can't help someone unwilling to learn the right way. You are dismissed. Live your life, and soon you will be ready. This was never meant to be a weekly occurrence. I will return when you are ready or need me most."*

"What about you?" I ask. "What are you going to do?"

"The same thing."

The ringing in my ears stops and the sounds of the river and outdoors return.

He's not here. I'm alone.

His teachings are incredibly hypocritical. So I'm supposed to reject my old lifestyle, but I must adhere to his definition of normalcy? He doesn't recognize a time of crisis, and for what? These vague platitudes can only take me so far, but he still owes me actual lessons on how to more effectively handle my powers. He's wasting my time, running out the clock of her life. What does he gain from Mother's suffering? His family must have been delighted when he left.

I climb over the gate out of I&MNG, narrowly avoid the barbed wire, and land safely on the ground outside the facility, then walk for nine minutes and hop over the fence into our boring backyard. There are no figs on the trees, no mishmash of vegetables or grapes; everything has been picked clean.

I slide open my bedroom window and crawl through. We live in a low-crime neighbourhood, so I don't worry about people sneaking in or stealing.

A small migraine envelops me. I get an aspirin from my bag, but I need to wash it down. At this point, I can probably condense the humidity in the air, but I don't want to exacerbate my migraine. It would be easier to turn on a faucet.

Sometimes it's hard to get molecules and atoms to orient themselves correctly, as they are unpredictable and fast-moving. Observing them at an atomic scale means that I only had a small window to see. I already know I can rip apart carbon dioxide molecules from my never-ending supply of breathing to make oxygen and carbon soot. Matter cannot be created or destroyed, but I can extract the elements from thin air.

I fill up a glass and walk back to my room. The light turns on. I freeze.

"Hey, bro," someone on the couch says, but it's not Mother; it's Mindy. She's lying on the couch upside-down, reading on the Kindle, head on the floor and feet on the window. Seeing her home on Friday night is a surprise. "You know I could see you climb over the fence from our couch."

She might as well have told me to get on my knees. She's going to own me for life. "What do you want?" I hold myself up and decide to be the bigger man. I won't use my powers on my sister.

"Nothing." She frowns. "I was just saying what I saw outside. You have a valid reason to be out at this hour. But maybe you want to dispose of the evidence." She gestures down to my torn pant leg, then somersaults off the couch and stands up straight.

I walk up to her, and after one whiff, I deduce that she, too, has been out.

She reeks of fruit juice, peppermint, and something eighty-proof or higher. As far as I know, she has never consumed alcohol. She doesn't even drink caffeine to heighten her senses or get massages for relaxation because it would mess up her natural circadian rhythm, and waiting in lines is too unpredictable with her well-crafted schedule.

Now, she's standing up straight, her hair is blown out, and she's wearing a dark shade of lipstick smudged on the left side of her face. The pronounced concentration wrinkles on her forehead are gone. She's practically glowing, and that's before I even notice the figure-revealing, dark blue sequined dress she's wearing.

"What have you done to my sister?" I cautiously back away. She runs to me, grabs my hands, and pulls me into her warm embrace. She places her head on my shoulder and rubs her cheek against it. It's more affection than I have gotten from her in a year: two hands, each hand placed firmly on my back, constricting me as painfully as Mom does.

"I dropped out," she proudly announces.

I release myself from her hug and drop my jaw.

"After getting a call from Kat, I realized that I have been a bad sister and an even worse daughter. I need to be more involved."

"What. The. Hell," I scream. "So life gets too real and you decide to drop out and drown your sorrows in alcohol?" I shake my hands, gesturing to her sparkling dress. "You are way too intelligent to become a teen mom, and this family has too much on our plate." Her expression doesn't change.

She smooths the creases in her outfit. "I only went out once. My friends took me for a night, and I never felt better. But I'm back now, and I'm going to take care of Mother for as long as she needs me."

I don't believe what I'm hearing. "Do you know how to take care of her? Do you know what she needs? Does Mom know?" The pitch of my voice rises with every question.

"Mom knows. I can learn everything she needs. It will be a lot of work, but she deserves it." She keeps her joyful tone.

"Why can you not just reduce your workload? People find ways to prioritize work, family, and life."

"You know I can't do that." She frowns. "I keep telling Mom, 'One more paragraph', but she sees through it. I always overexert myself, leaving our family on the back burner. You went to the hospital a month ago and I didn't even bat an eye. And for that, I'm sorry, Sidney." She takes a breath and then smiles. "But now I can focus one hundred percent of my energy on us. And I'm just putting my future on hold until Mother no longer needs my help. It's only fair. She did it for us." She drags me to the kitchen table and we take our usual spots. She lifts the glass candle off the table and examines it. It surprisingly has more than ninety percent of its wax. "She made this from the stuff in our garden. This is what she wanted to do with her life; it's why we spent so much time there as children. I saw old videos of her on *Dragons' Den*. She tried to pitch her products and get funding from the Dragons, but none wanted the opportunity. After starting up an online store and going into debt, she stopped selling at boutiques and took a job at the nuclear plant, working long hours, but making enough so we could live comfortably. Our mother took a job that gives her PTSD but made the world a better and safer place, just for us." She puts the candle down. "I know she was tough on you—"

"She's hard on me because she's MY mother," I cut her off. "So why don't you fix your failed relationship with your mom?"

Our parents believed it was best to raise Mindy and me without revealing each other's biological mother. They hid pregnant pictures of themselves as well as medical records so we could never figure it out. They even got donors of the opposite race so Mindy and I would look like each other. I only figured out who my biological mother was because Mindy already knew her biological mom.

"You dick!" Mindy leans across the table, inches from my face. "I have known them for two more years than you. When we went to South Africa, Mother took care of Mom and me when we got malaria. She's not my stepmother. She's OUR mother." She stands back up but looks away from me. "Despite every terrible thing that has happened this year, I thought the one thing I could count on at home was my little brother happy to see me, to have everyone together for the first time in months. Let me know when he's back, because I don't know who you are."

She storms off but only makes it a few steps before freezing at the sound of keys unlocking the door. Mom walks into the foyer and takes one good look at Mindy.

Mom's eyes are bloodshot, her cheeks a palish-red, and she starts sniffling even more when she sees the two of us just getting out of a fight. My heart sinks.

"Hi, children." She wipes off a tear. I mentally prepare for the tantrum Mindy is about to receive. Mom wipes the left corner of her cheek. "Well, I'm happy you had fun today." She struggles to produce a smile but produces one. "Maybe this is what we need right now."

"What?" I whisper and shake my head in confusion.

Mom enters the kitchen and grabs a bag of sleepy-time tea while opening the fridge for the leftover sushi. She stuffs a couple of pieces of leftover sushi into her mouth. "Imitation crab?" She holds a few pieces for the two of us. I politely refuse, but Mindy backs away in horror. She takes some pieces and stuffs them into her mouth. She pours the boiling water and dunks the tea in the mug to infuse the water.

She exits the kitchen and joins us in the dining room with her mug of tea. She doesn't look at us. "Your mother has been diagnosed with a Grade III tumour in her occipital lobe. It's pushing on her skull."

I guess I was wrong. It wasn't in her frontal lobe.

"Best case, she will need an eight-hour procedure to remove a piece of her brain, which could mean she loses vision in one eye. Regardless, we will be starting radiation therapy soon. The oncologists say there's a low probability it will do anything, but she wants to try." She takes a large sip, but her mood does not change. "I'm so sorry, guys; this is my fault. We've known these new growths would come for weeks, but I didn't want to upset you. And I didn't expect the tumours to be so aggressive." She finishes drinking the entire mug in less than a minute.

"We're sorry, too." Mindy keeps her hand on Mom's shoulder. "But no more secrets. We can handle it."

Mom rubs Mindy's cheeks, and they both smile. "What great thing have I done in my life to get a daughter like you? Between you and the oncologists, I know Mother will be in good hands."

"Wait, what?" I yell.

The two of them break from their hug.

"How are you okay with this? She's giving up her future—"

"Sidney," she whispers. "I know you're upset. I am, too, but times have changed. And I cannot deal with this energy right now. If you do not have anything positive to say, then go to your room."

"No." I object as I still have grievances. "I mean—"

"Now, Sidney," she screams in a commandeering voice that she usually only reserves for her patrols.

I storm off, stomping my way into my room, then slamming the door shut behind me and jumping on my bed. I feel the urge to punch something or scream into my pillow, anything to release some anger, but I have nothing left. All my rage had been dealt to my sister and Mom, and neither deserved it. I told Mindy she was my mother because I thought it would give me seniority in determining what she needed. And I wanted to tell Mindy she was stupid for dropping everything to help her when it wouldn't do anything.

The only person I'm angry at now is myself. I thought just checking in on her once a day would be enough. I should have been doing more research and testing. I was just dicking around for the past month, enjoying my life and spending time with my friends and girlfriend. If I had learned faster, I could have saved her, Mindy could have finished her final year of school, and everything would be back to normal.

Mom knocks on my door and lets herself into my room. "Hi." She sits right beside me on my bed. I don't look at her.

"I have nothing to say," I pout, turning my head away from her.

"Well, I do." Mom puts her hand on mine. "I get you are mad; anyone would be. Mindy might say she's happy, but this was the last thing she wanted." She takes in another deep breath. "This. Sucks. And sometimes that is all you can say or do. But what do we accomplish by yelling at each other?" Mom's no longer looking at me. Instead, she focuses on her feet, only holding my arm and spreading her fingers around my forearm. Much like her cop tone, everything sounds sincere but rehearsed.

"So?" I ask, still looking away. "What do you want?"

"I first want to apologize for yelling. Second, I want you to cool off and talk to me, or someone else." Mom lets go of me. "You deserve to live the life of a normal teenager. You can have the car again, and have fun with your friends."

"Okay." I turn my head to her. "I thought you wanted to do something as a family."

She smiles. "I'll be working late tomorrow. Maybe, next Friday, we could eat at Mr. Ganatra's restaurant. However, tonight, I'll sit with you for as long as you want." She lifts my head to look at her. The tension in my face melts as I look upon her tear-stained cheeks, but there are no more tears in her eyes. She's mimicking my face, trying to cheer me up.

"I'm alright, Mom. Thank you."

She kisses me on the cheek. "I love you." She holds me for a few seconds, then exits my room, leaving the door open. I should apologize to Mindy, but she probably doesn't want to see me now.

I call Harriet and tell her I want to join her tomorrow. She shrieks in delight before hanging up. Maybe I need an honest, unfettered reality check and consolation talk. She has been right about a couple of my fears. I do have some unresolved issues to work out. And she's probably my closest friend. Out of everyone in my friend group, she's the only person who's not sick, hospitalized, or Tikha.

A delightfully cheesy movie could help me with some much-needed escapism. And with the car, I could also check in on Yasmine; maybe I will bring her some sushi; horseradish helps boost immunity and deal with nasal congestion. There are some things I can fix.

I lie down on my bed and look up at the ceiling. My head no longer hurts, but my hair is still a mess. The power is out of my hands and in Mindy's and a couple of oncologists.

I promise I'll do more research when Mother comes back. But right now, I'll progress, with Harriet.

Part 4.5: Dazed and Confused
Vritikha, November 13th, 15:30

Fortunately, I have been getting nine hours of sleep for the past two days. Unfortunately, it has been at the expense of not getting any visions.

When I spoke to Mr. Riviera, he knew some things about clairvoyants. He said not to give my visions attention if I didn't want them. I have wanted this for the longest time, but the day is fast approaching and I need to know if I'll die in the upcoming days.

Our family is preparing our restaurant for our annual Diwali party. We are expecting around a hundred people. Guests would come in, immediately take their shoes off, bow before the gods, say a quick prayer, and then eat and socialize. We've set up candles, homemade sand Rangoli, and the many different idols of Ganesh, Shiva, Brahma, etc. around the vigils, covered half the floor in a bedsheet to section off a sacred space, and hung up strings of lights on every wall. There will be a large open area for people to walk around separate from the sacred space and also designated tables for the uncles and aunties who can't stand for too long.

Once everything's set up, we arrange a video call with Veera, Ammi, and Vipesh, and say a quick prayer. Afterwards, I make it to my room and note the time: three-thirty in the afternoon.

I step into our closet and put my backpack down. My sari is hanging at the back of my closet. The top and bottom are made of orange Kota fabric that, when worn, exposes my midriff. It's a sacrifice I'm willing to live with as it would draw attention away from my legs. I also have a thin shawl that wraps around my shoulder, covering my waist and hips. I like wearing it because when I put it on, I embody my other half, one often forgotten by my existence in Canada. To complete my look, I place a Bindi between my eyebrows, bangles around my wrists, and a stone-studded necklace. I put on enough makeup to even out the dark circles around my eyes. But when I look at myself in the mirror, something doesn't feel right.

From my neck down, I looked like a young Vaishya set up for her arranged marriage, minus the mehndi tattoos and rings. But from my neck up, I look and feel like I am appropriating someone else's culture, even though it's my own.

The hijab isn't me; I'm only wearing it to hide my bald spots. And I look like my Nani on her wedding day.

Sarita Mir was the same age as me when she married a twenty-two-year-old merchant named Prakash Ganju from her village. They hadn't met before being arranged but she gave him one daughter, and they lived together in Jammu for fifty years. They had spent their entire lives in the village. She warned Ammi that terrible things would happen if she left, and right in the middle of the immigration process, Nana died.

Diwali was a hard time for us. He not only died on the day of Diwali, but it was also the last time we saw my older brother. Nani would later give us her blessing to move away because I would require better medical services. Abba and Ammi told her to come with us, but she wanted to be with Nana in spirit.

I remove the yellow hijab out of respect. The colour belongs to her. Veera fortunately has a whole set of drapes.

"*Oh, mon Dieu.*" Harriet walks in as I free my hair.

"Woah," I exclaim to her. Harriet has removed her hair highlights, and I'm not used to her normal medium brown hair without the green or sky-blue dye. Also, since I cut my hair back and hers grew over the past few months, we had very similar hairstyles. I dread more people will confuse the two of us now.

"*C'est magnifique.*" She brushes her bangs away from her eyes. "T, can you just pass me your other sari?" I give her the other red sari I own.

She leaves and tries it on in Veera's room. I go into the other side of the closet and find a silky gold scarf. Veera doesn't use it, and it matches my shawl's colour. I wrap it around my head. It feels softer on my skin, but it's even more slippery. I should be fine, provided I don't make any sudden head movements. I tuck a loose end into my top and grab my realistic prosthetic. I can't wear my carbon-fibre one because the dhoti is thin and translucent.

The prosthetic rattles when I pick it up. A clear, disposable bag containing a joint and an arc USB lighter falls out of the socket, the same one Harriet had given me on election night.

A terrible thought immediately comes to me: I need to stay calm, I need to relax, and I need clarity. I need to know what happens within the next few days. I take off my leg, roll out Harriet's yoga mat, and sit down. I would have taken out Veera's prayer mat since it would have been softer on my knee and butt; however, it's in another room, and I want to minimize the number of religious rules I'm desecrating at the moment.

I dump out the bag's contents, take the electric lighter, place the two prods, and light it. Once it cinders, I put the other end to my lips and inhale. I drop the lighter on the area rug. I gag from the smell, and recoil in a coughing fit as the fumes kick me in the throat. How does anyone enjoy this?

I inhale again, using my nose and mouth. It's a little smoother. I hold it in for nine seconds before throwing another coughing fit. The third time I breathe through my nose and throat again. It's just as painful as the last two times, but I persevere. I hold it in until I sink into the ground. I exhale slowly while pursing my lips and exhaling.

Ashes scatter all over my sari, and in hindsight, I should have put a towel under my door. I lean over and place the joint on my desk. I sit on one foot and look at the ceiling, then forward into the darkness of my closet.

I close my eyes, put my hands on my thighs, and hum. My sight blurs and my brain starts to drift. I can already feel the joint numbing me, but I'm calm.

* * *

I will be on the bridge again, walking toward two people in a fight. Sid will be dragging the white-hooded figure by the arm. I will walk up to them and will see the white figure with some red streaks in their hair and an indent in their head; they will still try to hide their face from me—

I will get a beat in my vision. Sid will be yelling to himself, spinning around. We will feel the ground shake, and the white figure will drag me off the bridge. Chunks of asphalt will fall into the river below us, but we will get off right before the bridge collapses. The figure will take off her hood; it will be Harriet. Sid will emerge from the water.

Another beat in my visions happens. A police car and an ambulance will show up at our scene. Sid and Harriet will not be around me anymore. I will be hiding out by the riverbank. There will be one gurney taking a fully zipped-up body bag into an ambulance. After everyone leaves the scene, I will walk home. My hands will be covered in mud and my ears will ring. When the scene clears, I will get home and open the door.

I will walk into chemistry class, and everyone will stare at me. Yasmine and I will be performing titrations in the lab. Neither Harriet nor Sid will be there. Then I will freak out while performing our experiment and break a beaker. I will open the cupboard to grab another one.

I will enter my room, and after staring at my whiteboard for a prolonged period, I will feel a hot rage inside me. I will toss my whiteboard across the room. It will hit Harriet's desk. Then I will tear up some papers on my desk, and after tripping and falling on the ground, I will shut my eyes and whimper to myself, crying on the floor again, alone. I will close my eyes.

I will open my eyes again, finding myself in my kitchenette. The six of us will be together, which will include Ammi and Veera but not Harriet. We will be eating dinner. Ammi will tell us about Nani's last few days while Abba will tell us about Vipesh's resignation. The door will ring, and Krishna will be on the other side. I will smile.

* * *

"T!" Someone on the other side yells. I get up, not realizing I only have one leg, and I collapse on my bed. I crawl on the soft mattress and feebly reach to the door and turn the knob. Harriet runs up to me and grabs my face.

"Shiny," I giggle as I poke her nose. She has a small piece of glass on one of her nostrils. It creates a wild display of colours when I reposition my head and view it from varying angles. I remove my hand from her face when I realize it's just her diamond nose stud. She sniffs around our room.

"Well, I guess I know why the smoke detectors went off." She gestures to my desk.

I start giggling. "I didn't start a fire, did you?"

She picks up something off my desk and holds it above my face. The joint is still lit, and our room is full of smoke. I fan the smoke around to see Harriet more clearly; she seems upset.

"Don't blame me." I point in her direction. "You gave that to me. You told me to clear my head and take a few deep breaths. Remember?"

She smokes the joint but doesn't cough.

Startled, I fling myself backwards at the wall. "Please don't tell Abba."

Harriet smiles. "I won't. But I guess you didn't last too long. It's good to know your limits, and this particular strand had a high

THC percentage." She extinguishes it on the table, puts it back in the bag, and throws the whole thing under her pillow. It's a little disorienting, watching her teleport around the room. Am I still sitting on my bed? I feel for the mattress below me and sigh in relief.

"How are you feeling, T?" She gets my attention.

I open my mouth.

"It has been about thirty seconds, and you haven't said anything. I asked how you are feeling."

I close my mouth and then open it again, but no sound is coming out.

"You are really out of it. You need some food and water."

My stomach growls, and I hug my right knee.

"Give me your phone for a second."

I try to find my phone and crawl over to my nightstand. I pass it to her.

She shows me the home screen, and it lights up. The time is six-thirty p.m., which means I have been out for around three hours. The phone unlocks itself, and the six flips around and becomes a nine. Is it half-past six or nine? Was I asleep for three or six hours? She turns it back towards her and types something.

"What are you doing?" I try to snatch my phone back from her. She dodges my arm and I end up falling on the floor. I feel for the bristles around me, and then sink my fingers into the rug. "Never mind, I don't care." I nestle my face and purr.

Harriet rolls me into a sitting position by grabbing my arms and leaning me on my bed. "I just texted a special someone to bring up a food delivery. He should be here in about ten seconds or thirty minutes, depending on how baked you are."

I take a strand of her hair and twirl it around my fingers. Her hair is very soft, but not red.

We hear a knock at the door. "Here's your special delivery."

"Is it Krishna?"

"*Oui,*" she stands up and her strands fall out of my grasp. She walks to the door.

"Why do you want us together so badly?"

"I told you; I want you to be happy. I want you to be walking on your own two legs."

Her joke isn't funny, but I cannot resist the urge to laugh again.

"Speaking of which, let's put this on." She picks up my realistic prosthetic.

"Can I have some privacy, please?"

"*Tiens.*" Harriet leaves our room, and I quickly slip on my leg. I still feel like I can blank out occasionally. The experience would probably be more fun if I had another high friend.

"Are you done?" Harriet yells.

"Yes," I inform her.

"Perfect timing. Because look who is here." Harriet enters with Krishna; he's holding two plates of food and he looks a little different. He's wearing a gold jubbah from my flash-forward visions. He cut his hair to about two inches and shaved his face completely. He looks five years younger. Could this be the flash forward I kept seeing him in? I don't remember setting up any canopy.

The smell of the food fills our room and makes me forget about my scent. But he recoils at the smell.

"Is she...?" He turns to Harriet. "*Est-elle gelée?*" he whispers.

"It's the festival of lights," Harriet says while holding her arms up, and I start laughing uncontrollably. The joke is bad, but her delivery is hilarious. "*Oui, elle a fumé un peu de hasch,*" she explains. "*Et vous devez l'occuper.*"

I don't know if I'm just really high or if they're speaking some incomprehensible dead language.

"*Me fais-tu confiance?*" Krishna asks her.

Harriet walks up to me and lifts my chin. We smile at each other. "*Non,* but I trust my cousin. And we tell each other everything." She lets go of my face and walks back to him. "If anything happens to her, even if it's not your fault, I will know." She looks over at me, tilts her head to the left, and nods, and I nod with her in unison. Harriet takes a fistful of his jubbah and drags him down to her height. *"Mon père peut te renvoyer à Kashmir."*

Krishna falls silent, nodding to her.

I sit myself back up and giggle in her direction.

"What's so funny now?" he asks me.

I point to Harriet. "Hari." And then to Krishna. "Krishna." I alternate between the two of them repeating. "Hari Krishna. Hare Krishna." I fall to the ground and laugh.

Harriet scrunches up her face. "Those are just our names; I don't get it."

He rolls his eyes. "How do you not know? You'll get it when you're older. Anyway, I guess I can watch over her." He comes next to me, two plates in hand. I pick myself off the floor.

"You kids have fun." She leaves the room, closing the door behind her.

"Here." He sits on the rug in front of me and hands me a plate of Vegetarian biryani, Chana masala, and Mattar paneer. I rip the naan bread and shovel it into my mouth. I moan with every bite, and as soon as I finish, I lick the plate clean, but it's not enough—my stomach growls again. So I take the second plate and start devouring the dahl and naan. Partway through eating the second plate of food, I realize what I'm doing and stop.

"This was your food, wasn't it?" I ask. "I'm sorry."

"No," he smiles at me. "You texted me to bring you everything available downstairs. I already ate with your brothers. They are fascinating individuals."

"Yeah, one of them has no filter, and the other one thinks he's so witty when he's irritating. Well, they're both irritating, but in different ways."

"Not like that. They're pretty funny and sweet." They are to him because they like him. "Although, I got confused when people kept calling them Rajya and Anuj."

"Abba calls us what we all call each other, Veera, Vritikha, Varshil, and Vijay, all Vs. But Ammi calls us by different names, Natasha, Talibah, Rajya, and Anuj. I'll let you guess who filled out the immigration paperwork for us. Outside the house, we use our Hindu names, but inside, we use our Muslim names. All of Ammi's friends and relatives call me Talibah, and everyone else calls me Vritikha or Tikha, or T or V." I cough into my hand. "I need to have some consistency as to what people call me." I get up and sit on my bed.

"Wonderful." He gets up and touches my fake knee. His fingertips trace my socket, towards my hips. "You have a captivating upbringing, Vritikha." He starts to look down at his lap. I hold his hand and feel his pulse slow down.

"You miss your family, don't you?" I deduce.

He nods to me. "Harriet said you were really smart. I guess I can't hide anything, even from high Tikha. A part of me wants to reach out to them because it's been more than six years. But the longer I stay here, the more awkward I feel about going back."

"*Sayonee*," I say. "You should call them. Any family would be lucky to have you; mine certainly would. And if they don't respond, at least you put in more effort than they did, and they don't deserve you."

"Did you call me 'soulmate'?" He raises both eyebrows.

"Ummm." I forgot he knows Urdu. I look up and away from him, but he tracks my gaze. I stop at the whiteboard and all the Urdu markings. But before he can read them, I distract him by loudly shovelling the remaining food into my mouth. The Shahi Paneer and Dahl drip all over my bed. I finish the second plate of food within a minute.

"You got a little something." He points to my right cheek; I touch it and feel a thick blotch of Shahi curry on my face.

"Oh." I giggle. "I got it." I rub my face.

"You just made it worse," he informs me.

I'm spreading it on the right half of my face. "Hang on." I take some residual curry from my plate and spread it on my left cheek. "Is that better?" It's soothing. Hopefully, it won't give me breakouts in the future. I close my eyes and try to see the future.

He laughs. "Let me help you with that, Trudeau." He takes a serviette and wipes my face clean.

"Thank you." I reach out to touch him and feel his face. "Woah, your face is so smooth." It can't be the flash forward; he will have a beard in my vision and a longer and fuller one, not just patchy stubble when I first met him. I don't know why he wants one. He's not Sikh, and he looks much better without one. I lean forward and press our foreheads together, trying to figure out our future. The sudden impact of our heads hitting causes me to jerk back and causes my headscarf to fall off.

"What did you do to your hair?" he exclaims.

"Why, do you not like it?" I say calmly and confidently.

"No, no, no. It's great. I, I didn't expect I—"

I interrupt his panicking by laughing, and not because of the weed. "I want to remember this moment where I made you stutter, where I was the cool one and not the person constantly tripping over herself." A twinkle develops in my eye, and my heartbeat quickens.

"I like this new confident Vritikha," he quips. "What are you feeling now?"

"I'm feeling sober enough to do this," I throw my shawl around his neck, grab both ends, and then hoist myself onto his lap.

I can't believe my body moved without my brain analyzing every thought and path of my present and future, but when I look at his clean-shaven face, nothing else matters.

I caress his face and stare deeply into his eyes, but close them as his tongue enters my mouth. I know I smell like a strange mixture of different kinds of herbs and spices, which I'm sure is the last thing he wants to taste. Krishna's shoulder is very toned, and I trace his arm until I feel my hand on my bed. However, he brings it back up and touches my inner thigh. I immediately get up and fall off my bed.

I can't say a word; I can't move after landing on the floor. I grab my chest. He places a hand on my shoulder, but I push it off.

"I thought you..." He tries to explain himself. "...wanted to..." He gives me space. "Listen, if you don't want to, that's fine, I understand." He raises one of his hands in realization and points to my left leg. "I forgot you're an amputee. I know why you freaked out." He stands up and gives me his hand. "I thought you wanted me to move forward, but I guess you don't have feeling in your left leg. Until I got to your thigh, then—"

"Stop," My heart races. I use my bedframe to stand myself up. "How the hell do you know about that?" I take a furious step forward. "Who told you? Vijay? Varshil? Harriet?"

"It doesn't matter. I was going to find out eventually."

I take another step forward. "But you don't get to decide when that is."

"It's not a big deal. It doesn't matter to me."

"Oh, it doesn't matter, you say?" I mock his words. "I'm so glad it's not a big deal...to you. You don't know me."

"You're right. I don't know you." He inhales. "But I have been trying to get to know you. I was curious, so I asked around." He clears his throat. "Are we good?"

"No," I answer. "You know what? I do think you are moving too fast." There are many things he has not told me, specifically how he fits into my visions. "And if you are such an open book, how can you speak nine languages? How do you own a car? And what job do you have? Why are you trying to seduce me? Maybe you're trying to get me to let my guard down so that I can reveal something in my visions. You're not getting that out of me." I slide my foot backwards and put myself into a box stance. I can take him on if I need to. I close my eyes so I can anticipate his moves, but I get nothing.

He grabs both my arms and lowers them to my side. "I work as a dishwasher in the cafeteria of Algonquin College. I must take jobs where I can get them. Look at me. This is the first time I got a decent haircut in a long time, and this is the nicest outfit I own. I also chauffeur part-time, and the Corolla that you look at with such disdain gave me the biggest return on my investments. I'd like to have a cleaner car, but I need to eat, too." He opens the door. "It's almost ten. I should go, and you need time to cool down." He exits through the door and disappears around the corner.

I should have seen this coming. *Sayonee* didn't end with the boy finding his soulmate. He sat alone and cried in the street.

He didn't attend Vipesh's victory party because he probably didn't have anything to wear if the jubbah was the nicest thing he owned. I sometimes forget how hard my family had it a decade ago, and how far we have come in this country.

Abba worked as a cab driver for the first four years of living in Canada. In those days, we would sleep at Vipesh Kaka's house during the summer because we could not afford to run air conditioning in our apartment building. Driving a cab was stressful, and the pay was terrible. There were days he slept in his car because he worked sixteen hours straight and didn't have the energy to come home. And he didn't earn enough money to exit the company. He got a loan from Vipesh to rent the space downstairs and turn it into our restaurant.

But Krishna didn't let the cycle get to him. Even when I was yelling at him, he kept his composure. I want to go up to him, grab his hand, and make eye contact, trying to find out what our future holds, but I can't move my leg as quickly. I climb on Harriet's bed to look out the window. He has already left, but someone else enters our restaurant below: Sid.

It's ten-thirty, and Krishna could not have been in my room for three hours. He must have entered at around nine-thirty, which means the vision lasted six hours. Maybe I'll see him again in six weeks.

But something else changed. I'm alive by the end of my new visions. I walk over to my whiteboard and write down the following: Harriet in trouble, Sid yelling, dead body, Chemistry class, trashing my room, family dinner. In my frantic shuffling, I accidentally knock the whiteboard off the wall, and it falls behind my bed.

I'll fix it later. Now I know that Harriet's life is at stake. No more distractions.

I can see everything. The weed is no longer in my system. I head downstairs into the restaurant to find Vijay, as he is one of the few people left. "Have you seen him anywhere?"

"Krishna's long gone," he says.

"Not Krishna, Sid." I correct myself. "Where is he?"

"He took Harriet to see a movie together. Why do you want Sid?"

I didn't go to the theatre in Islington, I went to Manotick. It was on the other side of the Morrisette Bridge.

The bridge is going to collapse today.

I exit the restaurant and call her. The phone rings for a few seconds, then she picks up. "Hey."

"Harriet, please listen to me. I don't know what's going to happen in the next hour, but you cannot cross that bridge, get home—"

"Slow down," she cuts me off.

"Listen, Harriet, remember the web I had on my wall; it's all leading to this moment. I'll explain when you get home. It won't end well for you or Sid."

"Really? Okay, I understand."

"Tell Sid you have a migraine or something. Get. Home. Now."

"Thank you. Bye." She hangs up, and I go back in.

"Vritikha." Abba approaches me as soon as I walk back into the restaurant. "I could not find you all night."

"I was talking to Krishna until he went upstairs with two plates of food," Vijay answers for me. "But I'm just going to keep my mouth shut."

"He left early, looking extremely guilty." Varshil retorts. "So screw him, you deserve better, Vritikha."

Varshil and Vijay are taking my side? And most surprisingly Varshil didn't make some smart-ass comment. He makes the same jokes every time I bring someone over to help them with math or science, like, 'they were probably studying anatomy or French' or something stupid.

Abba gasps. "Please tell me you two were safe." He places his hand on my right shoulder.

I force a smile. "Nothing happened." I keep it short and simple so as not to arouse suspicion.

"Well, as long as nothing—" Abba suddenly stops talking. He tightens his grip on my shoulder and smells the smoke on me. And then he peels my top right eyelid upwards and frowns. My heart beats faster. "Are you alright? Did he hurt you?" He spins me around but releases me from his clutches. "I am going to kill him."

"It was mine." I bow my head to him. "For the past couple of days, I wasn't sleeping properly. I'm sorry, Abba."

"क्या?" (What?) Abba lifts my hands and smells my fingers. He knows I'm not lying, and his concern turns into fury. "You are grounded until Ammi comes home. You are to attend school and immediately come home. The only exceptions are band practice and the restaurant. But you are not to leave this building for any other reason."

"That's not fair," Varshil defends me.

"They were just having fun," Vijay joins in as well.

Abba takes one step forward, and the three of us collectively step back. "Do you two want to join her?"

My brothers shake their heads.

"Once every year, we are expected to serve our guests and act sensibly for the people in this building. It's the least I expect from you three." He sighs. "It's hard enough without your Ammi or Veera, then you pull this stunt." He waves his hand at us. "You have ruined our holy day."

I bow my head to Abba. "I accept...my punishment."

After Abba's rant, I help my brothers clean up. We bring everything back to its original position, vacuum the floors, and pick up discarded litter. Meanwhile, I keep an eye on the entrance, wondering where Harriet is. After an hour, I count my losses and head upstairs.

* * *

I can't sleep. I check my phone; it's midnight. Harriet's still not in our room. She should have arrived half an hour ago. Did I make things worse by calling? Would I be held accountable if I didn't show up? My cousin has always helped me. I have to be strong for her. We are more than just comrades, and if the time comes to put Sid in his place, I will. I've tried being nice to Sid, but nothing has changed. He will pay for everyone he has hurt and will hurt in the future.

I grab a black scarf and cover my head. With my keys in hand and my phone in my side pocket, I head to the bridge, knowing I'm going into the future blind.

Part 5

Part 5.1: Hard Right Turn
Sidney, November 13th, 22:00

Yesterday was rough, but I did get through it. I managed to complete all of my homework, and even though Mother, Mindy, and Kat are all still furious at me, Mom still let me go out tonight.

I have spent time in Islington, in Kyle's affluent neighbourhood or Yasmine's high-rise condominium building. But I had never spent much time in the rundown low-rise parts of Islington. I drive up to Ganatra and Ganju: Indian Cuisine and Sweets, and park right in front. The smell of curry, spices, and incense makes its way outside before I open the door.

The vestibule is lined with Christmas lights along the front window, and many different kinds of dress shoes, slippers, and Birkenstocks. And on the far end of the vestibule, there are many different-looking statues of Hindu Gods and rhythmic chants playing on a loop over the speakers.

Harriet told me Tikha's family is throwing a party for the Indian New Year. I had always thought her family was Muslim, based on her and her sister's hijab, but I guess I was wrong; maybe it's a fashion choice. Everyone is wearing long, flowing robes or simple dress shirts and pants. I feel underdressed, wearing my black hoodie and nylon pants.

An Indian man with the build of a bouncer at a nightclub greets me. "You must be Hari's friend. Welcome. You can call me Mr. Ganatra, I'm Hari's uncle." He talks in a deep and smooth Indian accent, places his hand on my back and pulls me through the crowd to the buffet table. "Eat some food, *chhote*. You look very thin." He passes me a plate and leaves my side.

I scoop some rice and what looks like chickpea curry and blended spinach. My appetite has increased since the explosion because my brain consumes more energy from using my powers.

I grab a spoon and start eating a dish with chickpeas. It overpowers my taste buds with an incredible amount of spice. I pride myself on having a decent spice tolerance. I can handle wasabi, which is spicier, but its intensity is short-lived. Indian food, however, will stay on my tongue for the rest of the night. Parts of my body I didn't know had pores open up. I pour myself a glass of water and immediately down it.

While I'm eating, someone taps me on my shoulder. Harriet stands behind me wearing a red, Indian sari. The sarong stops at her knees and is adorned with small, thumbnail-sized mirrors, which serve as the centre of the flower embroideries, while small beads and threads outline the stem and petals. She's also wearing thin cloth leggings, and a thin scarf around her left shoulder, neck, and head.

"Wow. You look different, in a good way," I correct myself. "I haven't seen you embrace your other half before; you look great."

She stares at me for a few seconds. "You're supposed to use the bread called Paratha, tear off a bit, and scoop the food to eat it." She walks away.

I grab some bread and more food. Tikha's two younger brothers approach me, they are both dressed the same and bear a strong resemblance to their father, however, instead of a beard, they both have a little bit of brown fuzz on their upper lips.

"You can eat this however you like," the younger one instructs me. "We don't care how, as long as the food goes in the mouth."

"She has no authority on what Indians can or cannot do," the older one continues. "She's about as Indian as the people who first settled here. She's effectively a Métis."

"The colloquial term is 'coconut', but he's right," the younger one adds.

The food enters the wrong opening and I cough. "I don't think you're allowed to say that," I say once my airway clears. "But

I will try it both ways." I rip the bread and pick up everything together, the chickpeas, spinach, fried rice, and bread all in one go. It breaks my brain. None of these flavours clash with each other. The dishes' overall spiciness diminishes while the savouriness rises. It's a little salty, but an incredible amalgamation of all four food groups.

"If you came here earlier, the food would've been much better," the younger chirps.

"When it's fresh, it burns as it goes down. And that's where a lot of the flavour comes in," the older one adds.

I'm not trying to overeat because I want to save room for treats in the movie theatre. But I'm enjoying myself here, and have taken my mind off my home. I like listening to these two boys talk about food as I finish my plate. "No, it's fantastic." I continue to eat the way Harriet suggests. "My parents want to come here, so look out for us next week."

My stomach churns, but not because of the food. Mother probably can't eat anything here, even if she were released early. She will be starting her new round of radiation therapy on Monday. Mom briefed us on what we should expect. Mother would need an eyepatch, but there is an outside possibility that she could be fitted for a prosthetic if the optical nerve isn't damaged. And that's assuming everything goes smoothly, which it might not.

"Let's go, Sid. *Dépêche-toi.*" Harriet snaps me out of my dark place and appears wearing her typical white zip-up hoodie and yoga pants, but also without any of her hair dyed. The change is more jarring than Yasmine's transformation. It would be as if Tikha stopped walking with a limp.

I take my keys out of my pocket and shake them at her, smirking.

Harriet turns to her cousins. "By the way, keep an eye on Krishna and your sister."

"He's gone, girl," the older brother responds. "He left before this guy showed up." He gestures to me.

"*Pardon?*" Harriet asks. "*Pourquoi?*"

"*Je ne sais pas*," the younger brother answers in subpar French. "He was embarrassed and didn't want to talk to either of us or say goodbye to Abba."

"Figures. We knew she was below his league," the older groans. "Can't imagine many guys lining up to date such a stilted person."

The young one nods. "What did he ever see in her, anyway?"

Harriet shoots daggers out of her eyes at her two cousins and flares her nostrils. "That does not mean anything. Most normal people don't pretend to know either of you after talking to you for more than three sentences."

"So, you're not normal?" they say in unison.

"I'm unfortunately related to you *tatas*. So, I have no choice." She darts her eyes back and forth, and then gets close to their faces. "But let me get something through those thick skulls. Your sister is a beautiful, kind person, and his drifter ass would be lucky to land someone like her." She points to them. "And you two little brats better appreciate her now, because when she's gone, you boys will never find anyone who will put up with your shitty behaviour as well as she does. Understand?" They nod in agreement without saying another word. She smiles menacingly and turns back to me. "*Désolé. Allons-y,* Sid."

I hastily consume the rest of the food and put my plate and utensils in a tray.

Without saying another word, we leave and get into my car. I remove my black hoodie and put it in the backseat behind me. Harriet inputs the directions into her phone and starts up navigation. "So...that was..." I pause, stalling to find a good connotation. "...interesting." I can't think of a better word.

"Those are my cousins," Harriet responds. "Varshil's the older one, Vijay's the younger. They're fun in small doses."

"No," I interject. "I meant you were a little mean to them. I get you're standing up for Tikha, but that's how boys behave." I drive towards the Morissette Bridge.

"Are you for real? Granted, Tikha has her problems. She can sometimes live in a bubble and space out for seconds or hours. But those boys can't treat their sister like that. It's unacceptable."

"What happened to the strong, intelligent Tikha you have been raving about? Maybe they're not alone in that respect." Maybe she's not alone, either. I wasn't the most charitable to Mindy yesterday. She's an adult who knows how to take care of herself.

"You know you can criticize someone and still love them. For example, you and your mother don't always have the best relationship, she constantly nags you about drinking water or getting your grades up. But that doesn't mean you want to see her go."

Keeping my eyes on the road, I mentally prepare for another monologue. "Okay, I'm ready now, I won't run away. Let's talk."

"*Pardon?*" She takes her second-to-last antidepressant and slips the bottle back into her purse.

"You were right about everything," I announce as she swallows the antidepressant. "You warned me about her worsening conditions, and I tried to suppress that feeling. But then it happened. You were right." I force a smile and side-eye her while keeping my head pointed to the road. "I'm just a scared little boy who cannot function without Mommy."

"What's with your tone? I'm not happy about this. I didn't want to be right. I'm so sorry, Sid."

We drive across the Morissette Bridge and enjoy the lack of traffic in Manotick. Harriet adjusts the mirror on her side, rubbing her eyes and blinking a few times. "All I wanted to do was be here for you. But today, I want to spend one-on-one time with my first real friend." I could feel her eyes maintain focus. I keep my eyes on the road. She closes the sun visor and mirror. "When was the last time we did that?"

"Well, there was that time at the beginning of October where—"

Harriet shushes me. "That was a rhetorical question. We don't talk about that."

During the first week of October, she needed a procedure done in Islington and couldn't go by herself. I was the only person she trusted with access to a car. I wasn't eager to lie to Kyle, Mr. Ganatra, or my parents about what we did, but Harriet would go through with the procedure regardless. She didn't want biological children, partly because they were bad for the planet, but also because she didn't have the right mindset to be a mom, as any child of hers would inherit her agoraphobia and depression. I drove her there and back, despite my disagreement with her philosophy.

I would love to be a father and hope to accomplish it while Mother is still with us. But I would be lying if I said some of her anxieties didn't resonate with me. Mother was admitted to the hospital soon after Harriet's procedure. It made me realize I could inherit her tumours, and so would any of my children.

Both of these events happened before the explosion, which was only six weeks ago. It feels like it was an eternity, but also like it was yesterday. I have traversed a large distance in those six weeks but simultaneously only displaced myself a few steps from the original starting point. Is this my new normal?

"Is it getting hot in here?" I move to turn on the fan, but Harriet slaps me away.

"Turning on the AC is wasteful. Open a window; it's still fuel-inefficient but not as much as air conditioning."

She's right, opening a window would not create too much drag. We are only going sixty.

"How much longer until we get to the theatre?" I ask as we continue along the long, dark, narrow road.

Harriet's phone suddenly rings. She picks it up. My body temperature drops a little.

"Hey," Harriet says. I cannot make out words on the other end, but the voice sounds shrill and anxious. "Slow down," she yells. "Really? Okay. I understand." She exhales softly. "Thank you. Bye." She inhales and exhales. Her expression seems unfazed.

"That sounded pretty serious. Is everything alright?" I ask.

"It was nothing." She frowns. "By the way, just make a right." Harriet points.

I look in my rearview mirror. We have been heading south this whole time, but if I take a right, I will be heading west. "Is this some secret shortcut?" I ask.

"Just do it, Sid. I know my directions."

I make a hard right turn.

"Thank you." Harriet smiles, and I start to feel a little sweaty again. Luckily, the road's empty.

We drive along Rideau Valley Drive North. I know this neighbourhood; this is where the nuclear plant is. I have spent every Friday walking southbound on the lonely road. My stomach churns.

"Stop here," she orders.

I press gently on the breaks until we stop by the soon-to-be-demolished I&MNG. Harriet unbuckles herself as I put the car in park, keeping it running. "You see that over there?" Harriet gestured to her right, pointing at the plant.

"You mean the dilapidated shack?" I ask, playing a little dumb. My core temperature rises slightly. Small deposits of sweat accumulate in my armpits and legs.

"No, the plant. It was where our story began, our new story." She sighs and turns her head to me. "When were you going to tell me about your powers?"

My heartbeat is now audible. How the hell could she know?

"Were they the ones you wanted?"

When we were at Kyle's summer house in Orillia, the four of us talked about what kind of superpowers we would want. It was a balmy thirty-two degrees outdoors at night, and we were sitting by an unlit and drafty fireplace. However, the blackflies still made their way into his cottage. Kyle wished on one of them, saying he wanted the power to communicate with animals. I said I just wanted super healing to help sick people like my mother. Harriet said telepathy so she could control the rich and powerful and make them willingly give up their massive wealth. Yasmine wanted to read minds to know who she could and could not trust.

Harriet woke up from her coma earlier than I did. "You were affected by the explosion as well?"

"Sure." She puts her hand over the vent blocking the warm air. "You can absorb any kind of energy, thermal, photon or radiation, and your body holds it. You don't need to eat, although it doesn't hurt. Just think about it, it's a new way to harness energy from the sun, and we are like solar panels. No need for this shitty technology that's killing your mother. We need more people like us."

I have heard her diatribes about climate change and how inefficiently the government is handling it. But that's why her father ran and won the election, what more could she want? To be fair, I always thought it was stupid for people like us to stay in the shadows.

"You're getting it, Sid." She laughs. "I know you have been wondering what your career path will be ever since the closure of I&MNG. This could be it."

My body cools down a little. Wait, when she said, 'You're getting it', how did she know? Riviera did the same thing. She's reading my mind.

"It's just one friend looking out for another," she explains. "And together, we can help this planet. You know how dire the circumstances are. It's mid-November, and it hasn't dropped below ten degrees. There are a record number of hurricanes, floods, and wildfires happening all around the world. Not to mention, every year, we break the record for the hottest year ever recorded and the shortest winter. Most leaders of the most resource-rich countries don't even care. They have sold themselves out and garnered enough money to find a sustainable shelter, but what about the rest of us who cannot sell our homes and move? We have about eight years until our brains stop developing, and before we run out of nuclear material. Then every use of our power will shorten our lifespan, not to mention our planet will be burnt into the ground even further to meet our energy needs."

"Hari." I inhale and exhale. "I understand the consequences, but I just want to help my mother. Any small telekinetic blast is painful. Cleaning up the planet would kill us."

"We need to leave the world better off than we found it. If it kills us, then so be it. Doing nothing is selfish. Do you only care about saving people who matter to you personally?"

I lean back. "Woah, what the hell is wrong with you, Ayn Rand?"

"You're acting like—" She rubs her face while she collects her thoughts. Her nostrils flare and she balls her right hand into a fist.

I wanted to call her a psycho but thought it would be too mean. However, I think she would have preferred it based on her reaction.

"Alright, do it for me, then. You owe me. I got Yasmine to take you back. Also, I visited Kyle at the hospital. They said his lips were frozen shut. Why did you do it?"

I gulp. It's not a great look to tell her about his bad joke about my mother.

"You almost killed him for that?"

I gulp again. "Well, you took Yasmine to a place where she is allergic to everything." I defend myself. "So, I guess we are even in that respect." Although I understand it's nowhere near as bad as what I did. I have no idea what she's planning, but it can't be good.

"Je ne sais pas ce que je dois faire maintenant. Il est mal dans la tête," she yells to herself in French, looking into the sun visor's mirror. *"C'est trop difficile, je ne veux pas le faire. Non."* She pauses. *"Si je dois, vive la révolution."*

"Let's take a moment to cool off," I calmly tell her, then push the ignition button, but the engine stalls. I hold it for a couple of seconds but let go before the engine floods. "What's your plan to save the world?" I ask. I know Harriet well enough. When she has her mind set on something, she will get it done.

"I know you're bullshitting me. We don't have time to cool off. So let me be a little more *gauche.*" Harriet unbuckles herself and leans over the gearshift. "I see how you have already used your powers. Do not think for a second that you are any better than I am, because you are not. I will get you to see the world for how it is. You will hate it at first but come to realize that disasters, bloodshed, and rigged systems changed this world for the worse and they are the only way to bring balance."

I slowly lean back until my head hits the cold window, and unbuckle myself as I feel hot again. The sweat trickles down my neck, between my shoulder blades, and down to my ass.

How did Harriet plan this? Did she know the heat exchanger would blow up? And that it would blow up just as we walked in front of it? I'm an idiot. It was no accident. I wipe a layer of sweat off my forehead. "I guess Tikha was right. It wasn't just a technical malfunction." How was I supposed to know she was right the whole time? It still sounds insane.

"You'll be able to ask her pretty soon," Harriet answers.

"What does that mean?" I ask, not expecting an answer.

How could she do this? Does she not know what pain she brought to hundreds of thousands of lives in this city? My body temperature rises by the second and I sink deeper into my seats. My head gets heavier and heavier until I collapse onto the steering—

Part 5.2: Attempt #8
Sidney, November 14th, 00:00

"Can you hear me, Sid?"

The first thing I remember is falling onto the steering wheel and hearing the horn start to blare. Everything's dark now. My arms ache and my eyes will not open.

"Stay still, do not twitch your eyeballs or move a muscle."

I hear another voice in my head. It's low-pitched and a little raspy.

"You are unconscious. You have just been knocked out. Play limp until you can figure out what is happening."

It's Mr. Riviera. Is he here with me? And where is Harriet?

"Good, it's working. I am in your mind. I have implanted a piece of my subconscious next to your brain stem. We have had clear lines of communication since October twenty-second."

"It was the fourth meeting we had, why only come in now? Can you take care of her? She's abusing her powers far worse than I ever have. Use the EpiPen on her."

"Harriet Ganatra? Vipesh's daughter? I didn't teach her; I haven't even met her."

Mr. Riviera's health kept getting worse every time I saw him. His nose bled, and he even got my name wrong. I must be the reason he lost, why Mr. Ganatra won, and why she feels so emboldened. "I had no idea; I am so sorry, Mr. Riviera."

"This is not your fault, Sid. I knew the risks of teaching again."

"Why teach again? I know he does not want us in the light. She's dangerous, we need some system in place to counteract people like her. She managed to indoctrinate all my other friends."

"Don't get political right now. I never said I didn't want people like us to suppress our powers. When you use your

powers to harm others, it makes us look bad. It makes you look dangerous. Keep calm and content, no matter what gets thrown your way."

"So you're not going to help me fight her?" I ask.

Silence.

Every part of my body is sore, but primarily my arms and head. I shake my hands and open my eyes to pitch blackness. My body involuntarily shakes.

"Morning, Sid. It's a new year, which means time for resolutions and revolutions. And for you, it's a time for a revelation."

Warm air hits my face. She's next to me.

"I'm giving you one more chance."

I must be chained to the pipe again. The weight of my body is stretching my arms out. This time I'm blindfolded. "I didn't plan for this meeting to be on Diwali, it just kind of worked out that way. I know this could be uncomfortable, but I needed to take some necessary precautions. I can still feel your hands wringing my neck as they did on October twenty-fourth."

My friend is now a murderer. I play limp. I will not say anything.

"Sid, I can hear you thinking right now. I care about your safety and warmth. That's why I gave you back your sweater. And I had access to the plant's blueprints from when my dad's consulting firm worked on it and made sure what I was releasing into the air would create people like us."

"There's no way you could know that," I yell. "You could have killed everyone."

"But why were you the only one affected? Hundreds of people were in that building, but only you came out stronger." She sighs softly. "It's disappointing seeing all these powers squandered by someone like yourself. Someone with no real ambitions or original thoughts, conditioned to uphold the status quo. I should have expected no different from the son of a cop and a nuclear technician. But who am I to walk away from a challenge? I've been helping you with your parents, Yasmine, and schoolwork. Now it's time to pay me back. Why are you being so stubborn?"

"Why are you doing this?" I scream. "There are better ways to get your message across."

She lets out a loud, angry scoff. Some of the spittle hits my face and the wood sidings creak. "You're such a naïve boy. You don't think I've tried? I spent the majority of my life trying to think of better ways to get my message across. I thought companies and politicians would listen to science. When they didn't, I protested their greed. When that didn't work, I organized people to vote them out. Yet they tried to blame all of us for the earth's problems and used the free market as a scapegoat. They said we needed to wait until alternative sources became cheaper and more reliable. So what do the polluters do next? They lobby to keep their power, capital, and inefficiency.

"I thought this country was one of the good ones, not like those capitalist pigs down south. But beneath the stereotypical friendliness are some of the biggest mining and fascist groups on the entire planet. These heartless lobbyists love throwing money to prop up ineffective politicians while they masquerade 'concern' to avoid transitioning. 'What's done is done, you're going to be screwed either way. There is no point in changing, so just live your life.' Which means: 'Buy more shit that poisons the world'. So what could we do now? Shutting down I&MNG is the one thing that worked in my life. So can you think of anything that could satisfy the greater good? I'll wait, but our planet cannot."

Is she expecting me to answer that? Even if her morals were altruistic, she still killed people.

"Oh," she interrupts my thoughts. "So it's bad when I&MNG kills one person, yet oil rigs, nuclear disasters, and fracking earthquakes are all allowed to constantly endanger wildlife, thicken the air we breathe, and even kill the people who work for them? Neither the Chairman of I&MNG nor the former MP would set foot in this death trap, they just rake in the profits and scrap the parts when their polluting nightmare is no longer lucrative. We will fix this power imbalance and create more people like us."

There are only two ways out of this. Either I join her, or I fight. I have been looking for someone to fight ever since the Tuesday after Thanksgiving, and I found her. She's very emotional, and I know ways of getting under her skin. "How would your dad react to this?" I smirk. My cheeks flush, and my body warms up. "Unless he's also in on this. I should have known; he must be the ringleader of the operation. He has plans and knowledge of government systems. But since he could not get anything done, he recruited his—"

"Holy shit, you are dumb." She cuts me off; my smile disappears. "Can you imagine him being a part of this? I love my dad, but one thing he is not is tough on white-collar criminals. He won't even consider punishing eco-terrorists who lobby for deregulation."

"What are you talking about? What do they have to do with the destruction of the nuclear plant and creating more people like us?"

"One hundred companies around the world create more than two-thirds of global emissions, six of whom are in this country. Their existence is incompatible with a healthy planet. They've known for almost a hundred years that they're killing us and hid that information. They only care about money and keeping other people poor. This means a sizable portion of the population is too focused on economic survival to deal with the deadliest crisis facing our planet. They love to point towards the gas-guzzling poor person with a huge carbon footprint because it takes the blame off of them long enough to keep drilling, fracking, or mining.

"And when the earth is destroyed, they'll retreat to their decked-out doomsday shelters and sell the masses extremely marked-up supplies to make even more money. You could help me take them all down and give real power to the people. I know how to stay hidden, and you are a fast learner. That little altercation with those three newspaper boys did not go unnoticed. If you help me, those things will stay buried, and better yet, I can help you with whatever you want. We are, unfortunately, going to miss that movie. It would have been a nice treat after two friends joined forces to save the world. But it took a while for you to wake up and set up this apparatus. It was very convenient to have this equipment already in the shed. Anyway, I'm getting off-track here. It's time for your awakening, Ms. Pontellier. There are choices you must make. You can return to your boring life with Mr. Pontellier, meaning we all die in eight years from heating the planet by eight degrees. Or we can exact real change; the choice is yours."

She already read *The Awakening* during summer school. Edna Pontellier is a housewife who goes on vacation with her family. She meets an assortment of people: her best friend, Mme. Ratignolle, tries to remind her of her duties as a mother, while the talented and hermetic Mlle. Reisz tells her not to conform to society's expectations. In the end, she kills herself by swimming into the Gulf of Mexico, trying to recapture the small amount of independence she held when she had her awakening. Its themes are about feminism and societal norms, not climate change, but I couldn't explain things to a crazy person.

I can still use my powers, but without my vision, I'd just be shooting blindly. I need another way to see around me. Eyes are only sight receptors. My brain processes these images and can shoot low-amplitude waves. These waves then feed information to me by rebounding off the large atoms.

"You know I'm right," she continues. "Your mother went into debt trying to do something she loved. Now she is killing herself trying to get rich at the expense of the planet. If she could do what we do, do you think she would be slaving away in this death trap?"

"Stop monologuing, bitch. You're not the good guy here. Just look at what you are doing to me, to this town."

"And you think you are the good guy? You're a passive observer and consumer."

"That's better than being a murderer."

"It's funny that you keep resorting to hollow labels rather than trying to refute anything I say."

"Refute? I'm not going to debate with a sociopath."

"That's another hollow label. I still care about you. No matter what happens, you're still like a brother to me. And you know deep down that I have not told a single lie."

She can still read my mind. I need to stop internalizing my thoughts, and I need to find a way out. If I could block out my thoughts, she would have nothing. So if I clear my mind, think of nothing. There are only millions and millions of moving particles floating in mostly-empty space colliding with each other. When there are no collisions, there is silence.

She turns away and sits in a corner, rocking her head. I see her reach into her hoodie pocket and pull out her pills, shaking them, except there's no rattling sound. She has taken her mind off me. If I shake off my hood, I can look all around me, everywhere except down.

My brainwaves tell me the proximity of every particle around my head, creating a clear monochromatic picture three hundred and sixty degrees around me. The gradients resemble an old black-and-white television set, while the picture quality is of a detailed Optical Gas Imaging Device. It is far superior to looking at the atomic level, because my frame of vision is much larger. Air particles come close before their opposing charge sends them whizzing through the air. Sometimes they rebound off the deteriorating planks of wood that make up the shed or other particles. The wood sidings rain down particles, deteriorating and falling to the ground. And through this picture, I could see her, made up of particles. The back of her neck is made of gaping pores, blotches of oil, and beads of sweat. Not even makeup could cover it up.

I'm on a wall, chained up similarly to when Mr. Riviera had me the same night I accidentally gave Liam a bloody nose. My arms lift above my head, and the handcuffs loop around a metal c-channel fastened to the wall, this time with two bolts. Both are silver, a little more than an inch long. I turn the bolt counterclockwise, very slowly and quietly.

It's working. I can feel them moving, although she might notice. I need to get her to talk so she does not read my mind.

"Let's say I do agree to partake in your scheme, and let's say we do kill the execs of the one hundred biggest companies around the world," I ramble. "Ignoring the fact somebody just as bad will replace them, it's only a matter of time before someone else finds out. Say Tikha? She's almost as persistent as you. She will put the pieces together."

"I think I'll be able to get her onboard easily. She's as passionate about the issues as I am. She, too, is like us, but cannot shoot waves out of her head." The grin on her face grows wider, pores on her face close.

"What about your dad?" I ask. "If it gets out that the daughter of an MP who ran on abolishing nuclear energy blew up a nuclear plant, think about the optics. Nuclear energy becomes much stronger. The plant might even reopen." Unlikely, but it would get under her skin.

She doesn't respond for a second and paces around the shed.

Où est T?

Oh shit. She's scared, she's calling out for her cousin.

"Scared?" she asks. "I don't get scared." She spins away from me and paces back until she turns again. The first screw detaches itself from its pilot hole. I wait for her to face away from me so it can fall.

It's almost too easy now. "So, your dad knows nothing? He doesn't know you're the reason he won." I stroke her ego. "What would she do if he resigned?" It's clear she needs a man on the inside.

"No. How does any parent feel about their child getting superpowers? Have you told your parents?"

I have not told them anything; the waves propagating out of her head decrease in frequency and increase in amplitude, which means she's less nervous.

"I have spent the better half of a year earning a glowing reputation. I'm not the girl who publicly assaulted three students or his girlfriend."

I keep my cool and remember when Yasmine and I got back together. I have to stay focused on unscrewing the bolts.

"But that does not matter anyway," she says. "Stop stalling, Sid. Have you told your parents? Have you told Yasmine or your sisters?"

I breathe in and out. My breath forms a laminar stream of particles from my mouth. "I know how they feel about big sudden changes, and I know they can handle it. And at the end of this, I'm sure they will be grateful for what I will have done for them." The second bolt falls, as well as the c-channel. I create another point cloud in my head and see the outside of the shed. There's no one in proximity. We are alone.

Watch your head.

"*Pardon?*" she exclaims.

I step to the right and yank my chains downwards with my sore arms. The creaking pipe falls in a quarter-circle arc. She's positioned slightly to the left of me.

Three distinct sounds ring throughout the shack. The first is the sound of the c-channel detaching from the wall. The second is the sound of a rusty pipe colliding with Harriet's head, and the final is the combined sound of a body and pipe hitting the ground and rebounding before settling.

With my hands finally free, I stretch my arms, rotate my shoulder blades, and let them dangle until sensation returns. I zip up my hoodie and place my hood over my head. I need to preserve as much energy as I can.

I remove my blindfold. It's hard to believe that she thought a thin piece of fabric would have stopped me from using my powers. I didn't need Mr. Riviera to fix my eyesight. Maybe I would have felt hopeless sometime in the future, but not today. I stand next to the unconscious girl on the ground with blood spilling out of the top of her head. She's just lying on her back, almost motionless. Her right ear is drowning in a growing pool of blood, and the bump on her head is swelling. Her fingers twitch a little, while her ribcage is moving up and down. Her heart beats weakly, but it's not slowing down. Her white clothes start to absorb blood and change colour. She'll wake up eventually.

I'm still wearing the handcuffs, so I scavenge her pockets, trying to find my phone, car keys, or key for the handcuffs. I check her sweater, her pants, bra, and shoes, but I can't find anything. I search the entire shed. But the only thing in the shed is my old pair of glasses.

After a month of sitting in the shed, they're a little rusty, and the cracked lenses started to pick up some fungal growth. The boy who wore these glasses would have done anything to get the life he had, but he's a superhero now.

I drop the glasses and they shatter again. Without a key, all I can do is let the handcuffs wither. I zoom in on an atomic level, and in less than a second, each particle drifts away and disintegrates.

Even though I don't have my car keys, I can still make it home, unless that's where she would expect me to go. I need to go somewhere she can't find me. I exit the shack and avoid the jagged nails by the entrance.

I need to talk to the real Mr. Riviera. He's in bad shape, so I head to OHG. It's across the bridge, north of Islington. Regardless, I need to get far away from this shed and from her.

The wall sidings are almost entirely rotten, the roof is practically one giant hole, and the door is minutes away from falling off its hinges. I will never return to the shack.

Using one large amplitude wave, I look down and shoot the wave at the ground. It rebounds as I jump, and the wave then pushes me upwards. I hop over the fence without snagging any articles of clothing, land safely on the asphalt of Rideau Valley Drive North, and run away.

Part 5.3: Meeting #9 (Attempt #8 cont.)
Sidney, November 14th, 01:00

"Can you hear me, Sid?"

I run far away from I&MNG and towards Islington. Islington's impressive structures guide me away from my dark hometown. The streetlights are warmer in colour and more concentrated.

The ambiance noises get louder as I travel east along the Morissette Bridge.

"Where are you, Mr. Riviera?" I ask him in my head.

"You told me something the day after the election. Is this the path I wanted to follow? Anyway, if I know myself, I will take this as an indication to go back to my family."

"Where would that be? Can you send an e-mail or call me?"

"I have no connection to my former body. All I have is his memories since I installed myself."

"Then what are you?"

"I am just a piece of his subconscious who will guide you. I cannot control you or look through your eyes. I cannot make you do anything you do not want to do. But I can still hear your thoughts and will pester you to complete some unfinished work."

"I'm not going to kill her. She will wake up again, possibly with a concussion and some memory loss. Maybe she'll forget about tonight."

"You need to help her."

"After what she did? She'll get a lot of people hurt or killed, and she will double down and get even dirtier."

"Not with that. You hurt her and need to help her back up."

"She wanted you dead."

"Do you have any idea how many death threats I've gotten from people like her over my thirty-six years of public service? Other than her powers, she's just like any other entitled radical

activist. They'll get everything they want and still find a reason to complain, and she gives people like us a bad name. But every time someone like her creates havoc in the world, we have more of a reason to stay hidden. We are creatures of emotion, and teenagers have the strongest emotions, but Harriet will grow up eventually and change because you have. Be mindful of everything you do, and your surroundings, and choose to see the good."

Suddenly, a cold breeze flows through my t-shirt and hoodie, chilling my back and creeping up my neck. I turn around to find Harriet; she has a small indent on the top of her head, and some of her hair near the right is stained red. Her white clothes are clean, instead of being drenched in the same red shade as her hair. She walks towards me, and I walk backwards, keeping my eyes on her as I cross the bridge.

A devious smile grows wider on her face. "I don't appreciate you leaving me for dead." Her eyes meet mine. "Good thing I got out of that shack before it collapsed."

"Where's my car?" I walk backwards, trembling.

"It's at your home. I took it back along with your phone, wallet, and keys." She smiles. "I want you to return home safely, but after what you did, you should forget this."

"You're a terrorist," I blurt out.

"I prefer the term 'anarchist', but you can call me whatever you want. You can refuse to say my name. But I know who I am." Her smile fades a little. "Someone who would rise against the tyranny of our money-hungry government."

Her definition is wrong, but the word perfectly describes what she is. "You killed people." I stop moving backwards. "You bring a bad name to your cause. This is not the way to move forward."

She laughs and wipes a tear from her face. "Have you ever noticed that it's always people in power that tell us that? It's the language of an old white man who never had to face any consequences for his actions. They tell people to 'turn the other cheek' but forget to acknowledge they support the people who dealt the first slap. You remind me of every do-nothing lip service, bad-faith actor who takes up space in our Parliament. You're Guillaume Riviera."

"I don't want to hurt you—"

"It's too late for that." She runs her right hand along the top of her head. A stream of blood falls next to her eye, down her cheek, and drips off her chin. "Besides, your inaction brings me more pain than any copper pipe could. You think you're civil, but really, you're just lazy. You think just because you're comfortable, it means we don't need to progress any further. We have reached a point where people only respond to apocalyptic events, and people like you need to be pushed out of their comfort zone. Case in point." She moves her arm, pointing towards I&MNG.

I lunge forward to grab her arm. She smugly narrows her eyes, staring at my grip, and smiles. After a couple of seconds, her eyes widen. She doesn't move. Her mouth trembles as she begins to breathe nervously. She can't use her powers against me. She slaps my arm, but I refuse to let go and twist her arm behind her back.

"We are going to the cops. And you are going to tell them everything." I let out a large exhale of relief. "I want you to be better. Please." I escort her back towards Manotick.

"Alright. I want us to be good by the end of this." She looks over my shoulder, and her frown turns into a smile. "But you just blew your chance, and I can't trust you yet."

My arm gets violently twisted behind my back, pushing my shoulder blade up to my neck. I release my grip and my field of vision shrinks down to pinholes. A black-hooded figure wearing grey sweats kicks me in the back of my right knee, so I collapse face-first onto the asphalt. Some aggregate embeds itself into my face and my ears start to ring. One sharp jolt of pain bursts throughout my right leg and arm.

The pain cripples me as I lie motionless on the ground. This person doesn't do anything else to me, and instead holds Harriet's hand; she looks grateful to be by their side.

I push myself off the ground, cringing at another jolt of pain shooting down my leg. I take a few seconds for my vision to return, and then I try to sweep the grey person's legs. The figure jumps. I try to uppercut the figure, but the person leans back and dodges. I try to kick the figure in the chest, but they grab, put their feet in a box stance, and push me to the ground.

The person slowly walks to me and yanks my head backwards. "Go to sleep," they whisper. My eyelids flutter.

I close my eyes, push my fingers into the asphalt below me, and with them firmly in place, push myself up. I look down and angle my forehead to the figure, then I shoot a large and invisible wave forward.

The masked figure shoots upwards and lands on their back. As they lay in pain on the asphalt, they grab their left knee, unable to move. I approach them and try to unravel their hood.

But my arms and my feet grow stiff. My body slides towards the north side of the bridge. My shoes grind on the sidewalk until they hit the cold steel cables near the base of the bridge. My hands jerk involuntarily until they meld to the surface of the handrail. My shoes also heat up and melt into the concrete. I can't move.

"Thanks for the distraction, T." Harriet helps the black-hooded figure onto their feet. "I needed time to recover from the head injury he gave me." She grabs their wrists, crosses both her arms, and hoists the person upwards.

"Are you okay?" they ask. "Let's *just* go home."

Those dark cat eyes, how she pronounces the 'j' differently, and the firm grip on my arm. "Tikha?"

"I'm sorry, Sid," Tikha apologizes. "This was the last thing I wanted, but when you hurt my cousin, my comrade, you hurt me. I did what I had to do."

Two of them share the same mind, and I should have kept an eye on the quiet kid. But why was she acting so clueless about the explosion? Why did she draw so much attention to herself and ask everyone so loudly? Nothing makes sense. Also, Tikha has to protect her family? All the families her cousin hurt need protecting. I grunt and try to lift my hands from the railings, but doing so would tear the skin off my palms, so I give up.

"Look around you. You can see it. The difference between Manotick and Islington?" Harriet asks. Tikha looks at her confused.

She pushes my head to the right, to Manotick. It's a quiet town full of very few dwellings, home to one hundred thousand, and a nuclear plant attacked by a terrorist. Then she pushes my head to the left to Islington. It's a livelier town full of soulless condominium buildings, pumping tons of light into the night sky. It's one in the morning, and despite the dense city centre being kilometres away, the city is loud enough for us to hear.

"You can either be like Islington, a town that can move with time, or like Manotick, left in the dark." She exhales deeply. "Attempt eight failed. We'll try some other time."

My hands warm up immensely, yet my body cools. I start to shiver. She's trying to knock me out cold this time. My energy leaves through my hands into the metal railing.

"Do you..." I give myself some time to breathe. I try to get a few words out before I blank out. "Have...any remorse for what you have done?" I take another breath. "To this town. To all the lives you affected?"

She rolls her eyes. "Does anyone have remorse for the collapse of a malevolent institution? It rarely ends in tears." She has been conditioning us far before this moment. She thinks her happy ending is blowing up the system, tearing down the metaphorical bricks in the wall, and doesn't care if anyone gets hurt.

"Enough, let's go. He learned his lesson." Tikha backs away slowly and heads towards Islington.

Harriet grabs Tikha's left leg, stopping her in her tracks.

"They are good people. My mother..." I mumble. "She was trying to provide."

"People do need to make money." She grabs my face. "But she had every opportunity to leave after paying off her debts. Instead, she got comfortable and chose to get rich over the planet's health, so she could also learn a lesson. Unfortunately, she will have lasting damage she won't recover from, but everyone goes through this." She releases her grip on my face.

"What are you talking about?" I ask.

"You wouldn't have saved her. Getting rid of tumours is easy, but curing cancer? You would have to rewrite her entire genetic code. And even if you were fully developed up there, you don't have the medical knowledge to save her; no one does." She seems almost apologetic. "All you can do is delay the inevitable. I'm sorry about her disease and that she got fired. But we all go through this, you can either—"

"What?" I scream. A sharp stabbing pain cuts through the back of my head like someone forcibly removed an already-impaled object from my brain. The back of my head drips onto my back and the railing behind me. I rip my hands from the railing. The duress helps me separate my skin from the metal. Metal splinters protrude from my palms, and the skin from my hands is partially missing around my fingertips and palms. I look at them on a cellular level and get rid of the fragments. I try to clench my fists, but it's still too painful.

The ground underneath me sinks. Four metal cables on the bridge behind me are severed; the lower halves fall into the river, while the top halves dangle from the arch, a few centimetres below my head. The two girls move backwards. Tikha is petrified, but her cousin takes her hand and drags her back to the Islington side.

My head falls below the railings on the south side. The road crumbles around me. I break the asphalt below my feet and free my shoes. The soles have lost traction, but I run to the south side of the bridge. When I touch the back of my head, blood coats the tips of my fingers. The metal railings deform, and the girder holding up the road yields under the stress of excessive loads.

The bridge continues to growl as more cables snap under the weight. Every cable on the north side snaps sequentially from the middle of the bridge outwards, one by one, creating a loud, low-pitch ring.

Mr. Riviera told me about a skull-fracturing power; it's a wave so dense and powerful it can slice through physical objects, including the back of my head.

For the past month, I wanted one thing, and no one told me it was impossible. I had been learning for months, and all I wanted to do was help her. And now I have been feeling incredible amounts of physical and mental torture, just to be told no.

"You got your second opinion, Sid. And I did tell you, there's nothing we can do that a machine has not already done. If we could have helped your mother, we could have done something without our powers."

Someone's got to pay.

"There's nothing you can do."

"I'm not going to do nothing," I say out loud.

"I understand how you are feeling."

"Don't give me that bullshit!" I yell. "Do you know what she put me through? Do you know what you put me through to deny me the one thing I wanted?"

"You need help, but if you don't get off this bridge, you will die."

"Get out of my head! You have no power over me."

"You can either learn to move on and accept it or let the emotions stirring inside you—"

My eyesight blurs as I collapse onto the asphalt. A deafening crash travels through me as the road underneath me shatters. The sudden quake upsets my vertigo. I regain my footing, then run northeast and jump off the bridge, diving below into the Rideau River.

I plunge into the cold water, and while fully submerged, I swim north, trying to keep up with the current so as not to be hit by any rubble. Fragments of concrete obstruct the flow of the Rideau. The remaining cables dangle from the red arches: the bridge that took about two years to build and stood for almost a decade fell because of the senior structural manager's daughter.

I touch my thumb to my index finger, then my middle finger, then my ring, and finally my pinky. My fingers respond to the painful, skinless touch. I swim upstream and east towards Islington. I have some unfinished business.

Gasping for air, I streak my hair backwards to see and get a feel for the cut on the back of my head. My head feels less hot now than when it produced the cable-splitting wave. The wound is about the width of my pinky nail, and thinner than a millimetre. The pain doesn't disappear, but I ignore it and the migraines.

I make it to shore and step on the gravel by the riverbank. I quickly shake myself off. The water on my body and clothes vaporizes within seconds.

The two girls are together, standing across from each other, talking.

"I thought about what happened and—"

I send a mind pulse and knock her backwards. She rolls across three lanes. I stand over her as she groans in pain. She bends her right leg but not her left, and rubs her back in pain. I unfurl my hands, and even though my palms sting as I wrap my fingers around her neck, I still find strength to squeeze. It hurts to grab her, but I feel a rush as I crush her throat.

But as the adrenaline starts to wear off, I look at the girl in my grasp. She's not struggling or trying to grab my hands. She's just lying on the ground and closing her eyes as if she's accepting her fate. The unblooded colour of her hair and her two dark brown eyes come into focus; this isn't Harriet, it's Tikha.

I let go of her. She's complicit, but I will deal with her later.

I turn around. Harriet stands in front of me. She raises her hands and the streetlights increase in intensity, shining directly at my eyes. The metal pole bends down to my level. Blinded, I fall to the ground. Tikha scampers away on her butt towards the river and disappears behind the riverbank.

"This is for your own good," Harriet declares. "But after what you have done to me, to my cousin. We all should forget about this." My body temperature rises. I start to feel light-headed; the lights and migraines paralyze me. "But I finally understand you. There is an issue you care about deeply." She grins. "There is a problem in your life so grand that it takes up every moment of your existence. Anytime you aren't thinking about ways to fix it, that moment is wasted. You cannot properly function until it is made right, and you would even break the law to fix it. You'd never give up on helping your mother, and I'm not giving up on you." She squeals in delight. "I know what it is like to feel powerless, knowing there is no real-world solution to help the ones you love. But the fight is only over if you give up. You are like me."

I clench my fist in anger. How dare she equate us? But the rage keeps me from passing out.

"Lights," a voice in the distance yells. It must be Tikha.

The lights serve two purposes: letting Harriet see, and giving her energy to use her powers. The high concentration of photons hitting my black clothes also helps. I can absorb ample amounts of energy and concentrate in a few powerful, yet painful waves. Also since I'm larger than her, and I ate and she didn't, I know I have more energy to use.

"It's a new year, time to turn off the lights." I concentrate on this feeling of rage and release three light pulses. The waves are silent as they exit my head, but as soon as the sound of the shattering light bulbs hits the asphalt, I know it works. The three closest lamps turn off within a second. The metal base of the streetlamps screeches as they contract toward their original positions.

Harriet lets out a pathetic grunt as she topples. I rub the sides of my head and look to find my whole palms coated in blood. I feel three new cuts on my head—all a little smaller than the first one. I shake my hands dry. I manage to power through, pushing myself off the ground. I feel a little disoriented from the blood loss. However, everything comes into focus when I see her, completely confused, grabbing her right ear.

She slowly manages to get two feet on the ground. The brainwaves exiting her head decrease in frequency. She's losing energy to the cold outdoors. I look up and condense the air around us, creating a fog around her and her surroundings.

"I know what you're trying to do," she stumbles in place. "You still need an energy source. There's no sun, or radiation, or photons, so you're going to pass out eventually, too."

"Don't worry." I walk up to her and place my right hand on her cheek. "I got one. You're so warm." She has energy stored in her, and I absorb it through skin-to-skin contact. If I were looking through an infrared spectrum, I would see her skin changing from a warm red to a cool blue. Instead, goosebumps cover her arms while her body hair stands up.

Her teeth start to chatter as she loses balance again. I release my grip.

"S-s-s-s-s-s-s-o-o c-c-c-c-o-l-l-l-d." She shivers and drops her arms, letting go of her ear, revealing a cut between her head and the helix of her ear. She's about to faint, but I hold her up without touching her.

I won.

"Harriet Isabelle Ganatra," I finally say her name. "It's over." She tries to touch my face, but I turn the other cheek, and her hand falls off. I grab her by her now blood-stained shirt. "Were you trying to absorb some energy?" I condescend. "Poor, little rich girl, it must be exhausting not getting one thing because you're so used to getting everything else handed to you. You have not suffered a day in your goddamn life. So let me get something through that thick skull of yours." I stare directly into her bulging brown and blue eyes; her lips quiver, and she hyperventilates. "It's your turn to feel powerless."

I lift her above my head, and with one swift motion, I throw her body onto the asphalt. She cries as she hits the ground with a loud crack. After a few seconds of whimpering, she tries to slither away.

I pin her to the ground with my melted shoe. "This is for your own good." I stomp on her back. She unfurls herself and wails.

I use my foot to flip Harriet on her back so I can look at her as she struggles to breathe. "If today has taught me anything, it's that you don't care about the planet, people, or even your friends or family. You want to play God." I stomp on her chest.

"And why; do you crave power? Do you like seeing my status-quo family suffer? Did you give my mother that tumour?" I stomp on her chest again. "Did you?" I scream. "You were the person who started this whole chain of events."

She shakes her head.

I kick her left arm; the scar opens up and blood starts to run from it. "Well, you are going to feel every bit of pain she felt." I walk over to her right side and kick her so hard that she tumbles a few times on the asphalt and lands on her front again. "You know, calling you a terrorist is too good for you. You are just a spoiled child with a complex." I wind my foot up for the final blow to the right side of her head, near her almost-severed ear. "No more destruction. No more power outages." I exhale sharply. "No more pain."

"Sidney!" I freeze, my leg still up in the air. Harriet doesn't move. We both look at where the sound originates; towards the riverbank, where I can barely see a hand waving through the fog, Tikha crawls out.

"Nothing will get better if you kill her."

Harriet weakly positions herself into a semi-upward-dog position.

"I know she hurt you. She hurt us both." Tikha tries to push herself up. "But she's not the single source of all our problems. It's much bigger than just her." Tikha's entire body is above the riverbank. "Please, Sidney. Some people don't get time to analyze what they have done, but you do, and she will, too. This is not your fight; she's just a victim of terrible circumstances."

I put my foot on the ground, step back, and look around. The broken bridge between the two towns continues to crumble. Even though the arches remain, the roads and supports are gone. I did that, not her.

Harriet's lying on the ground in filthy clothes, covered in the gravel, blood, dirt, and the rubber from my shoes. She only has enough strength to turn her dismembered face to me. She looks at me with her black eye as her right ear dangles a couple of centimetres off her head.

It would have been so easy to kill her with my powers, just freeze her lips or push her to the bottom of the river. But I want her to look at the face of the person she hurt the most. I want her to suffer, but she has always been suffering. She has to take antidepressants so she could function properly. Her mom's dead, her father's no longer there for her, and her cousins and boyfriend didn't always know what she needed, but both Tikha and I do.

No one would recognize her in this state. But I saw a little girl constantly in pain: she couldn't unsee a world plagued by imbalance. A world where the powerful ravage the powerless until they are weak, repressed, and miserable people stripped of everything they ever had. I did what I wanted to do to her, but it wouldn't change her awakening.

Harriet tries to get up, but her left arm is too weak to hold her weight; her right arm tries to make the difference, but because of the broken bones in her body, she strains her face. She manages to crank her head off the ground and meets my eyes. "S-s-s-s-s-i-i-d-d. I'm-m-m s-s-o-o-r—"

A siren breaks her stuttering, and the police's red cherry and high beams blind us.

I fall onto the ground; Harriet receives a small jolt of energy and pushes herself off the ground. She grabs onto my pant leg. "RUN," She yells without a French accent. I look at my hands and see them trembling, as I have never felt more energetic. My sight blurs and my breathing devolves into short rapid breaths. "You have ten minutes. Run," she orders, then promptly collapses on the pavement.

I get up and sprint southbound, past the entrance of Islington. Tikha has hidden beside the gravel ridge near the Rideau; her left leg is all mangled.

The adrenaline courses through my veins. My heart races. I can't hear the river or the armed officers, I can only hear my heartbeat. I'll be fast and focused, but in nine minutes, it will reach my brain.

I have to leave, like Mr. Riviera wanted, alone and floating around the world. I can dematerialize and disappear. I start with my hands. I look down and zoom in, separating the atoms. I don't need to memorize their structure. When I look away, they return to their original composition, and they even heal themselves with new skin. I must dematerialize myself long enough for the cops to lose sight of me.

The tips of my fingers start to vanish until they form stubs, then my palms disintegrate. Particles flake off my hand until they are gone. Mother always caressed my face with her hands. She told me I needed to be there for our family and act like the man of the house. When she grabbed my face, she showed me what it's like to be firm but also warm.

I fight it; my hands are gone. I keep pumping my handless arms. The adrenaline keeps me going. The next part of my body to disintegrate is my arms. My wrists go, then my forearms, then my upper arms and shoulders. My sweater is hanging on my torso with the sleeves flapping around my body. Mom embraced me with her arms when we were going to visit Mother. Mom always hugged me tightly. She wanted to keep me close. And Kyle. He held on to me, and even though he may have changed his entire personality, he was still my best friend and I know he will never forgive after he finds out what I did to his girlfriend.

This is what I need to do. I suppress any urges to rematerialize. My legs are the next to go. My shoes lift off the ground and disappear with my legs. I float off the ground. And I remember Mindy. We would run across our backyard together. She would not run away if it got tough and was always there when we needed her. She would give up her entire future for her family. And I remember Mr. Ganatra, the father I never had. He ran for office because he knew what his wife and daughter loved above all else. He asked me what my mother loves above everything, and now I know.

It's getting harder to disappear. My pants and shoes fly off behind me, but I am halfway there. Next are my chest and stomach. I look down to see my skin flake off to reveal my rib cage and internal organs, and slowly, they disappear. My sweater flies off behind me. I think of Kat and how her biological family vanished from her life. She could not live through that again. Her heart could not take it. And then I think of Yasmine. I know it will be over between us after she finds out what I did to Harriet. But I will always be grateful to her for the best two years of my life. What we had was real; we tried this time.

They both will have family members who will care for them. They don't need me. I look down and do not see a shred of my original body. The last thing to go is my head. This is when I think about Mr. Riviera, who opened my mind to new ideas, and even though I forgot everything during my rampage, I know how to keep myself grounded. And Tikha, whom I only knew for a couple of months, left the most impactful change in my life. She saw the worst thing I did and still chose to reason with me.

I can't leave my home, family, or friends. There's too much grounding me here. I could never be like Mr. Riviera; I will have to pay. I breathe, inhale, and exhale, then shut off my mind.

I crash into the ground, and a jolt of pain hits my rib cage and skull. My head starts to numb as my heart slows down. The adrenaline is out of my system. I lie facedown on the ground, naked. Unfortunately, my brain doesn't memorize the atomic configuration of my clothes or body hair. My heart beats silently, and the faint whispers of the cops get louder. The fog falls onto my face. The suspended water atoms collect on my skin and cool me off.

I breathe through my nose and out through my mouth. It's my last breath as a free person. All the pain and agony I cause collapse in on me.

I'm sorry, Mother, I cannot heal you.

The police stand over me. I place my hands over my head. They gently help me up and cover my body with one of their jackets as they escort me to their squad car. Another massive migraine shrouds my entire head and blinds me.

One of them places their hand on my head and shoves me into the backseat. The other officer looks away and gives me my discarded clothes from the ground. I blindly put them on in the backseat, then rest my bleeding head on the cold window, trying to mitigate my migraine.

As they read me my rights, I look in their rearview mirror. An ambulance picks up the girls.

"Sidney?" one of the officers asks.

Everyone's gone.

Part 5.4: Six Weeks
Vritikha

A blinding blue light appears behind Sid as he screams "What?" Four steel cables behind him splash into the water. The bridge below us sags. Harriet grabs my hand and drags me off the bridge to Islington. While she tries to get me to run, my headscarf flies away. I try to retrieve it, but it's lost in the wind.

"We need to get out of here right now." Harriet's panicked words are barely audible over the sounds of deforming metal and crumbling asphalt splashing into the river below us.

My feet try to pick up the pace. I haven't moved this fast since physiotherapy. After we make it safely to the ground, all I can hear is the bending of metal, churning of the bridge and road debris into the Rideau, and pieces of the bridge falling into the river.

Everything is gone except the two red arches and half-cut, dangling cables. There are no roads, sidewalks, or railings; our towns are disconnected.

Harriet escorts me away from the entrance of Islington, northbound. "Tell me what's happening." I forcibly remove my arm from her grasp.

She looks at me, lowering her line of sight until she stops at my waist. My phone, keys, and earbuds exit my pockets, levitate for a few seconds, and fly to the riverbank's edge. "I want to trust you, but at the same time, I thought I could trust him. Anyway, Sid got telekinetic powers from the power plant explosion. He was hoping he would help his mother. After realizing that it's impossible, he's now going full-Akira." She giggles to herself. "Or should I say half-Akira?"

"What the hell is wrong with you?" I yell. "How are you making jokes right now? Sid was going to kill you, the bridge just collapsed. But he's dead now. What have I done?" I never wanted him dead. I wanted the madness to be over. I lose my balance but stop midair as Harriet raises her hand and, without touching me, stabilizes my feet to support myself.

"Relax, Sid's not dead. And in the end, this will all be a pleasant dream. The bridge complicates things, but it's fine. This is fine." She smiles half-heartedly. "He'll be fine."

She seems unfazed by everything that happened. She wasn't exactly joyful in the plant's explosion, but she did try to downplay the tragedy. "You're responsible for all of this," I deduce. Of course, she would benefit from the explosion. Riviera and her father are figureheads, not masterminds. "What did you do?"

"I brought about real change. But we need to band together to stop the psychopath who capsized the bridge. You have seen the future; Sid's going to strangle you." She shakes her head. "Hide, I'll take care of it."

"How do you know that?" I ask. She can't read Urdu.

"I can't read your board, but a translator app can."

I grew up with this girl. I let her stay in my room. I shared my most private thoughts and feelings with her. She was always there for me. She's always there for me. "What happened on Thanksgiving Sunday at Kyle's house? Why doesn't anyone remember anything?"

"The first failed plan. I had no proof anyone had gained powers from the explosion. It was easier to wipe the slate clean before trying another attempt. With every iteration, I learn something new." She holds her head high as if she realizes something. "And I think I know how to get Sid."

"Who hurt you?"

"The largest polluters in the world." She ignores my rhetorical question, but it's on me for not expecting a genuine answer. "While this plant isn't one of them, it's emblematic of a larger, systemic problem. People are too comfortable."

I step away from her, but she raises an arm and I freeze.

"I thought you could've changed Krishna, but apparently he changed you. I'm so disappointed." She forcibly quivers her lower lip. "Kyle and Yasmine were only involved in our movement for the community service hours. But not you. We think alike, act alike, and fantasize about ways to save the planet. The only difference between us is that I did something. I want you to join in secretly making the world a cleaner place, using your ability to see the future to tell us successful and foolproof ways to shut down dangerous polluters—"

"People are dead because of you," I interrupt. "Not the dangerous polluters, but the nine-to-five middle-to-lower-class people."

"That tour guide killed himself by saving us. He chose to become a hero. But his sacrifice was not in vain." She holds her hands in mine. I shiver, as I still can't move. "Someone has to get hurt, otherwise nothing will change. If you help, I promise only the elitist pricks and lobbyists will suffer. We will form a revolution, better than anyone has seen, because no one even knows we exist. Take a stand, and for once in your life, stop being a pitiful little bitch."

I forcibly jerk my hand away. Vipesh has every right now to fear what his daughter is becoming.

"That was mean. I'm just in a lot of pain right now." She pulls the hair away from her eyes and blood drips down from her stained bangs. She looks into my eyes, tilting her head and fluttering her eyelids while a smile slowly creeps onto her face. I mirror her expression for a second before I break free from her gaze. She did the exact sequence of movements when she moved in; she's playing with my emotions.

This is the real Harriet. Everything's an act to her, and she's been playing me since moving back to Ottawa.

"I know what you're thinking, T." She moves closer, but I'm still frozen. "I meant everything I said when I moved in, and I know you did, too. We have a lot of work, but we are not alone.

People who have their affairs in order get to live a life of complacency. It takes a broken person to see what isn't right with this world; it takes a headstrong person to do something. I know you're broken, but I'm both. So what do you say, sister? I am trying to save the planet, while Sid is only trying to save his mother. Who will you fight for?" Harriet extends her hand to me. I lean on my real leg to take pressure from the knot in my back.

I inhale and exhale softly. "I thought about what happened and—"

A blast of wind knocks me off my feet and tosses me across the asphalt. I fall onto my right shoulder and roll into a ridge next to the river, underneath a streetlight. I wince as the knot in my back spreads and shoots up my spine. I reach to push my spine back in order. Sid stands above me, blocking the bright light with his head.

He stands on top of me, lunging towards my neck, wringing his hands around me for a second. I close my eyes; I don't know if I could have stopped her. I deserve this.

After a few seconds, he releases his grip with a horrified expression. He takes a step backwards and turns around.

Harriet comes up behind him. The streetlights bend down to their level and brighten immensely. He shuts his eyes hard and collapses on the asphalt next to me as I crawl away from the two of them.

I roll myself behind a ridge beside the river, barely hiding from them. I can't hear Harriet, but Sid is submitting to her. Nothing will change if she wins again like the other seven attempts prior. I need to help him.

He can destroy the lights the same way he destroyed the bridge, so I yell at him, "Lights." The sound of glass shatters and the lights go out. But I could not have predicted what he would do next.

I try calling out for him, but it doesn't work. He continues to stomp Harriet within an ounce of her life. But when I shout his full name, he freezes, with his foot in the air. I say everything I can to stop the carnage, and when he puts his foot down, I exhale in relief.

Sirens approach. He runs past me as I put my leg back on. The two officers pursue him as I hide below the ridge. My leg socket won't bend. I roll up my pant leg and inspect the damage. The mechanism that locks my leg is destroyed.

The police officers are not looking in my direction but call for an ambulance to pick Harriet up. I try to make an exit when the police are not looking.

"T?" she whimpers. "Help."

She's still family, and maybe I can get her to confess. She laces her fingers around my wrist. "You're so warm." My hand gets warmer, but the rest of my body cools.

I hold on to her. "What is going to happen to him?"

"I'm going to stop," she answers, trying to get up on her knees, screaming in pain.

I slip my fingers down to her wrist. "He's going to be okay." Her pulse accelerates as she continues to speak. She looks into the distance at him and frowns.

She's lying. She's not going to change. "You can have your obsessions," I repeat her words. "As long as you're not hurting yourself or anyone else." I grab her hideously deformed face, peel her black eyelid open, and stare at her angrily. Her eyes roll backwards, and she collapses onto her chest.

She lies motionless on the asphalt in a pile of rubber, glass, and blood. I hide behind the ridge as an ambulance arrives on the scene. I step on something slippery; it's my black headscarf. It's soaking wet and covered in dirt and sand. It doesn't smell like anything else, so I lather myself in the same soil and sand and curl into a ball next to the riverbank, shivering, trying not to make a sound.

Once everyone clears the crime scene, I peek out from the ridge.

Everyone's gone.

I shut my eyes and suppress the urge to scream. How do I explain to anyone what happened tonight? My arms and back are covered in road rash, I can't stand up straight, and my stump is giving me phantom cramps again. The invisible knife stabs and severs my limb.

Why don't I feel better? I stopped them, I'm still alive. I got everything I wanted; it's not a small victory. But they were my friends, and they showed me their real colours. He's the violent psychopath in my visions, and she's a sociopathic manipulator. He ran away like a coward while she didn't learn anything, even after getting the shit kicked out of her. She was trying to save the planet, he was trying to save his mother, but in the end, I got to save myself. Why does the universe reward selfish acts? And why am I accepting it?

My phone and headphones lie in the gravel next to the riverbank. I pick them up and see that it's almost three in the morning. I prepare for a thirty-minute walk home on a broken prosthetic. Connecting my headphones, I play the song *Wolves Without Teeth*. I turn the volume up to try to drown out my internal monologue. I limp back home; every other step inflames my phantom pain.

I have also received a few texts from Krishna:

<u>I understand now. I invaded your privacy.</u>

<u>I know this is relatively new territory for you.</u>

<u>I apologize for overstepping. Can we talk?</u>

He was in my room for a while. He could've read what was on my whiteboard. He could deduce that I'm responsible for everything.

All I can do now is forget about it and work on something else. I could start by dedicating all my time to school and work, which is what I should have been doing in the first place. I'll pass out in the restaurant and lie to Abba about waiting for Harriet. I could wear heavy clothes to cover my scars and a hijab around my neck for the bruises.

My phone dies, and the music stops with it. But even when I go to recharge it, I won't reply to Krishna. According to my visions, I'm supposed to marry him. But I can't be with someone who would go behind my back as he did. And he overstepped? I heard that excuse before. My visions don't chronicle forever; they change so quickly and cruelly. It's not up to me. Why did I ever think it was?

I finally make it home. I unlock the door.

November 15th, 9:00

I open the door to Chemistry class. I was listening to *I Heard I Had* before entering. I remove my headphones from my ears as Yasmine runs up to hug me. I'm greeted with a thousand sympathetic eyes. Ms. Stone doesn't call me out for being late, as it now takes longer to get to school since the Morissette Bridge is no longer standing. The bus I usually take rerouted itself through Long Island. Yasmine walks me to our lab bench and tells me she's one hundred percent on my side. She has disowned Sid forever.

We begin our titrations. Yasmine tells me about how she's done with everything in Manotick. Being hospitalized from the explosion and bedridden from allergies was terrible, but after what Sid did, she's taking it as a sign to move to Barbados at the end of the year. She explains that she's only known half of her life by living in Islington and needs to change.

She seems excited and tells me about her plans to put her hair in cornrows, drink from coconuts, and bicycle around the island. She assures me we will still be friends, and for the next nine months, I'm all hers. Afterwards, we will still video-chat and go to Bluesfest, and she will visit Ottawa twice a year for a week to be with her father.

I perform my titrations and dispense too much sodium hydroxide into the vinegar, making the mixture too basic. The phenolphthalein indicator turns dark pink or dark red. I grab the beaker of dark pink liquid and dump the blood-coloured liquid down the drain. I lose grip for a second and accidentally drop the beaker in the sink, breaking it.

I hyperventilate at the broken glass in the sink. I collapse and almost break down, but not before Ms. Stone comforts me, telling me it's not a big deal.

I get up and find another beaker by opening the cabinet.

November 19th, 15:30

I open my locker and get my guitar while listening to *Black Water*. I close my locker, and Kyle seemingly appears on the other side. I look directly at his neck and the fresh x-shaped scar on his trachea, and then look up at his hair, now free of those ugly blond tips. I remove my headphones and put them around my neck. He asks if I have any news about my cousin. I don't have news, and I walk away, refusing to get involved in the school drama.

Most people took Harriet's side because of how rough she looked in the pictures from the hospital, but not everyone did. Some people took Sid's side because she's just so goddamn annoying.

Harriet has not woken up but is in stable condition, which is more than she deserves.

I stop in the middle of the hallway when I realize I don't have my guitar. Kyle brings it for me. I try to grab it from him, but he insists on carrying it. He continues to walk by my side. I have been wearing my realistic prosthetic, so it's harder to maneuver around with it.

Kyle tells me he should have trusted Yasmine when she said she got pushed. He didn't know whether to believe his ex-friend, thinking Sid would never do such a terrible thing. He then tells me he didn't like the person he was when dating Harriet.

We make it to the music room. Kyle holds the door open for me and hands me my guitar. He tells me briefly that he feels guilty about not stopping their little movie date.

All I can think is, 'Who is this guy?'. He seems almost reasonable and courteous, and nothing like her prick of a boyfriend. He seemingly reverted to his old, indecisive, and rigid self. He changed because of her—she forged the man of her dreams.

I enter through the doors and join band practice.

November 22nd, 11:00

I enter Ms. Phillips' English class and stop listening to *Tongues*. We receive our graded essays. I got an eighty-one, the best mark I have ever gotten in any English class.

But it wasn't the essay I wrote two weeks ago. I came home early Sunday morning and distracted myself from the incident. I rewrote my entire essay in one night. The most evident example is my introduction. 'While Macbeth had the option to change his faith, King Lear never had a chance to change. Both tragic heroes experienced their self-fulfilling prophecies by succumbing to their tragic flaws'. My conclusion stated: 'Both tragic heroes exemplify the terrible reality of one's conquest to gain power; it was ultimately their tragic flaws which led to their respective downfalls'.

My essay has changed. It used to say that the works were more different than similar, and now I say they are more similar than different.

Ms. Phillips gives everyone a copy of *The Awakening* by Kate Chopin. I take the book, put my headphones back on, and exit the class.

November 26th, 16:00

334

I open the door to our restaurant and Abba walks me through the aisles and up the stairs to our apartment. I take off my headphones. Varshil and Vijay are sitting at the dining table, watching the news on one of their phones. The lower third news chyron says: 'Former MP Guillaume Riviera has passed peacefully in Quebec, surrounded by his loving family at age seventy-eight'.

Varshil turns off his phone as the four of us sit at the dining table. Both Ammi and Veera are video conferencing with us. Ammi tells us she will be coming home in a month as Nani has given up on her treatments and has a couple of weeks left to live.

After being dismissed, I enter my room and take out my guitar. I sit upright on my bed, remove my prosthetic, and try to recreate the bass line to *Live Through the Night* on my acoustic guitar. After a couple of minutes, I hear a knock on my door.

Varshil enters with teary puppy eyes. Without saying a word, he sits on my right and nestles under my arm, laying his head on my chest. I pat him and rub my fingers through his hair like Veera does to me. Soon after, Vijay joins us. He puts his head on my stump, looking up at me, and I start to rub his head and Varshil's at the same time.

They both want to listen to me play. I have never felt close to them until now. I hum the tune of the song to them. After almost two hours, they both fall asleep. I slowly maneuver myself out from underneath my brothers as they lie peacefully on my bed. I put on my black button-up, pants, and shawl to begin my shift.

I open the door from our apartment and walk downstairs.

December 2nd, 18:00

I enter our restaurant. I take out my tablet and put on a phony smile. I don't say anything, but the first family tells me they want water. More and more people have been coming in since Harriet got sent to the hospital, as they want to pay their respects. Abba even put out a small vigil in front of the restaurant for her and Nani.

While moving to another table, I hear a tap on the window and turn around to a little girl through the glass, waving her hand and summoning me outside. I put down the tablet, exit our restaurant and see Sid's little sister, Kat. She runs to the rest of her family. I had never really seen Ms. Tamashiro until now. Her bald head is wrapped in a scarf and covers her right eye as well. She needs the support of another woman, whom I would guess would be his sister. They look alike; she's wearing the same glasses as Sid.

Ms. Adams immediately apologizes for his actions, claiming she knows everything. I want to unload on them, but they didn't do anything wrong. Besides, no apology could ever make up for what he did.

Instead, I shake my head, but they apologize again. Ms. Tamashiro hands me a gift bag, telling me that she knows no gift can make up for Sid's behaviour, but he's now getting proper help to deal with his issues.

Abba comes outside looking for me, and the four women leave.

I pull out the gift to see a green candle with a tranquil scent that reminds me of Harriet and Sid's neighbourhood. I would almost assume it was homemade because there is no label or a receipt. Abba suggests I put it next to Harriet's picture. We enter our first set of doors. I strike a match and light the candle instead for Nani.

I pretend to be sick, quit my shift, and then open the door to the restaurant.

December 16th, 18:00

I enter the restaurant again. Veera is taking what should have been my shift as she has returned from Toronto for the winter break. I'm listening to *Little Talks*, before I take off my headphones; not even the sight of her cheers me up. She caresses my face and touches my scarf. She smiles, as she always wanted us to match like this.

She deduces that something's troubling me and asks me if I have seen Harriet. I shake my head.

She tells me Kaka goes as much as he can. The next time he will visit her is in a couple of days. She says it's almost therapeutic to tell her things you would not usually tell her if she was conscious, and she would convince Abba to rescind my grounding for one day.

I close my eyes.

December 18th, 11:20

I open my eyes. It's the first Sunday of winter break. Harriet has been in the hospital for over a month now. Vipesh signs me in. I have one earbud in my right ear, listening to *The Clearing*. We enter together; she's hooked up to a ventilator. Her heart rate beats around forty beats per minute, but she's still breathing, very slowly. The doctors have no idea why she's still asleep. I scratch behind my neck; my earbud drops to the floor.

Vipesh tells me that he has always regarded the boy who nearly killed her daughter to be like a son to him, and he couldn't believe that Sid would do such a thing. He then asks if I want some time alone with her. I nod.

Everyone leaves the room. I circle the bed and walk to her left side. The bruises on her eye and her shoulder have turned a yellowish-brown colour, but the most attention-grabbing deformations are the surgery scars on her right ear, even more than the casts around her mid-section and left arm.

I want to ask her if she is in pain and if she's suffering from being trapped in her mind's prison. Then tell her she deserves it.

I want to tell her everything about her is a lie. Her hair and accent are fake, and so is the boy she 'fixed'. Her entire personality is manufactured; everything...except for her politics.

She's a comrade, but not family.

But even now, I know I didn't want to see her die. I didn't want him to keep kicking until she became motionless. The last time I felt this powerless was when my Nana died right in front of me.

Harriet has done horrible things, and she told me why. I know why she blew up the plant. I understand why she wanted me to be another pawn in her devious scheme. The small explosion didn't make that much difference in how the world operated, but it still affected hundreds of thousands of lives.

The confines of this world don't allow us to grow, only assimilate. She did think she was making the world better, in a Machiavellian way.

I look at her broken face and stare at the scar that starts on her nose and ends next to her right eye. I interlace our fingers holding her broken arm and kneel next to her bed.

"You don't deserve this."

I can say no more. Her fingers twitch, and her heart rate speeds up. I release my grip and walk out with my head down. Vipesh runs into the room, alongside a couple of doctors.

"She's resurfacing," one of them says.

The intercom turns on, and I pick up my earbuds off the floor and shove them deep into my ear canals, turning *Six Weeks* on full blast. I cannot believe it. She'll wake up feeling vindicated, while everyone else she hurt still suffers. She's the problem. I chose the wrong side.

"I'm sorry, Sid."

Every step I take intensifies my phantom pain as I exit the hospital.

December 18th, 16:00

I re-enter our restaurant while listening to *All to Myself* when Abba hugs me. "Great news, Vritikha. Hari has woken up; we will be able to see her again." I get as far away from him as I can.

Everything kind of just blends. I have been living on autopilot and haven't been able to remember one vision since that night. I start in one place and end up in another. Every terrible vision I dream of happens, and if it doesn't, it explodes into something much worse. Bad people win, lives get destroyed.

I enter my room and sit on my bed, sliding against the wall and dragging my head down until it hits a sharp corner. I find my whiteboard sandwiched between my bed and the wall. I pick it up; the writings have not changed in five weeks, and are in English.

Harriet in trouble: She's a powerful and resourceful girl. She was never going to be in trouble, because she is trouble.

Sid yelling: He's a monster. Everyone kept telling me he was a nice guy. How could everyone be so wrong? How could I have let my guard down around him? He's dangerous, but also the lesser of two evils, and I still chose wrong.

Dead body: These visions keep lying to me. But she could have been a martyr if she died.

Chemistry class: This is one of the nine moments where I am reminded there is lasting damage to the people around me, and it's also my fault.

I couldn't look at it anymore. I throw it across the room towards Harriet's desk. It shatters the glass picture frames of her parents and Kyle. Shards of glass rain on the carpet. I tear my essay up into a million pieces. It's my so-called best work, yet I don't believe the words I wrote. Harriet doesn't have a tragic flaw. A flaw is minute and can be fixed. She has a rot, and I almost let it infect me.

In my rampage, I forget about the pieces of glass, so I slip and fall on the carpet. I look at everything around me: my broken prosthetic, the pieces of shattered glass, and ripped-up paper; I'm the one lying in it now.

"Don't cry, don't cry. She does not deserve it," I whisper to myself.

Part 6

Part 6.1: Ammi
Vritikha, December 19th, 8:30

Another night passes and I wake up in my room by myself. Our family's going to the hospital in a few hours. I wake up feeling like every other day in the past six weeks.

I take my crutch and a towel to the bathroom. Once in, I let the water dribble over me. I know it's wasteful, but I struggle to care.

My neck starts to sting the longer the water trickles over me. A small cut underneath my ear and on my neck stings. Since I cut my hair, I haven't had anything to play with, so I scratched the back of my neck and must have broken the skin. All of my rashes and bruises along my arms, neck, and back have gone away, but not this one. I vigorously scrub behind my neck, and the water turns a reddish-brown colour as it goes down the drain.

My stomach growls and churns, and then something shoots up my throat. I vomit directly into the shower drain and groan at the sensation. I rinse out my mouth with water, gargle with it, and wash everything down the drain. Once I'm done showering, I wrap that towel around my chest, place my crutch under my shoulder, and open the door.

Veera's waiting on the other side, half-asleep and rubbing her eyes. "Hari?" Her name brings another pit to my stomach. I push her aside and limp to my room, slam the door, and lock myself in.

I cleaned up my room as much as possible yesterday, which meant putting back every broken frame where I found it and throwing away all the shards. I wasn't going to leave my room a wreck after my outburst. I don't want to step on the broken glass again, and it's bad luck to step on paper.

After the clean-up, the only intact pictures on Harriet's desk are the ones with Auntie Isabelle, Vipesh Kaka, and her four cousins. We were just so happy back then. Nine to ten years ago,

"

we spent every weekend together. We would play in her massive backyard when it was pleasant outside. And at night, we would stay up late, watching movies suitable for children. Once we watched a horror movie, and were all scared of monsters lurking in dark places. But Harriet protected us while the rest of us could sleep easily.

What happened to her? There must be more than just Auntie Isabelle's death. Auntie was always radical, but how much of an influence did she have on her daughter before she died?

"Can I come in?" Veera bangs on my door. "Vritikha, I was just surprised. Please?"

I rub my hair until it's dry and messy, then use the towel to hide my whiteboard. I put on sweatpants, an oversized shirt, and a zip-up hoodie. They are all grey, faded, and ill-fitting. Even though the outdoor temperature has not reached zero degrees, I always feel cold. I open the door.

"I'm worried about you," she says before entering. "Your room is a mess. You have been missing your shifts, and..." She takes her hand and turns my head ninety degrees to the left. "I just noticed this. How did these scratch marks happen?" She looks at me with tearful and heavy eyes.

"This isn't what it looks like; I just tripped because I could not get used to the weight of my realistic prosthetic leg."

Veera stares at me until I give in to the urge and start scratching the back of my neck again. I wince at the stinging sensation.

"You have a very obvious tell when you're lying." Veera sits on the floor. She pats the carpet beside her and I join her. "It's been a bad year for a variety of reasons. And you aren't making this easy. You know that?"

"I know." I sigh and look down at my waist. "I should have called you when Nani passed, or when you and Neel broke up, or..." I exhale sharply. "...when she got hospitalized." I still didn't want to say her name. "I'm sorry."

"I don't mean that." She moves in front of me. "I'm the big sister, I don't expect you to help me." Those words hurt me. Don't I owe it to her to help her? "And maybe it's my fault as well. I chose to go to school in Toronto instead of staying here. We used to talk every weekend. It didn't matter what the topic was, or if we had nothing important to say. I loved hearing your voice, and I'm only hearing it now for the first time since I've been home." She gently lifts my head. "We have not seen Vishatan in more than a decade, not even a video or a voice call. He just disappeared. And I hate to say this, but I fear you might follow his path." She sighs. "I was so close to giving up on you, but circumstances outside my will won't let me."

"You mean, her hospitalization."

"*Inshallah*," she tells me. It can't be God's will.

"You are allowed to be mad at God, or even...Sid." I swallow his name.

"I'm not mad at Sid. I feel sorry for him. He can't hurt anyone in juvie. Nothing can undo what he did. But I have been praying that both he and Hari get better."

I understand her point, but faith is reserved for people who don't have real power, unlike Harriet and Sid. Although, if Veera can forgive Sid, maybe I should be more like her.

"Can you wrap my head and make it like yours?" I don't know what to do, but it's a start. I want to feel some comfort.

Veera smiles and instructs me to sit in my desk chair. She leaves my room for a few seconds and comes back with a couple of scarves and pins. She shows me a black scarf, the same one from that fateful night. I shake my head, so she grabs another scarf, a green polyester one, similar in hue to Harriet's dyed hair. Veera walks around me and brushes my hair backwards and around the sides. The bristles scratch my scalp. I close my eyes, feeling a little bit closer to my sister.

"I know I'm probably the worst sister ever." I pause for a moment, hoping she will disagree with me, but she lets the moment hang. I guess deep down, I know it to be true. "And I don't know how to make it better. But I want to try."

"Sorry, I just had a pin in my mouth." Veera breaks the silence and raises her voice. "Don't ever say you are the worst sister ever." She sighs softly. "A bad sister would hold a grudge for years about moving away from India. A bad sister would violate your trust by telling the guy you like about her condition, even if she thought she was looking out for her best interests. And a bad sister would do this." She pokes me in the arm with a safety pin. I wince and she wraps her arms around my torso.

She places the scarf on my head and the pin underneath my chin; it's cold. "You would freak out when you saw anything sharp, and I know you still don't like sharp objects. But much like this symbol of oppression on your head, it's only oppressive when you give them power."

I understand. I can rise above fear.

"If you walk out the door like this while keeping your chin up, no one can hurt you." She takes her phone out and shows me my reflection. "Typically, you wear a cap to hide all your hair, but it's up to you. Maybe bring your bangs out. It will frame your face well." She reaches over my forehead and pulls some strands forward.

But I don't see myself. "Harriet?" I mutter her name.

People confuse the two of us constantly, not just because we look alike, but because we share a mind. I'm reminded of how I let her down even though she's the one who betrayed our movement. I was in denial when she said we were the same, and I latched on to the idea that I was better than her because I wouldn't participate in terrorism. But I trespassed, tampered with evidence, annoyed people, did drugs, betrayed my morals, put her in a coma, and lied to figures of authority with the selfish endgame of preventing my death. It's so easy to condemn an evil person for doing terrible things, but I still feel the same way she does. I see myself in this dangerous person, and maybe if I had the same abilities as her, I would have done similar things.

How could I live with myself?

A tear falls down my cheek and I break down. Veera picks me off my chair, laying me on my bed. I whimper and slobber all over her.

"Let it out." She pulls me up and wraps her arms around me.

My sniffling lessens a little.

"I get it. You must be feeling some terrible survivor's guilt. You might think it should have been you on that bridge instead of Harriet. But it shouldn't have been anyone. It won't be easy, but all six of us are here, and we'll be here when we go see Harriet."

"Six?" I ask.

"Natasha? Talibah?" Ammi's almost angelic voice travels through our walls. Hearing her voice in person, instead of through an electronic device, propels me off Natasha. She happily walks into our room, fully dressed in a long, flowing yellow sarong and a dark orange hijab. The soft wrinkles around her eyes and forehead look crisper now than on a phone screen. She greets us with the biggest smile. I wouldn't expect her to be so well-rested after spending twenty-four hours travelling back home on multiple planes.

"I missed you two," she says in Urdu while hugging us, me resting on her left shoulder while placing Natasha on her right. If I could stay in this moment forever, I would.

"Come to the kitchen." Ammi leaves the room to greet our brothers.

"Thank you, Natasha," I say to my sister.

"Great, whenever you can..." She smells my face. "...brush your teeth." There's still some vomit on my breath.

Natasha gets up off my bed. "By the way, I replaced the locking mechanism on your carbon-fibre leg. You're welcome."

I don't deserve her. I slip the sleeve on my stump and put on my carbon-fibre leg, performing the necessary checks before going to the bathroom to brush my teeth.

Abba, Rajya, and Anuj are eating in the kitchenette. I join them at the table while Natasha goes into her room to freshen up.

"You think it's hard for you? Imagine what Harriet's going through."

I catch them in the middle of their conversation. "You put your trust in someone, and then for no reason, he almost kills you," Abba continues.

"We probably should have seen it coming," Anuj comments. "There was something off with his face. He just looked like a bad guy."

"Also, his name's Sid. Like Sid Vicious, Sid Phillips, Sid the Sloth, Sid Powell." Rajya counts all the bad Sids on his fingers.

"One of those is a real person, but the other three are fictional characters," Anuj corrects.

"Do not speak his name," Abba silences his sons. "Anyway, think about your uncle, who's considering stepping down because of his actions."

"Vipesh Kaka's resigning?" Anuj shouts out loud. "Is he giving in after the bridge collapsed? Or the plant explosion? He had nothing to do with either."

As it turns out, his firm designed the glass lobby for the nuclear plant. They never went near anything remotely radioactive. But someone made the connection and ran with the story. And coupled with the bridge collapsing, it made some stupid yet damning evidence of engineering malpractice.

"It's because of Harriet," Rajya answers. "You know he almost dropped out of the race because she spent two hours in the hospital, right?"

After every conceivable reason, he resigns because of Harriet. Vipesh swore an oath to serve this country but would drop it because of her. If he does drop out, he loses, Harriet loses, and our message is gone. I want to tell them what Harriet is capable of, but how can I? What proof can I garner to make such a horrific claim?

"It's just a thought right now," Abba clarifies. "He hasn't submitted anything yet."

"We have doctors," Anuj says. "Don't we?"

"Hari's not as lucky as you guys. Her only parent has a hard and time-consuming job. She's still in a rough condition. He wants to be there for her. He still feels guilty for being gone when Auntie Isabelle passed. He wants to be with her like your Ammi was there for Nani."

I pull out a chair to join my family.

"By the way, I need to tell you about Nani's final moments," Ammi says in Urdu as she joins us at the table.

"Harsha, do you think now is a good time?" Abba expresses his concerns in Hindi.

"Yes. Because this will help them." Ammi summons Natasha to the table. We all sit around and listen to her intently. Rajya puts down his phone. Natasha holds Anuj's hand while Rajya holds mine.

"On her last day, she would not get out of bed and started grunting and rambling. She thought she was on a bridge and then a hill."

My heart starts to beat faster.

"But in the end, she looked at me, and I was the only person in the room, she said, thinking I was Nana. 'I'm proud of you and what you have done for our family. We have made the right choices in our lives; we raised the perfect daughter. And she raised perfect children Natasha, Talibah, Rajya and Anuj to live long and happy lives'. Then she closed her eyes for the last time and smiled."

Ammi doesn't shed a tear as she repeats Nani's words. I would have if I were there. She looks at each one of us around the table. None of us understand what she means. Rajya releases his hand from mine.

"*That's it?*" Anuj asks.

Ammi pours herself a glass of water. "*What else do you want to know?*"

Anuj shrugs. He didn't have much else to say. And neither does anyone else. Ammi continues to drink her glass as the rest of us eat.

Once everyone is done, we all go our different ways. Abba goes downstairs to prepare for the lunch rush. Natasha, Rajya, and Anuj head to separate corners of their respective rooms. We have about two hours before visiting Harriet. I sit still on the sofa in the living room. I have my headphones and phone with me, and calm myself by listening to *Organs*. At this point, there's nothing else I can do other than take in the air around me and sink into the sofa, waiting for our upcoming visit.

"Talibah?" Ammi taps my headphones. I pull them down around my neck and shuffle my body from the indent on the sofa. "What happened on Diwali?" She speaks in English.

I gulp. Ammi hates speaking in English; it's her third language. On top of everything, she hates the idea of conforming to British rule.

"Why were you on...bridge?" She narrows her eyes into slits and stares at me.

"I don't know what you're talking about." I reach underneath my hijab and scratch my neck. It holds its shape, yet the scratch marks continue to sting.

She takes out her phone and swipes through her photos, then shows me a screenshot of a map showing all of us on her family tracking app. The icons of Rajya, Anuj, and Abba were all in our building clustered together, but my icon appeared next to the water, near the Morissette Bridge. The invisible knife cuts through my stump. "I check midday in Jammu, but morning in Ottawa," Ammi explains. "I saw you on...bridge first, then saw news about...collapse." She frowns. "Then, Vipesh Kaka told Abba and me you were with Hari when she woke." She moves close to me and holds me down. "Talk."

It's now clear from where I inherited my paranoia and persistence. "You could have asked me over a video chat or a phone call."

Ammi firmly places her hand on my prosthetic. "I want words. Now." She holds my head with her other hand, caressing the back of my hijab. Making this simple gesture made an intrusive gesture seem comforting. *"I've been through similar things."* She pushes our foreheads towards mine and looks into my eyes.

* * *

I will be onstage again. Krishna will be next to me. He will wave me away and Ammi will approach me in a golden sari. She will be pulling me off the stage and snatching the microphone from my hand.

* * *

"Natasha's wedding. After you give a speech, I...give mine." She tells her as soon as I exit my trance.

"Natasha's?" I ask. "Not mine?"

She shakes her head. *"You're not wearing a flower garland like Krishna. Also, the two of you are matching."* Either she can read my mind, or she has the same abilities as me. The latter makes more sense, because she wouldn't need to ask me to tell her anything.

So, I tell her about how I temporarily disarmed Sid to protect Harriet. I tell her about how I told Sid to snuff the lights out so he could gain the upper hand on Harriet. And how I talked Sid out of killing Harriet, and then I told her about how I put Harriet in a coma. I can't explain how my visions are inconsistent, but I tell Ammi that Harriet is the reason the plant blew up.

351

"Thank you for telling me, I am not surprised but I'm disgusted."

She takes the glass of water off the coffee table and gives it to me. I take a sip from it.

"You know, I was the first person in nine generations not to have an arranged marriage," Ammi recalls. *"Once I got to know Abba, I saw how beautiful our future would be together. That's when I knew I could tell him anything."*

I take a long sip of warm water. I point to myself. *"Does he know about mine?"*

"No," she relieves my worries. *"I would not tell. But maybe I should. Children don't tell parents anything; you think we don't understand. I will handle Hari. You have a bigger job, helping Sid."*

Could I talk to Sid? I know where he is. After pleading guilty to aggravated assault, he was detained in the William E Hay Centre near Alta Vista, about ten minutes north. As bad as my state of mind is, he's likely worse off because most of the world is against him.

"I arranged the visit but won't force you. Meet us at the hospital later." She walks away from me towards the stairs. *"You are a good girl and will make the right choice."*

"I'm not, Ammi," I hang my head. I'm just like Harriet.

"You would not wake her up if you didn't care. Don't let anyone take your heart away." She walks down the steps into the restaurant.

It's only nine-thirty. Ammi is right; I still have empathy, even for Harriet and Sid. I don't want to stay in the dark. I close my eyes.

Part 6.2: Cannot Go Back
Vritikha, December 19th, 10:00

"Vritikha Ganatra?" I open my eyes and find myself in a waiting room. "He's ready." An officer escorts me to the visitation area. The chair below me rattles as I sit down.

Sid's wearing an orange jumpsuit and looks decent. His hair is buzzed, his biceps and triceps look bigger, and there are four closed-up wounds on his head, one on each temple and two on the back of his head, each comprising four or five stitches. In total, he had eighteen sutures, two more than my leg stump after my amputation.

Our table is small and made of a thermally-conductive metal that cools my hands as I lay them bare. And nothing is separating us. I expected we would have a glass pane and communicate via telephone. And he's not even attached to the table with handcuffs. The walls of the room are made of large, concrete blocks. I couldn't locate any climate control devices. I shiver.

"How are you doing?" I awkwardly ask while giving him a fake smile.

He doesn't respond.

"It's pretty cold outside, eh?" I cringe. I have never said 'eh' in my life. I hate reinforcing stereotypes, like apologizing too much, but sometimes I can't help it. "Still hasn't snowed yet. What's up with—"

"Why are you here?" Sid cuts me off. "You can stall all you want; we have a whole hour. But I'm guessing you want to get out as soon as possible."

I inhale and exhale. I already know why Sid almost killed Harriet; he made it very clear. I already know why he ran; I don't understand why he just gave up running afterwards. I know he has some supernatural ability, but I don't know the limits of it.

"I called the cops," I blurt out. "I knew something bad was going to happen on that bridge, so I did what I had to."

"That's understandable," he comments. "Harriet had to be restrained, and whoever got the upper hand probably would have to face legal consequences."

"No," I respond. "Before what you did. I was at home. I couldn't sleep because I knew she would be in trouble, so I called the police, letting them know something bad would happen on the bridge at midnight, but I still wanted to protect her."

"You knew before it happened? Like a clairvoyant?" He looks deeper into my eyes.

My heart beats faster. "I guess if anyone deserves the truth, it's you." I look around to see if anyone is close; a couple of guards look at us intermittently, so I lean in. "Ever since the explosion, I have been having these dreams about the three of us on a bridge, fighting. The prophecy, if you want to call it that, was supposed to happen after my uncle lost the election, but he won. I thought it was over, but it just got delayed by three weeks. You were not the reason Harriet ended up in a coma. She was still conscious when you ran away. I had to stop her, but then I accidentally woke her up six weeks later." I close my eyes but am unable to get any vision. "I'm sorry. I'm sorry you're here. I'm sorry I ruined your life. I'm—"

"I don't know what you want me to do with that," he interrupts me. "And why are you apologizing? I almost killed your cousin, because I thought she made my mother sick."

"She did?"

"I never got an answer. But I also didn't wait for one, either." He looks down at his reflection on the table. "How is she?"

"I don't know." I shrug. "We're going to see her later today. But why aren't you swearing revenge on me?" I ask. "Just jump across this table and strangle me again. Promise to break out and threaten to kill me. I don't know." I groan. "But do something. You got revenge on Harriet, and frankly, she didn't get it bad enough. And I deserve something for playing a part in your imprisonment." I almost tear up, but I hold back and close my eyes. He can get a bit of closure if it's what he wants.

He clicks his tongue on the roof of his mouth. "I will not do that for several reasons. There are witnesses here that would make my punishment worse. Also, I saw you close your eyes just now. I remember what happened on the bridge. You were able to anticipate all of my attacks." He sits up straight. "If you could see the future, is that how you get perfect scores on all your tests?"

I nod.

"But since we are here. I want to know something about you." He lowers his voice and looks around before saying it. "What explosion or lab accident gave you your ability?" He maintains a blank expression during our entire conversation.

"None; I've had them since I was at least two years old, and so do my mother and grandmother." I answer with some skepticism, as I don't know everything yet.

We exchange looks. "Okay. Maybe it is different for different people," Sid reflects. He touches the table. "But something has been on my mind for the past few weeks. How did Harriet cause the explosion?"

I shrug my shoulders; even though I saw the security camera footage on the news, Harriet only appeared on the day of the explosion. She acted alone. The pressure gauge on the heat exchanger began to shoot up when she was within sight of it.

He strums his fingers on the table and I copy him, perfectly matching his rhythm. Harriet, as far as I knew, could always get what she wanted, despite my father's stubbornness. We would stay up all night just because we could. I tap my hand faster in excitement out of sync with his rhythm, but he quickly matches mine. "Maybe she was born with them like me." I look down at my reflection on the table. The sight of my green hijab is still upsetting, but I force back more tears. "And if she was always born with it, maybe you are, too?"

He shakes his head in disagreement. "That's not possible. I only started using them after the explosion."

My mind starts spinning again. I knew my overactive paranoia was good for something. "Hang on. I remember what happened in tenth-grade science. We were both taught by Mr. Glass, and he screamed at you for not submitting your homework on time. He went on a long tirade about how you were always late and ineffective." Sid finally changes his expression to one of bitter resentment. "I'll get to the point. During his rant, he suffered a heart attack. Did you do that to him? I would think about doing the same thing."

He fakes a smile, humouring what I say. "I don't know how I could have. My thoughts at the time were 'I wish he would shut up and I would maybe think about him clogging an artery on his—'" He suddenly stops speaking, leans backwards in his chair, looking upwards, eye popping out of his skull. "No no no no no no no no...NO." He deflates and laughs to himself, and his mouth hangs open as he slides downwards, dissociating from his physical body.

"Sidney, are you okay?" I reach over to touch his arm, looking him in the eyes. He immediately wakes up. Once he does, I sit back down.

He rests his head on his hands and elbows on the table. He looks at his reflection on the table and breathes short and quick breaths. "Mr. Glass, Yasmine, Gerald, Topher, Alex, Liam, Kyle, Harriet, Tikha." He puts his hands over his face and silently whimpers. A single tear falls down his cheek and onto the table. "Oh, fuck me, I'm a monster."

"It's okay, Sid." I try to reach for his hand, but he moves it away.

"No, you don't understand." He wipes his face and nose. "I keep hurting people. I'm worse than Harriet." He looks at me with bloodshot eyes. "I deserve to be here." His voice quivers as another tear falls from his chin.

"Harriet didn't have any remorse for what she did," I tell him. "But you do." I lay my hands open and face-up on the table. I try to force a smile but give up after he fails to produce one. "When I asked for your help on that English essay, I was trying to get some insight into who you were, because my visions showed you as some dangerous strangler. But something changed. You revealed yourself to a stranger. I said I believe your story about Yasmine, and I meant it. Even though you did unconsciously push her." I inhale and exhale deeply. "But I know you will now take responsibility for your thoughts. And I mean that. You will get better."

"Thanks," he softly sniffles, his eyes no longer red. "To answer your earlier question, I guess I always had these powers and didn't know. But I don't understand. If it's genetic, why didn't my parents tell me?"

"Maybe they didn't know, either." I strum my fingers on the table lightly and point to him. "Because your father passed it on to you."

He shrugs. "Maybe, never met him. He's not important to me, just some guy who gave me twenty-three chromosomes."

"Really? But it's half of your life you have not discovered yet." I realize my hypocrisy, because I internally criticized Yasmine for leaving Ottawa, despite not knowing half of her life back in Barbados.

He shakes his head. "Never needed to. I have two great parents and that's enough. But now I have something to look forward to when I get out." He smiles. I haven't seen him smile in a long time. I lean forward, off the backrest of the chair. "When..." I want to ask when he gets released but I feel weird about it.

"Nine months," he answers. "And I was lucky to get that. They could not find any way to link the bridge collapse to me. Even though I told them it was my fault, they found no tangible evidence. Maybe I can get out earlier for good behaviour. But I'm not sure I need it. My mom has approved furlough if I need to be with my mother in her final moments."

"Oh no." I remember seeing them at the restaurant; his mother is going through some treatments. "Your family came by to see me. Your mother looks pretty good." I scratch the back of my neck again and wince.

"I know," he informs me.

I stop scratching and lower my hand.

"My parents and sisters come to visit me once every weekend. It's the first time all five of us have been together in one room. And Mother is hanging on. She's not in remission yet, but my mom tells me the treatments are working." He points to his head. "I shaved so I could be more like her. I like to think it helped a little." Sid looks away and down to his feet. "Mom joked that ever since I came here, I was helping to reduce her stress levels, and as a result, the treatments are more effective..." He inhales and exhales softly. "...maybe there is some truth to that."

I shake my head, even though Sid's laughing. I'm glad he can find some humour in all the pain. But the only thing I can think about is the pain. He'll miss winter break, exams, prom, graduation, and the first month of university. I have no idea when his birthday is, so he could turn eighteen and get transferred to another facility. "Of course, she's joking. But I can help you."

The two guards are not paying close attention to us. I signal for him to lean in. "I just need to close my eyes for a second and I'll help you get out. You deserve to be free just as much as Harriet or me. We are all in this mess, and you don't deserve to bear all the punishment."

He shakes his head and leans backwards, raising an eyebrow. "Thank you for the offer, but I'm not busting out."

I lean back, unable to understand why. It's minimum security, and he is wrongfully charged with crimes. People need to know the whole story.

"Tikha, have you heard the rumour of me beating up Gerald, Topher, and Alex, the three students who run an online blog on the school grounds?"

I nod.

"Unfortunately, it's true. I didn't get into trouble, even though people saw what happened. I hurt people, including you."

The only time he even came close to hurting me was on the bridge, most of which was in self-defence. However, there was the time I tumbled across three lanes of road, and it busted my artificial leg.

"Just for the record, you didn't break my leg."

"I know, but I was not referring to that."

"Wait, you know?" I raise my voice at him.

"When I was working last summer, I noticed your limp. Everyone did; we spoke to Harriet about it, and she told us to shut up. Then, about two months ago, Yasmine hopped over my fence easily. When it was your turn, you climbed over it very awkwardly. And finally, then there was election day, your left leg was cut, which tore your leggings, but there was no sign of blood. I know there's something..." He breathes through his teeth. "...different about your left leg." He used the word 'different' so charitably that he could use it as a legitimate taxable write-off. "I have had a lot of time to think here."

"About my leg..." Am I going to tell him? I figure he revealed so much about himself, and as of now, there's no one else I feel more comfortable talking to about it.

"You don't have to tell me if you don't want to," Sid politely informs me.

"I do. You bore your soul to me, it's only fair." I tell him while noticing the guards around us, far away. "I don't feel comfortable saying it aloud." Maybe there is a way I could tell him. "You can read my mind, right?"

He nods.

I know Harriet can because she always knows what I am thinking, so I figure Sid can, too. I put my hands and arms on the table. They cool down significantly, and I shudder as it chills my core temperature. I cross my legs, putting my right leg over my carbon-fibre prosthetic. Sid stares at my forehead. I slowly breathe in and breathe out.

I don't know where I should begin. The story of my amputation, intertwined with the death of my grandfather, my older brother's departure, and a lively Diwali celebration which turned into the worst day of my life. I can't tell one without telling them all.

"So, let's just start at the beginning."

Part 6.3: Three Broken People
December 19th, 10:51

Vritikha let Sidney into her mind. She thought about why she got her prosthetic leg and her childhood: growing up in Jammu with her siblings and living in a mountain region with a lot of snow. She thought about one Diwali night and what her brother did to her and her grandfather. Sidney read her thoughts and visualized her stories. While Vritikha didn't say a single word, she relayed every graphic detail as she remembered it.

Upon finishing, she sank into her uncomfortable chair, her hands grazed the floor, and her shoes extended to Sidney's side of the table. Her neck bent over the backrest as she could not support the weight of her head. She balled up her fists, but the muscles in her eyebrows and cheeks relieved some tension; she felt freer.

"Holy shit, Tikha," Sidney corrected his posture. He reached across the table to her. He knew the real Vritikha Talibah Ganatra. "I am so sorry for everything, I am sorry you had to go through that."

Vritikha rose in her chair. Even though she knew telling someone her story wouldn't solve any of her problems, she knew she could trust him. "I'm not trying to get sympathy, and you don't have to apologize. When people discover my leg, I can get defensive, because in my experience, when they see it, that's all they choose to see, and I suddenly become 'the crippled girl'. I usually tell people: 'I got a bacterial infection and noticed it too late'. It's true, but I don't tell anyone my brother made me this way. What you read was real and I'm never going to forget what happened."

"I just cannot believe I am one of a handful of people that know—"

"The only," she quickly corrected him.

361

He waited for her to respond with some clarification, but when none came, he leaned back towards her. "You barely know me."

"I know you, Sidney," she corrected him again. "I know you are a cheery, optimistic boy with a short fuse. I know you want to do good things for the world, but you want to protect the people around you. I know you would have done anything to help your mother, not just because you love her but because she's the toughest person you know, and because you're scared of living in a world without her. I know you are well-read, love bubble tea and anime, and above all else, love your family and feel the need to protect them as the only male. Most importantly, even with all your abilities, I know you feel powerless. Because while your powers are vast, they still have many physical limitations, like a powerful engine inside an old car."

Sidney sat there, initially annoyed that she was trying to boil down his entire life into one short speech, but after ruminating on what she said, was impressed by how accurately she summarized his personality, and how far he had drifted from the boy he was before the explosion. "How?"

"Harriet told me once that she and I were the same person, and I know she told you that the two of you were the same as well. So there must be some similarities between us as well. And before you say it was Harriet being manipulative, I think there's some truth to it."

"No, I agree with you."

"The point is I know you, Sidney Tamashiro-Adams." No one had ever called him by his full name, not even his parents. His mother had shortened his surname so he and his siblings would not be overburdened, but he liked the sound of it. "I told you because you're the only person I could tell who wouldn't be completely devastated by hearing it. You deserve to know the real me and why I am the way I am. My grandfather died trying to save me from 'him'."

"And you have just been sitting on it." He lowered his tone slightly.

"I never got an answer as to why he did what he did, and I will probably never get one in the future," she whispered. "I have not seen him in almost a decade. He's been running ever since, even though I never reported him. He might be dead."

Vritikha finally unfurled her fists; at the beginning of her monologue, her hand turned a bright red. Her skin now changed back to its regular light, brownish-red colour. She checked circulation by tapping her thumbs on her index finger, middle, ring, and pinky fingers; her capillary refill was still responsive. "My naïve, six-year-old mind thought nothing terrible would happen to me." She looked at her reflection on the table and cringed. "After that moment, I just had to accept my fate no matter what happened; like Louise Banks in *Story of Your Life*. Then a couple of months ago my visions kept changing, sometimes nightly. I thought, maybe I was like Donna, the precog from *The Minority Report*. I had a few different outcomes, and I had to choose the least bad option. The only problem is, I didn't even know why or how it was changing."

While Sidney had read those short stories in his past, he still didn't completely understand what she was saying. "Those stories dealt with aliens and deformed mutants. They are much more sophisticated at programming well-defined paths for the future, but people aren't like that. We are random and limited to our singular point of view. Maybe that's why visions change?"

She shook her head. "My grandmother told my mother right before she died that we are on the best path and we made the best decisions, but why doesn't it feel like it?"

"Because nothing in the future is definite." Sidney smiled. "Predictions are based on a limited scope, and we can't know everything about everything at any given second of the day. Remember when the so-called climate experts determined that the world was supposed to end in 2030? I mean, it wouldn't have ended, but due to the effects of—"

"I know what you mean. And yes, I remember tenth-grade history." Vritikha riled herself up. "They weren't wrong, we still missed the deadline, and we are on track for four degrees of warming by the end of the decade." She unfurled her fists and noted where her fingernails dug into her palms.

"What I'm trying to say is, so much can happen over eight years, or four and a half months, or even ninety seconds. We're not screwed because we are still here."

"We have always been screwed." Vritikha raised her voice. "But this is not comparable to my grandmother; we had the answers back then, but I don't." She shut her eyes in frustration, coming to terms with what her cousin went through every second of every day of her life.

"You still tried to figure out how your visions work, and that's better than just doing nothing." He rolled back into his chair, unsure about what he just said. He thought back to what he did to Harriet. "Maybe." He looked to the window and noted the sun peeking around the corner, shining directly on him.

He redirected his attention back to her. "I was just thinking if delaying was better than doing nothing. My mother's treatments are only delaying the inevitable, because she'll die someday. But I hate the idea of losing her to something so benign, way before her time, and the idea that I caused her stress and worsened her condition. If I had done nothing, maybe we would've been better off." He hung his head in despair.

"You wanted to help her. You wanted to solve the problem even though it was hopeless," Vritikha reassured him. "You tried to do something unconventional, and it didn't work out. But you haven't given up, have you?"

"I haven't exactly given up, but I'm not researching experimental procedures. I still check her condition when I can, and I have stopped lying to her. So far, she hasn't had any problems."

She smiled at him. "I think you just learned from your mistakes."

The realization suddenly dawned on him. "You're right, Vritikha," he exclaimed in delight, and felt the urge to get up from his seat, but knew it wasn't a good idea, given his confinement. "Although it might not work forever. I don't know what the future will hold."

Vritikha, while listening to Sidney's optimistic soliloquy, had a moment of clarity, and thought about how they could combine their powers. "I could show it to you. You can read my mind, and I can show you where we would end up together."

"I don't want to know," he told her. "If this whole experience has taught me anything, it's that I shouldn't rely on magical solutions to real problems while ignoring real solutions. Besides, I would rather see these changes unfurl—"

"Hey." A guard banged his baton on their table lightly. "Visiting hours will be closing soon. Wrap it up. And next time you're not allowed to touch each other. I'll make a pass just this once, but you better stop it next time, lovebirds."

"Oh, we're not—" Vritikha tried to explain the situation to the guard but found that he had already left. "Pig," she muttered under her breath.

"He means well. It's for your protection, mainly." He sighed. "I guess this is it."

"Yeah." Vritikha was sure she helped him, but still felt the need to ask. "Are we good?"

Sidney glared at her. "Oh, you thought just because you came here and we had a pleasant conversation about mutual suffering, it suddenly means we're good? I'm just supposed to disregard the fact that you put me in this shithole?" He slowly inched closer to her. "When I get released, I'll get you and your cousin to pay for everything." He laughed menacingly. "But thank you, Vritikha, for showing me my final form. Get some rest, but be warned, when your visions get cut short, I'll be coming for you."

She got up from her chair and backed into the metal divider separating the visiting room and lobby, while clutching her left arm.

Sidney could not contain his amusement anymore, broke his stare, and produced a high-pitched girlish laugh, curled up into a ball, and fell out of the chair. Vritikha quickly realized his threats were not serious, walked up to him, and slapped his arm. "Dude, you're such a dick. I was about to summon a guard to take you out."

"Sorry." He wiped a tear off his cheek. "I went a little too far with that. To be fair, you did ask for it. And I haven't been able to joke like that with someone in a long time. It felt nice." He stood up again. "Yes, we are good. You don't have to worry about me. I know it will get better. The people here are nice. I was an asshole for the first month, but that's about to change because of you. And if you can do that for me, maybe you can help Harriet as well."

She walked back but winced with every other step. She brought her hand down to her stump, massaging it as she sat back down.

"Are you okay?" Sidney asked.

She nodded. "It's my phantom pain. I think it's dying down a little." Over the past thirty-six days, Vritikha had gotten used to the invisible knife cutting through her stump. A small relief felt unpleasant and off-putting to her. "But what is it you said about helping Harriet?" she asked, raising her voice a little.

Sidney summoned her back to the table and leaned closer to her. "I wanted to play the part of a hero ever since that explosion, to find my exact equal and opposite. I thought that was Harriet. I saw her as a villain, someone who needed to be defeated. But she isn't what I built up in my head. She's broken, similar to us or even people in this facility. It's probably too late for me to help her, but not for you. I know you still love her."

Even though she didn't want to say it, she agreed. "What's wrong with me? She's a terrorist."

"Nothing is wrong with you." Sidney kept his hands on the table, but raised Vritikha's head gently so their eyes met, and noted a couple of small tears falling off her cheeks. She had never heard someone tell her what Sid had just said. "I told my family everything I did to Harriet, and they still loved me despite it. They were mad at first, don't get me wrong. They could have disowned me, but didn't. I had burned down almost all my goodwill that night, but I would be nothing without them. Before the explosion, I was this happy-go-lucky guy, but I now realize I wasn't happy, just comfortable. She challenged me and made me realize that catastrophic events can come out of nowhere and could happen to anyone, and that we can't always be prepared for them, but we can learn from each other."

After his lecture, he stopped using his powers on Vritikha. She held her head up and looked into his eyes.

"You know her better than anyone else now," Sidney continued. "And I know her capabilities and supernatural limits. There are millions of people like Harriet, but only a few who would go as far as to be a terrorist. What you did for me, you need to do for her."

"How?"

"Let her know you don't approve of what she did, but you haven't lost sight of what she's trying to do. Let her know that she is not beyond saving and that you won't stop trying to save her. Tell her as often as you can that she isn't alone and that you love her. Her father will eventually find out what she did, but no matter what happens in her life, she'll always have you. Does this sound like something you can do?"

"Okay." She pushed herself up from the table. "I can do that."

Sidney stood up. Vritikha gave him a polite half-smirk, reached out, and shook his hand. He watched her leave with a huge grin on his face.

The guard escorted Vritikha out of the visiting room. An alarm buzzed and the metal door opened. She walked into the lobby.

Sidney sat back down, knowing he had found a person he wanted to keep in his life. He had felt a connection he never felt with anyone else. He was not attracted to her like he was with Yasmine, nor did he form a brotherly bond as with Kyle, but he knew he found something deeper he wanted to explore once he got released.

As she disappeared from his sight, a guard approached him. "Get up, Sid. Your private tutor is waiting for you."

"Can I just sit down for a couple more minutes?"

"Ninety seconds." The guard reluctantly allowed him to stay a little longer. He had only seen the detainee during recreational time, sitting underneath a tree far from everyone else in the facility, meditating.

Regardless, Sidney was doing the same motions he was under the tree. He sat down and looked through the window at the sun. He nodded to himself as if a voice in his head were instructing him, staring contently at the glass pane for those ninety seconds. He absorbed some of the sun's warm energy and deeply breathed in and out in nine-second intervals.

The guard started to fan himself. When his short seconds were finally over, he got up. "I'm ready."

The two of them walk out of the visiting room.

* * *

Vritikha walked into an empty lobby. She managed to use up the entire hour with Sidney; all they did was talk. She unzipped her sweater, feeling a little warm.

"Excuse me, miss," the receptionist called for her attention. "You still need to sign out." Vritikha walked over to the front desk and scrolled through the list of names signed right beside hers, along with the current time. The receptionist reached underneath his desk and brought out a basket of her belongings: purse, winter jacket, earbuds, and phone. "You must mean a lot to him. I have never seen him in such a good mood before."

She backed from the front desk, feeling a little breached.

"I wasn't paying attention to anything the two of you said, but I saw his expressions when he entered and when he left."

"Yeah." She reapproached the front desk. "We go back a while. I guess he just needed a little reminder of who he was." She took her belongings, put on her jacket, left it unzipped, and connected her earbuds to her phone.

"Good," the receptionist responded. "Have a good winter break. Do you want me to call a cab?"

Vritikha politely declined.

"Alright, I'll buzz you out."

The exit door's alarm buzzed and she promptly exited the building. She inputted the address to OHG and saw a text from her father.

<u>What is your plan?</u>

<u>Ill meet u there</u>, she texted back.

Vritikha appreciated the natural beauty now that she got some closure from Sidney. She looked up at the sky full of clouds. The winter season was just beginning, and both the deciduous trees and shrubbery had shed their leaves. The pine trees and cedar bushes bordering the property were perfectly manicured, and were a beautiful shade of green. A gentle fall breeze swept across her face, inside her hijab, and around her neck. She needed to seek shelter soon.

She slipped her earbuds on and looked through her music. Seeing that she had listened to the song *Six Weeks* one hundred and seventy-eight times since Diwali, she instead played the album *Traveller* on shuffle. And as soon as she heard the first notes played on the sitar and the proceeding chants accompanying it, she was instantly reminded about another 'traveller'.

Krishna had texted Vritikha for over a month asking her if she wanted to talk about Harriet's hospitalization or Nani's passing. On average, she got about two texts per day from him. He eventually stopped, understanding he had been ghosted.

She dialled his number, and as it rang, she looked at herself in her phone's reflection, still feeling a little uneasy about her reflection.

"Good morning," came Krishna's gleeful greeting.

She brought the receiver of her headphones to her mouth. "I know the last time we spoke was over a month ago." She said the first thought in her mind; it wasn't the best opening line, but since he didn't hang up, she took it as a good sign.

"Thirty-six days," he answered. "I knew I was invasive, but you were—"

"Rude, unnecessarily protective, batshit crazy? I know," she interrupted. He wouldn't have said those words to her directly but was thinking of at least one of them. "And I understand all you ever wanted to do was try to get to know me. So I'm sorry for yelling and ignoring you. And I'm apologizing, not because it's my go-to response, but because I messed up...with you. And I hope we can still be friends." She stopped in the middle of the sidewalk, feeling a little winded.

A large pine tree appeared to her, so she decided to rest underneath it for a couple of minutes. "You made me uncomfortable, but in a way that made me emerge from my shell, so for that I thank you. You deserve more in a..." She swallowed the word. "...girlfriend. I was not ready for that. But I will say a part of me wanted this to work."

"That's very mature of you, and yes, we can still be friends. We were family friends before anything. But I didn't want to make you uncomfortable; you have secrets and I respect that."

Krishna had read the writings on her whiteboard on the night of Diwali. He didn't have the full context because they were just random list words, but she knew he knew about them. Since he did not bring it up, it was all the proof she needed to know he let it go.

"It's not just because of my leg. I'm just naturally guarded. I have been since I was young, and after a decade, it felt too weird to change course." Vritikha moved her hand to scratch her neck. "Well, there is a process I go through." She lowered her hand out of her hijab. In the distance, she saw some white specks fall in the distance, and stepped out of the comfort of the tree's protection as she needed to seek better shelter.

The drops fell slowly, landing delicately on her eyelashes. She lifted her hand to catch a couple, but they melted on her palm. Some were bigger than others, but none stayed longer than a few seconds.

She looked up, and to her delight, saw it was snowing. "That does not mean I never just act on impulse; sometimes, I do." While keeping her head up, she blinked a few snowflakes into her eyes. "And some were the best decisions I have ever made."

The last time she had seen snow in December was the year before her family moved to Canada. After half a minute of continuous snowfall, it became heavy enough to accumulate and change the colour of her jacket and hijab. She laughed and spun around the sidewalk.

"Vritikha?" Krishna asked. "Are you alright?"

"I don't think I have been alright since immigrating here, but maybe I can be for the first time in a decade." She continued to laugh. "Maybe for the first time, I will be. Next year will be mine, I can feel it."

"Should I be worried?" Krishna asked. "About...your sudden change in mood?"

She walked a bit faster; snow started to stick to the bottoms of her shoes. "If you want to know, come to my place. Six-thirty, on the dot."

Krishna shuffled through papers in his room, trying to find his schedule. "I have an exam tonight, but after writing it and driving to your place, I can make it there around..." He calculated travel time with his phone's GPS. "Six-thirty. But I would have to leave your place early. I'm going back to Pakistan tomorrow."

"You're going back?" Her smile disappeared.

"For the break." The night after Diwali, after upsetting Vritikha, Krishna felt lonely and decided to call his parents up. They had a pleasant conversation and he agreed to book a flight to see them right after exams. He was excited to tell them about his world tour and how he finally finished his secondary education and started college, later planning to transfer to a university after two years and perhaps permanently settle in Canada, depending on certain factors.

"Of course, that makes sense. I guess you should have a good trip back home."

"That's a yes," he told her. "Vritikha, I would love to pop in for a while. If it's alright with your family."

"Yes. My mother hasn't seen you yet. And I know Veera would love to see you once more...and more times after that." Snow had started to accumulate on her head and shoulders. From a distance, her hijab and jacket appeared to be white. She removed the safety pin from under her chin, took off the scarf, shook off the snow, then retied it around her head, but left her neck exposed. She placed the pin behind her head to secure it and continued to walk, hoping more snow would reaccumulate on her head.

"Perfect. But can I ask you something? Not related to this conversation?"

"Sure, what do you want to know?"

"Why is all the music you listen to from the 2010s?"

"Oh," she laughed. "Thirty-year cycle? I guess more of a forty-year cycle. Don't think about it too much. I know I won't. I'll see you tonight. Bye." He hung up as she made it to the bus shelter. The bus pulled into the stop.

But she had a sudden change of heart and decided to walk to the hospital. The bus slowly finished loading and unloading passengers, and while the driver waited for Vritikha to mount, she waved him off and the bus drove off without her.

Vritikha looked at her reflection on her phone screen, at the scars on her neck: the new style suited her. She took her headphones out of her ears and put them back in her purse. Instead, she listened to the natural ambiance around her: the winds blowing, the rustling of branches on nearby trees, and the subtle noises of snow falling and crystallizing on nearby objects. The natural elements were having a little conversation of their own. There was no rhythm or mathematical order to the conversation, just a tempo that accelerated to guide her steps; and eventually, she picked up the pace.

It was only three-point-six kilometres to the hospital; not a short distance, nor a long one. The winter winds washed through her ears and chilled the exposed scars on her neck. As the wind accelerated, she matched her steps to an imaginary beat.

It was initially uncomfortable, but her prosthetic could handle her speed and the sleeve kept its place. And as the wind continued to speed up, she started running. She decided to take a long way around, veering off-path as much as she wanted and running for as long as she could. She set herself free and wandered around a snow-covered sidewalk.

* * *

It's only one moment, but they are both alone with their thoughts, looking at the sky, uninhibited by migraines or phantom pains, exercising their small amount of power.

THE END